THE HORN OF DAWN

Symphony of the Sephira: Book 1
Hadder Martinez

For Astrid, of course.

Illustrations by Changmen "Chilidraw" Zeng

Copyright © year 2019 Hadder Martinez

ISBN: 978-1-7344651-0-5

This is a work of fiction. All characters and events portrayed in this book are fictional, and any resemblance to real people or events is purely coincidental.

Prologue

"Death is not my enemy, it is my home," Miira whispered under her breath. "Fear is the body's burden. Its passing only a door. I live on. I live on."

Every time her bare feet touched the stone floor a chill ran up the back of her legs. Fear coiled in her stomach, tightening and churning. A few more steps, and she would pass into the light beyond the temple's arching doorway.

She bit the inside of her lip nervously as a cool morning breeze crept through her thin linen gown, making her shiver. The ancient Seeress with her feathers and beads, the Shapka in his ceremonial furs, and their loyal, painted acolytes stood outside, glaring at her impatiently. Gathering herself, Miira stepped into the light and beheld the Vale of Azilial for the last time.

The Vale yawned out from the mouth of the temple. Lush, green, and bountiful — its jagged mountains dotted by dozens of homesteads built into the rock and linked together by meandering roads.

The entrance to Miira's family home lay within view. High on the Vale's eastern wall, its entrance draped in fragrant gogi moss and honeysuckle, and its floor littered with generous offerings of oats, goat cheese, and ampules of fish oil.

The people of the Azilial crowded at the bottom of the temple steps, naked and painted in the sigils of their clans. They stood in rapt attention as Miira stepped before the Altar of Renewal. Her family stood at the front of the congregation, granted a place of honor and draped in strings of beads, bones, and flowers. Except for her eldest brother, all smiled up at her, beaming with pride.

Perched on the altar before her, held by an ornate stand of bone, awaited the Horn of Dawn. White, delicately curved, with masterfully chiseled scrollwork, the ivory horn was a divine relic, gifted to the people of the Azilial by Ariel himself. Once she blew the horn, the Shapka would cut across her throat with his ceremonial knife and sever her link to the world of flesh, releasing her spirit through the horn's mouth.

The clans would sing her into the soil and into the water. They would paint her name on their livestock and on the stomachs of women wishing to bare child. Even her own mother had done so, in hopes of replacing the daughter she now sacrificed to the gods. They would drink wine, dance, and sing her into the fire, asking the gods to revitalize the valley's barren soil, purify its water, and nourish its dying fields.

Afterward, her body would be bathed in oils, wrapped in sacred texts, and entombed deep within the temple. Her name would be carved into the Tablets of L'en and remembered forever. She would join the sisterhood of those who came before her, made eternal and beloved by Ariel.

Miira had passed the first trial meant to weed out the false and unworthy. To be chosen was the most coveted of honors in the Vale, as only the purest could blow through the Horn of Dawn, or it would anger the gods and bring about a terrible doom.

To prove her worth, they lead her into the Chamber of Prophesy and gave her the black lotus milk. She did not cough the milk back up, which would have shown her to be weak of flesh. Though the viscous liquid made her nauseated as it drove her deep into the dreamsilk, she held it down.

The milk showed her a prophet's dream, revealing the future she would sacrifice for the Vale. She saw herself as a grown woman, and the path her life would have taken, had her first blood not come on the night of the equinox, marking her as Ariel's chosen sacrifice.

"What did you see?" The Seeress asked when she awoke.

"A beautiful life," she replied breathlessly.

"And do you give it willingly, child? For the sake of your people?"

She had sobbed bitterly. She wanted to be strong, but to surrender the promise of such unachieved wonders was heartbreaking.

"I want to live!" she cried.

"And you will, child." The Seeress ran a gnawed hand through her hair. "With this act you earn eternity, for yourself and your family. You are awaited in paradise."

The final test would be performed here, before the people of Azilial and the effigy of Ariel himself, which sat on its regal haunches high above her head. She did not dare look back at him, fearing his emerald eyes would be filled with disapproval.

The Shapka took her left hand and spread it open, palm up, speaking the words of stone before cutting her skin with his ceremonial flint knife. She bit back her cry, wanting to appear strong before her family and her people.

Her blood fell into the wooden bowl, mixing there with milk, wine, and the Shapka's seed. In a useless gesture, the Seeres wrapped Miira's wound while the Shapka brought the elixir to his lips and drank.

Miira's chin touched her chest in silent shame. While she had come this far, she knew she would not pass this trial. She had always been different from the other children, though she could not understand why.

When she was five winters young, playing by the pond near her home, she came upon a mother duck and her half dozen ducklings. The hen had been protective of her young — hissing, craning her neck, and flapping her wings menacingly.

Miira felt insulted and challenged by the animal. An undeniable, fervent urge overtook her.

She grabbed the mother duck by the neck, pinned her on her back, and squeezed her feathery neck with all her strength. The duck squirmed and kicked under her but Miira held on, pressing down until she ceased her hideous gargling and lay still.

The act filled her with an immeasurable thrill, leaving her blushing and breathless. Terrified, the ducklings tried to flee but never wandered far from their mother's lifeless body. She caught and broke their little yellow necks one by one.

When she realized that her father watched from the shade of the nearby ash, a stab of guilt and terror struck her so tenaciously, she wet herself. What she did was wrong, and she understood this without being told. When her father noticed the rivulet running down the inside of her leg, he knelt and took her into his arms.

"It is all right," he said, holding her close. "Do not cry. Your actions held no wrong, my little huntress. These animals were placed here for this."

They took the ducks home that day and father showed her how to feather and dress them. From then on, she always brought her kills home.

Her mother was disquieted, giving her wary glances when she returned home with her hands covered in fresh blood. Her father however, beamed proudly and placed her on his shoulder, telling her brothers how she would become a renown huntress and bring the family fortune.

At eight winters, her eldest brother grew jealous and attempted to beat and shame her. An overwhelming urge to strike the life from him overtook her. She did not act upon it. She only stared at him as he struck her, considering the many ways to go about ending his useless life.

Her brother must have sensed something, seen something of the truth in her eyes, because his fists loosened, and he backed away. He never hurt her again afterward, and only spoke to her when needed. He learned to fear her without her having to injure him, and this made her feel powerful.

Despite her father's approval, Miira knew she was different. She did not kill for the sake of meat, bone, feathers, and furs. She took life because only this act brought her any joy. Something ravenous and enraged lived curled up inside her, begging to be fed, growing stronger by the day.

Once the Shapka tasted the taint in her blood, everyone would know. He would deem her unclean and unworthy, bringing shame to her family and clan. She would be forced into exile, but at least she would live.

In her prophet's dream, brought on by the lotus milk, she saw what her life would become were she not chosen. There were impressions and feelings in her vision she did not fully comprehend. Words were spoken which held great meaning. Words like betrayal, incest, poison, and murder. The rush of power those strange adult words inspired in her was intoxicating. Her heart swelled and a current ran through her, pulsing like a fire in her chest. She wanted to live to experience them.

"She is pure!" The Shapka bellowed. "She is clean!"

The people of Azilial cheered. Her mother and father embraced with a joyous kiss. Her eldest brother's lower lip dropped like fruit from a tree, his eyes going as wide as blood oranges.

"No," Miira muttered. "No, I cannot be."

"Stand strong, child!" The Seeress hissed in her ear and removed her linen robe, exposing her thin, painted body. "Take hold of your destiny!"

But I am not clean!

Willing herself not to cry, Miira stepped forth and took the Horn in her hands. She looked out at the naked, cheering masses of the Azilial and a wave of disgust flushed through her. Why did the Shapka not see the truth of her heart? She squeezed the Horn between her fingers, shuddering with fury. Her brother pleaded with their father, pointing at her, his face anxious and fearful. Her father scowled at him, speaking through grinding teeth.

"Blow the Horn, Miira, daughter of Nuvren, son of Balko!" The Shapka called so that all would hear. "Renew our land, so we may reap what you sow!"

Miira took the Horn to her lips. She did not want this. She wanted to live. The Shapka stood behind her, the flint knife gripped tightly in his hand. He did not find her darkness because he could not see. This ritual was a lie. She looked pleadingly towards her mother and found her smiling brightly, already celebrating her meaningless death.

"Blow the Horn," the Shapka growled under his breath.

I hate you. I hate you! I HATE YOU ALL!!

Miira blew the Horn of Dawn as hard as she could. As the long, low blast filled the air, something within her released its crushing hold.

The long serpent's totality revealed itself as it slowly uncoiled from around her spine, the tip of its tail curled around her tail-bone while its broad head rested on the back of her tongue. It bared its fangs and slithered forward, sending a ripple of pleasure through her center as it slid into the Horn's ivory length.

Tears flowed down her cheeks as a glorious physical release pealed through her, leaving musical color-patterns painted behind her eyelids. When the serpent had nearly completed its escape, her bitter hatred was replaced by cavernous emptiness and loss.

Torn in two, separated from something integral to her being, she felt a desperate urge to force the thing back inside herself — to chew and devour so it would become one with her again. She bit down reflexively on the mouthpiece, chipping her tooth.

The serpent completed its escape, transforming into the sound made by the horn, leaving her behind, encased in hollow flesh.

The Shapka ran his sharpened knife across Miira's throat. The shock of the blade's bite and the heat of her blood washing over her bare chest passed quickly. She crumbled before the altar, cold, dying, and alone, while the Shapka raised his arms in bloody triumph. The last thing she heard in life, was the rising voice of the Azilial, singing her hatred into the soil.

ACT I

1

The Devil's Spine

Captain Dorav Minos stood at the bow of the *Kajak* and peered into the encroaching darkness of The Devil's Spine; a forest of wet, black rock as tall as his ship's topgallant. Behind the Spine, the black peaks of the Norvan Mountains rose, stark and imposing — their shapes revealed by flashes of sheet lightning above their tips.

For hours, they had been running dark, guided by the mepsien who stood beside him.

"How much longer?" Dorav asked, anxiety stirring in his voice.

"Not far now," Nihengale said, his calisthian clear but heavily accented. "Keep to the current course."

"I don't wish to go in there blind," Dorav said. A sensation of helplessness had been coiling itself around his bowels since the ship had gone dark. This restless, unfamiliar sea tasted pungent on his tongue.

"And I have no wish to swim to shore, Captain. I'll let you know when we're clear." Nihengale resumed the strange, nearly inaudible clucking in his throat which somehow helped him navigate in the dark.

Swallowing his frustration, Dorav turned to his midshipman. "Keep the current course," he said. "Furl the mainsail and man the oars. Nice and steady now."

"Aye, sir." The man walked astern with his hand on the port side bulwark.

The *Kajak* was a war-tested frigate which had seen her share of battle in three different wars. Built and baptized in Palidor's shipyards, her slender shape and smooth angles were designed for sharp maneuvering, even in unfavorable weather. Her ironbark hull had once been clipped by a Calimport fire-galley at full sail and held true. His girl could take a beating, but one mistake in that maze of jutting rocks, and she'd be reduced to flotsam.

Nihengale made a series of hand signals to his kindred perched in the foremast crow's nest. "There are no other ships in sight, Captain," he said, his eyes shining like a stalking alley cat's. "And the *Merrigold* has reached Relm's seaway. We are clear."

"Lights!" Dorav cried out. "All lamps and bulls-eyes on deck!"

The boatswain, an old cruel looking bootstrap named Tundy "The Terror", was quick to pick up the call.

"Move, you quivering cunnies!" Tundy bellowed, the sharp angles of his face pinching angrily. "Keep those lights steady or by God I'll cane your knuckles bloody!" He blew his shrill pipe to echo the command.

The *Kajak* came alive after hours of silent running. Bare feet slapped wet timbers and sailors groaned as they climbed the shrouds and masts, oil-lamps in tow.

"Stay here Nihengale," Dorav said, "and keep your man in the nest. If you see anything my lights can't, I would know at once."

"Aye, sir," Nihengale replied calmly.

"Have him stick his head in the water and check for reefs!" Lieutenant Kartecus called out from the quarterdeck. "And don't let him rise for air until he sees one!"

"They've served their purpose so far, Lieutenant!" Dorav cried, his men hurrying around him with the tenacity of flies on a carcass.

"Pack of mother-raping, godless jackals, I say!" Kartecus spat, speaking loud enough for all to hear. The old man's cracked voice could still carry.

"They still have work to do, old friend," he said, standing by his lieutenant on the quarterdeck. "I'd rather have them alive for it."

"We'll all need to atone after working with those godless things," Kartecus said.

"Noted, Lieutenant," he said, and waved his navigator over. "Master Myrkin, I want you at the helm."

"I can handle this, sir," First Mate Dessa protested, squeezing the spokes on the wheel possessively. She was young, sharp-eyed, and competent, but tonight required a more experienced hand.

"I know you can, Dessa," he said. "I'd rather Myrkin steer all the same."

"Aye, Aye, sir," she said, reluctantly surrendering the wheel and rubbing her umber colored hands. She had been squeezing the spokes with a death-grip.

"Check our depth," Myrkin told her. "I want to know at once if we go anywhere near eight fathoms."

"Aye, Aye, sir." Dessa hurried off the quarterdeck.

"For God's sake." Dorav placed a hand on Myrkin's shoulder. "See us through this alive."

"Sir!" Myrkin spat on his callused hands, rubbing them together before gripping the wheel's smooth wooden spokes.

"Ser Isa, is the seaguard in place below?" he asked.

"Ready and waiting," she said. "Are you expecting armed resistance from those scary looking rocks, Dorav?"

Ser Isa had her blond hair braided tightly against her skull. Her sun-baked face was etched in shallow white scars and deep frown lines. Her hard blue eyes regarded him evenly.

"Always best to be prepared." He matched her glare until she nodded and moved away.

The rowers below followed their drummer's slow, deliberate pace, thrusting the *Kajak* cautiously towards The Spine. The topsailmen picked the rocks out of the darkness with their bulls-eye lanterns so Myrkin could gauge their path. The rowers pulled their oars in before the threshold, leaving them at the mercy of wind and wave.

"Harbor-furl the sails!" Dorav cried. "Steady now!"

The Kajak held its breath as it slipped into the Devil's Spine.

Myrkin's steady hands moved the wheel inches at a time, as whitewash lapped against the *Kajak's* hull, making her sway. Sailors moved gingerly about the weather deck, whispering to each other and flinching whenever a beam creaked too loudly or a line groaned on its tether.

"Ye know why they call it the Spine?" One man whispered to another as they secured a line below the quarterdeck. "Daemons live out here. If they catch us, they'll put their claws up our arses and rip out our backbones."

"Quiet down there!" Kartecus barked and they shrunk away.

Dorav observed the tumultuous sky above his masts. A pregnant, troublesome pattern of gray and pitch hovered above. A single arc of purple sheet-lightning danced across the heavens, followed by a low rumbling filled with promise.

"Don't you rain on me now," he whispered.

"Captain!" Nihengale cried out from the bow, "sharp turn ahead, due south!"

The mepsien on the crow's nest, called down to Nihengale in their winding language.

"The masts have room if she leans, Captain," Nihengale said.

Even at its crawling pace, if the ship did not adjust in time, they would smash her bowsprit into the rocks. There was just enough room to turn, if they used haste.

"Ahull! I want her ahull port side!" Dorav shouted.

"To port! All hands port side! Now, now!" Tundy bellowed and blew his pipe.

The sailors ran across the deck and stood on the port side bulwark, pulling back on the rigging with all their might. The topsailmen straddled the yards to add their weight to the maneuver. The Kajak began a slow, steady turn around the rocks, her bowsprit sliding into the new passage.

The pillars on their left gave way to a cluster of squat boulders and half-sunken stalagmites near the turn, giving her masts just enough room as they dipped.

"Do we drop anchor, sir?" Myrkin growled, turning the rudder as far as it would go.

"She's almost on her beam ends!" Tundy called out.

"No, she'll make it!" Dorav said. "Be ready to straighten her beam."

He gripped the bulwark for balance as his ship made the slow pitch to port, angling itself into the treacherous turn, her stern clearing the northern rock wall by less than a foot.

The foremast topgallant shattered against a towering pillar further along the turn. Sails and rigging dangled from broken perches. Two topsailmen screamed as they fell, dislodged by the impact. One man collided against the rocks in a bloody splatter, dead on impact. The other sank beneath the waves.

"Drop my chair!" Tundy cried out as splintered wood, rope, and belay pins rained down on the deck. "Get that man out of the drink!"

The water came alive with the frenzied feeding of piranha sharks — each one, three feet of slick gray muscle and gnashing teeth. The sailor's terrified screams were swallowed by the waves as he was dragged under — the sharks' tail fins smacking against the *Kajak's* hull. Her deck crew stood stunned and silent in the murder's wake.

"What are you doing?!" Dorav shouted, seeing the mainmast headed for the same fate. "Straighten her beam!"

"Move, ye bilge drinkers! Move!" Tundy stood amidships shouting at the top of his lungs. "Anyone I see slackin' gets used for chum!"

The sailors scrambled athwartships, climbing up the weather deck and across the yards while Myrkin righted the helm. The *Kajak* straightened herself with a groan of ropes and creaking timber. Sailors aloft screamed, clinging to the rigging for dear life as she rolled on her axis before righting herself.

"Torchfin whales don't swim this close to shore," Dorav said. "What are those piranhas doing here?"

"They shadow ships that enter their hunting grounds, sir," Kartecus replied. "Damn things are clever that way."

The men aloft gripped the yards,frozen in fear and deathly quiet.

"Get those men moving, Mister Tundy!" Dorav said.

"Ye can change yer knickers later, lassies!" Tundy barked. "Brace the rigging! Secure the sails! I want my canvas crisp! And someone clean this up!" He pointed a meaty finger at a broken belay pin laying at his feet.

"Captain!" cried Denirce, the ship's carpenter, as she reached the weather deck. "What have you done to me baby!?"

"It's just a flesh wound, Ms. Denirce," Dorav said.

"Flesh wound? You just flicked me off me cot with that stunt!" She raised her gaze to where the sailors were scrambling to secure the loose sails and rigging. "Terra's sweet tits! Just a flesh wound you say!?"

"God's name!" Kartecus rasped, pointing. "Dorav, look!"

The broken ruin lodged between the rocks ahead made Dorav quietly thank God for his crew. A Padivian war-galley was wedged between two stone pillars and cracked open like an egg. Her broken masts and wasted bowsprit jutted out of the water like the fingers of a drowning woman, covered in tattered canvas and rigging.

"Keep the course, Master Myrkin," Dorav said sternly. "Eyes on the rocks."

"Aye, sir."

If they had not made the turn in time, or if their hull had struck the rock wall, this could have been their fate.

"Help," came a chilling whisper as they inched past the wreckage. "Help."

"Sir?" Myrkin glanced towards the broken ship.

"Help! Help! Help us!" The desperate cries came from inside the broken ship's hull, growing suddenly in number and urgency. "Please!"

Dorav could hear people moving around within her hull, pressing against the planks of the partially sunken forecastle. "We have injured! We're trapped in here! Please, help us!"

"Sir?!" Myrkin's eyes betrayed his fright.

"Eyes on the damn rocks, Master Myrkin!" he barked back.

Kartecus and Isa walked to the starboard bulwark, studying the wreck somberly.

"How long do you wager she's been there?" Isa asked.

The damage suffered over time was extensive. Her canvas was in tatters, her timbers had rotted, and her archboard swarmed with so many barnacles he could not read her name.

"Since the war," Dorav said sourly. "Fifteen years at least."

A few sailors crowded astarboard, gaping at the terrible fate they had avoided. Dorav dug into his coin pouch and pulled out three silver marks, each embedded with Zenthien's holy scepter. He put them to his lips and threw them to the water.

"May God's golden light find you and lead you to the City of Splendor," he said before turning to watch the ship's progress. Isa and Kartecus each took out a single silver mark, kissed it, and tossed it, repeating the prayer of passing. A few sailors retrieved their iron chints with trembling hands and threw them into the waves, their faces haunted.

"Wait!" The voices cried out. "Where are you going?! We have children here! You can't leave us! Wait! Please!"

"Back to your posts!" Ser Isa cried out. "Stop listening, unless you would have them follow you into your dreams!"

The sailors returned to their posts while the cries carried on behind them. Women howled, men spat profanity, and children wailed at the top of their lungs. The wind gave their voices a hollow, inhuman tone until the sounds finally died away.

"No good omen," Kartecus said, watching the ship's wake.

"No," Dorav said, his mouth like cotton. "Best not to dwell on it, Kartecus."

"Aye, Aye, sir."

"We're clear The Spine, sir!" Myrkin said, once their bowsprit passed the last towering pillars.

"And not a moment too soon," Dorav said, the first drops of rain falling around them. "Nihengale, what do you see?!"

"A cove, quarter mile west of our position," Nihengale called back. "No sign of the enemy."

"Depth!?" Myrkin glanced towards the bow.

"Twelve fathoms, sir!" Dessa cried.

"Drop anchor and prepare the boats!" Dorav called. "Ms. Dessa, come relieve Master Myrkin at the helm."

"Aye, Aye, sir!" she cried.

"Master Myrkin, once I'm ashore, the ship is yours," he said.

"Aye, sir."

"Ms. Denirce, I apologize for the trouble but I need those masts duly repaired."

"Once we are out of these troubling rocks, sir," she said, "but don't worry your pretty head. I'll have her mended double-time."

"Make certain you do."

"Have I ever let you down, sir? I'll go raise my crew." She vanished below deck.

"Probably best if you attempt your escape during the day and with clear skies, Myrkin," he said. "And stay clear of that wreckage."

"Agreed, sir," Myrkin said.

"You know your orders from here. Let Kivan know that I want him stitched to the alchemist girl..."

"Marca, sir."

"Right, Marca. He is at her disposition from here on."

"Aye, sir. And the spook that shadows her?"

"She is Marca's responsibility, but keep one eye on her."

"Aye."

"Ser Isa..." He let the statement hang in air.

"I'll prepare my men for the boats."

"Nihengale!" Dorav called out. "I want you and yours on the first boat out. Scout the area and secure the landing for my marines."

"Aye, sir." Nihengale nodded and studied the cove.

"You're going with them, Kartecus," he told his lieutenant, ignoring his sneer of dissatisfaction. "Give us a signal when we are clear to approach."

Kartecus nodded, his eyes oozing resentment. "Aye, Aye, sir."

Lieutenant Kartecus glared at the five spooks standing at attention on the sand. The creatures stood in a line as ordered, staring with their beady, inhuman eyes. With his hands behind his back, he strolled before them, taking their measure as he would a gaggle of freshly pressed recruits. They wore cured leather armors the color of wet slate, with recurved direwood bows strapped to their backs. As much as he loathed to admit, they exuded the dangerous air of trained killers.

The first on the line was their leader, Nihengale. Like all bajies, his skin was pale as eggshells, though unlike city bajies, his black hair was long and braided behind his head. His facial features were as sharp and feral as the rest of his kind, but his viridian eyes displayed a piercing intelligence Kartecus rarely saw outside of the Admiralty. His thin nose and chiseled jawline gave him an almost aristocratic air, and he wore a thin scar on his left eyebrow. A thick leather belt with two recurved daggers at each side, and eight throwing knives in individual sheathes hung from his waist.

The next spook on the line was half a head taller than Kartecus, with raven-colored hair and cobalt eyes holding lethal promise. The damn pybem's gaze was difficult to hold, but Kartecus held it all the same. He had seen that look before, in the eyes of men who shed so much blood, they became as dangerous as the weapons they wielded. He had the merest hint of crow's feet near his eyes, and his mouth was a knife cut. His face was that of a man unaccustomed to cheer or laughter. The pybem's hands were disproportionately large with vicious claws peeking through his fingertips. His equally clawed feet were shaped like a man's, but had padded soles, like those of a cat. He wore a slender sword tied against his right shoulder-blade, a battle-worn, black metal gauntlet on his left forearm, and a throwing knife belt across his chest.

Kartecus snorted in derision and moved down the line. Up next, the gray-skinned nebi also had padded feet. In every way, she reminded him of an overcast sky. Her long, white hair held a dull silvery hue and her eyes were a haunting mix of ivory and polished galena. Her face was angular and striking, like a high-born lady of court. If she was not little more than a two-legged beast, he might even call her beautiful. She was muscular and lithe, and either lacked breasts entirely, or had wrapped them behind her leathers. There was nothing delicate about this nebi. She stood with the coiled tension of a seasoned warrior, her features hard and fearless. She wore a xiphos sheathed on her belt and a reinforced wooden shield strapped to her back.

Otherwise decent men fancied plowing nebies like her — even paid top coin for the privilege. The thought made his skin crawl. Kartecus smoothed his long white mustache with his gloved hand and continued his appraisal.

He could tell the dali at the end of the line was a specialist. His composite bow was an exotic looking contraption of bone and lacquered wood. The smallest of the males, he had their same jet-black hair, but his skin was more ecru than off-white, and his oval eyes were a mixture of polished amber and tangerine. His facial features were as predatory as the other spooks, but his hawkish nose, rounded eyes, and thin neck made him appear effeminate. Kartecus knew a deadeye sniper when he saw one.

Adding to their already savage appearance, thin scrollwork tattoos marked their hands, necks, and faces. They looked like humans who had spent too much time in the wilds and been reforged by nature's cruel hands. Mepsiens, the fucking spooks called themselves, from the wilds of Helicartia. As much as he hated all xial, he loathed these wild, tattooed freaks the most.

"What was your name again, baji?" Kartecus asked.

"Nihengale," he replied.

"You lead these beasts ?"

"Yes."

"Yes sir, you godless abomination," he said sharply.

"Yes, sir." Nihengale's face remained calm, his tone even.

"How is my perimeter?"

"Secure, sir. No enemy patrols in the area for two miles."

"Good. Now, there is a guarded outpost standing between us and Sharn. Captain Dorav believes you four spooks can clear it without warning being sent."

"Yes, sir."

"There will be around twenty men, and more than one way to relay a message."

"I am aware of the numbers, sir," Nihengale replied. "They will not be given time to alert Sharn."

Kartecus bit back his rising ire. He did not like how calm this bastard whoreson was acting. The only advantage the crew of the *Kajak* had over the fortress of Sharn was surprise. If word reached the garrison that an armed contingent was marching towards them, they would drop their portcullis and the mission would fail. They did not have the manpower to besiege or overtake the city if she closed her legs to them.

When Kartecus went to speak, his throat tightened and choked his words. He coughed into his fist and tried again. "How long?"

Nihengale squinted against the steadily falling rain. "There is still time before the sun rises. We can clear the outpost before first light."

"We will see," Kartecus said bitterly. "Listen well, baji, if wounded or captured, do not expect rescue. If Sharn is warned of our coming, so help me I will fuck your corpses in turn and feed them to my dogs."

Nihengale did not react to his taunt.

"Dismissed!"

"Yes, sir," Nihengale stated flatly and quickly moved away, the others following closely behind.

Kartecus watched them go, wanting nothing more than to draw his blade and bathe in their blood. Taking a deep breath, he carefully lit the wick of his lantern. He swung the lamp three times in each direction, informing the *Kajak* the beach was secure. A lantern on the ship repeated the signal in confirmation.

Kartecus stood in the rain and waited as the *Kajak's* rowboats made their way towards his light. His good, loyal men, following orders without question or reproach, sent to this miserable country, only to die.

2

The Blades of Mepsia

Murciel stood at the edge of the precipice overlooking Sharn's outpost, absorbing its details. Six cordwood cabins with tepid candlelight shining through their windows, huddled within a twenty-foot enclosure. Sentries patrolled the wall's parapets, shielded lamps in hand.

Two men scanned the surrounding area using bulls-eye lanterns from a single watchtower rising forty-feet into the night sky. Another pair guarded the southern gate, wrapped in oilcloaks to fend off the rain.

A flat dirt road led from the fort's southern gate to a nearby boathouse and pier where six flat-bottom keelboats floated, held fast by wet ropes.

Murciel edged away from the lip and headed back to where the others had taken shelter, huddled under a concavity in the mountain's face.

"Two gates, six cabins, a boathouse, and a watchtower," he said in xiasi, the age-old language of his people. "Their stable is near the north wall. The horses are in shelter with no sign of a stable-hand. Most of the anthrops are inside, but my guess is there will be around four to eight to a cabin, not counting the two in the watchtower, two by the gates, two on the parapets, and whoever resides in the boathouse."

"Having them indoors will make the job easier," Nihengale said pensively, "and the rain will cover our approach. We will need the tower and the wall sentries silenced first. Can you do it from this far?" Nihengale's green eyes studied him.

He nodded, shuffling his feet. "I can see them well enough, and the wind is thin."

"We cannot afford a miss," Escara warned him sharply, tying her long white hair in a loop, revealing the smooth chiseled features of her truculent contours. Her face was like the sea, calm and beautiful one moment, turbulent the next. He sensed her iron glare piercing his skull.

"I won't miss," he said, keeping his tone level.

"The rest of us will wait for your signal," Nihengale said. "Are you certain there are no other sentries?"

"No, but the north gate is likely guarded, from without."

Nihengale nodded.

Buio's cold gaze fell on him. The D'kirn's silent demeanor and hard icy stares could unnerve the most seasoned warriors. Nihengale could stare right into those dangerous orbs without flinching, but Murciel was quietly cowed.

"I'm not going to miss, Buio," he answered the unspoken chide.

Buio stood and padded into the downpour, heading for the outpost.

"Nihengale," Escara said, "what did that foolish old anthrop call you at the beachhead?"

"Baji? It's a...demeaning slur. They have one for each of our clans."

Escara's brow furrowed. "I think I'll kill that old trolker."

"You don't have my leave to do so, Escara," Nihengale said, "as much as I desire to give it. Let's move, before Buio kills everyone without us."

"I'll handle the boathouse," Escara said, and unsheathed her xiphos.

They walked out of the enclosure, leaving him to his thoughts. "I won't miss," he whispered.

On their last mission, he had become overzealous and missed twice attempting to take down an outrider. That one horseman prolonged their stay in anthrop lands for another month. Nihengale made no mention of it, but Buio and Escara had yet to allow him live it down.

Murciel made his way out and around the black-stone mountain face. As he reached the lip of the precipice, Buio and Nihengale dispatched the two gate sentries and dragged their bodies away. Escara exited the boathouse, the blood on her blade washed away by the downpour.

21

Murciel drew his bow and measured the range. Knowing his arrows would need more power to clear the distance, he pulled the weapon's limb extensions into place, doubling her profile. With practiced hands he strung her and tested the tautness of her queen's silk string.

His Manticore was a beautiful, black-lacquered bone and direwood composite bow. Master Bonen made her capable of extension and retraction, giving him a weapon he could use in both skirmishes and long distance sniping. She was his prized possession and the envy of many an archer from his cadre.

Unsealing his quiver and securing his grip on his bow, he eyed the watchtower. The observation platform was four hundred feet of rain heavy sky away, and covered by a conical roof of thatch. The rains pushed down on the packed straw, revealing the location of the wooden support beams underneath. The silhouettes of the two guards in the tower were betrayed their lamplight.

Murciel retrieved two arrows with heavy-headed piercing heads called *beaks,* and inspected the markings on their heads. Satisfied, he pinched one with the index finger of his bow hand and knocked the second.

Every muscle in his body was soaked, cold, and tense. His breathing was hurried and his heart raced in anticipation.

When he pulled the queen's silk cord back, his muscles relaxed into the motion, his feet rooted to the earth, and a ball of power expanded within his stomach. By the time the string was fully taut, his body was at ease.

The *Kiyo'ezat* was practiced by only the most devout archers in Helicartia. It gave him a profound link to his weapon, but would also take a toll on his body over time. The chill wind on his skin and the water soaking his leathers became distant memories. Only the Manticore and her intended victims existed in that moment.

The movements of the men in the dimly lit tower slowed with his every inhalation. He angled his aim up to compensate for wind and distance, patiently following his target until a single bolt of sheet lightning exploded in the horizon, brightening the leaden sky.

His first arrow flew, followed instantly by his second. The arrows arched in air and fell towards their targets, gaining speed as they dove like birds of prey. His first beak punched through the thatch and pierced one sentry's throat cleanly. The other tore through the flimsy roofing and sank into the second man's torso, between neck and collarbone. The anthrop grabbed at the arrow and stumbled against the squat wall, blood gushing on to his leather gloves and polished mail.

The men on the parapets turned to regard the tower's erratic lamplight.

Murciel fired two fast-flying strikers at the guard walking towards the south gate. Both missiles drove through the man's leather armor and he crumbled. The last sentry moved to unstrap the signal horn on his belt. One beak plunged between his ribs as his arm came up, another burrowed into his pelvic cavity just above his hip bone. The anthrop collapsed, his left leg kicked twice, and he lay still.

Murciel took measured breaths as the *Kiyo'ezat* faded. All four targets were down. He lowered the Manticore.

"All clear, Escara," he said as loud as he could without shouting.

Below, more than three hundred feet away, Escara gave him a hand signal to verify she heard him. Murciel's head throbbed from the exertion of the *Kiyo'ezat*. The weight of his flesh and the chill of the pelting rains returned in unison. Forcing himself to focus, he pointed the bow at the camp's center and waited for the others to enter.

"I won't miss," he whispered once more.

Buio studied the six anthrop mercenaries from behind the cabin window's shutters. The largest of them he dubbed Polisher. He was a fat, broad-shouldered man, polishing a breastplate near the southern wall.

Sleeper was a mere cub, snoring soundly on his cot by the door. The other four anthrops sat at a table in the middle of the room, playing cards. Eye-patch was the eldest, with only a wisp of hair on his spotted head and a worn leather patch over his right eye. His thick white mustache twitched as he studied his hand. The other three were young and lacked any distinguishing marks.

Buio reached into his pouch and retrieved three purple-skinned orbs the size of walnuts. Holding them gingerly in his left hand he gripped the hilt of the slender sword strapped to his back.

Made from mitiri, mepsien holy star-steel, the vrin was dull black except for its delicate scrollwork, which caught the moonlight as the blade cleared its ironbark scabbard. Putting his back to the shutters, he closed his eyes and calmed his body and mind, the markings on his skin tingling as he dropped into the *Alci'mavor*.

The tension in his muscles fell away and his heart slowed to a deep, stalling pace. The chatter of falling raindrops became a musical chorus, his ears picking out the minute differences of when water struck wood, water, or metal.

He opened his eyes and witnessed the rainfall slow its descent until he could observe individual droplets, glistening in the evening glow.

He took a moment to admire the raw beauty the enhanced state brought his senses. Sari's face was a pale, crescent apparition cloaked in living nimbus, her light riding the rain down to the pools of liquid silver by his feet.

A pang of guilt struck him at the thought that Sari, Child of Mercy, might weep for the lives he meant to take. A bolt of purple lightning danced above his head — the pulsing veins of Aeros Sky Serpent — painting the night sky in violet and cobalt.

Old Ren, guide my hand.

Buio took a deep breath and squeezed the chirk seeds in his hand until they cracked. In a single, fluid motion, he pulled open the cabin's shutters and flung the seeds into the room. The purple-skinned projectiles flew halfway to the far wall before pressure built up from contact with the air made them explode into a thin cloud of brown spores.

He leaped nimbly into the cabin with the anthrops — his pads making no sound as he landed, his senses peaked by the blood trance. Time's river flowed around him as a languid brook.

The startled men were in motion, but to him, they moved as if caught in molasses. The chirk seed spores were already taking effect, numbing their sensation of touch, gumming their eyes, and restricting the response of their adrenals.

Buio thrust his vrin through the neck of the man with his back to the window, cutting flesh like curd. A wet, sucking sound popped and a geyser of arterial spray took flight as he slid his sword back.

Eye-patch's one good eye and chapped lips widened as he fumbled for his weapon. Buio flicked a black throwing knife into the old man's gaping mouth. The aged mercenary fell back into his chair, grabbing at his throat while digging behind his teeth with his fingers.

Steel sliced across moonlight as the anthrop to Buio's left swung for his head. He blocked the kopis with his gauntlet and thrust the tip of his vrin into the young man's beating heart.

With a confounded look, the anthrop dropped his sword and stumbled, falling over his own chair. Buio's instincts flared. He bent at the waist, ducking under a diagonal slash meant to cleave through his torso.

Before he could turn on his attacker, Polisher threw his breastplate aside and stood, unsheathing his kopis with a burly hand. Buio snapped a throwing knife into the big man's groin. With a hissing wheeze, the soldier grabbed at his manhood and collapsed flat on his face. Buio rolled forward, avoiding a second vicious attack from the mercenary behind him.

He rose, facing the anthrop.

Terrified, the young man tried to call for help, but the cirk spores were deep in his throat now, constricting his vocal chords so only a tiny squeak escaped him.

Buio stepped forward into a devastating backhand slash, cutting through the anthrop's lower belly like a full sack of wine, spilling his steaming viscera at his feet.

As the man scrambled to retrieve his entrails in horror, Buio brought his black claws to bare and shredded his neck, releasing a gush of lifeblood.

Buio took a long, deep breath, releasing the *Alci'mavor*. His body insisted he vomit, but his training took hold. As he breathed to regulate his metabolism, he noticed the sleeping anthrop cub had his back pressed against the wall; a look of terror in his eyes, and urine staining his sheets.

A pained gurgle escaped Polisher.

Buio pointed the tip of his bloodied vrin at the boy. "Don't move," he spoke in calisthian.

The frightened cub shook his head.

Buio stood over Polisher, placed his left pad on the man's thick neck, extracted his claws, and raked back, ripping flesh and arteries to tatters, blood spraying on his leather schynbald. He yanked his throwing knife out of the dying man's groin and cleaned it against his shirt before sheathing it.

Eye-patch was dead, a rivulet of drool and blood oozing from his open mouth. Buio stuck his extended index claw into the mans throat, found the hollow ring at the end of the knife's flat pommel, and yanked. The cub on the bed did not move.

Buio sheathed his vrin and knife, reached into his pouches and retrieved a small blue flower — Mystwalker, his people called it. He presented it to the boy. At proximity, he could tell the cub had done more than piss himself.

"Eat this."

The cub shook his head.

Buio wrapped his fingers around the hilt of his vrin.

The boy hurriedly took the flower from his hand and put it in his mouth.

"Now chew."

The anthrop cub obeyed, tears streaming down his face. In moments, a dazed, faraway look entered his eyes, and he smiled. The boy's eyelids drooped sleepily, he let out a prolonged sigh, and slumped back into the bed. Buio checked his life signs.

"Sari's mercy, young one," he said. Mystwalker was deadly to anthrops, but it was a merciful, painless death.

Buio wiped the warm blood off his face and opened the cabin's door, leaning against its frame. Nihengale emerged from the neighboring structure, gripping his bloodied moonblades.

Fighting with the recurved mitiri daggers was a noble tradition among the Alci'tirnni, and was by far the most difficult of the combat styles taught at the academy, but Buio preferred his loyal vrin and shield gauntlet.

Buio pointed at the next building he intended to take. Nihengale nodded and headed towards his own target. Escara appeared, her shield strapped to her left arm. Buio tapped the throwing knives across his chest with two fingers. Reluctantly, she shouldered her shield and tapped her own knives.

She had hounded him for weeks to teach her how to use them in combat. Now that she was competent, she needed to put them to use. She depended too much on the forms taught by the Ren'koltor. She needed to learn diversity.

Near his next target, Buio found the body of an anthrop who had stepped out to relieve his bladder. He lay with his shriveled manhood in his hand and one of Murciel's beaked arrows protruding from his back. Buio looked towards Murciel's perch, but could not spot him through the rain.

The three men inside the cabin were still unconcerned for their missing companion. Buio spied them from behind their shuttered window, naming them in his mind; Reader, Frog-Chin, and Talker. He took a deep breath.

Old Ren, guide my hand.

Escara placed her back against the eastern wall of her next target, frustrated with the rain. She attempted to discern the different scents within and bristled. The overpowering aroma of moist earth was everywhere.

The rich, wet soil sang symphonies in her nostrils, but its revelry hampered her ability to sniff out her prey. She tried to listen to them speaking or moving around, but could not get a clear picture past the sounds of the downpour.

Not wanting to take risks, she returned to the cabin she had recently cleared and pulled the heavy oilcloak off an anthrop's corpse, wrapping it around herself. The large, cowled cloak enveloped her in its previous owner's scent; ripe with sweat, blood, and a hint of urine. She sprinted into the occupied building, turned her back to them, and closed the door.

"Oh get off it!" one of them said gruffly. "Rain ain't that bad."

"That you, Pip?" another asked in a well-humored tone. "Get outta' that cloak you little boot-lick and dry your man-cunnie!"

Escara took a long, deep breath through her nose. A bouquet of variant scents soared up her nostrils and into her mind, mapping the room in a breath. The damp cordwood walls provided the interior dimensions, the acidity of sweat lingering on the anthrop's sheets gave her the location of each cot, and the thick perfume of their wool-wax candles revealed every light-source. More importantly, were the multiple odors distinguishing the five anthrop males inhabiting the cramped quarters.

Three of them sat at a table to her left, drinking bullhorn. Two lounged on a cot to her right, eating pumpkin bread and pheasant boiled in corn broth. The three who had moonshine on their breath still wore their rain-soaked banded mail, and one of them had recently oiled his sword. The bed where the two unarmored males ate stank of sex-sweat.

"Pip?" the anthrop asked again, a hint of tension rumbling in his voice.

Escara closed her eyes and took a prolonged breath, entering the *Alci'mavor*. Her heightened senses sharpened exponentially — every sound and smell in the room rushing through her. She could hear the men's blood as it pumped fear through their veins and the shuffle of their uneasy bodies. Every flutter of their candles' flames was like a drumbeat. When she opened her eyes, the room was bathed in breathtaking, golden radiance.

Snap, don't throw. She reminded herself. *No spin.*

Escara dropped the cloak and turned. As the rain-soaked garment floated away, she snapped two throwing knives at the unarmored men on the cot, catching one in the eye and the other in the center of his chest. The men at the table sat stupefied, mouths agape at her sudden appearance. She threw two more knives near the end of her rotation — one bouncing harmlessly off the wall's mortar, the other gashing the side of one man's head before nailing itself to the log beside him.

Rodent's luck!

The *Alci'mavor* fell away, leaving her dazed and nauseated. She leaned against the door for purchase, fighting back the urgent need to vomit, a cold sweat coating her skin. She was disoriented and dangerously drained.

"Fuck my sister's ass!" The man with the fresh gash across his skull growled. "Kill it! Fucking kill it!" He pointed a dirty fingernail at her.

The other two men stood from their stools and rushed her, kopis swords scraping from scabbards. She ducked under the first man's swing, drew her xiphos and cut a deep gash into his inner thigh in a single motion. Hot blood erupted from the femoral artery, drenching her face and blinding her left eye. She immediately regretted not keeping her shield.

28

As the first man fell, bleeding leg in hand, the second anthrop's kopis sped for her torso in a violent downward slash. She parried the attack and used the coiled power of her legs to thrust her sword upward, slicing behind his chin, up through his tongue and palate, and into his gray-matter.

The man let out a wet, gurgling whine, cutting his hands open on her blade as he tried desperately to pull it out. When he dropped, limp and lifeless, his weight tore the xiphos from her hand.

"Cock and ass!" The last one shouted, running for the back door. "Alarm! Intruders!"

Escara leaped on his back, wrapping herself around him, and using her forward momentum, to peel him off his feet. They hit the floor in a crash, the man's metal breastplate slamming painfully down on her left arm. Before he could react, she put her hand firmly over his lips and sank her teeth into his neck, biting down until she tore tender flesh and hot lifeblood flushed into her mouth. He screamed impotently into her hand, squirming in agony until death finally stilled him.

She pushed him off, coughing and spitting out his blood. "Trolker!" she said, and stood.

The throbbing pain in her bruised arm and the scents of unwashed skin and emptying bowels, only worsened her nausea. The man with the fatal leg wound whined, still clinging to life. Escara recovered her xiphos and buried it in the back of his neck.

She retrieved her weapons from around the room, making certain everyone was dead before stepping out to rejoin the others. When Buio came into view, she tapped the knives across her chest, put up two fingers and then four, revealing her success rate. He nodded flatly and looked away, deadpan and unimpressed.

She narrowed her eyes at him.

"Bastard."

Nihengale watched Ser Isa as she entered the sacked outpost, flanked by armed seaguards. She wore her full Ashuran battledress; masterfully crafted steel breastplate, helm, tassets, gauntlets, and schynbalds over a padded gambeson and light chainmail. Over her shoulders she wore a thick leather oilcloak to protect her metal

29

plating from the rain.

Nihengale had never faced an Ashura in battle before. Their armors were expensive and laboriously detailed, made with the finest steel and custom fitted to each wearer. Every symbol and length of scrollwork engraved on the metal was emblematic to the zoniran faith, which spared no expense to equip their knights.

The ornate, round shields they carried were bonded with an alchemical agent called aegis, which made them both light and nigh indestructible — making Ashuras notoriously difficult to kill.

He casually took note of the small weak spots in the cumbersome armor, surmising that it would take some feinting and swift maneuvering, but he could kill her, if he had to. He simply needed to wear her out first.

With a series of quick hand gestures, Isa sent two of her men into each cabin to inspect their work. Nihengale waited with Buio and Escara by the fort's north wall, while Murciel sat on the parapet above their heads.

"Report," Knight Isa said, the flat, sharp angles of her helm enhancing her grim features.

"The outpost was cleared without incident, Ser Isa," he said.

"Ser, everyone's dead." Lieutenant Commander Kathor announced as he approached. "There were more than thirty mercenaries here."

Isa eyed them in turn and looked up to Murciel's perch. The rain had washed most of the blood off them, but he could tell she was disquieted. "Are you certain none got away?"

"They had four caged carrier-pigeons in the watchtower and eight horses tied in their stable, one of them saddled and ready for quick escape. They are all still there, awaiting your inspection."

"Seems the Captain was right to trust you," she spoke begrudgingly. "Think you can manage this same trick at Sharn?"

"Not with just the four of us. We will need every man you have trained in silent killing."

"My men are trained in honorable combat, mepsien." Ser Isa's stony demeanor became menacing.

"Of course."

"I will grant you men, but they are not yours to expend. You will sacrifice your own before you risk a single one of mine. Understood?"

30

"No, that I will not do," Nihengale said, mirroring Isa's icy stare. "We work together, and I will protect them as I would my own, but we live or die as a unit. Your men's lives are worth no more than ours."

"So it is true," she said with a scoff. "You wild spooks really believe yourselves equal to humans."

"No, Ser Isa. I would never reduce my people to such a level."

"Cretin!"

Knight Isa wrapped her fingers around the hilt of her sword. Before she could draw, the tip of Buio's vrin landed above her wrist, pressing softly against her leather glove. Had Buio completed the strike, he would have taken her hand.

Ser Isa stared at Buio in surprise. Her men came pouring out of the cabins, swords drawn.

"Hold!" Captain Dorav called out forcefully. "Stand down!"

The marines begrudgingly sheathed their weapons. Dorav made his way into the outpost with Kartecus by his side. The captain wore the same style of armor as Ser Isa, except for his cloak being purple cloth and bearing the head of a snarling white wolf, distinguishing him as a Vinergalian naval officer.

Kartecus wore pernoit armor along with his own long officer's cloak. The flat wooden disks tucked between two layers of boiled leather that protected its wearer from neck to knee was named after the master of the enslaved xial who created it.

Mepsiens used a similar kind of armor on river war-vessels because it not only provided protection, but kept whoever donned it afloat if they fell into the current. Anthrop sailors had dub it "woodmor", or "barkskin". While effective in naval combat, the armor made the old lieutenant appear noticeably less imposing than the clanking Ashuras.

"Put it away, Murciel!" Nihengale called out in xiasi without bothering to look up. He knew how fast Murciel could draw and knock arrow.

"I told you they were not to be trusted, Captain," Kartecus growled as they approached.

"Not now," Dorav admonished. "Mind explaining this, Ser Isa?"

"It's nothing, sir," she said. "Just a misunderstanding."

"Is that true, Nihengale?" Dorav asked dourly, looking between them with eyes as sharp as cut sapphires. They built them hard, these Ashuras. He had to respect that.

"Yes," he said.

"Good, consider the matter resolved then. Someone, give me a status report. Was anything sent to warn Sharn of our coming?"

"No," Nihengale said. "As I explained to the Commander, all methods of alarm were disabled."

"Ser Isa, does this meet with your satisfaction?"

"I've yet to check the stables and bird cages, sir."

"Then do so. Have the men set up a perimeter and establish a command center...there." He pointed absently to the cabin on his right. "Nihengale, I want your people a mile up the road in case we have unwanted company. Both of you report to me once you're finished."

"Sir," Nihengale and Isa said in near unison.

"Dismissed. Kartecus, with me." Dorav turned on his heel.

The old man gave them a withering look before following his captain.

"This isn't over, mepsien," Isa hissed at him when Dorav was out of earshot.

Nihengale eyed her evenly, accustomed to eyes more dangerous than hers. Ser Isa turned and walked away.

3

A Life of Stone

"If you could live anywhere, where would you travel?" Tynisia asked, wrapping her arm around his chest.

Caige stared up at his home's thatch ceiling, pulling her closer against him. "To Ticondria."

"Where you grew up cutting trees?"

"Yes. To be among the oaks and erawa trees again. To walk the hills, crooks, and meadows."

"To be with Erin and Marin?"

"Yes, and so that you can meet them." He nibbled at the tip of her nose.

She smiled and kissed his chest. "Do you think they'll like me, Caige?" She rubbed her leg against his groin, stirring his lust.

"They'll love you, Tyn." He pushed her hair behind her ear and kissed the crown of her head. "Who could bear not to?"

"Would we have land?"

"I know the very spot. A hill I frequented as a boy. A stream flows at its foot and the soil is rich for planting."

"And your father? Will he come with us?"

"No," he said. "We leave him here."

"Beneath the heavy stones?"

"Yes, beneath the heavy stones."

"What about Maggie? She must come too."

"No... no, Tyn, she cannot."

Tyn graced him with a beautifully tragic smile, her amber colored eyes staring. "If she cannot come, then this is goodbye, my Cairn," she said, flowing out of bed and walking naked out his doorway.

"No, Tyn wait!" Caige stumbled uneasily after. Outside, the sudden glare of the morning sun pierced his eyes like arrowheads. He raised a hand and steadied himself. His beloved ran over the cracked earth of Kaira, making haste for a two-horse carriage waiting beyond a thin sheet of heat-blur.

"Tynisia!" he called after her, the sound of his own voice cutting through his skull. "Tyn! Wait!"

A startling roar answered Caige's call. An enormous apparition of woven muscle, sharpened claws, and a full black mane left a trail of dust as it sprinted for Tynisia's back. She screamed in terror, running frantically for her life as the predator closed the gap between them.

"No! NO!"

Caige ran after them, his feet heavy and awkward on the uneven street.

The massive beast pounced, bringing Tynisia down in a cloud of whirling sand and horrified pleas. It snapped its head back and forth, drenching the sand with her blood. Tynisia's struggles became feeble and her screams gurgled.

Caige's heart clenched like a fist. "Tyn! Tyn! TYYYYN!" All around him, his world began to shatter like broken pottery.

He woke, the thundering in his chest leaving him momentarily breathless.

"Fuck," he spat.

Whether pleasant dream or nightmare, he loathed dreaming of Tynisia. The joy of seeing her, touching her, only to awaken alone on his straw, gutted him, leaving him like an abandoned furnace recalling a warmth it would never know again.

Caige stood, stretched his sore back, and walked to his tiny kitchen space. Using a ladle, he scooped warm water from his barrel and drank his fill. A family of black cave beetles were inside his bread crate, sharing one of his loaves. He flicked them off and took a hearty bite , shaking the remaining critters out of the container before resealing the lid. The insects crawled away, deprived of their meal.

As he ate, his gaze wandered to his meager possessions within his small, dactwood hut. A woodcutting ax, an empty clay pot, a hunting bow, and a dusty quiver holding six forgotten arrows — all remnants from his years in the woodlands of Ticondria.

He had happily sold everything that belonged to his father, but now his hut felt lonely and hollow. Shaking the dust out of his shaggy hair, he grabbed the clay pot and headed towards Ricker's claim — the morning's light bearing down on his back.

On the Earthly Road, the Antep family worked their flax field and the Pirils nursed their dact palms. He stopped at the Piril's fence,waving to little Rinna. The girl ran up to meet him with her enchanting smile.

She was ten, with shining black hair and eyes like honey. Her white smile shone against her walnut colored complexion.

"Hello, Caige!" She climbed the short fence and wrapped her small arms around his neck. "Ugh! You stink!"

"Because I'm old," he said, smiling at her. "Wait eight years and you'll smell too."

"I will not!" She made a bitter face but never lost her smile.

"Have any dacts for me today?"

Rinna looked over her shoulder and lowered her voice to a conspirator's tone. "I'm not to give anyone dacts. Father's word."

Caige placed his chin on the fence, matching her whisper. "I'm not anyone. I'm your friend, Caige. We are friends, no?"

"Stop swindling my daughter, Caige." Gimen Piril approached with a grin. He wore only his trousers, calceus, and a battered straw hat.

"No swindle. This is fair exchange."

"So you eat free dacts every morning. What do I get?" Gimen asked.

"You get nothing, but Rinna here gets a big wet kiss!" Caige planted a kiss on Rinna's forehead. She laughed, wiping her head with the back of her hand.

"Go ahead and give him one, Rinna. Just make sure he pays what is due."

"I will!" She tutted at her father in annoyance. "Here you go."

Caige took the little fruit with a smile.

"Now go help your mother," Gimen said.

"Bye Caige!" Rinna waved and ran back towards the field.

Caige waved back before putting the brown, wrinkly bulb into his mouth, savoring its sweetness.

"How's the mining coming along?" Gimen asked, wiping his hands on his trousers.

"Lousy. Your dact palms appear healthy."

"Appearances only. Won't be much harvest this year. It's too hot, even for them. Might have to go without dact wine."

"Madness. We'd sooner go without bread."

"I am serious, Caige. If change does not occur in the next month or so..."

"Well, gods be praised for palm sap." Caige grinned and presented his clay pot, swinging it by the handle.

Gimen chuckled. "I tapped you boys some an hour ago. Should be ready. How can you stomach the stuff this early?"

"We drink bullhorn, Gimen. Sap is nectar by comparison."

"As you say."

After saying his goodbyes to the Pirils, Caige made his way up the Kafra Road. The sweet palm sap numbed his pains and soothed his mind. The rest of the team sat at the box cut of Ricker's claim, looking hung-over and half asleep. They wore the same torn breeches and crusty layers of mine-grime they left with the day before.

Ricker sat in the shade with Sifran, sharing a cuksar. Ricker's black beard sprouted more gray hair every morning. While his body was knotted muscle from a lifetime of mining, the old man's skin was beginning to sag.

"Rough morning?" Ricker asked from under thick brows while passing him the cuksar.

"Aren't they all?" Caige traded him the clay pot for the smoke and took a deep drag.

Cuksar was a soldier's tool during the war. Each man was given a ration of it with their gear. The acrid smoke helped them withstand long marches and prolonged melees. After the war, the leaf found its way into the common market and became a favorite among farmers, sailors, and miners.

Caige held the thick, pungent smoke and released it with a hearty sigh, instantly feeling its alchemical effects. His muscles loosened, the fog in his head began to clear, and his heartbeat increased. Two more long drags, and he was ready to begin his day.

Sifran held out a four-fingered hand for the smoke. The wiry miner's lusterless black eyes were partially obscured behind his disheveled blond hair, and the small necrini pock scars on his face were dark and sunken this morning. He smoked the cuksar with relish, as if his life depended on it. "Bad dreams?" he asked.

Caige nodded.

"Me too," Sifran said. "All of us, it seems."

"We must be closing in on a vein," Ashen said. "I dreamed my hut was on fire. I tried to rise out of bed but I was tied to it by a length of living rope, black as tar."

Ashen was a good friend, who had seen him through a black time in his life. He had the same black hair and amber eyes as most Norvan born.

"From your lips to divine ears." Ricker passed Ashen the sap. "The vein, not your hut burning."

"David?" Caige asked.

"Where do you think?" Ashen drank from the pot.

"Decent a way as any to spend your chint," Sifran said with a shrug.

"Funny hearing that from you," Ricker said. "You never take any of the girls upstairs."

"I don't like paying for cunnie," Sifran said. "And I don't cherish the idea of my cock crumbling from my sack."

They shared a laugh.

"If cunnie's how David wants to lose his chint," Sifran said, lighting up a fresh smoke, "who am I to judge?"

"Especially since you spend all your chint on cock!" Ashen chortled.

Sifran grinned, blowing smoke through his nose. "Deadluck's a hard cock to beat. Two weeks of his victories have earned me good coin."

"Well if there's one thing David's proved," Ricker said, "is Leina's slit is clean. His dick would have fallen off months ago otherwise."

David heard the swarming of flies long before laying eyes on the village of simple thatch huts, shoddy and threadbare, each with rotting human heads staked three to a pole outside their thresholds. Tanned human skin curtained their doorways, stitched together with sun-baked sinew. Overlapping coats of blood coated the thatch as a ward against malign spirits. The reek of carrion was everywhere. At the village's center, they found what was left of David's men.

Three Queen's Storm Talons hung crucified on the branches of a mocatis tree, disemboweled, with their viscera wrapped around the branches, left to dry like strings of sausage. David's stomach lurched but he stubbornly kept his food down. Two of his men doubled over and retched.

"Cut them down," he said through sour cottonmouth. "Please, for God's sake."

One of the crucified corpses raised his head and glared at him with eyes gleaming like roseate quartz shards. David's heart caught in his throat.

When he woke, he was squeezing his linen covers in a death-grip. Leina lay beside him, her naked back to him. His dirk-caked skin and red beard were drenched in night-sweat and a layer of moist grime was soaked into the threadbare bedding. He put his bare feet on the floor and tried to calm his racing heart. He was in Leina's room above the Pick Rock Tavern. He drank too much bullhorn and blacked out again.

"You alright?" she asked, drowsily.

David had seen his share of horror during the war, but the memory of his men strung up like pigs for a banquet was a scar which never fully healed.

"I'm fine." He stood and cracked his weary bones.

Leina turned and pinched her face at him. "I swear by Terra's stone, you're not touching me again until you bathe, David. You stink like a fucking kafra."

"That's what you said last night, yet here we are again."

"Well, I don't normally refuse a man who pays up front, but for you I'm willing to go without."

He knew she didn't care about how he smelled. She was luring him — trying to rile him up enough to give her another rough tumble and a bit more coin. He quietly put his ragged breeches and leather caligae back on before placing a silver mark on her counter.

"I said you already paid me, you fat drunk." She stretched her thin arms above her head. Her sun-kissed skin, youthful curves, and dark, hard nipples made him reconsider leaving.

"I know," he said and walked out.

The musty tavern below was as silent as a tomb — littered with empty bottles and dirty mugs. He helped himself to the last dregs of an abandoned bottle of dact wine before stepping out into the stifling heat of Kaira's dusty streets.

The Coppertooth Road was sparse this morning. Citena unlocked her clayworks shop while Dendor diligently tempered a flat piece of hot iron by his forge. David waved to each in passing and made his way through the narrow alleys that crisscrossed the town.

Thoughts of his nightmare followed him on his walk up towards Ricker's mine. Though the war had ended fifteen years ago, he took pieces of it with him, like shrapnel in his mind no medicus could remove. The others lounged in the box cut, waiting for him.

"Hey red," Ashen called out. "You finally decide to roll your fat ass off Leina and put in some work?"

Ricker smiled behind his salt-and-pepper beard and offered him a half consumed cuksar.

Ashen sat throwing stones at a discarded beer stein with Caige. Corren's boy was two stone of muscle heavier and three years older than Ashen, but they looked like they could be brothers.

Ashen became a man of fifteen yeardays over a year ago, but remained a child in mind. David longed to beat the boy into some sort of shape, but Ricker always defended him.

When the earth-god Tarrak tore through the tunnels of Kaira two years back, he devoured everyone who did not flee their claims in time. Ashen's parents and Caige's father, Corren, all died during the attack.

Ricker had kept Caige on the team and brought Ashen into the fold. The boy would have ended up in the hands of the Magalian Miner's Guild otherwise. Anyone else would have put a boot to Ashen's ass for his daily antics but Ricker tolerated him and even carried his parents' debt to the Maggs.

People whispered that Ricker had been in love with Hajira, Ashen's mother. Some believed Ashen might secretly be Ricker's boy, but no one would speak it to the man's face.

"What's a pin-dick like you know about work?" David retorted. "I saw Dendor's boys playing stick ball by Fort Kai. Why don't you run along with them instead of stumbling around our ankles?"

Both Caige and Sifran chuckled at his remark.

"You look like shit, David," Ricker said. "Bad dreams?"

He nodded. "A cursed price to pay for mining shinn. We must be getting close to some."

"Pray we find it soon."

"Caige, there any wine left?" David asked, pointing at the clay pot near the boy's feet.

Caige shook his head.

"Fuck."

"Next time get here earlier," Ricker said, pushing himself off the wall. "Alright, everyone up! It's another beautiful day in Kaira!"

The others grunted their enthusiasm.

The wide Kafra Road was the busiest thoroughfare in town. It bordered every claim pockmarking the mountain's face, allowing miners to drag wagon-loads of discarded earth down to the deep stone bowl on the range's western base. Grunting, sweating merchants pushed loaded carts up and down the road, peddling dact wine, kafra stews, honey pastries, and secondhand mining supplies.

Every morning, Nianah walked her route on the road, calling out for her father's freshly baked breads. Nikos knew the men would spend their coin so they could speak to his daughter, and that no one would dare cross the line with her.

A man called Dunan who mined for old Meros had taken things a little too far with Nianah once, and was never seen again. Rumor was, Nikos used him as patty stuffing. To this day, people in Kaira still jokingly called meat pastries "dunans".

Ashen bought two thick loaves from Nianah every morning, and was never short for words. David watched them smile at each other while Ricker inspected the mine's rusty metal fence and lock for tampering.

"Ashen!" David shouted. "Stop wasting the girl's time and get back here!"

Ashen returned with a warm piece of bread lodged between his smiling teeth and gave each of them a half a loaf. They muttered their gratitude and put them away for later.

David had never seen a kafra before coming to Kaira. The bulky, shaggy beasts had six muscled legs and flat, black, wrinkled faces — like a six-legged buffalo beaten over the face with a broad beam. They were slow, stupid, incredibly strong, and ate anything you put under their snouts.

Ricker owned two: Colp, who'd belonged to Ashen's family before Tarrak's attack, and Craptank, who he'd purchased from the Reens. Every mining team in Kaira needed at least one kafra, which made the Reens one of the wealthiest families in town.

The kafras lumbered up from the drift and into the light of day, snorting impatiently. Caige and Ashen dumped buckets of greasy slop into their trough, which the beasts lapped up greedily.

"Say it and mean it," Ricker said, kneeling.

David and the others knelt, taking handfuls of dirt from the shaft's floor and rubbing it over their unwashed skin.

"Cala-Terra, I beseech you," they chanted in unison, "hide me from your brother's eye. Grant me safety from his eternal hunger during this needed trespass." They remained on their knees while Ashen grabbed the small knife tied to Colp's thick, shaggy leg.

"Easy, boy," Ashen said, stroking the beast's coarse brown coat as it ate. "You know the routine." He cut a shallow line into Colp's exposed skin, right under a dozen thin scars. Colp was impassive during the assault, letting out a puff of nostril-air in protest before returning to his meal.

Each miner stood and took a dab of the creature's blood, smearing a vertical line across their foreheads. "By this blood I do plead," they said in turn, finishing the ritual.

A visit from the earth-god was something none of them could risk. Tarrak's undying hunger for human flesh was renowned. He devoured anyone who dared intrude in his domain, grinding their bodies to bloodied mulch between his countless dragonglass teeth. Terra, the goddess of the harvest and fertility, was their only protection from her brother's wrath — so you always spoke the words.

The bird, which no one would bother naming, fluttered excitedly inside its wicker cage at their approach. Even when Tarrak did not rise from the depths to consume trespassers, his poisoned breath coursed through the deep veins of the world, odorless, yet deadly enough to kill. The bird would be the first to die if his venom wafted through their mine shaft. The Dinzeni family made their living raising the little yellow angels, which had saved many lives over the years.

"How's the bird?" Ricker asked.

David lifted its cage and checked its seeds and water. "Fine."

Whenever Ricker told the story of their narrow escape during Tarrak's visit to Kaira, he always claimed their bird's death had saved them, but there was one other sign he failed to include. Caige had acted strangely right before the attack, hitting the wall erratically. The breath had addled him, which was why Ricker thought to check the bird at all. Little such details never made for an entertaining yarn however, so he left it out.

Corren did not escape the claim that day. David managed to pull Caige out in time, but Tarrak's breath left the boy a confused, forgetful mess for days after. He had wept like a child when they told him about his father's demise.

"Ashen, you're on point today," Ricker said, shouldering his pickax as they walked deeper into the drift. "Sifran and I are your flanks, Caige is clearing, and David has the tug."

"Can I get the tug instead?" Ashen asked, lighting his oil-lamp. "Nikos wants me to help out at the bakery after sundown and I'll be too exhausted if I have to break today."

"You can give me a tug, you lazy dick-sheath," David growled.

"You had the tug two days ago, Ashen," Ricker said tiredly.

The tug shift was Ricker's way of giving each man on the team a rest. The shift still shoveled an exhausting amount of rock debris during the day, but leading the kafras down to unload their overflow at the pit was a welcome respite from the sapping heat of the mine, and an expected break was taken after. The duty got its name from Corren, who boasted he would "give himself a tug" before coming back up with the kafras.

Ashen used the tug to visit Nikos' daughter, which they could not blame him for. Caige had done the same with Tynisia.

Now Caige was Ashen's willful accomplice — retrieving the kafras and wagons from the pit, and working harder to fill in for the absence. Ashen would return before the day was done with the dumb, content gaze of the hopelessly lovesick.

"I'll take point," Caige said.

"Caige, don't." David glared at him. Caige was a good friend and a hard worker, but ever since he lost Tynisia, it seemed like he was trying to break himself against the stone.

Everyone in Ricker's team loved Tyn. Her smile could sweep away a foul mood, and she had a whip-fast wit, especially when she drank. They all missed her, but no one loved her, or agonized over her absence more profoundly than Caige.

"I want to," Caige said, walking up to the shredded wall.

"Thank you," Ashen said. "I will owe you."

"Are you truly certain?" Ricker asked, raising his dark brows.

"I am," Caige said, shouldering his pickax.

"Fine," Ricker relented. "Ashen, you're on clearing. David still has the tug."

"That little wank-stain is using you, Caige," David said.

"No, he's not." Caige took a few warm-up strikes against the earth. "It's fine, David. I've had a lousy morning and am my mood is sour. A little hard work will help clear my mind."

Ashen ignored David's bitter glare as he retrieved Caige's shovel.

"All right," Ricker said, grabbing his pick with both hands. "You know what you have to do. Let us see about becoming rich."

Caige and Sifran led Colp and Craptank by their coarse hemp ropes up the drift of Ricker's claim. The kafras groaned with the effort, filling the cave with the echoes of their frustration. The array of rusted chains holding the loaded wagons together rattled as they made the climb, adding to the chorus.

Outside, they found the sun only a few hours from setting. Caige smiled in gratitude as he guided the beasts down the Kafra Road. His back and arm muscles ached and his callused hands bled from a long day of clearing. Relief flooded him seeing the day nearly done.

They reached the stone pit and aligned the wagons, so they stood parallel to the quarry's lip. Unhooking their restraints, the containers turned on their pivots and dumped their payloads down the batter into the steep bowl below. Sifran helped him shovel out the remaining debris before pushing them upright and locking them back in place.

The waste dump was once an open pit-mine the Maggs had dug dry. For years, prospectors dropped their overflow here without threat of filling the chasm.

Tarper Reen's body swung limp from the petrified tree nearby, flanked by half a dozen empty nooses. The miners dubbed the prodigious sandwillow Maggie, since the Magalian Guild hung their debtors and cheaters from her branches as an example.

Tarper's dangling corpse reminded Caige of a pair of smaller feet, swinging in the air, toes curled in with rigor mortis.

A tide of terrible memories threatened to rise and assault his senses. A pinching tingle rose behind his eyes and his stomach curdled and groaned. He shook his head and pinched his eyes closed, denying the memory's entry. He could not let himself remember.

"Caige?" Sifran asked.

"Tarper's still ripe is all."

"He really is. What an unpleasant way to die. You don't cheat the Guild, no matter how rich your family is."

"No you do not," Caige agreed.

"Remembering him as anything other than this rotting, bloated, corpse is difficult. Did you hear about Galgis?" Sifran lit a fresh cuksar.

"No, what happened?"

"Failed to repay his debt to the Maggs. They locked his team in their claim with a meal-a-day ration until they either pay back what they owe, or Galgis gives them the mine."

"What are they doing?"

"They're fucking digging. The Guild always collects, one way or another." Sifran passed him the cuksar. "Galgis should have fucking known better."

"Fucking cock-licks," Caige said, spitting on the ground and taking a drag of the acrid smoke.

"How much do you owe them, Caige?"

He passed the cuksar back and studied Tarper's bloated, maggot-ridden body. Corren always believed they would find a thick vein of shinn here someday, sail west to Nortain, and leave their life of hardship behind. His father died crushed by Tarrak's maw while still owing the Maggs a small fortune. Caige inherited a rundown dactwood hut, a few old mining tools, and his old man's debt.

"Unless we strike rich core soon..." he said, pointing at Tarper.

"So much?"

"Enough to hang for."

"You won't let me end up like that, right Caige?" Sifran asked. "You'll cut me down before the crows and maggots find me?"

"And get strung up beside you for defying the Guild? Enjoy being fucking dinner."

"You ass," Sifran chuckled.

"Take your time getting back. Day's about done." Caige tugged at the ropes and the beasts lumbered obediently behind.

"I intend to." Sifran sucked on his cuksar.

Caige heard the sharp banging of the team's pickaxes long before he saw the murky light of their oil lamps.

"Sun's almost gone, Ricker," he said, reaching the end of the drift. "Do we keep digging?"

"No. Enough for today," Ricker said, rubbing his shoulder.

As the sun descended behind the Norvan Peak's western foothills, Kaira's miners stored their picks, secured their claims, and made their way down the Kafra Road towards town. David sat outside Ricker's claim with the others, watching the sun's last rays paint the sky indigo and blood orange. Below those thin, sun-drenched clouds, sat the bowl-shaped town of Kaira.

At the town's southern entrance stood the walls of Fort Kai, erected by the Sickle Talons to ward off Padivian attack during the Greenfire War.

Padive's Raptors put the fortress to the torch and razed its inner buildings. The armory was the only structure to survive the Battle of Kaira, which the Maggs now used as their personal vault and counting office. Most of the misery in town today, emanated from the counter's vault.

From the ruined walls of Fort Kai, two main roads spread out in a V towards the mountain. On the east side lay the Coppertooth Road, flanked by all the important shops — Ladan's tailoring, Nikos' bakery, Sol and Kile's leatherworks and carpentry store, Citena's clayworks kiln, Dendor's smithy, and of course, Noss' Pick Rock Tavern.

To the west, wound the Earthly Road. On this broad stretch of land, the Antep family grew flax, the Reens herded kafras, the Danpors farmed leck wheat, and the Pirils tended to their dact palms.

Kaira's homes huddled between those two thoroughfares, surrounding the Temple of the Calusian Brotherhood. The blue-domed temple sat at the heart of Kaira. Here the Korgur, Minkar Slen, gave the weekly sabbath mass and performed funeral services. His son, Acolyte Nirr Slen maintained the grounds and gave the daily morning sermons.

David attended every mass without fail. He did not dare miss one. Neither the Pick Rock nor the Grit Mug taverns opened for business on the night before the sabbath, by order of the korgur. The Mug marked the south end of the Earthly Road, near Fort Kai. The mining teams all frequented the Pick Rock, but the farmers, traders, craftsmen, and the damn Guild counters, all preferred the Mug.

Minkar's weekly rebukes towards the work Leina and the other girls did at Noss' tavern warded decent folk away. The korgur softly shamed the girls and Kaira's sinning miners every sabbath, while the congregation muttered approvals under its breath. People with families and safer trades found comfort in looking down on girls like them and men like him. They did not understand how whores and miners kept each other alive and sane out here.

David confessed his transgressions and purchased his penance disks at every mass besides Leina and the other girls. Every week they sinned together and then sought forgiveness together. The Temple condemned them and took payment for its lenience in an unending cycle.

Nianah walked up the Kafra Road, dragging him out of his reverie. She gave them each a small piece of sweet bread and sat with her back against Ashen's chest, watching the sun's dwindling light.

David could not understand why Nikos allowed Ashen of all people to court his daughter. The little runt made some kind of impression on the man, and there were rumors of a possible betrothal. David did not believe them.

The rough old baker had nothing to gain by letting his only daughter marry a poor, orphaned rock-farmer like Ashen. He would be wiser marrying her to either Kile or Sol, who both made more coin on Coppertooth Road than Ashen would ever see. One of the Danpor boys would be a better choice. At least their family had coin to fall back on when times became difficult.

"Nianah," David said, clearing his throat. "How did the runt here convince Nikos he was worth the time of a pretty girl like you?"

The others turned to glare at him, but he kept his eyes focused on Nianah. She gave him an inquisitive look, her dark Teplian features pinching. "Father loves Ashen," she said with a smile. "He says Ashen's the only man in Kaira who doesn't have rocks for brains."

Ashen turned towards him, his face obscured by shadow.

"Hmm. The rumor's not true though, right?" he asked. "That he's thinking to let you two take vows?"

"Ashen!" Nianah said in genuine surprise. "You haven't told them?"

Ashen shrugged. "Not their business."

"They're your friends!" She pinched his side, making him chuckle.

"Fine, fine. Yes, it's more than true. We're to marry next spring."

"Shit-heel!" Ricker scolded through a bearded smile.

"Ashen, you fuck-twig!" Sifran laughed. "Why didn't you tell us?"

Again, Ashen only shrugged. David noticed Caige was smirking. He knew. Ashen had already shared the news with him in secret.

"Your father must not be thinking straight," he said. "We miners make for lousy husbands."

The group quieted and shared startled glances, but no one spoke.

"Is Nikos teaching him how to bake at least? Is that why Ashen's been next to useless lately? He's being mentored in the coveted secrets of dough and yeast?"

"Fuck, David..." Caige said.

"No, it's fine, Caige," Ashen said, his voice icing with every word. "This is why I didn't tell them, Nia, because of big, red, and ugly here.

"Yes David, I'm learning to be a baker. Mining means breaking your back for scraps, and I don't want to die between Tarrak's teeth like my parents. Is that reason enough? Do I have your permission to not end up a fat, lonely sack of shit like you?"

To everyone's surprise, including his own, David started laughing. The others watched him, glancing between themselves in uncertainty.

He raised his hands in a show of surrender. "I didn't mean to sound like such an ass," he said. "Well, perhaps I did, but I enjoy seeing you find your stones, boy. Amazing what the right woman will do to a man. I'm happy for you both, truly."

47

Everyone relaxed, smiling nervously and shaking their heads. They returned to congratulating them, asking where they would live and how many children they planned on having. David pushed the noise into the background, watching his cuksar burn between his stained fingers.

As the final rays of sunshine disappeared into the west, the waxing, crescent moon and her accompanying stars materialized in the sky.

"The day is done," Ricker said. "Let us grab a drink."

"Or two," Caige said.

"Or ten," Sifran said, wiping his hands on his trousers.

"Enjoy, you scoundrels," Ashen said, walking down the mountain, holding Nianah's hand.

"Lucky little shit," David whispered.

"He is," Caige agreed, placing a hand on his shoulder.

"Good to know that come next spring, we'll finally be rid of the lazy little fuck," David said.

"Oh, you will miss him when he's gone," Ricker teased. "I wager you'll bawl like a girl as he walks away."

"I'll take that wager!" Sifran laughed.

"Shut your pig-hole," David said.

"Ashen my love, don't leave me!" Sifran cried in mock grief.

"I'll fucking kill you, Sifran!"

Caige and Ricker laughed as he chased the scrawny miner down the mountain towards the Pick Rock.

4

Sharn

Aside from Ser Isa, Nihengale, and himself, the command tent was vacant. Dorav purposely kept Kartecus out of the briefing to keep his old mentor's venom from spoiling their chance at a cohesive plan. He could almost hear the old man's teeth grinding for being left out in the rain.

Isa and Nihengale gave each other uneasy glances while pouring through his maps and charts. While she did not bare the naked disdain Kartecus held for the xial, as an Ashura raised by the Knighthood, she was implanted with unyielding opinions about the Helicartian clans, especially the mepsiens.

When he had brought the xial aboard, north of Palidor's shores, Isa and Kartecus both protested. Even after explaining that their joining the mission was the will of the King's Eastern Rook, neither of them seemed appeased, and their temperaments toward him had grown strenuous since.

"Is this Ship-Breaker-Pass?" Isa asked, pointing at a thin line just south of Sharn.

Dorav looked at the map and nodded. "During the war that entire seaway was defended by ballista, catapults, and trebuchets. It swarmed with archers, here and here, armed with longbows and fire-arrows. So many ships burned attempting to penetrate that strait, their carcasses became another obstacle for the Padivian navy."

"And now?"

"It is an undefended trade port."

"And how are we taking this undefended port?" She raised her eyes to meet his.

"Once the *Kajak's* masts are repaired, Master Myrkin is sailing her out of the Spine and making quiet approach to the mouth of the Pass."

Isa's blue eyes widened. "Dorav, the patrols will catch them out there."

He smirked at her, which only made her frown lines deepen. "I have faith in Myrkin," he said.

"He is a fine navigator, Dorav, but he's sailing with a skeleton crew, and is still young and inexperienced."

"Far from it. The *Kajak* is hardly the boy's first commission. Few know this, but before I brought him aboard my ship, Myrkin served as second mate to Captain Malcion Madgier."

The name gave Isa pause. "Madgier? The Black Eel of Calimport? Myrkin was a second mate on the *Mako*?"

"The very same. And no, I never asked him to divulge his old Captain's secrets about how he hid from us and eluded our embargoes during the war. However, he assures me that if he does not want the Kajak found, she won't be, and I believe him."

Isa's face was a dour mask, but she offered no retort.

"They will wait here at the neck." Dorav touched the map. "Out of range and out of sight, until we strike."

Myrkin needed to come through in this. If he let the ship be seen by a Teplian patrol, or if word of their presence reached Sharn, they were all vigorously fucked.

"Let's take this a step at a time, starting here," Dorav said, motioning towards the lines and squares symbolizing the first measure of defense. "This outpost is used by the Magalian Guild to purchase raw shinn brought in by the surrounding mining towns, so it will be well guarded, even at night."

"The trade post is of no concern," Nihengale said. "My team can clear it."

Dorav eyed the mepsien. "You've shown a deadly efficiency up to point, but this is not the time to be flippant. A single warning reaching Sharn's ears means the mission fails. There can be no mistakes."

"Understood," Nihengale said. "We will not fail you, sir. What are these two large structures just beyond?"

"Sharn's refineries. Before the Purge, they both ran at capacity, purifying and shaping shinn. These two long buildings flanking the road once produced numerous goods to sell on the open market. Now, only this refinery on the right runs, and only during the day. The other buildings fell into disrepair."

"So they're negligible?" Isa asked.

"Yes. Once we're past the trade post, our next objective is the gate."

A thick black line ran parallel to Sharn's entryway, representing the iron stake filled ditch serving as the city's final siege defense.

"Nihengale?" Dorav said.

"We will need your seaguards for this," Nihengale replied. "While the four of us can handle the sentries quietly, we cannot hold the bridge alone."

"Ser Isa?"

"I could guarantee victory with a unit of Archonwolf Knights in full battledress, but my marines are not equipped to maintain a defensive line."

"Can your men secure the bridge or not?"

"Yes, sir." Isa's brows furrowed. "And they will."

"If anything goes wrong, Nihengale," Dorav said, "I want your people deep in the shit with the others. Clear?"

"Of course." Nihengale nodded.

"Once the guards are handled and the signal given, the vanguard will ride straight up this road to assist in holding the gate until our full force is loosed from its scabbard."

Isa nodded pensively. "Once inside the walls," she said, "we can contain the city, street by street, in quadrants. Here, then here, then here."

"Exactly right, but your primary objective is here," he touched the rectangle at the end of Sharn's central thoroughfare. "House Magalia. Every enemy we face in Sharn will be hired steel, but their best will be guarding this manor."

"My team and I can neutralize the house after-" Nihengale began.

"No," he cut him off. "The job of securing high priority captives is one my own people will handle, Nihengale."

"Aye, sir."

"Ser Isa, once the wall is secured, you'll detach with a unit and make for the compound. No harm is to come to any member of the noble family or their servants — not even their damn pets. Neutralize their guards whichever way you deem fit but the damage to the manor is to be kept minimum. No looting. Choose your most reliable men and ensure they follow my orders completely."

"Aye, sir."

"Nihengale, you and yours will help me pacify the streets. When the fighting is done, I'll want you to make yourselves scarce until I call for you."

"Aye, sir."

"All right, let's fill in the details," he said, putting his finger back on the mark of the outer trade outpost. "Once more from the beginning."

"How is it you manage to walk with balls as big as yours, Dorav?" Lord Metzial Renot asked him on the night he was given the mission to Sharn — shot like an arrow at a rampart.

Not knowing how to respond to the Lord's rhetorical question, he remained standing silently at attention.

The air in the Aegis of Man's war-room was warmed by the crackling hearthfire and smelled of burning oak, ink, and pipe smoke. The window shutters and long, white curtains behind Lord Renot and Lord Admiral Selliaro were shut against the pelting rains falling on Palidor's streets that fateful night.

"Well?" Metzial asked.

"I am not certain, sir," he said.

Metzial's icy blue eyes watched him with spiteful intensity. The Host of Knights had grown old. His face sat on its bones resentfully, his liver-spotted head was wrinkled and hairless, and his right eye drooped, as if hoping to find sleep without the rest of his face noticing.

If anyone took these physical nuances as signs of weakness however, they would be gravely mistaken. Under his warm councilor's robes, the old man was wrought iron. Even with the years he carried, he could still wield a sword better than most seasoned knights, and his wrinkled hands were monstrously strong — able to crush walnut shells in their vice-like grip.

"You and Kartecus are making quite a name for yourselves on the Sea of Crowns," Metzial said. "What did you rename your vessel again?"

"The *Kajak*, sir," he said.

"Did you find something wrong with the name *Cidraster*, Commander?"

"No, sir."

"Why did you not just dub her the *Iridia*? Why be coy with your petulance?"

Dorav remained silent, striving to display no emotion.

"I asked you a question!"

"Lord Renot," Admiral Selliaro interjected, sitting back in his tall chair in unabashed boredom. He sipped on his goblet of mulled wine and tugged absently at his salt-and-pepper beard. "If you would like to charge Captain Minos with something, please do so. Otherwise, I would prefer to go about my evening."

Metzial shot Selliaro a withering look before turning back to him. "Your orders, Commander, are to take your ship and escort the vessel *Merrigold* down into Relm's northern trade route. You will be given all the necessary documentation before departure.

"Once this is completed, you are to turn your ship towards the Norvan Peaks, and with your crew, sack the fortress city of Sharn. Have your marines plunder if you like, but the important nobility must be secured until the contents of Sharn's fabled vaults are safely in your hold."

Dorav felt his face go cold, staring at the Host of Knights in silent disbelief. When he opened his mouth to speak, he found his tongue limp and useless.

"You have something to say, Captain?" The Lord Admiral coaxed dismissively. "Go on man, spit it out."

"Sirs," he finally managed. He wanted to state the obvious — that attacking Tepley was an act of war. While the entire Norvan region belonged to the Magalian family, they were lands protected by the Queen.

This mission was reckless and ill-conceived — something a fleet of privateers should be sent to do, not a renown war-galley flying the banners of the Archonwolves and Holy Ashuran Order.

He knew he would be rebuked for making mention of such, so he chose another path.

"The crew of a single ship cannot hope to overpower a fortress that withstood the full force of the Padivian Armada," he said.

"Sharn is no longer defended by the Queen's Talons, Captain," Admiral Selliaro said. "As you know, it was purchased by the Magalians years ago and is now guarded by mercenaries. Are you saying you cannot sail through defenses manned by a handful of mangy sell-swords?"

"Of course not, sir, but this mission is no task for-"

"We're not here to listen to your griping, Minos!" Metzial's open palms slammed the table. "These are your orders. Are they clear or do you need me to repeat them?"

"No sir, they are clear," he said, straightening his back.

"There will be another joining your crew once preparations are made," Metzial continued. "A young alchemist by the name of Marca Kaitner. She will be in charge of cataloging and making estimates on the stores of Sharn's wealth. You will provide her with the use of your clerk and any other assistance she might need."

"Yes, sir." He attempted to sound firm despite his swimming mind. There existed places at sea that sailors considered damned and unapproachable. During the Greenfire War, the fortress of Sharn with its Ship-Breaker-Pass had gained such a reputation.

"This mission is of the utmost importance and is to remain a secret, Commander," Lord Renot said. "No one is to know of your intentions to sack the Magalian stronghold. No one.

"There will be no written command or writ of passage for you or Ser Isa. You will take this operation unto your own flesh and if you fail, the stain of your actions will remain with you." The Host pointed a callused finger at him. "You will raise your hand before us and swear the Oath of the Black Wing."

Dorav breathed in deeply, summoning himself to display no trepidation. "I stand before the Eye of God," he began, raising his right hand. "With mouth stitched and fingers sewn, by virtue of my faith. I become the Lord's Black Wing, heart and soul surrendered to his light. No mortal act shall taint me while my stitches hold. No living being will know my true intent and all secrets will die with me. If I break these threads of my hallowed service, with glad heart I relinquish my soul to the Vorx."

"Good." Metzial nodded, his body visibly relaxing.

"You will take Lieutenant Kartecus with you on this," the Lord Admiral said. "That is a direct order. If I find out you left him behind for any reason, he hangs for desertion. Am I clear?"

Dorav looked to Lord Renot who nodded his acquiescence to the command.

"Yes, sir," he said and stared dutifully at nothing, keeping his storm of emotions at bay.

"Consider this as a test of your faith," the Host said, his grin of satisfaction making Dorav's skin crawl. "This is your opportunity for atonement. Succeed, and I will forgive the taint of your past transgressions against the Order and strike them from our records in their entirety."

"And Kartecus?" Dorav asked.

"No!" Metzial said with a tremor of rage in his voice. "He is forever unforgiven! He will never regain what he has lost."

"Yes, sir," Dorav said, clearing his throat.

"I grant you this one opportunity for redemption, but fail me, Commander, and I will stake your head on my balcony and hang your balls over my mantel as trophies! Am I understood?"

"Yes sir!"

"Good. You are dismissed."

Stunned, Dorav made his way towards the war-room's exit.

"Commander," Metzial called to him as he reached the door.

"Sir?" he asked, turning back to his lords.

"I believe this is check-mate."

Dorav clenched his teeth but could do nothing to keep the blood from racing into his face. He stared hard at the Host until his breathing settled in his chest. "Check, perhaps," he said calmly, "but far from mate, sir."

"We shall see." Lord Renot replied.

"They have tallied too long, Dorav," Kartecus said, bringing his horse up to his left flank.

"Patience," he replied.

"I should have gone with them," Isa grumbled from his right, her stallion bobbing his head as if in agreement.

"In full battledress? You would have given everyone away. Have faith in Kathor, Ser Isa. He can handle this just fine."

"My Lieutenant Commander is not who concerns me, sir," she said, rubbing her stallion's neck to calm him.

Dorav sighed and glanced at the seaguards saddled behind him. Isa had chosen five of her best to ride as the spear-point of his vanguard charge.

They sat straight-backed, holding their reigns tightly, and anxious to prove themselves. The other marines stood in unsteady attention, shuffling impatiently inside their banded mails.

Behind their ranks, stood every blooded crew member the *Kajak* could spare. They were armed with looted weapons and donning a hodgepodge of Caliman, Telkan, and Qanalarian armors, taken from dead enemies over the years. The rest wore only the clothes on their backs, yet stood no less bravely. His crew was no stranger to combat, but now they appeared ill at ease, whispering nervously to each other.

"Stand firm!" he called back at them. "We've been through tighter straits than this. Be at the ready!"

The men sullenly shifted into more organized lines.

Dorav had waited until well past midnight to send the mepsiens and his marines to pacify the trade post, and the long hours of the evening had waned considerably since. A chill mist rose from the south, announcing the imminent arrival of dawn.

"We've been sitting here so long my ass is beginning to chafe," Kartecus growled, shifting his weight on his saddle.

"Not in front of the lady, Kartecus," he said, reflexively adjusting in his own seat.

"Call me a lady again, Dorav," Isa said.

"I wouldn't dare."

A horn blast echoed on the night's winds, coming from Sharn. This was not their designated signal, meaning the attack on the fortress had been discovered. Dorav cursed under his breath.

"Time to prove our worth before God!" he shouted at the men. "For the glory of Zenthien! For the might of Vinergale!" He kicked his horse's flanks and led the charge forward — patches of dark earth flying in their horses' wake.

His stallion's hooves thundered beneath him and a chill wind snapped his purple cloak like an unfettered sail. He could feel the animal's power as it gained speed, its head bobbing rhythmically before him. They banked north around a sharp turn and Sharn's southern trade post rose just ahead.

Dorav looked back at Kartecus who rode furiously at his side, long white hair dancing wildly behind his weather-beaten face. The old man noticed the glance and nodded, drawing his sword. Dorav held the reins as loosely as he dared and unsheathed his sharpened wolfbert. With this signal, the entire vanguard drew steel.

A dozen armed mercenaries littered the sandy earth of the outpost, lying in pools of their own blood. The sprinting horses trampled over their corpses, but one snagged its hoof and toppled headlong, sending its unfortunate rider flying. The man hit the dirt with a baleful crack, but they could not stop to assist him.

The unlit buildings flanking the road past the trade post sat lifeless, observing their progress through blind, blackened windows. Behind the empty edifices rose the soot-stained smokestacks of Sharn's refineries. The night here was quiet but for the rumble of their horses.

The city of Sharn's imposing wall stood before them — a thick, oppressive barrier made from the Norvan Mountain's own black rock. As they neared it, Dorav could see lit candles on the parapets but no archers stood manning their posts. Grateful to not be riding through a hail of arrow-fire, Dorav focused his attention on the battle raging beneath the gateway.

Kathor's seaguards and the four mepsiens struggled ferociously against Sharn's growing mercenary force. The heated clash inched back from underneath the wall and on to the drawbridge. His brave men were taking heavy losses in the desperate effort to hold the archway and keep the portcullis from being dropped.

One seaguard screamed as he was shield-bashed into the spiked trench below. The mercenaries held the upper hand on his men. At any moment, they would be sealed out.

I grant you this one opportunity for redemption, but fail me, Commander, and I will stake your head on my balcony and hang your balls over my mantel as trophies!

57

Dorav stopped his horse at the edge of the drawbridge and dismounted, the weight of his plates making him grunt with the effort. This stallion was no warhorse. He could not take the risk of having him panic and buck him off during battle.

"Vanguard! On me, on me!" he shouted as he strapped his aegis to his arm. His marines cheered their arrival, redoubling their efforts.

"Make a hole!" he cried.

Isa and Kartecus flanked him as he charged, shields up and swords thirsting. When his shield struck the first of Sharn's mercenaries, he screamed and leaned into the mass of bodies with all his might. Isa and Kartecus put their heads down, stabbing with their swords from behind their shields.

"Push, damn you! Push!" Isa cried.

The vanguard pressed up behind them, adding their weight to the human battering ram. Steel blades hit Dorav like hail, striking his helm and armor plates. Boiling with battle-lust, he stabbed out blindly, Teplian blood dripping down the length of his blade. He dug his boots in with every step until his forward momentum halted.

"Kill!" he cried. "Kill them all!"

Dorav swung with sword and aegis, cutting through one man's collarbone and crushing another's nose with the edge of his shield. He swung in bold arcs, forcing the mercenaries back.

Though Kartecus no longer wore the formidable Ashuran armor, the old man stood his ground fearlessly, as if his skin were ironbark. The seaguards howled, inching the enemy back under the wall and into the city.

"Now!" Came a shout from somewhere beyond the gate. A tall man stood at the mercenary rear, wearing mailed half-plate and raising a bloodied bastard sword above his head.

Behind Dorav, the heavy oak and wrought-iron portcullis made a dry click-clunk noise and dropped, scrapping against stone as it fell. His marines screamed and tried to evade, but too many of them were packed into the narrow archway. The bottom of the portcullis hit the floor with a boom, pulping four men under its massive weight. Blood and entrails burst upward, painting the survivors in gore.

His forces were now cleaved in two, the smaller of which stood within Sharn's walls. Four men to one were their odds, with more quickly joining the enemy ranks.

"Archers! On the wall!" The mercenary leader shouted to his men as they arrived. "Kill the ones outside! The rest of you form lines and bring the oil!"

"Phalanx!" Dorav cried and raised his shield.

The archway was spacious enough for five men to fight abreast, which was to their advantage, but the call for oil meant they meant to burn them out. They needed to attack now, before they were cooked like caged pigs in a barn fire."

"Xial! Rii! Rii!" Nihengale called out in his strange language from behind the lowered portcullis. The mepsiens sprinted up the taunt chains of the drawbridge towards the parapets, their speed and balance unnerving.

Divine Father! What are these creatures?

"Spearhead formation!" he called. Isa and Kartecus gave him incredulous looks.

"Dorav," Isa hissed. "We have the bottleneck. We can hold them here!"

"Dorav is right," Kartecus said. "They will cook us feet-up if we remain here. We must take the fight to them!"

"Spearhead! Now!" Dorav cried.

They were sorely outnumbered. The moment their line punctured they would be slaughtered, but better to die fighting.

"The only way out is through!" he shouted.

"To live is to die!" his men called back thinly. They were frightened.

"The only way OUT is THROUGH!"

"To LIVE Is To DIE!" They roared.

"CHAARGE!!"

They met the yet unorganized mercenaries in a crash of wood and steel. Their backs were up against the hard place now. Either they gave this their all, or they died.

Dorav deliberately overextended, slamming into their center mass, pushing into their ranks and forcing their attention on him. Kartecus and Isa stitched the gap in the line and pressed forward.

The mercenaries stabbed and hacked at him from all sides. The blows he could not block or parry dented his plated armor. There was no finesse to this kind of fighting. He summoned brute force to bash their weapons aside and push them back, bullying them out of formation and granting his line a stronger foothold on the field.

Now and again his blade would catch a forearm or a thigh, drawing blood and cries of pain. The clash of battle rang in his ears, and he began to sweat profusely inside his armor, forcing him to blink the salty drops out of his eyes.

He parried an incoming sword blow, and thrust his wolfbert deep into the man's crotch, making him bleat like a goat before he crumbled into a ball of misery. Dorav cracked his skull open with the heel of his boot.

Something sharp struck him in the back, hard enough to carve through his steel plates and chainmail. He spun around and broke his attacker's jaw with the edge of his shield. The woman fell holding her ruined face while two mercenaries quickly took her place.

Dorav swept the legs out from under the first, stabbing him through the chest as he hit the ground — blood sprayed up his sword arm and face. Another heavy blow landed, absorbed by his shoulder-guard but strong enough to send a wave of agony down his arm. Biting past the pain, he raised his aegis in time to catch the second blow.

A man with a crude, iron mace went to take a third massive swing. Dorav's wolfbert plunged into his belly, scraping the undercarriage of his sternum and breaking his spine. Dorav twisted the blade inside his flesh and extracted it diagonally, blood and feces-stained entrails tumbling out of the massive wound. The man crumbled, blood-spittle gurgling from his trembling lips.

Raw instinct forced Dorav's shield up in time to catch the deadly strike of the mercenary leader's thirsty bastard sword. Dorav crouched and swung for his enemy's hip but struck the bottom of the man's hoplon.

They circled one another, both winded, their armors thick with blood. They kept their shields up and ready, watching for weaknesses in each other's defense.

Dorav came in with a four strike pattern designed to test his opponent's reach and reactions. The mercenary leader responded using an antiquated *Claddis* defense. Dorav switched his footing and feinted a low slice. As predicted, the man dropped his shield to block instead of letting his tassets deflect the blow.

Dorav redirected his blade and brought it up, cleaving halfway through the thick muscles of the man's broad neck and striking his lower jaw. The mercenary released his sword, his hand groping at the terrible wound.

Dorav sank his wolfbert under the man's armpit and into his torso, plunging through his lung. The man fell on his side, wheezing for air.

The four mepsiens stood on Sharn's parapets, bows in hand, raining death on the enemy below. Nihengale and the female killed anyone attempting the stairs while the other two concentrated their fire on the melee.

On the exterior of the portcullis, his men shouted, struggling in futility to lift the obstruction. His main force was closing in at a full run, almost to the drawbridge now.

"Nihengale! The crank!" he yelled and pointed towards the hefty wooden spool wrapped in heavy chain. "Kill the ones by the fucking crank!"

His seaguard spearhead formation was now a misshapen oval, but it held. The death of their leader did not slow the opposition, and they still maintained numbers and momentum on their side.

"We need to open the gate!" Dorav shouted over the storm of screams and steel. "Isa, with me!"

When Ser Isa pulled away from the formation, Kartecus and Kathor quickly stitched the hole. Kartecus breathed heavily, his hair and mustache damp with sweat and blood. Kathor's young face was flushed and furious, a long, angry wound indenting his engorged right eyelid.

"Hold the line! Hold the line!" Dorav screamed and barreled into the enemy, forcing them back with sword and shield. Isa stood beside him, hacking at their limbs, her teeth bared and her blue eyes shining with battle-lust.

Few of these mercenaries wore anything better than doublets and boiled leather, but even those in chainmail stood intimidated by their fearless onslaught. The mercenaries inched back and swung halfheartedly, hesitant to take either of them on directly.

Overcoming battle fear was among the first things taught to Ashuran Initiates. Dying in combat guaranteed them a place among the Ashkandar, the celestial elite of Zenthien's divine legions, destined to fight in the eternal war against the Vorx. If Isa died here today, a Diva would guide her spirit to Celestia and her name would be remembered in the Halls of Ascension.

He would face a much crueler fate, having forsaken salvation long ago. His ability to overcome fear in battle was not a matter of faith, but one of discipline and loyalty. For his crew's sake, he could not allow fear to overpower him.

A sharp sting ran up Dorav's left leg whenever he put weight on it. At a glance he saw blood running over his tassets, but he could not see the wound. Ignoring the pain he pushed forward, using his shield and sword in trained unison.

As they reached the crank, Nihengale, the larger mepsien with the blue killer's eyes, and the female, dispatched the last of the mercenaries guarding the spool. The thinner spook with the tangerine eyes remained in the parapets, firing his bow with frightening accuracy.

"Spool the chain!" Dorav called to them. "We'll cover you!"

They turned to face half-a-dozen charging men. Dorav was woefully exhausted. His limbs were heavy and his breathes came as if through wet cheese cloth. The mepsiens behind him grunted as they wound the crank.

Fearful cries and a sudden surge of movement erupted near the archway. His men's formation had collapsed, and they were being decimated.

"Back!" he heard Kartecus and Kathor call out from within the madness. "Back to the gate! Form the phalanx!"

"Get that fucking thing open, Nihengale!" he shouted and raised his aegis to block an incoming heavy ax.

The enormous impact made his teeth rattle and his left leg buckle beneath him. He thrust his blade up through the enemy's meaty forearm.

Dorav reversed his grip on his wolfbert and used the man's arm like a fulcrum, twisting it in at an angle. He jammed the edge of his shield against the back of the mercenary's shoulder and leveraged him off his feet and into a forward flip. As the man spun midair, Dorav yanked his sword clear and plunged it down, impaling it through his unprotected chest. The man death-rattled beneath him before going limp.

The female mepsien joined their line, fighting back their would-be assailants. Her shield-work was surprisingly efficient, blending perfectly into their defensive structure.

The mepsien archer's black arrows slammed into the mercenaries rushing to outflank them, punching through hard leather and chain mesh. Dorav roared and swung at anyone who came close, pushing them back, clawing for time. Isa and the mepsien female guarded his flanks, sharing the burden.

Another shift in momentum — howls of rage and diaphragm screams. His men were under the portcullis. As they poured into the fortress in a spiteful wave, the mercenary line turned tail and ran back into the city, some of them dropping their weapons in their haste to flee.

For the first time in what felt like hours, Dorav lowered his arms, his tense biceps pinching painfully in protest. He took three long steadying breaths.

"Ser Isa," he said dryly. "Gather your men and make for House Magalia. The wall is ours."

"Aye, sir," she said breathlessly. "Oh and, Dorav?"

"Yes?"

"You have an ax sticking out of your back."

He glanced back and saw the wooden handle of a handaxe protruding from his left shoulder-blade, slick with his blood. Only now did he feel the ache of its presence.

"Duly noted," he said.

5

The Embers of Murder

Before the first rays of daybreak touched her southern parapets, Sharn fell to the bloodied and tired crew of the *Kajak*. The surviving mercenaries surrendered once they accepted that victory was impossible. The smaller, less problematic citizen militia ceased resistance once Ser Isa took the Magalian manor.

Except for the city nobility, which was locked away at House Magalia, Sharn's populace was disarmed, pulled from their homes, and locked away in the domed Calusian cathedral at the city's heart to await their fate.

"I cannot believe we just sacked Ship-Breaker-Sharn," Kartecus said, walking beside him through the corpse-littered streets, his pernoit armor sticky with drying gore.

"A hard-won battle," Dorav said. His left leg had received a nasty gash behind its plating, forcing him to walk with a limp. The handaxe which was plunged into his back now hung from his belt as a keepsake. "What are our losses?"

"Thirty-two dead or dying, forty-seven badly wounded, and half our seaguard out of commission. I fear Hedego might give birth to puppies if one more man is brought to him."

"And Kathor?"

"He lost the eye," Kartecus sighed. "Hedego wants him resting but the boy won't sit still. He is already back on his feet, snapping orders."

Dorav nodded approvingly. "Good lad. What of House Magalia?"

"Ser Isa placed the nobles under guard at the palace. Lady Rubena requests an audience with you."

"She will have to go without."

"Captain, tradition demands that a noble family like the Magalians be afforded-"

"I know the damn protocol, Kartecus! There's nothing I can disclose to that woman, so why bother infuriating her further? Which one is she, anyway?"

"Rubena is Lord Lucra Magalia's niece on his second sister's side."

"An inheritor?"

"No. The Norvan South was granted to her husband as a dowry. When he died, Sharn became her only claim to the family estate."

"An entire fiefdom as a dowry? Is that all? God, how much gold do these damn people control? They could redeem the souls of all eastern Obsal, if they so wished."

"And still live comfortably, I imagine," Kartecus said.

"Keep everyone under guard until this is over, but make certain they are comfortable and afforded every consideration, within reason."

"Aye, sir."

"The harbor?"

"Secured. The dock masters and guilders attempted escape on a private barge with Sharn's administrative coffers — including the mercenaries' pay. When the sell-swords discovered the betrayal, they handed the guilders and port over to Master Myrkin without scuffle."

"Now we must capture the surrounding towns." Dorav loosened a few armor straps to ease his breathing. "Sharn's tendrils spread around the Peaks and our presence will soon be discovered. We cannot allow word to reach Nevine."

"Sir, we lost nearly a third of our crew here," Kartecus said. "We don't possess the manpower to hold all territories around Sharn."

"No need to hold them at all. I will take a hundred men and sack the lands along the south-western Counter's Road. Civilians will be put in chains and brought here under escort. The only resistance we face now are vault guards and local militias."

"And the north and eastern roads?"

"All lead here. The only path anyone can use to warn Nevine of our presence is the west. The hard part is done, Kartecus. We won, at a price, but we fulfilled our duty to God and the Order."

The old man pulled at his mustache. "What about the spooks?"

"They accomplished their mission. They will remain here until I return."

"They're treacherous, Dorav," Kartecus said. "We cannot trust them. Allow me take a unit to their campsite while they sleep-"

"No."

"They are mepsiens! Their knives will be in our spines the moment we let down our guard. You know this!"

"They are under control. Have faith, man! There is bitterness between us, distrust, but we *can* work together. We proved as much here."

"I do have faith!" The old man's voice was coarse. "I carry this mark as proof!" He pulled down on his leathers and bared the thin scar across his neck. "My faith alone kept me alive when blade kissed flesh."

"Forgive the intrusion," Nihengale said as he appeared from around a corner. He wore his hood up, obscuring his features. "The sun will soon crest the mountain face. May we be relieved to seek shelter?"

"Yes, of course," Dorav said. "Take you rest, Nihengale." Considering Kartecus offered to murder them for their efforts, Nihengale's voice carried no bitterness.

"I overheard you plan on traveling to the towns of the western trade road-" Nihengale took a cautious step back as Kartecus moved in on him.

"You sneaky, spying little fuck!" The old man growled, gripping the hilt of his sword.

"Kartecus! Enough!" Dorav's order halted his old mentor, but the embers of murder remained in his eyes.

"Yes, Nihengale, I will ride out as soon as things are settled here."

"We would like to accompany you, Captain." Nihengale's gaze never left Kartecus. "Our oath was to ensure your safety and success. We would be going against orders if we do not come with you on this final leg."

"Filthy mongrel!" Kartecus barked before a fit of coughing assaulted him.

"While you are under my command, your orders are mine to give," Dorav said stiffly.

"Of course, Captain," Nihengale said.

"A few more blades will not be a wasted precaution, and with you I can afford to bring less men. Yes, bring your people along."

"Dorav!"

He stared hard at his lieutenant. Taking the hint, Kartecus backed down.

"Nihengale, you will be guarding my prisoners at the temple tonight. Inform the others that we leave tomorrow, but I want your alchemist..."

"Rairi, sir," Nihengale said.

"Yes, right. Tell Rairi to remain with Marca, clear?"

"Aye, sir." Nihengale gave him a stiff salute and returned the way he came.

"If they are going with you, so am I."

"You remain here to lead in my absence, Kartecus."

"Not to be difficult, sir, but I'm not leaving you alone with them." He pointed a gloved finger at Nihengale's departing back. "I swear by Zenthien's sword, I will drop my emblem of the Archonwolves at your feet and become a damn camp-runner if I must."

"By God's good name, Kartecus!"

The old man was genuinely afraid for him around the mepsiens. Truth be told, he had fair reason to be. Arguing the point was pointless, and short of putting the old bastard in irons, he knew he could not keep him from coming along.

"Fine. Tell Ser Isa, Sharn is hers until we return. Mr. Myrkin retains command of the *Kajak*, and the port."

"Sir," Kartecus saluted and turned on his heel.

"You will be the death of me some day, old man." Dorav muttered under his breath.

Rairi walked beside Marca and Kivan as they made their way towards Sharn's shinn vaults. The hall they traversed was nearly twenty feet wide and thirty feet high, with a steep incline curving right. Three broken wooden portcullises and the remains of two vicious looking bladed traps lined the walls.

"Someone certainly wanted to keep this place safe," Marca said.

She was a young anthrop with boyish features punctuated by her short auburn curls, freckled face, and petite breasts. She wore leather riding boots, doeskin trousers, and a cotton shirt under her alchemist overcoat.

"They still do," Kivan said. "Not an easy thing, to repair and replace defenses like these."

The ship's clerk was taller than them both, with long, fair hair and clear blue eyes. He wore a simple tan doublet, mended linen pants, and well-worn boots. He carried a leather satchel containing two thick ledgers around his shoulder and their torch in his raised hand.

The doorway into Sharn's vaults was only accessible from within House Magalia. Ser Isa had ordered two men posted at the entrance in case they were required, and to dissuade the curious family members and upstart nobles from wandering in behind them.

At the end of the hall stood two massive ironwood doors with alchemical symbols carved into their faces. Four grown men could stand on each other's shoulders and still pass beneath their frames.

The attention to detail in the intricate craftsmanship gave Rairi pause. The rune-inscribed copper arrowhead tied to Marca's belt rose, pointing at the center of the door and pulling at its anchoring leather string.

"The shinn is behind those doors!" Marca smiled.

Kivan chuckled.

"What is so amusing?" Marca asked.

"You appear to be hard," he said.

Marca glanced down at the springfinder protruding from her waist and blushed deep crimson.

"You are a pig, Kivan," Marca said, tucking the arrow behind her belt.

Kivan shrugged, returning his gaze to the doorway. "What are those?" He motioned to the indented markings on the doors.

"Binding wards!" Marca said, her eyes glimmering.

"Yes," Rairi said, flat-pan. "Binding wards."

Marca sat at the foot of the doorway and opened her travel journal, muttering quietly as she scribbled.

Rairi had been wary and distrustful of Marca during the first leg of their journey. The excitable anthrop girl was so enthralled to work with a mepsien, she began sleeping by day to attempt conversation. When Rairi had refused to answer the girl's questions, Marca volunteered details about her own life, home, and training in the alchemical arts.

Their mutual love of alchemy eventually bridged their many differences, and by the time they sailed past Enelysion and into Teplian waters, they were sharing notes and theories like classmates from the same academy.

While Kivan waved the torch high above his head, marveling at the craftsmanship of the door faces, Rairi focused the glyphs. They were an old, complex mechanism of interlacing energies, each symbol serving as a small part of a larger equation. To bypass them, they would need to resolve how each marking correlated with the others, and in what order. The decrypting plate at the door's center held nine sigils, each representing a different alchemical reaction. The number of possible combinations was staggering.

Rairi released a heavy sigh. Their best course of action would be to visit the vault-keeper's office and force him to relinquish the sequence. Otherwise, this door could take them days or weeks to crack open. To add to their troubles, if they made any mistakes, the wards would reset and lock them out. They needed to be certain that the key they used was-

"I believe I have it!" Marca cried, flying to her feet and joyously tapping the glyphs on the decryption lock. She struck five of them before Rairi found her voice through a fog of disbelief.

"Wait! Marca, no!"

Too late. Marca touched the ninth sigil.

The plate in the center spun on its axis, sank into the door, and split into four parts. A series of clangs and clicks sounded as the door's inner steel bars moved from their locked position.

The enormous doors swung out gently.

"Marca, you idiot!" she shouted. "You almost...you could of...do you not realize..." Rairi stammered, unable to complete a single argument — not with the damn door looming idly ajar.

"I'm sorry?" Marca said meekly. "Did you not want it open yet?"

To her horror, Marca made to push the doors back together.

"No! Stop!"

Marca froze, her face a mask of confusion.

"How?" she asked, rubbing the bridge of her nose. "How did you do that?"

"You mean solve the puzzle?" Marca shrugged sheepishly. "The sequence was the *Avanty Mercy Equation*."

"Solve the puzzle? Marca, the number of possible combinations... show me your notebook!"

Marca retrieved her journal from the ground and handed it over.

Rairi could not make sense of the girl's sloppy calisthian script, but her alchemical symbols were clear. She had pinpointed the essential elements in the equation and deduced their order through induction. An unfamiliar formula was scribbled near the bottom of her notes, which she had used as a keystone.

"What is this formula here? You did not pull something like this from the ether."

"No." Marca shook her head. "That's the skull key."

"Explain."

"Tepley's great shinn vaults were built by Grandmaster Dossan Mun'vel during the reign of Queen Aviedeen. Risking his life, he secretly built a decryption for all his binding wards and hid it within his works. The formula has no name, but it opens every vault he ever made, like a skull key."

Rairi scanned the markings carefully, committing them to memory before handing the journal back to Marca. "Such secrets are jealously guarded treasures among alchemists. How did you come upon it?"

Marca glanced between her and Kivan, blushed, and turned away, leaving the question unanswered.

Fascinating creature. Rairi fought to keep a smile off her face.

"So are we going inside?" Kivan asked. "Or did you two wish to speak about the door some more?" The young anthrop raised his brows at Marca, ignoring her completely. Kivan did everything in his power to pretend like she didn't exist, which suited her fine.

Sharn's shinn vault was a circular chamber, sixty feet in diameter and forty feet high, lined from floor to ceiling with iron-reinforced oaken shelves, each holding a number of sturdy witchwood chests.

As Kivan busied himself lighting braziers and Marca gaped in childish awe, Rairi counted one-hundred-and-twenty-one containers in all, with only fifty-two of them currently sealed. The rest sat open, revealing the white quartz lining of their interiors, like silent baby chicks waiting to be fed.

"This is supposed to be the greatest shinn vault in Tepley," Marca sighed.

"You are surprised it stands half-empty?" Rairi asked. "What the Kragten did not destroy, you people poisoned."

Marca gave her a bewildered look. "Why do you sound angry? The Neterian Purge was long ago, Rairi, before either of us was born."

"It still occurred," she said, "and our Elders remember it well."

An uncomfortable silence sat between them.

"How do you think they placed those heavy looking chests up there?" Kivan asked, scanning the room.

"I'm not certain," Marca said, "but we must figure it out. Captain Dorav requires all shinn counted, categorized, and put inside the *Kajak's* hold with haste."

"I'm surprised you anthrops still find value in shinn," Rairi said, "since everything you ever built with it now lies in ruin."

"Humans, Rairi," Marca said. "We are called humans."

Rairi ignored her and walked towards the center of the chamber where a single black chest wrapped in iron chains lay on a flat block of gray marble.

"Shinn does require purification now," Marca said, walking beside her. "And much potency is lost in the process, but we are still capable of producing wonderful feats of alchemy with enough clean shinn. If anything, shinn's value has increased due to its rarity."

"I will take inventory," Kivan said, sitting on the stone floor by the far wall. He retrieved a thick ledger, inkwell, and quill, and began writing.

"What do you make of this one here?" Rairi asked the girl.

Marca ran her bare hand confidently over the chain.

"Marca!"

"What?" Marca jumped back, startled. Kivan's eyes shot up from his ledger.

"What are you doing?! The markings! Are you blind?!"

"Oh..."

"Oh?! Arisia help me..."

"They are not alchemical wards," Marca said. "I would know if they were."

"There exist older languages than alchemy! Some far deadlier!" The reprimand came out sharper than she intended.

"My apologies." Marca's girlish pout made Rairi sigh.

Seeing no immediate danger, Kivan returned to his ledger.

"This will be our task for the next few days then," Rairi said, attempting to change the subject.

"No, I plan to go west with Captain Dorav," Marca said.

Rairi stared into the girl's large brown eyes and tried to find some kind of answer. "I thought your priorities lay with the shinn in this vault. The Captain is going off to clear a road and round up a few witless miners. What interest could that possibly hold for you?"

Marca's mischievous grin peaked her curiosity. The girl lowered her voice so Kivan could not overhear.

"No one has entered those mines with a springfinder in untold years." Marca tapped the sigil-covered arrowhead trapped behind her belt.

"Why?"

"Because they are outlawed. The Inquisition labeled them heretical after the Kragten War."

Rairi bit her lip to keep from smiling. The girl had salt. "Are you not concerned with Kivan knowing you own one?"

"No. Kivan threshes the purser's ledgers and secretly smuggles molki and shiver for the crew. We met in Palidor's black market years ago. He and I have an understanding."

"A dangerous arrangement, Marca."

"A safe one, trust me."

"That still does not explain why you wish to do this."

"Because, these chests," Marca said, pointing at them, "have an owner awaiting delivery. The shinn inside the mines are no one's property...well perhaps the miners', but that changes once Dorav herds them all back here.

"The Captain was given command to see I complete my objectives, and I am expected to survey as many of the shinn-producing claims around Sharn as possible."

"You will lie."

"I will."

Rairi admired this young girl's audacity.

"Come with me," Marca said.

Rairi shook her head and spared the chained chest a glance before turning her attention back to Marca.

"No," she said. "We stay with the contents of the vault. That is our mission. The shinn we take from here is destined for your academy regardless."

"Yes, but I will never be granted its use!" Marca sighed and lowered her voice again. "Apprentices are not allowed to experiment with shinn. We may draw up theories and present them to our professors for evaluation, but they decide if our goals are worthy of their shinn stores being tapped. My formulas have sat on Headmistress Dyrcei's desk for two years. She shows no sign of ever allowing me to prove their worth."

"Then steal some of this shinn," Rairi said, waving a hand at the chests. "No one is going to miss an ingot or two they never knew existed. You say you have an arrangement with Kivan, so he is obliged to keep your secret, yes?"

"I cannot use this shinn," Marca said.

"Why not?"

Hesitation appeared on Marca's face. "It has been cleaned." She licked her lips. "I work on a method to purify shinn without losing potency in the process. I need raw stone for the trial."

"I see. Tell me more about these formulas."

"I will, on the road. If I can find enough raw shinn to prove my theories, I can force the academy to validate my work. Will you help me, Rairi?"

She shifted uncomfortably. This was not the plan. Her eyes betrayed here and glanced back at the chained box. It was a colossal effort to not stare. "What about our counting and labeling of the vault?"

"That is covered." Marca conspicuously pointed at Kivan.

"You are a malicious one, Marca."

"We will assist him on the journey home. He need not do all the work, only most of it."

"I may not sail back with you. My place is with my kin, and our service to Dorav ends once he releases us."

"Oh." Marca's crest fell.

"However, my current orders are to stay by your side, so I will come with you, and guard the secrecy of your quest."

"You will?! Oh, praise you, Rairi! You will not regret this!" Marca moved to embrace her.

Rairi's hand went reflexively for the hilt of her knife, stopping Marca cold. The girl retreated a step, her smile faltering only slightly.

"Sorry," Marca said, "I forgot."

Rairi did not believe Marca would hurt her, or could if she tried, but she did not enjoy the idea of being embraced by an anthrop, even one as interesting as her.

"Before we go," Rairi said, "we must make certain these chests are being moved to the ship and secured — starting with this one." She pointed at the chained box. "Once that is done, I will accompany you."

"A deal well struck!" Marca said brightly. "Let's see how to bring those boxes down, and give Dorav the good news."

"You should give Kivan the good news first."

Marca's smile was full of mischief.

Dorav stood with Isa and Kartecus under Zenthien's Banner of Atonement while his men opened the indigo doors to the Calusian temple. The masterfully crafted cylindrical edifice was fifty feet across and sixty feet tall. Its blue, domed ceiling was upheld by thick marble pillars, each depicting once of the seven seraphs who guarded the pools of Kahalma, where petitioners bathed away their worldly corruption before entering the kingdom of light.

Time and devotion went into this building's construction. Master builders were consulted and paid a mountain of gold. Marble and shale were sailed here, along with blackwood and brass. The majestic building was meant to last the ages as an eternal symbol of Calusian might and prosperity.

As an emblem of intent, the Banner of Atonement had stood vigilant at the bottom of the temple's stairs since Sharn's capture. Made of royal blue cloth, the banner displayed a golden disk encircled by white T'korin sigil-script which stated: *Those who kneel before mine light are atoned of heresy and granted mine forgiveness.*

"My men prepared a wagon for you and yours, Nihengale," Dorav said as the mepsiens approached. "She may prove a bit stuffy, but will keep the sunlight out during our journey west."

"Appreciated, sir," Nihengale said.

"You are dismissed."

The mepsiens departed, their hoods pulled up to hide them from the morning's approaching light. Dorav understood why the Blades of Mepsia were treated with such care and animosity by most. Their unnatural presence and proficiency in killing was unnerving. Domesticated city spooks were a far cry from their wild cousins.

The temple's korgur came to the threshold, draped in his finest ceremonial robes of white, red, and black, gripping his gilded Calusian scepter tightly against this chest. He was being defiant.

"Have your people decided on my proposal, Korgur?" Dorav asked. "Have you shown them the path away from damnation?"

"You are the only ones who are damned, Zonirans!" the korgur said, his voice uncertain.

"I call to those inside the temple!" Dorav shouted. "The time to choose has come! Step away from this! Kneel before the banner and receive atonement! Purge yourselves of this heresy!"

The captured sell-swords who protected the city walls stormed past the korgur and knelt beneath the banner. Merchants, tradesmen, and simple folk who did not believe their misguided faith worth dying for, also joined them.

"You have chosen wisely," he said to their bowed heads. "Lieutenant Kathor, escort these people to my ship. Put them in irons and have Master Myrkin conduct a screening. Those he finds useful are to be pressed into service. Those he does not, sail on the Red Fleet."

"Aye, sir." Kathor raised a hand to his bandaged head in a stiff salute.

The mercenaries gave each other disquieted glances, but did not resist. They knew Dorav would kill them to a man if they tried. Their only recourse now was to prove useful and avoid the slave ships. Kathor and his armed contingent led the new converts to the port where the *Kajak* awaited.

"Anyone else?!" Dorav called. "I will not ask again!"

The korgur straightened his back and raised his chin, looking down at him with unhidden disdain.

A few people's curious heads poked out from behind the doorway. A little boy almost stepped outside before his mother scooped him up and carried him back into the temple.

"You make a grave mistake, Korgur." Kartecus said. "Tell your people to choose atonement."

"They have atoned!" The korgur cried, raising his arms in a flourish, "and Kahalma awaits! Do what you like, false prophets! Our souls remain clean!"

Ser Isa's lips pressed to bloodless lines, and her brow furrowed. She gave him a silently pleading stare.

"How many are in there?" he asked her.

"Over two dozen, sir."

Dorav nodded his consent, and she took a deep breath of relief.

"Bring out the children!" Ser Isa cried.

The korgur stared,confounded as Dorav's marines entered the temple and pulled the children out of their parent's grips, striking anyone who intervened. A score of mothers and fathers followed their wailing, reaching children outside and knelt before the banner in supplication.

Others however, remained behind. They hovered at the threshold, watching the soldiers take their pleading children away, unwilling to abandon their faith. They looked to their korgur with stricken faces.

"You said we could choose!" the korgur shouted. "You break your word! You said we could choose!"

"And you've chosen!" Dorav shouted back as his soldiers closed the temple doors and barred them, locking everyone else inside.

Dorav was loathe to do this, but Ser Isa, Kartecus, and his men would all question his faith and allegiance to the Order if he shirked his duty. The zoniran scriptures were specific about the prescribed fate of heretics, apostates, and infidels.

"Burn it," he said sharply.

Dorav did not seek refuge or turn away. Like a man in the path of a brush fire, he suffered their pleas, bloodcurdling screams, and the scent of their burning flesh. He stood at the foot of the temple's steps, as motionless as a marble statue, until the only sounds remaining were the low roar of the flames and the crackling of smoldering timbers — until only embers remained, dancing in the wind.

6

The Screams of the Kafras

"Get yourself up that mountain boys,
"But best you take heed!
"For Old Horny Goats,
"The Old Horny Goats!"

Singing helped the time go by. The repetitive strikes of picks, the rumble of rocks, and snorts of the weary kafras could drive a man mad without some form of distraction. David had point today, with Ricker and Sifran at his flanks. Ashen had clearing and Caige had the tug.

"They'll dance on their hind-legs,
"They'll give you the eye then,
"They'll kick in your head!"

His pickax tore into the familiar stone, creating small sparks which lit the oily gloom. Flint was mixed with the rock, which was a hindrance. He would need to take a whetstone to his tools after they got through this patch.

"They'll piss in your mouth!
"They'll shit down your neck!"

Unexpectedly, David's pick struck something soft and brittle, sinking almost to the shaft. He stopped singing and lifted his oil lamp, realizing he hit a bulbous, red and black mushroom, buried in the cave wall. Pulling a few rocks free, he discovered a cluster of fungi surrounding a thin layer of flint and loose stones.

"They'll bugger you,
"They'll bugger you!
"The Old goats'll bugger you!"
"If you don't pay their toll,
"They'll fuck every hole!"

"Hey! Look at this!" he called out.

The singing and clanging died down as the others came to investigate.

David examined the fungus by the light of his lamp. "These are redstone mushrooms."

"Are you certain?" Caige asked suspiciously.

"Not our first time finding some," David said, taking a bite and chewing tentatively. The rough, grainy texture and sour aftertaste were unmistakable.

"I remember that day," Ricker said, picking one out of the wall. "We figured water might be nearby but never found it."

"What is their taste?" Ashen asked.

"Try it." Ricker tossed him one.

While the others inspected the mushrooms, David dug his thick fingers into the dirt. "The earth is moist here," he said. "Soft. Might be we find the water this time."

"Worth a gander at least," Ricker said, through bites. "Ashen, grab a crate for these. We can give them to Nikos to bake into his bread for us."

"All right." Ashen walked up the drift, his oil lamp swinging in the gloom.

They continued to dig into the wall, pulling out patches of mossy stones and flat, red mushrooms. The farther they dug, the softer and damper the earth became.

David scarcely remembered the pungent sweetness of moist earth. He took a handful to his face and inhaled its aroma, recalling early mornings on the march, right before the sun rose and the legions broke camp.

A swarm of beetles scrambled out of the dirt, startling them.

"Shit!" Sifran cried, jumping back.

"Ease," Ricker said.

"You know I fucking hate beetles!" Sifran pushed himself back against the far wall, stomping his feet restlessly. "Shit! Shit!"

"Easy, Sifran!" David growled.

Ashen returned with a small crate. Noticing Sifran's distress, he muttered something under his breath.

"Speak up, dick-sheath!" Sifran barked, either hearing him or assuming he was being made small of.

"Enough!" Ricker said. "Pinch your turds, both of you! We keep digging. Caige, Ashen, grab your shovels. Now!"

As they tore through the wall, Sifran kept looking around, nervously slapping at his neck and shaking his trouser legs.

The digging became easier the deeper they went, allowing them to turn their picks around and use the ax heads to plow the soft earth, raking two feet of dirt-wall before finally breaking through.

Tearing away at the final layer, they formed a hole spacious enough to step into. A cool, pungent draft chilled David's tired muscles. He lifted his lamp and peered into the newly discovered cavern. A broken clay pot lay nearby.

"A dwelling of some kind," he said, squinting.

"Ashen, grab the bird," Ricker said.

David gripped his pickax and entered the oblong chamber of mossy stone walls. Shattered clay pots and vases, rusted farming equipment, and other odd items lay scattered haphazardly about the floor. Six hempweave mats lay on the earth around a cold fire-pit and twice as many hammocks cluttered the space above.

"What is this ?" Sifran asked.

"Some kind of habitat," David replied, moving his light around.

"What's over there?" Sifran pointed.

At the far north end of the cavern hung dead, desiccated vines ,clustered in a corner from floor to ceiling. Dozens of skeletal human remains jutted out from every angle of the dead plant, like a macabre altar.

"David, what in the Vorx is that?" Ricker walked beside him with Caige.

"Python vine," he said.

"Did that thing? No." Sifran made a worried face.

"It did," David said. "They eat anything or anyone that comes within reach, but Kaira is too dry for them. It should not be here, unless..."

"Unless?" Ricker asked.

David shrugged. "It was planted here and kept well fed."

Ashen returned with the bird and inspected the cave warily.

"How is he?" Ricker asked.

"A little excited, but fine."

"Give him here." David put his hand out.

Ashen passed him the cage and went to eye the remains inside the knotted bulk of dead vines before taking a few cautious steps back.

"I found the way out," Ricker called. "Come see this."

The cavern's entrance stood overlooking a thickly wooded valley of petrified trees. The sky was tinged with hints of tea-leaf and honey over the valley's western crests.

"What did we dig ourselves into here?" Ashen asked.

"I don't know," David said, the red hairs on his arms standing on end. "But I don't like it."

A disquieting pressure sat on Caige's chest. The air was filled with a sense of quiet danger, making his every instinct plead caution. "Ricker, we should probably head back," he said. "I don't think it safe here."

"Agreed," Ashen said.

"The boys may be right, Ricker," David pressed. "This place has an ominous smell."

Ricker had a faraway glint in his eyes, as if searching for something. "There!" he said, his eyes widening as he pointed to the mouth of the valley. "Something stands down there!"

Caige squinted and scanned the canopy until he caught sight of a stone structure at the edge of the forest — some kind of ancient ruin, obscured by overgrowth.

Ricker started down the dusty path.

"Ricker!" David called after him. "What in the Vorx are you doing? This is dangerous. We cannot walk into this all brass and balls. We're miners, man, not fucking explorers. Lets head back and grab a few more hands. We'll summon the militia and-"

"No!" Ricker turned on them, his face pinched in anger. "No, don't you understand? This is where the claim leads!"

They shared glances of quiet confusion.

"Tarrak brought down the eastern tunnel, remember?" Ricker said. "The western drift led us here. There's nowhere else for us to dig now except fucking north!"

Ricker had a point. They had skirted hard bedrock for months now, being herded westward by the unyielding stone. The north end of Ricker's claim could not be breached without fire-setting and sluicing — both impossible in Kaira.

"Everyone who works hard bedrock in Kaira fails, without exception," Ricker continued. "We will break ourselves against that stone before we find any shinn."

"Wait," Ashen said, his brows climbing his forehead. "You mean this is it?"

"Yes!" Ricker shouted, shoving the handle of his pick into his mining belt and raising his thick arms. "Yes, this is fucking it! We've dug as far as my claim goes."

Concern clung to everyone's faces. They had reached the end of Ricker's claim, and would now leave empty-handed. The mine had refused to repay their grueling effort.

A chill hand gripped Caige's heart remembering the small fortune he yet owed the Guild. With no more mine to dig, he was well and proper fucked. He turned to contemplate the valley again and an idea struck him.

"What about all this?" he asked.

"I can't claim an entire fucking valley, Caige," Ricker replied.

"No," he said, "but some of these caves might lead around the bedrock, or hold a little shinn behind their walls. There might still be a chance here."

Ricker scratched his bearded cheek. "Perhaps." He looked the vale over once more, this time with a more focused, critical eye. "I read the maps that show every claim west of Sharn. This valley does not appear on any of them, which means this is not Magalian land."

"And what the jolly fuck does that mean?" Sifran asked.

"That we need to keep this find between us," David said. "Whatever is in here; shinn, jewels, a giant golden cock with fist-sized diamonds for balls, belongs to whoever lays hands on it."

"We may find jewels here?" Ashen asked.

"One possibility in many," Ricker said.

"So we might not be completely fucked?" Caige asked, receiving odd glances from the others.

"Listen," Ricker said, "we must be careful, but we cannot go back. I won't go back. We still have daylight enough to see what might be down there. If you wish to leave, leave. No one holds a knife to your throat, but if do, you are out."

"Of the team?" Sifran asked.

"Yes," Ricker said.

They shared meaningful looks between themselves, a dangerous tension hanging in air. Someone deciding to leave now would be troublesome and dangerous. If one of them went to the Maggs or another crew with this find, there would be conflict, and bloodshed.

"Well?" Ricker crossed his arms. "Are you lassies coming or are we going to eye-fuck about it some more?"

"I'm with you," Sifran said without hesitation.

David scoffed loudly. "What the fuck else am I to do, dig for the Salkas?"

Caige nodded at Ricker when their gazes met.

"Ashen?" Ricker asked.

Ashen's face darkened. For a moment, Caige thought he might turn away. He had other options after all.

"I'll stay," Ashen said softly.

"Are you certain, rat-dick?" David growled. "Unwrap your tongue!"

"Yes, fuck, I said I would stay!" Ashen growled back.

"All right," Ricker said, starting down the dirt path. "Then follow."

Caige extinguished his lamp and made his way down the dry, curving path behind Ricker until they stood by the shadows of the petrified forest.

The sun finished clearing the valley's western peaks, casting hard shadows on the earth. A partial human skeleton lay sprawled on the ground before them, facing away from the darker depths of the vale. Only its smashed-in skull, part of a brittle torso, and one outstretched arm remained.

"Appears like something bit him in half," Sifran said.

"Shut up, Sifran," Ashen said. "Nothing grows that large."

"You could not be more wrong, boy," David said.

Caige sensed eyes on him from somewhere within the silent forest. He scrutinized the woods but found nothing but a dense stillness, heavy as lead. "Feels like something is watching us," he said dryly.

"Stop scaring yourselves," Ricker sniffed. "The ruin should be up ahead. Keep close."

As they walked into the chilling shade of the deadwood, Caige focused on repressing how scared he felt. He refused to be the first to turn back, but the old, nightmarish stories told around Ticondrian campfires were scratching at the corners of his mind.

He recalled the tale of Bittertooth, the foul vagrant who fed on men's bones if they met him in dark places. He would whistle through his broken teeth, taunting his prey because he liked his marrow spiced with fear.

The Chikorko was a ghostly giant spider capable of walking through solid stone and snatching you away in its poisoned mouth. Children who did not heed their elders were its favorite meal, but if hungry enough, it would eat dogs, cats, and pigs.

The worst of them was the Shrix; a sinister mist which melted your flesh and trapped your soul after it killed you, growing larger and stronger with every kill. Entire towns had been left desolate by a visit from the Shrix, and you never knew where the monster would appear, until it was too late.

Further along the path they found the remains of a blackened grove. Desiccated skeletons hung from the encircling tree's branches. The broad, petrified oak in the center had a gaping, hollow scar in its trunk resembling an open maw, under a pair of grieving vacuous eyes.

They ducked under the dangling feet of the dead and entered the grove.

"Tell me that's not a man-eating tree," Ashen said.

David shook his head. "Plague Tree. We ran into a few in Blackmeadow Wood during the march to Sentinel. This is Old World magic, meant to halt the spread of sickness. The tribes hollow these trees out, carve that pained face on them, and char their insides.

"Sacrifices to Kaxxil are chosen, put in the tree's mouth, and burned alive."

"Does it work?" Caige asked, strangely intrigued by the macabre ritual. He knew the name Kaxxil. The plague-bringer, god of pestilence, one of the Four Winds of Doom. To not pay respects at his shrines was to court disaster.

"If the tree burns down," David said, "the offer is accepted, otherwise more sacrifices need to be made."

"Is that why they strung those people there up?" Caige asked. "The tree wouldn't burn?"

"No," David replied, his tone leaded and the lines on his face deepening. "That is...something else."

He considered probing David further but thought better of it. The man had experienced more during the war than Caige could wrap his head around. Better to leave him be.

"Whatever happened here," David's scowl deepened. "Made this place wrong...unnatural-like."

"This place is cursed is what," Ashen said. "Coming here was a mistake."

"You're free to go fuck a hen, Ashen," Ricker said with a tired sigh. "But we keep moving."

As they passed the Plague Tree, Caige noticed something half-buried among the bones and ash inside its jagged mouth.

"What are you doing?" Sifran asked, looking back at him.

"I found something," he said.

"What is it?"

"Not certain."

"Caige, no!" Ricker said.

He pulled the object from the ash, smacking off a thick layer of soot. The ivory hunting horn was old, covered in intricate carvings and the visages of various tiny, faded animals. There were snakes, ants, herons, ravens, bats, wolves, falcons, bears, hunting cats, and a few others he did not recognize. A fierce lion's open maw formed the horn's mouth, and a long, jagged crack ran down its ivory center.

"It's broken, but it might still be worth something," he said.

"Fucking half-wit," Ricker muttered. "You should never disturb the dead, Caige."

"Mind if I see?" Sifran asked, holding out his four-fingered hand.

He handed the horn over and watched Sifran appraise it.

"Lighter than I thought." Sifran turned the item over carefully. "Has a white marble mouth piece, and these engravings are masterful, if worn down."

"Does it have value?" Caige asked.

"If it wasn't broken perhaps." Sifran wiped the little mouthpiece with his thumb and put it to his lips. The horn let out a pained, garbled sound.

"No, useless," Sifran said and spat.

"Here, let me." David held out his hand. "You have smoke for breath."

David blew a deeper groan that echoed back through the deadwood. The big man shook his head. "Here Caige, this is your find. A little caulking will fix that break right up."

"Let's keep moving." Ricker said, walking further down the path.

Caige turned the ivory horn in his hands pensively, prepared to drop it, when he caught the glimmer of something hiding inside.

Digging his fingers into the crack near the mouthpiece, he touched something cool and smooth. He found a rock on the ground, and struck the horn against it, pulling its wound open wider. After the third blow, the horn snapped in half. Something shiny rolled out. He tried to catch it in midair but missed.

On the earth lay a small, green, sphere. He pinched it between thumb and index finger, and studied it in the light. Roughly the size of a knuckle bone, he held a flawless, perfectly cut emerald.

Caige did not know much about gem shaping, but he had never seen one cut without facets before. It was a breathtaking little thing.

"Now what were you doing in there?" he asked the little gem.

"Caige, are you coming?" David called back.

"Hold on!" He tucked the emerald into a pouch of his thick miner's belt.

When he reached the others, he had to bite the inside of his cheek to keep from smiling.

To David's dismay, the obstructed building they spotted from the mountainside was an abandoned Neterian temple. Standing under its oppressive mass, an unmistakable surge of dread filled his gut.

The Plague Tree in the grove was a ritual tradition of many Calic tribes. The corpses tied to the trees however, were indicative of ritual cannibalism — something Neterians used in their daemonic rites. He was correct in fearing this valley as a home to Neterian vorxcraft. Seeing the temple, brought back a wave of unwanted memories that he bit back and swallowed.

A deep ravine cut the valley like a scar at the foot of the temple's broad stairs, putting twenty feet of empty air between the ziggurat and themselves. Rope bridges once stitched the divide, but now dangled uselessly against the chasm walls.

Despite his disgust, what held his eyes in place was not the dread temple, but the massive broken statue lying at the head of its steps. The high, rectangular portal leading into the ziggurat was flanked by two muscular lioness statues, sitting regally on their haunches, poised and as tall as the doorway they defended.

The male lion, which once sat on the temple's ceiling, had been wrapped in ropes and vines, pulled down from his vaulted perch, and shattered into five uneven parts. Everyone stared at the broken statue, and for a time none spoke, too afraid to dispel the illusion. David's own disgust could not drown out his rising elation. He believed himself ready for anything, but not this.

Ricker took a deep breath and let it out through his nose. "I suppose you lot are glad you didn't cunnie out," he said.

"We're rich," Ashen whispered, his young face lighting up. "We're fucking rich!"

The enormous broken idol, laying smashed against the ziggurat steps, was sculpted entirely out of shinn. David could imagine how such a sight might appear divine to a primitive people — a towering lion, perched higher than the valley's tallest trees, refracting the silvery brilliance of the rising sun. Now the statue lay ruined, covered in grime and moss, but the shinn it was carved from was worth a queen's ransom — perhaps more.

"Terra's stone! Sifran cried out sharply. "Draw an eyeful of it all!"

"Our long search is over." Ricker smiled brightly. "We found our fucking fortunes!"

They cheered and embraced each other, laughing uncontrollably.

David's mind raced with so many possibilities, he could barely keep track of them all. Only now, after years of arduous labor in Kaira, did he realize, he never truly expected to find a significant amount of shinn. Certainly not almost two goddamn tonnes of it.

Caige was the only one not celebrating. He stood apart, staring at the broken lion with a far off, haunted expression.

"Caige?" David asked. "You all right?"

"Look, there!" Caige pointed.

A wiry old man was perched on the cracked altar-stone, glaring at them. His long unkempt beard was gray and stained with crusty patches of orange and brown. He wore dense bones as ornaments around his neck, arms, and waist, and his small, puckered phallus poked out of a thicket of white pubis between his thin, naked legs.

When he spoke, his foreign words were short and crinkly, like stones rolling over dry twigs. He knelt and prostrated himself, facing the door, giving them a clear view of his shit-stained ass.

"Who is this dick-eater?" Ashen asked. "If he believes he'll keep us from our shinn he can-"

"Ashen, be quiet!" Ricker hissed. "Listen!"

The bird chirped and bounced off the bars of his cage, clearly terrified.

A deep, baritone moan accompanied by a dry, hollow clunk, like boulders cascading down a hillside echoed from within the temple's gaping entrance.

David felt the sound surround him, slither into his every orifice, and wrap his guts into a sailor's knot. The subsonic vibration of it struck him at an instinctual level, burrowing into his marrow and ceasing his muscle fibers.

This fear was familiar to him. In the instant before a battle charge against a screaming horde of enemy spears, his body would bite down, threatening to evacuate his bowels, and pinch him into a trembling, useless heap. The flesh sensed when death's shadow fell over it, and never failed to give warning.

His battle training kicked in immediately.

Don't freeze up. Don't freeze up. Don't freeze up!

"Run!" he cried, snapping the others out of their horrified paralysis. "Run, gods damn you! RUN!!"

David's heart pounded furiously as they fled the temple. He did not dare look back at whatever was making that horrible noise. Menacing shadows followed as they ran headlong through the petrified forest, the rattling moan growing louder and closer.

He was accustomed to long hours of hard labor, but not running. His lungs screamed for air and the muscles in his legs burned as they pumped.

"What is that fucking noise?" Sifran's voice was cracked and manic.

"Shut up and run!" Ricker barked.

The bird's cage snagged on an outstretched branch, yanking it out of David's grasp. "Wait, I lost the bird!"

"Fuck the bird!" Caige screamed back at him.

They cleared the forest and ran headlong up the dirt road towards the claim. The noise was everywhere now, echoing off the valley walls. It wrapped itself around David's chest like a stone fist, insisting he drop to the ground and embrace his knees.

They plowed through the cave dwelling, trampling over ancient pottery and sending old tools flying in their haste.

"We need to close this hole!" Ricker gasped once inside the mine shaft.

"What about the shinn?" Sifran wheezed.

"To the Vorx with the shinn!" David tried to recover his breath. He was sweating profusely and he had a stitch on his left side.

The swiftly approaching rattle-moan entered the cavern beyond the wall, filling the enclosure like a death knell.

"Close it!" David shouted. "Close the hole!"

"Too late!" Ricker said. "Everyone out! Move! Now!"

They scrambled up the black drift, not breaking stride until they cleared the entrance and were on the Kafra Road. Ricker hastily chained and locked the makeshift gate behind them.

The group took a step back, caught their breath, and waited, uncertain of what to do. The Kafra Road lay dark and silent, the other mining teams having already left their claims and gone down the mountainside. For a moment, there was only silence — then came the horrible screams of the kafras.

Snorts, groans, yawns, and farts were the only noises the docile kafras ever made. Now their cries filled the mine with echoes of such terror and pain, it made David's eyes well up. He stood horrified, staring helplessly into the darkness of the box cut.

"Colp...Colp!" Ashen cried.

He felt a sudden pang of pity for the boy. The lumbering kafra was the only thing left of his family after Tarrak had killed his parents.

"Ashen, don't," Ricker said, putting a hand on his shoulder. "I'm sorry, lad...it's too late."

The kafra's painful cries became wet, throaty gurgles, then silence reigned once more.

7

A Stranger Walks into Town

The Pick Rock tavern reeked of cheap spirits, dried piss, and vomit. Its grimy walls were decorated with twenty-eight picks hanging on long, bent nails — each with the name of its previous owner engraved on its handle.

They were markers, left behind by prospectors who had made their fortunes and moved on to greener, cleaner lives. The picks filled the tavern's patrons with burning envy and the hope that one day, their names would be among them.

David took his favorite stool on the corner of the bar, closest to the door. Caige sat at the other end, by the wall, while the rest of the team sat between them. Everyone who frequented the Pick Rock knew that these five seats belonged to Ricker and his team, like the oval table on the southwest corner belonged to Galgis and his boys, and the circle of stools around the limp oak table belonged to the Salka brothers.

It felt odd coming here after what occurred at Ricker's claim, but they all needed a stiff drink to calm their flailed nerves.

"Bullhorn?" Noss asked with a rot-stained smile.

"Yes," David said and tossed two iron chints on the bar.

Ricker and the others each tossed two chints as well. Noss took their money, served each of them a measure of dark amber liquid in five dusty tins, and left them the bottle.

David turned and scanned the tavern, taking note of who else was here. Fanten, Elmir, and Benny Salka sat at their table playing cards with a small cask of ale between them. Leina sat on Benny's lap. She gave him a playful wink before turning back to their game.

Sordon and Vesser Reen talked heatedly in the corner while Illa worked on them from beneath their table - her head bobbing rhythmically between Vesser's legs while her left hand stroked Sordon.

Loklis and his men sat in their usual place and were already on their second bottle of bullhorn. Mita and Sepi sat with them, rosy-cheeked and laughing.

Ricker raised his tin. "To health, wealth, and wanton fuckery," he somberly recited their habitual drinking cheer.

David raised his tin and drank the bitter spirit, savoring its stinging spice. Bullhorn tasted like peppered lemon peel dipped in kafra piss. Only a seasoned drinker could resist coughing the stuff back up in a fit of tears and snot.

Sifran downed his drink stoically and lit a cuksar for them, his thin hands trembling. They each took a few long pulls of the acrid smoke before Sifran retook possession of the stub.

"I'll speak with the Maggs in the morning." Ricker stared down at his empty tin, speaking only loud enough for them to hear. "Tell them what we found and ask what they might offer."

"Ricker," David said, "they won't offer much of anything. Besides, whatever butchered the kafras still lurks in the drift."

"Whatever is in my claim is Sharn's problem now," Ricker replied. "The Maggs can hire as many swords as they need to clear whatever that was out. I will make sure we all receive a fair cut of everything."

"Wait, everything?" Caige asked. "Claim and all?"

"That's right," Ricker stated flatly. He refilled their cups and they each drank again.

"Uughah!" Vesser exclaimed from behind them. Illa stood, spitting into a rag cloth.

"You cannot sell the claim, Ricker," Sifran whispered. "That broken statue is worth a fortune, and was only one thing we found. What if there's more wealth inside the old ruin? The Maggs will spit in out mouths and call it fair trade."

"That statue alone was enough to keep us all living like landed lords for the rest of our days, Sifran," Ricker said, " but it does us no good if we're dead. We barely have enough chint between us to buy rations and tools. We don't hold coin enough to hire the kind of muscle we need to kill whatever is in my mine."

"Then we borrow from the fucking Guild," Ashen said. "We each take out as much as we can, and hire the militia to kill whatever they find. Ricker, consider this before you sell."

"Ashen's right, Ricker," Caige said, serving them another round. "This is the find we worked all these years for - you longer than any.

"Remember when Willar's' team found the rock-eater in their claim two years ago? The militia charged him two sovereigns apiece but they killed the damn thing."

"Paying that loan back almost ruined Willar," Ricker said.

"Perhaps, but he hadn't just made the kind of fucking find - ow!" Ashen glared at David in surprise.

"Lower your fucking tone," David said, pulling his elbow from Ashen's ribs.

"Right, sorry," Ashen said.

David glanced back around the tavern. If anyone heard the outburst, he could not tell. Gratefully, Noss was still on the floor clearing tables.

"What do you think I should do, David?" Ricker asked. "You have been with me the longest."

David downed his drink in a gulp and poured himself another. "We assume whatever killed the kafras is still in the mine, but what if it went back into the valley? Like you said before, if we bring the militia into this, they'll want a piece of whatever they find, and if they see our shinn, they won't settle for a cut. They'll want everything."

"Which means killing us," Caige said.

"Right."

"Fuck!" Ricker wrapped his hands around his tin cup as if wishing to strangle it. "The fates fuck me!"

The distant sounds of shouting reached them, rising above the tavern's chatter. A commotion of cries, barking dogs, and women's shrieks slowly rose from the town around them. Everyone in the room quieted down.

"Chen's teeth," Sifran's lusterless eyes opened wider than David had ever seen them go.

"It's out," Ashen said, his voice choked. "It got out. We need to go. We need to go now!"

"Ashen, cork your cunnie!" David said.

"No! I have to find Nianah!" Ashen stood and sprinted for the doorway.

"Ashen, get back here!" Ricker shouted.

As Ashen opened the tavern's door to leave, a booted foot struck him squarely in the chest, throwing him back on his shoulder blades.

A tall man dressed in a dust-blasted suit of plated armor and wrapped in a bloodstained purple cloak stepped into the Pick Rock. He studied the room quietly before undoing the leather strap of his helmet's face-guard, revealing his yellow stubble and thin mouth.

"Listen well!" he said. "My men and I subdued your militia and secured this town. Your women and children are safe, but if any one of you drunks gives me any trouble, I'll hang you in front of them as an example."

The Pick Rock fell eerily silent as the Ashura's blue eyes scanned the room from behind the sharp angles of his helm. Everyone stared at the knight, shocked by the tenacity in his iron voice. The oil lamps gave fluttering pops in the silence, their greasy light dancing off the man's armor plating.

Caige had never seen an Ashura before, but David had told him stories about them from the war. No weapon could break their divinely blessed aegis shields and their holy swords cut through leather armor like warm bread. When they entered the field of battle, taking one down required a squad of Talons working in concert.

"You're all going to follow my marines down to the remains of Fort Kai," the Ashura said. "The road has not been kind, so do not test my patience."

Nobody moved or spoke out.

"Bring them down," the knight said, striding into the Pick Rock.

A dozen armored men, each brandishing a sharpened xiphos, ran into the tavern, their foreign caligae slapping against the floorboards. They pulled everyone out of their chairs and stools, pushing them roughly towards the door.

"Get moving!" one man shouted.

A bearded soldier walked up and put the tip of his blade up against David's hairy chest. "No trouble from you or yours, big man," he said in a thick, northern accent. "Clear?"

"No, no trouble," David replied and stood, his hands in the air.

"Keep calm," Ricker told them as he stood, mimicking David's movements. "Everything will be fine."

Caige stood and raised his hands like the others, keeping one eye on the knight, who was carefully inspecting the picks on the tavern walls, as if searching for something.

As they marched down Coppertooth Road, Caige saw soldiers rummaging through people's homes, cracking open chests and barrels with their sharpened axes, and taking anything of value. Loklis shouted something at the men inside his home and stormed off the line.

A line guard threw a handaxe and lodged it between Loklis' shoulder-blades. The ornery old bastard cried out and hit the dirt face first. Before he could crawl a foot away, the same guard drew his xiphos and stabbed him four times in the back.

"Anyone else have a complaint?" The tired young soldier asked, gripping his bloodied sword.

No one else expressed complaint.

Along the road, people were taken forcefully from their homes and shoved into the growing procession headed to Fort Kai.

Roughly thirty soldiers stood behind the old fort's walls, with three of them conducting searches at the entrance. Remembering the emerald in his belt pouch, Caige quickly retrieved the stone, shoved it in his mouth, and swallowed, nearly choking in the process.

"Caige?" Ricker glanced back at him.

Caige hacked for breath a moment and nodded back. "I'm fine."

He wiped the tears out of his eyes as one of the soldiers took off his mining belt and emptied out its pouches. Finding nothing of interest, the man pushed Caige into a line behind the others.

A large tent was being erected on the empty sand lot which once served as a Talon sparring ground, and the soldiers were setting up their camp around the fort's shattered barracks and mess hall.

The Magalian's vault had been raided - its desks, chests, and ledgers lying in a careless pile outside the door. The Guild's counters knelt before their own building, draped in their coats of office with their hands tied behind their backs. Seeing them on their knees with their heads bowed brought a guilty smile to Caige's lips.

Served them right, the greedy assholes.

He would prefer to see them dangling from Maggie's branches, but this suited him fine.

An old man with long white hair and a carefully groomed mustache walked by and sneered at them. "Lieutenant Kathor!" he called out.

"Sir!" A young man, only a few years younger than Caige, jogged up to the older man and saluted. Half the boy's head and right eye were tied in thick bandages, flecked in red seepage.

"How many head?" the old man asked.

"Almost two-hundred in all, sir. Largest town of the lot by far."

"And the vault?"

"Marca and her spook are counting it up now."

"I want a full report, by them, and you."

"Aye, sir," Kathor said.

"And put these beasts to work." The old man thumbed at them. "I want to be away from this hole come first light."

"Aye, sir!" Kathor said.

The young lieutenant made them load wagons with the heavy crates of bounty looted from their town. The women and children waited, huddled under guard inside the ruins of the old fort's mess hall while the men toiled.

An hour into the work, Caige felt queasy. His mind swam as if through a dense fog. His skin became slick with fever sweat and his mouth and eyes tingled. "Where did these whoresons come from?" he asked David, trying to distract himself from the discomfort.

"I don't know," David said. "Likely form the east."

"You mean...Sharn?" Caige's thoughts became jumbled and disorganized, making it difficult to focus on what he was saying.

David nodded. "The kid said this was the largest town they sacked so far. Kaira's the biggest town on the Counter's Road."

"Didn't you tell us that no one could ever sack Sharn?" Ashen inquired. His eyes held a strange amber glow in the lowlight Caige had never seen before.

He was a fine friend, Ashen. He would make Nianah a happy wife one day, and they would raise many children, and they would call him uncle Caige. He enjoyed the idea.

"No one ever has..." David grumbled.

Big Red.

In his younger life in Ticondria, Caige's hero was Erin Garo, the finest pelt hunter in the region. Caige thought of him as an older brother, and wanted nothing more than to be like him.

Caige ended up being better suited as a lumberman. He worked the trees without complaint, until Corren moved them here to mine for shinn.

He loved his father, but he never admired him. His abrasive, drunken behavior made most people either avoid Corren, or make small of behind his back.

David was different. He was a drunk and a lecher, yes, but he would put his hand in a forge-fire for those he cared about. David had risked his own life saving him from Tarrak's maw. He owed his life to the man.

Everyone in Kaira respected David...except for Ashen, but only because he knew David held feelings for Nianah, which was wrong, but it was not like David intended to take her away from him. David probably just felt old and fat around Ashen. He probably felt-

"What did they say about a spook?" Ricker asked, moving the crates along.

Caige blinked, certain that an hour had passed since the last person spoke. For a moment he forgot where he was, as if he were being swallowed alive by his own random meanderings. He tried to pay attention to the conversation but had already forgotten what Ricker asked.

Ricker was a good crew boss, but also the kind of man you learned everything about within two drinks. He was born here, like Ashen, and like...no he did not want to think about Tyn now. He could not face her memory.

"They have a pack of xial with them," David said. "Look up on the wall, careful-like."

Four shadowy figures manned Fort Kai's southern parapet, as still as sandwillows. Caige could not make them out from where he stood, but they did not cast the same silhouettes as the soldiers.

They were a part of the night sky, not a blot in the light's way, like everyone else. The moonlight glistened off their forms, embracing them, cradling them, like a mother would her child. Like his mother had once held him. He recalled her beautiful face, a face he had almost forgotten, and his eyes welled up with tears.

What was happening to him?

"What are they?" Sifran asked.

"The xial?" David shrugged. "I don't know. They look and talk like humans, but they're different. You'll understand if you see one in the light."

Caige startled at the sight of Sifran, working right beside him. Although he had been passing loaded crates to Caige for the last hour or so, the wiry blond manifested before him like a wisp in a fog. Black smoke seeped through the corners of Sifran's mouth, nose, and sinister, little eyes. He reeked of cuksar and spoiled cheese.

The thought occurred to him that Sifran did not appear to be a person at all, but some warped aberration wrapped in human skin. His bones jutted out at strange angles, his teeth were serrated black tips, and he moved like a puppet missing half its strings. How had he never noticed these things before?"

"Are you passing me that box or not?" Sifran hissed at him, holding out his bony, misshapen arms.

"Caige?" David stared at him strangely.

Big Red was drenched in blood, from head to toe. Like a feral beast after a kill, his blue eyes locked on to him with predatory hunger. Human skulls hung around David's chest and waist, and his broad stomach churned from within, as if some horrid parasite had engorged itself within his spoiled innards and now struggled for release.

"Caige, what's wrong?" Ricker's eyes were hollow pits in his withered skull and his tongue was a black length of slithering rope, covered in mucus. His beard was infested with maggots and something with deep red eyes observed Caige from inside its tangled mass.

Only Ashen appeared untouched by the corruption, except for his eyes, which shone with an almost golden intensity. "What's wrong with you, digger?" his friend asked. "You look like you've seen a murik."

Caige's eyes wandered to the ground where tendrils of light, like wispy roots, spread from everyone's feet and conjoined beneath the earth. The tendrils from his own feet fused with theirs, and he sensed the corruption they all carried slithering up his legs and into the base of his spine.

"No!" he cried, dropping the crate in his hands. "No! No! No!"

He leaped on the crate and stomped with his feet, but the roots would not sever. They crawled up into his back instead. Terror seized him as the foreign tendrils wrapped themselves around his heart.

"Caige!" Ricker's voice was an abhorrent growl, his thick tongue whipping the air. "Get a hold of yourself this fucking instant!"

"Daemons!" Caige cried, looking back at one of the soldiers who marched towards him, halberd in hand. "They are vorxed! Can you see? They eat me!"

Something swept Caige's legs out from under him and he landed on the crate, smashing through it. His torso burst open like a melon dropped from a great height, his ribs, blood, and bowels exploding around him.

He grabbed at his broken self, manically trying to pull his bloodied pieces back together. A menacing shadow fell over him, sucking the warmth from his decimated body. He glanced up an instant before the wooden butt of the soldier's halberd struck him on the head.

"What just happened?" David watched two soldiers drag Caige's unconscious body off by his legs.

"You four, clean this mess up," the man who hit Caige said, pointing to the broken crate of gourd melons laying smashed at his feet.

"Where are you taking him? Ricker asked.

"Why, do you want to go with him?" the soldier asked in a menacing tone, pointing the tip of his halberd at Ricker's chest.

Ricker furrowed his brow and pursed his lips.

"Then return to fucking work," the man said.

"David?" Ashen asked, looking up at him with haunted eyes.

He shook his head. "I have never seen someone act in such a way before."

"I have," Sifran said, in almost a whisper, "but it cannot be what I'm thinking."

"What can it not be?" Ricker asked, picking up the broken pieces of crate.

"Molki," Sifran said, kneeling to help him. "A paste made from dream-vine, patcha root, and mist walker petals. Terran holy men make it for their spirit ceremonies, but you can buy some if you know the right people.

"In small amounts, molki shows you things. Lets you peak under Terra's skirts. Take too much however, and you chance not coming back."

"How did Caige get his hands on such here?" Ricker asked.

"He could not have," Sifran said. "No one sells molki in Kaira. I would know if someone did."

"He did swallow something," David said. "Just before we came here."

"He did," Ricker nodded. "And almost choked."

"Fuck," Sifran said, visibly bewildered. "If he swallowed a ball of molki big enough to choke on, it would explain why he was acting such."

"Why would anyone eat something that makes you go crazy?" Ashen asked.

"Not crazy," Sifran replied. "Not really. You could say molki mines you. Unearths everything inside you that's broken and holds it up to the light for you to see. Not everyone can handle such a sight."

"To the Vorx with everything about that idea," Ashen said.

"Come on," David said. "Finish this up. We'll ask Caige later."

Once the wagons were loaded, the soldiers rounded everyone up, marched them back into town, and packed them into the temple. Caige lay against the far wall, fast asleep and with a patch of dried blood caked over the left side of his head.

David knelt beside him and shook him by the shoulder. He did not stir.

"David, don't," Sifran said. "Better if he sleeps, in case it *was* molki. You wake him up and he might have another fit."

"They hit him in the head," David said.

"He got knocked out, David," Ricker said. "Sifran's right. Best let him be."

"Korgur!" the Ashura called from outside the temple. "Make yourself known!"

David stood and followed Minkar as he shouldered his way to the

99

temple's threshold.

"I am the Korgur here," Minkar said firmly. "My name is Minkar Slen, Shepard to the Brotherhood's flock in Kaira. Whom am I addressing?"

The Ashura stood next to a long blue and white banner at the foot of the temple's short steps. "I am Dorav Minos," he said, "Knight of the Holy Order of The Aegis of Man, and Commander in his Lordship King Hervine's Archonwolf fleet."

"I fear we are not well met, Sir Dorav," Minkar said.

"No," Dorav returned grimly, "we are not. This is my offer to you and yours, Korgur. I give you until morning to renounce your heretical faith. Those who kneel before the Banner of Atonement will be forgiven all trespasses and be welcomed on the Golden Stair. Those who do not, will be deemed heretics and dealt with accordingly. Consider my words carefully. You have until first light.

"Close it," Dorav said to his men.

The soldiers barred the temple doors from the outside, sealing everyone within.

"What does he mean?" Gimen Piril asked from the back of the crowded temple. "What does he mean 'dealt with accordingly'?"

Minkar Slen turned, raising his arms against the rising din of concerned voices. "My good people,settle. Settle, please. I will not coat my words in honey, so listen carefully. What that man outside offers is a test of all our faiths.

"He seeks to divide us and force us to turn our backs on the promise of Kalhalma. Those who choose to condemn their immortal souls to save their sinful flesh have been welcomed to do so, but I beseech you to consider the outcome. Know that by kneeling under a Zoniran banner, you turn your back on salvation. You turn your back on the loved ones who departed before you and await you in paradise."

The din around the temple filled with whispered tension.

"Tell them, Minkar," David muttered gruffly to the korgur. "They deserve to know."

Until the moment they walked into the temple, David had hoped this would not happen. Dorav was a single Ashura, and this kind of thing occurred only when zoniran knights marched as part of a jihad.

"There are children in here, David."

"Children who will burn all the same!"

His words made the chamber go deathly silent. Minkar stared hard at him, his eyes poisoned-tipped daggers. David stared back, unwilling to back down. The tension in the chamber grew thick and pungent.

"My people!" Minkar raised his arms again. "What David says is true. If you choose to remain loyal to the faith, to seek the promise of Kalhalma, we will all be taking the journey together, at dawn.

"I understand, better than you may know, that the prospect of death is the cruelest, most difficult of life's hardships to accept! But remember, I have always been here for it with you.

"Laven, when you lost your brother to the wasting I sang his hymn and guided his spirit home. When Gonro Salka was bitten by that cascabel and perished to its venom, I tended to his body and laid his soul to rest.

"So many others. You have all lost loved-ones over the years here, but they are all my losses as well. Remember, these heathens make false claims! They have been seduced by Maemot in guise of our wise Zenthien. To kneel before their banner is to pledge yourself to the Vorx.

"This choice is yours to make, but those of you who remain true to your faith, who remain with me here and perish like true Calusians — I promise you on my own immortal soul, that I will guide us all to Kalhalma, and we will all meet our loved-ones again. There will be pain, yes, sharp and short-lived, but afterward, will come well-deserved, eternal rest."

David locked eyes with his korgur and felt sick for what he saw there. Minkar Slen, despite the unwavering tone of his brave, confident speech, was terrified.

"Of this sacred nectar you will all drink and receive your communion." The priest spoke with practiced solemnity, holding a bottle of ceramic crystal older than the stones the church was built on.

Dorav sat in a circle with eleven other hopeful initiates, garbed in their finest white ceremonial silks. At eight years old, he was the youngest of the group. He looked around at everyone's anxious faces, until his eyes found Iridia. She noticed his stare and tilted her head in silent question, making him turn his gaze, feeling foolish and exposed. He thumbed the silver thimble in his hand, nervously tracing along the tiny vines decorating the receptacle.

"A drop of divinity," said the priest as he carefully poured a viscous red liquid into each of their thimbles. "A drop of divinity."

The Chamber of Union was small, circular, and domed, lit by blazing torches whose light danced on the marble faces of The nine Bahal; the generals of the Ashkandar, charged to lead the eternal war against the Vorx in Zenthien's name. The somber statues guarded the ceremony and took silent measure of those who would one day become Ashuran Knights.

Dorav had been born under the star of Lorruskar, the Guardian of the Scales. Lorruskar would one day be his Bahal, but first he needed to prove himself here.

Once the priest finished pouring, he surrendered the ornate bottle to an awaiting acolyte and struck his staff on the stone floor three times. The choir's voices rose in perfect harmony around them. *The Valiant Squire's Canticle*, a beautifully haunting, almost mournful hymn, spread in sweet tendrils and reverberated off the stones until the sound enveloped the entire chamber.

"Drink," the priest demanded, and they did.

The liquid was thick, coppery, and vile. He swallowed dutifully and pressed his eyes tightly to keep from coughing until the bitter syrup passed his throat.

"Remember your love for God," the priest said somberly, "and you will be guided safely through all peril. If you are without faith, you will be undone and lost forever, so pay heed and seek mercy.

"Now, close your eyes." The priest's voice sounded far away and muffled. "Follow the song. Follow the song into the light."

Dorav's heartbeat slowed and his breaths deepened as he fell, deeper and deeper into himself. He lost the sensation of his extremities as he comfortably disengaged from his corporal self. The choir's song washed through him, filling him with light, unburdening him of his encasing flesh. When Dorav opened his eyes, he stood at the lip of the Vorx.

Every Ashuran initiate must either pass this trial or die in the attempt. If his faith proved true, his guardian would appear to protect and guide him through the trial. If not, he would be abandoned here to his terrible fate. The price of straying from God's path was unequivocal damnation.

Before this final ritual, the priests had taken them to the Sanctum Theater, where they housed the last year's initiates who were devoured by the Vorx for their lack of faith and virtue. Three pairs of black, soulless eyes had stared back at him from gaunt, sunken sockets. The Theater reeked of offal and sickness. When they approached, the chained children had made gurgling, keening noises from their greasy, mold-choked cells.

This would be his fate, if he failed here.

Elation flooded him when his guardian seraph walked up beside him. Unmarred, golden-spiral light in the shape of a massive bull stared at the terrors of the Vorx and wordlessly instructed him to bare witness.

Dorav's young mind struggled desperately for purchase as he stared into that blending, bleeding, landscape of indescribable horrors. Creatures beyond his mind's ability to comprehend slithered along a shapeless miasma, expanding and contracting while collapsing randomly into each other, creating new, impossible deformities. A raw, corrosive sense of despair echoed from that amalgamation, expressing itself in a discordant scraping his mind could barely tolerate. A cold terror crawled through him as his sanity buckled under the pressure of the Vorx's impossible geometry.

His guardian made a small gesture with its golden head and the maddening nightmare coalesced and assembled itself into a singular, identifiable shape.

They stood on the manicured lawn of House Minos, overlooking the rolling city of Palidor, perched at the crest of Silver Nectar Hill. Thick white walls and broad marble columns supported the manse's triangular ceiling. Fresh flowers decorated every windowsill and chalices filled with bright colored roses flanked every doorway. A neatly kept hummingbird vine covered the entire west face of the building which bloomed yellow trumpets during spring and summer.

House Minos possessed a vestigial beauty, but the guardians of the house's main entrance — two black-and-verdigris cast-iron bulls standing on solid black marble bases, caught his full attention. The iron bulls took on life and stared at him with molten iron eyes. The weight of the name Minos hovered oppressively over those two bulls like a curse.

Without his guardian having to mutter instruction, Dorav straightened his back and walked boldly between the massive cast-iron bulls. Their fiery eyes followed his progress, but once between them, their heads turned away and remained still.

He moved reluctantly towards the red ironwood doors of House Minos, wondering who would stand behind it. His grim, disapproving, older brother, Gigan? Or worse, their iron-handed father; Lord Mathis Argor Minos himself.

He went to grab the door handle and hesitated. He did not wish to open that door and face whoever stood beyond. Fear gripped him by the throat.

A warm light in the center of his mind gently prodded him to continue. He grabbed the handle firmly, but could not force himself to pull.

He tried to think of something pleasant to distract himself with, and Iridia's lovely features came to mind. Surprisingly, he sensed her presence somewhere nearby. He focused on the her and knew at once that Iridia was weeping.

A flash of light pierced through his mind. His guardian demanded he focus and continue on his path, but he could not pry away from the thought of Iridia being in pain somewhere near. He wanted to know why she wept. Turning away from House Minos, he moved towards the gentle sounds of her sobbing.

The world around him rippled like heat-blur. House Minos shook and slowly broke apart, slabs of expensively crafted masonry dislodged themselves from the walls and tumbled upward into a dissolving sky. He heard an inhuman moaning coming from within the manse, like some starving animal trapped inside a well, deprived of its meal.

The landscape around him shattered with every step he took. The cast-iron bulls howled like baritone wolves as they were obliterated. The manicured grass surrounding his home burned away and became scorching sand. The crisp night sky over Palidor melted into a kaleidescope of shattered abstractions, folding and refolding upwards into an all consuming black star.

House Minos exploded and rose in pieces, devoured by the void. Stubbornly, he ignored the nauseating shifts in his immediate surroundings and followed the sound of Iridia's sorrow. When Dorav found her, she huddled by a jagged rock with her bloodied knees up against her chest.

When she realized he approached, she wiped at her cheeks. "What are you doing here?" she cried. "Go away!"

"What happened, Iridia? Where is your guardian?"

"I don't have one!"

"What do you mean?"

"I don't believe! I've never believed in this nonsense, and now I am damned! I'm trapped here, cursed like those others in their cells!"

Iridia's anguish washed over him. He wanted to reach out, to hold and comfort her. She appeared so frail and powerless there.

"No!" He knelt down and grabbed her by the shoulders. "You are not damned! I will get you out of here."

She stared at him, surprised by his forcefulness.

"No one asked for your help!" She smacked his hands away. "Go away! Leave me be!" Her voice held iron grit.

He resisted the urge to smile. "I cannot do that." He sat down next to her. "If you truly want to stay here, I'll stay too."

"Then you're a fool!" She sneered at him. "A damn fool!"

"I know. My name is-"

"Dorav Minos." She looked away. "I know who you are."

She knew his name. For a moment, he felt so light he nearly forgot the terrible danger that surrounded him.

"You do?"

"Everyone does. You're a Minos. Wait, where is your guardian?"

The golden bull was no more. Only the encroaching madness of the Vorx, tearing away at the edges of the pocket they inhabited, remained. Fear screamed its way into him. The howling vortex of entropy sensed his terror and wailed in reply.

"He is gone," Dorav said.

"Gone?"

"It...doesn't matter."

"Doesn't matter? How did you think to get me out of here without a guardian?!"

"I will be your guardian," he said firmly.

"You?! You're no guardian. You've gone mad!"

"Perhaps, but think on the priest's words. When the damned are abandoned by their guardians, they can never find their way out because they are left here alone, but we are not alone. We found each other, somehow. I can be your guardian, and you can be mine. We can get each other out of here.

Iridia stared at him, incredulous.

"Come with me." He stood and held out his hand. Fear swam through every inch of him, but his hand remained steady. Iridia reached up and took it.

Dorav awoke in his dark command tent, his arm asleep and outstretched beneath him. He groaned and sat up, rubbing life into his limp, prickling appendage.

Beside his freshly oiled wolfbert, lay the age-worn mining pick he had taken from the Pick Rock tavern wall. He gripped it and walked wearily past his tent's heavy flap. A bright half-moon shone high in the western sky, surrounded by stars. Banor, Kathor's sergeant, stood outside his tent, standing guard.

"What watch are we in?" Dorav asked.

"Third, sir. Still some time left before sunrise."

"Some time indeed." He looked down at the pick in his hands, and the two names engraved on its handle.

Feayn. Arreln.

"That some kind of family heirloom, sir?" Banor asked.

"No. Yes...something of the sort. He stifled a yawn. "I won't be getting any more sleep tonight, Banor. Come help me with my armor."

"Aye, sir," Banor said and followed him inside.

"Are you certain you want to do this?" Rairi asked, as they made their way up the flat mountain road. "You have been yawning for the last hour."

"I'm fine," Marca assured her, rubbing her face. "I can sleep on the march back east."

"Why would this town be any different from the others? This is a waste of time, Marca."

"I need to be certain." Marca stretched her arms above her head and smiled.

As they came before the first box cut of Kaira's mines, the springfinder tied to Marca's belt rose lazily and pointed into the claim, tugging gently against its leather string.

"Perhaps not such a waste of time," Rairi admitted.

"Ramiel's bones!" Marca squealed triumphantly. "I knew this was a good idea!"

"Marca, remember these mines are hazardous. You twisted your ankle in the last one."

"That was nothing, and the springfinder began tugging from this far out. There must be shinn in there!"

"Perhaps, but the sun is less than an hour from rising and it would be foolish to go inside without proper escort. Let's head back and ask Captain Dorav for assistance."

"But we stand right here," Marca said. "Can you not do that...thing? Check and see if the way is safe?"

"That thing?" Rairi raised a brow at her.

"Like in Portan. The clucking."

"You mean ketter."

"Yes, could you check? If it appears hazardous we'll go ask Dorav for help, but if not, we take a look, all right?"

Rairi walked up to the wire mesh gate and rattled it, noting the thick chain and locking mechanism. "Its locked, Marca."

Not one to be dissuaded, Marca picked up the largest rock she could find and banged it against the contraption, making a rancorous noise.

"That won't work!" Rairi said in annoyance, just as Marca pounded on the old lock hard enough to snap it open.

Marca's freckled cheeks blushed in triumph as she raked the heavy chain away from the gate.

Rairi shook her head and peered down the dark drift, only able to see partially into the inky depth. She closed her eyes and clucked her throat rhythmically.

The ketter traveled neatly down the cylindrical opening, giving her a clear picture of the shaft's rough edges, beam supports, and discarded mining equipment, all the way to the end.

What she found at the cave's end confused her at first. She focused, clucking her throat more forcefully, thickening the waves. Her eyelids and lips parted in recognition.

"Dead kafras are down there," she told Marca in a whisper.

"Dead?" Marca asked.

"They've been torn apart — gutted." She licked her dry lips. "We must go."

"What else?" Marca asked. "Can you see the shinn?"

"Ketter does not work that way. Marca, we must-"

The sonic assault from within the mine hit her like a fist to the chest. It boxed her ears and lanced her stomach, doubling her over — her entire frame rattling from the aftershock. The urge to fall to the ground and roll into a ball nearly overcame her.

"Rairi?!" Marca's voice was coated in terror. "Rairi, are you alright? What is it?"

An unnatural moan, like the wail of some subterranean horror rose, accompanied by the baleful thunder of giant gnashing teeth on hollow stones. She had never heard anything like it, and wished with her heart never to hear it again, but the sound only grew stronger, drilling into her through every orifice it could find.

"Run!" Rairi screamed. "Marca, RUN!"

8

The Thing that Killed the Kafras

Caige yawned deeply as he led their wagon through the razorgrass hills. His father Corren sat to his right, fast asleep and snoring.

The wagon creaked and complained with every nook and rock it came across, the thick wooden logs tied to the bed clunking against each other.

He had traveled this winding road between Ticondria and Nevine twice a year for three years now. Not having the patience to become a hunter like Erin, he resigned himself to the lumber yards. The arduous work made him strong, and by the time he turned fifteen, Caige could down an oak in five swings faster than his old man.

The load of lumber they were hauling to Nevine was an entire season of backbreaking work. Once sold, they could buy enough supplies to spend the upcoming winter warm, fat, and drunk on mulled wine.

Ahead on the road, inside an ocean of burnt amber razorgrass stalks, was a patch of bright green grass, five-hundred feet across. The horses whined and stomped their hooves when they came to the edge of the strange patch. Caige snapped the reins against their flanks, but they refused to move.

"Corren." He grabbed his father's shoulder to shake him and felt a warm wetness soaking his shirt.

His father's neck was torn open. Blood poured from the gaping wound, drenching his shirt and dripping down to his linen trousers.

"Corren?" Caige's voice cracked. "Father! Father!" He covered the ghastly wound with his hands.

"Forgive me, Caige," Corren hissed, lifeblood squiring between

Caige's fingers with every word. "I was a fool."

"Don't speak! Oh gods, don't speak!" Caige took off his own shirt and pressed it down on the wound.

Corren turned to faced him, his eyes bloodshot and crazed. "I never meant to hurt you, son." Blood-spittle flew from his lips. "I never meant for any of it."

"Oh gods, stop talking! It's all right da', just stop."

"No..." his father put his head back against the wagon, his eyes rolling. "He is here."

A frightful roar rose an instant before the horses screamed in pain and terror. A cold sweat covered Caige's skin and his mouth went dry. He was almost too afraid to look.

The horses lay in bloody piles of torn flesh, steaming entrails, and protruding bones. A giant, black-maned lion with fierce emerald eyes stood over their carcasses, staring up at him with blood dripping from his panting maw.

"Run, Caige," his father's voice was a fading gurgle. "You must run!"

The lion padded slowly towards him, a deep menacing rumble emanating from his throat. Terror gripped Caige's stomach like a vice. He could not tear his eyes away from the creature's mesmerizing stare.

"Caige!" Corren coughed. His father's eyes shone like pink blood-mist caught in candlelight. He pointed a bloody finger towards the back of the wagon, which held the box cut leading to Ricker's claim.

"Go!" Corren hissed. "Caige, go!"

David woke and rubbed the exhaustion out of his eyes. His impoverished sleep was fitful and his dreams haunting. His last dream faded like candle smoke as he sat up and leaned against the temple's wall.

Eira Piril and Citena whispered to each on the pews, both with sleepless patches under their eyes. Eira had little Rinna cradled in her arms, fast asleep.

Before going to sleep himself, David had seen Colry pacing back and forth near the entrance of the temple, nervously wringing his black, callused hands. He was still pacing, still wringing.

The chill in the air and the thin light trickling through the temple's stained windows warned him of the sun's imminent rise. The time to choose had come.

He knew Dorav was not bluffing. The smoldering temples left behind by the Padivian Raptor's advance was a testament to zoniran madness. David remembered the blackened corpses, charred beyond recognition, laying in awkwardly sprawled heaps — overtaken by the madness of immolation. Some bodies clung together, their flesh fused into a single mass.

David had been inside this temple countless times but never truly appreciated the detail and artistry put into its construction. Every window and panel had been painted with a symbolic representation of his faith. The pulpit was solid marble with the Calusian Shield, Scepter, and Sword, carved meticulously into its face. Even the dactwood pews were masterly shaped, clean, and varnished.

Death's proximity always brought him a sense of tactile clarity. On the morning before every decisive battle during the war, the sun would rise and be more beautiful than any before it. His morning meal would be the most savory, and his every breath was a blessing from Aeros.

He wondered where he had gotten to all these years. Who was this fat, drunken, idiot whose flesh he now inhabited?

The evening prior, Minkar had brought out every pot, pan, and bowl he owned to give people something to relieve themselves in. Regardless, Wilkie, Benny, and Donner Salka all lined up against the temple's southern wall and pissed right on the fresco of *Darga's Pilgrimage*. The Salkas would not die for their beliefs. They would be the first to kneel beneath Dorav's banner when the time came. The korgur quietly watched them piss on his wall from his steeple, his troubled eyes far away.

The sounds of approaching soldiers rose around them. They gathered outside, muttering and calling out to each other in their foreign accent.

Minkar whispered a prayer under his breath and grabbed the temple's holy scepter, shouldering his way towards the door.

David stood and studied the marble visages of Tekuryo and Zenthien standing behind the pulpit, the twin pillars of the Calusian Brotherhood. He found it almost comical, to consider he was about to be burned alive, all because a handful of cultists once claimed Zenthien as the one and only true god of man. Their misguided belief germinated into its own religion and became fat off the coin of their herd.

The korgur always warned of the dangers of zonirism whenever that faith was mentioned. The Archdaemon Maemot, in the guise of a saint, had seduced the first zonirans into abandoning their faith. They were all damned, twisted by lies, and extremely dangerous.

The soldiers outside suddenly cried out, their voices pitched with fear.

"What's happening?" Ricker leaned on his elbow and rubbed the sleep out of his face. "David?"

"I don't know," David said, trying to make out the muffled noises.

All conversation in the temple ceased.

"Look!" Ashen pointed to a girder above their heads where a small yellow canary was perched, watching them.

"Is that? It is, "Ricker said sleepily. "The fucking bird. He's alive."

The bird shuffled on his perch a moment, then flew off through a small opening in the ceiling. With its departure, the dreadfully familiar rattling moan from the hidden valley filled the temple chamber.

"It's out!" Sifran cried, his voice spiked with panic. "It's out! It got out, and we are fucking trapped in here!"

David put a meaty hand on Sifran's mouth and pushed his head back against the wall.

"Quiet," he growled.

The nearest townsfolk observed them curiously.

"Just be quiet," David warned, looking around. Fear slithered through the room, as thick and foul as the effluvium of piss on the walls.

"I'm taking my hand away," he said, "but so help me if you shout out again. Understand me, Sifran?"

Sifran nodded meekly, rubbing his jaw when David released him. The hideous moaning grew louder, making David's heart race in his chest. The din of the soldiers outside became frantic. People crowded around the temple doors, trying to peek at what was happening.

"They're running off!" Ladan said. "Something chases them away!"

The temple doors shook on their hinges as something slammed into them. Ladan fell to his ass with a cry of pain, his left brow split and bleeding. The others took a cautious step back.

There was a second crash, then a third. A horrible scream came from beyond the doors. A thick, black, spike broke through the opening between them, covered in blood and gore. People screamed and crowded away. The bloodied spike retracted, dislodging the doors' thick barring beam. One blue door swung lazily in.

No one moved.

Creatures resembling a cross between a giant, wingless spider-wasp and a desert scarab, scrambled into the temple. They were as big as horses, sleek and long, with raptorial forelegs and glossy black carapaces highlighted by bright yellow knife-cut patterns.

Half a dozen of them crawled along the inside walls, their rapid movements knocking clouds of dust off the high rafters. Their thin thoraxes and tear-shaped abdomens were decorated with human skulls, held in place by fibrous webbing. The awful rattle-moan was coming from the overlapping, vibrating plates of their abdomens and the hollow skulls tied there.

The effect of that subsonic oscillation was overwhelming. It burrowed through David's flesh and sinew, boring holes into his spine and wrapping around his bowels like a living scourge. He drowned in the sound, his will broken by it. He was paralyzed — his heart and lungs seizing and his balls crawling up into his gut.

One creature thrust its abdomen forward, revealing a curved stinger, and stabbed it deep into Donner's stomach, lifting him off his feet. When Donner hit the floorboards, his eyes rolled back and his hands became stiff claws pulled up against his chest. He screamed his agony through clenched teeth, curling in around the pain, assuming a fetal position and going completely rigid. He continued to scream through his locked jaw, as if he were a prisoner inside himself.

Another creature bit down on Ladan's pelvis, dug its spear-like foreleg into his lower back, and pushed out, ripping the man in half at the waist. Ladan's torso spewed blood, gas, and long yards of bloodied entrails. Manic and in mindless shock, he dragged himself across the floor with his entrails trailing, refusing to accept that he was already dead.

Doko was skewered through the chest by one creature's foreleg, and stung in the crotch. He screamed and writhed in misery as the thing's poison raced through him.

Another bit Einadi in half at the torso. Her head and right arm fell away from the rest of herself, painting the temple walls with thick arterial spray. Little Rinna tumbled beneath the pews, screaming in terror.

David pulled himself out of his paralyzed fear, like a man crawling out of his own grave.

Don't freeze up. Don't freeze up! Don't freeze up!! Gods damn you, soldier, do not fucking freeze up!!!

"Move," he said through a biting effort. "We need to get out of here."

Ricker, Sifran, and Ashen stared at him blankly. Caige still lay on the ground, fast asleep.

"Caige!" David slapped the boy hard across the mouth. Caige did not stir. "Wake up! We have to go!" He slapped him again, harder this time. Nothing.

Caige continued to snore, his face reddening where David had struck him. He flung Caige over his shoulder like a sack of grain.

"Ricker, Sifran! We need to go! We need to go now!"

They snapped out of their trance.

"Do not look around," David said. "Just fucking run!"

They ran for the door, pushing through the mass of paralytic townsfolk who watched helplessly as their friends and family were butchered before their eyes.

"Run you idiots!" David yelled as they reached the doorway. "Run for your miserable lives!"

Rising panic overpowered paralysis. The people of Kaira screamed in chorus and swarmed for the exit in a desperate mass. As they evacuated into the dusty streets, the murderous creatures descended on the slowest of them. Their agonized screams followed them well beyond the temple's bloodied blue doors.

"Form lines!" Dorav cried. "Keep these things back!"

His remaining seaguard stood shoulder to shoulder near the north wall of Fort Kai, their wooden shields forming an uninspiring defense against the massive creatures' piercing forelegs and thrusting

114

stingers.

The bone-lancing noise they emitted had scattered the bulk of his men into the town. Soldiers who had survived a raging sea-battle off the coast of Magalao, helped secure and hold Port Usk during a grueling winter-long siege, and most recently captured the infamous Ship-Breaker-Sharn, had fled in a panic, making themselves easy pickings for these monstrosities.

Dorav had never felt more powerless than when these wasp-beetles descended on them, making their unholy rattle-moan. Like ravenous locusts they had slaughtered his men, each kill more gruesome than the last.

He had seen death before, but never like this. His poor marines, wide-eyed and brimming with adrenals, were torn apart and eaten alive before his own stunned eyes. In the span of four long breaths, his forces were all but decimated.

It was Kartecus, fearless, dauntless Kartecus who began shouting orders, forcing the remaining men to remember their training, to deny their instinct to flee, and band together. He followed his old mentor's lead, inspired by the old man's iron grit.

His surprised, overlong hesitation had cost him too many lives. He stood at the front of the phalanx, furious with himself. The surviving seaguards rallied, their xiphoi drawn, ready to live or die together. The creatures stalked them, still making their infernal noises. With his blood coursing hot and his men huddled around him, the sound was easier to bear.

One bulbous creature with massive, bloodied mandibles pushed hard on the line, scything its forelegs across their shields, looking to open their defenses. Others began climbing over the fort's walls, attempting to flank them. The idea of these ungodly things possessing some form of intelligence was too horrible to consider.

"Make for the vault!" Dorav shouted. "Form a bottleneck at the entrance! They have the advantage here!"

They attempted a tactical retreat towards the vault but two of the creatures cut them off.

"Chastity!" Dorav commanded. "Chastity belt, now!"

The formation formed a packed cube, defending on all sides. Five of the monsters surrounded them, thrusting their forelegs high and low, seeking to pry open their chastity belt and plunge into the pink flesh behind it.

"This is not right," Kartecus growled, blocking a swinging foreleg. The impact left a splintered hole in his shield. "Why are they not swarming over us like insects should?"

"There are too many of us," Dorav said. "They are being cautious."

"Cautious? You jest!"

The rattle-moan's intensity increased and became more difficult to deny. "More of them approach from the town," Dorav said.

"They are wrangling us?" Fear was painted on the old man's stony features.

"We will teach them otherwise," Dorav said.

Kartecus gave him a grim nod.

"Kathor, take command of the line! Get everyone into the vault!'

"Aye, aye, sir!" Kathor called out.

Dorav dug in behind his aegis and pushed forward, slamming one creature in the face and peeling it upwards and back. Despite their size, the things were not nearly as heavy as they looked. The creature's limbs lashed out, striking behind his shield and scraping against his armor plating. Dorav groaned and pushed it back away from the line.

Thick black mandibles pinched the sides of his aegis and lifted him off the ground.

"Aaaaah!" Dorav hung to his shield with both hands. "Kartecus!"

Kartecus put his xiphos through an opening in the creature's dense plates, between head and thorax. Black-red blood flushed out from the wound, making the giant insect gargle in pain as it released him.

Dorav hit the ground on his back, the metal fittings of his armor biting into his flesh and the air flying from his lungs.

The wasp-beetle swung its arm around, hooking behind Kartecus' wooden shield, and sending him into the dust. The other flanking creature barreled down on his old mentor, its piercing forelegs punching against the old man's shield. Kartecus came up quickly, using blade and shield in a defensive flurry, luring it away.

"Kartecus!" Dorav gasped, lifting his aegis in time to catch a pair of powerful mandibles as they came for his head.

The amount of pressure the thing's bite inflicted on the sides of his aegis was incredible. It stabbed at him with its raptorial forelegs, denting his armor. Its hollow stinger scraped against his schynbalds and tassets, seeking flesh, dripping with milky venom.

Dorav grunted as the monster lifted him off the ground by his aegis and slammed him down on the barren earth, white stars exploding in his blurring vision.

The wasp-beetle hooked his aegis, pulled it away from his body, and skewered his forearm against the back of it, sending a scream of pain up his left arm. Dorav hacked at the monster with his wolfbert, landing desperate blows on its mandibles and face, leaving shallow marks on its chitinous plating.

The creature's nightmarish maw bit down against the double edge of his upraised wolfbert, and with a whip of its bleeding mouth, yanked the sword out of his hand and into the dust.

"Cents!" Dorav shouted, reaching for his sword belt.

A black arrow sank into the back of the wasp-beetle's head, making it gurgle hideously. Dorav found the haft of the handaxe on his belt and yanked it free.

He swung hard, slamming the wrought iron head through the creature's plating and plunging it deep into the soft flesh beneath. He hacked wildly, slicing through the hard chitin as if cutting kindling. Hot blood spewed from the creature's grievous wounds as it scrambled back in pain, its appendages trembling before it fell flat on the dust.

Dorav stared at the plain, iron-headed ax in bewilderment. The female mercenary in Sharn had managed to open a gash in his armor with it, so he figured he would keep it, but he could not understand how he managed to deal such grievous damage with this weapon when his holy wolfbert could barely scratch-

He dropped the ax as a rush of hot agony rode up his right leg, into his crotch, stomach, and chest. He looked down and saw the puncture wound in his inner thigh, his blood mixing with the thing's syrupy venom.

"Leper's cock!" Dorav's body seized, crushed by an invisible stone fist. His throat became so constricted he could barely draw breath, and his veins pumped acid as his body's muscles cramped, pulling themselves into a ball.

"Negkrat!" he heard the word ripple through him like a bursting sack of spider eggs, crawling through his insides.

"Negkrat!" He screamed through grinding teeth and swollen tongue, his eyes rolling into the back of his head.

"Negkrat! Negkrat! Negkrat!"

Then nothing.

Nihengale crouched in the shadows outside of Fort Kai, struggling to keep the sun's piercing light from his eyes. Through the yellow blaze of dust, he spotted the silhouettes of Dorav and Kartecus standing shoulder to shoulder with their seaguards.

As much as he despised the idea, they had to leave this fray before those monsters noticed them. They could not hope to fight them off in full daylight.

With a regretful sigh, he lifted his recurved bow and aimed an arrow at the back of Dorav's neck, drawing his bowstring until it reached lethal tension. There was no reason to believe Dorav would survive this encounter, but he could not take the chance. A cloud of sun-drenched dust blinded him before he could let the arrow fly.

"Chastity," Dorav cried. "Chastity belt, now!"

Nihengale pinched his eyes and clucked his throat. The ketter painted a clear picture of the shield-wall now surrounding Dorav, keeping the flanking creatures at bay and blocking his shot. Cursing under his breath, he called out to the others.

"Detach!" he yelled out in xiasi. "We need to retreat from this light! To me! To me!"

"Where is Rairi?" Murciel asked.

Nihengale did not open his eyes, relying instead on ketter. Black and white silhouettes materialized into the echo-image as the others approached.

"She went to the mines with the anthrop girl," Escara said, pulling her hood around her face.

"Do you have her scent?" Nihengale asked.

"I cannot smell anything past this carnage."

"Buio?"

"She is not nearby," Buio said, "but she knows well to find shelter."

"Then so must we. She will need to stay here for now."

118

"Nihengale, no!" Murciel's voice was heavy with concern.

"We cannot stay here, Murciel. We'll be slaughtered."

"I'll stay behind and look for her," Buio said.

"No Buio. We need your eyes if we mean to escape with our lives. You know how resourceful she can be. Have faith in her abilities."

Buio's silhouette betrayed nothing.

"We will return after dusk and fetch her. For now, we must flee."

Escara gripped him by the belt. "Lead the way."

Before Nihengale had taken three steps, the sharp thwap of Murciel's bow rang in rapid succession. The bow sang, making its supple contours sharpen in Nihengale's mind.

When the creatures Murciel struck hissed in pain, the sound slithered into him as well, giving him a painfully detailed view of their menacing mandibles. One of the creatures had Dorav pinned to the ground. The other, which was harrying Kartecus, turned its full attention towards them.

"Murciel!" Escara barked. "What are you doing?!"

"Dorav and Kartecus needed help," Murciel said. "They were in danger."

"Now we all are!" Nihengale shot back. "Move!"

They headed west, away from Kaira, on a winding dirt road which snaked down the Norvan foothills. Escara held on to his belt with Murciel gripping hers. Buio followed them, his sight unhindered by the inferno of light.

"It gives chase!" Buio warned. "The thing is fast."

"We have no cover out here!" Nihengale said, his mind racing.

With nowhere to hide and blinded by the light, they were at a fatal disadvantage. The creature's terrible face and forelegs suddenly entered his ketter's imaging. It was gaining.

"Keep running!" Buio said, turning to face the monster. "I'll make time."

"Buio, no!" Escara released Nihengale's belt and turned, drawing her xiphos.

They were committed now. Nihengale drew his recurved bow and knocked an arrow. "Darrow trap!" he called out. "Buio, must call it!"

"Ten, front, source," Buio said, throwing something small and round at the thing's face. "Five, ten, armor, short!"

The creature hissed and pulled its forelegs back, attempting to rub the chirk spores off its face. Nihengale used ketter to position his shot, pulled his bowstring back, and let fly. His arrow struck the plates of the monster's torso and broke in half.

Murciel drew his Manticore and loosed an arrow in a single fluid motion, his eyes pinched closed. His arrow struck the thing's face plate — the arrowhead bouncing away and snapping clear of its shaft.

"Armor, armor," Buio called out. "At source. This is not working! Get away from here!"

The monster was on Buio, swinging its piercing forelegs erratically at him. Buio weaved around the swings, smacking the thing's carapace with his vrin to no effect.

With a throaty cry, Escara rushed in, shield leading. She shouldered her shield into the creatures side with so much force, its left legs buckled. She slashed blindly, her xiphos cutting shallow marks into the black chitin.

The giant insect regained its footing and scythed its foreleg under Escara's sword arm and into her ribs. She dropped to a knee from the blow, her shield falling at her feet. Escara wrapped her right forearm around the black appendage jutting from her torso and pinned it to herself.

"Buio!" Escara's cry was thick with pain.

Buio spun. Taking his vrin in both hands he swung down hard into the pinned foreleg's joint. The mitiri blade sliced between the plates, cleaving the foreleg in two in a brilliant display of spraying crimson.

The creature gave a gurgled hiss as red-black blood poured from its severed limb. Escara fell over, limp at Buio's feet with the thing's tibia still impaled in her side.

"Murciel," Nihengale called out. "Move forward, ten by two, left! Pull Escara out of there!"

Nihengale loosed a queue of arrows at the creature, trying to distract it while Murciel sprinted sightlessly into the fray. His missiles rebounded uselessly against the creature's dense plates, except for two. One sank into the flesh between head and thorax. The other went through the femur of its right hind-leg.

"The legs have weaker plating!" he called.

Buio was weaving and striking, keeping the thing away from

120

Escara, his outline appearing and disappearing between the swift intervals of Nihengale's ketter.

When Murciel reached ten feet he took two steps left and knelt, patting the ground just shy of Escara's head. The wasp-beetle vibrated its abdomen, sending a searing ripple of fear through Nihengale so fierce, it made his anus pucker. Both Buio and Murciel became paralytic in the wake of that terrible resonance. The creature reared up, slicing its remaining foreleg at Buio's torso.

Buio leaped back in time to keep from being skewered, but left Escara and Murciel under the monster's shadow. The creature thrust its abdomen forward, driving its stinger deep into Murciel's stomach.

A hoarse wail of agony escaping him, Murciel fell to the ground, curling into an arthritic ball and screaming incoherently through a locked jaw, his body spasming before going rigid.

Nihengale dropped his bow and ran headlong at the creature, drawing his recurved moonblades. Buio entered *Alci'mavor*, deflecting the creature's foreleg, dodging its snapping mandibles, and avoiding its stinger in movements so fluid, he blurred through ketter like an apparition.

Nihengale rolled under the monster and drove his knives up between its head and prothorax. With a gargled hiss the thing snatched him with the crook of its foreleg, squeezing his chest so hard, he was certain his rib-cage would crack open.

Nihengale kicked off his sandals and dug the rakes of his feet into its thorax for purchase, twisting his blades inside the thing's body.

Buio used the opening to cleave the creature's remaining foreleg at the joint.

The wasp-beetle curled into a ball around Nihengale, striking with its stinger and remaining four legs all at once. The claws at the ends of its tarsi, sharp as butcher's knives, plunged into his thigh, bruised ribs, and shoulder, making him cry out in pain.

One claw cut a gash across his head, drawing blood and filling his eyes with stars. The stinger punched into his back.

A violent lurch of the creature's head dislodged his hands from the blood-slick hilts of his knives. The thing wrapped its mandibles across the left side of his torso and bit down, cutting through his skerki leathers and into the muscles of his chest and back, hot blood

121

drenching his lower back and stomach.

Nihengale screamed in fury and dug his fingers into the thing's black eyes, blood and goo bursting on to his gnashing hands. He pushed his fingers in as deep as they would go, raking his small claws into its gruesome face.

"Nihengale! Nihengale!" Buio called to him from somewhere.

He desperately scraped and ripped at every bit of flesh he could grip, trying to cause as much damage as possible before death found him.

"Nihengale! It's dead. It's dead! Stop!"

The thing's mandibles and body was still wrapped around him like a chitinous cocoon, but it was not moving.

"Be still," Buio said. "The stinger is lodged in your leathers."

A light pressure pushed against his back, he heard a crack, and warm liquid ran down the back of his legs.

"Can you crawl out?" Buio asked.

"I'm in its mouth."

"Hold on then. I have to check on the others."

Nihengale wiggled inside the cage of stiff, barbed legs but was held fast. There was a scraping, dry clunking sound. Buio's knife appeared inside the bony cocoon, cutting away the flesh between its plates.

"How are they?" Nihengale asked. His ketter showed them both lying motionless on the dust.

"Alive for now," Buio said.

More blood hit him in the face and as Buio's knife severed the creature's head. A ripple of pain coursed through him when Buio pried the mandibles open enough for him to crawl out of the monster's embrace.

He searched his blood soaked skerki with his fingers and realized the beast had bitten him, but not hard enough to cause major damage. The hot blood rushing down his lower torso had been the creature's, not his own.

"How?" he asked.

Buio turned the hideous head in his hands and pointed to a spot under the carapace. Nihengale quickened the pace of the ketter to receive a clearer image.

"Dorsal vein," Buio said. "Saw it when it bent down to bite you."

"I thought that thing had killed me."

Buio nodded, holding the head up by its mandibles and staring into the ruin of its bleeding eyes. "As did I."

While David ran down the Earthly Road with Caige's heavy ass over his shoulder, Ricker pulled Sifran along like an unruly child. The wiry blond was little more than a stumbling rag-doll, muttering to himself with a patch of urine running down the front of his pants.

The things were already inside Fort Kai, slaughtering Dorav's men and barring their only way out of town.

"We're trapped!" David said, glancing back the way they came.

The monsters stalked the Earthly Road, chasing down the Anteps and Danpors, who ran frantically across their farms.

"Come on!"

They ran into the alleys of town, away from the main roads. Hidano ran behind them, lumbering and huffing in fear. A creature's forearm speared him in the ribs from behind, spinning him around and putting him on his back. The thing bit into his broad stomach, blood and intestinal gases blasting out of the lethal wound. Hidano beat his fists against the monster's plated head as it ate him alive. His gargled screams echoed through the street behind them.

Having to carry Caige was quickly sapping David's strength. He needed a moment to catch his breath. Shouldering the door of a nearby home, he stumbled inside with Ricker and Sifran following closely behind.

"Where is Ashen?" He put Caige down and barred the door. "I lost sight of him at the temple."

"He ran off with Nianah and the Birkils," Ricker said, gasping for air. "They headed for Coppertooth Road."

"Damn fools," he grunted, looking down at Caige who lay snoring contently. "What is wrong with him?!"

David put everything he had behind an open hand slap across Caige's face. The impact whipped the boy's head against the wall and drew blood from his lip, but he did not wake.

"Sifran, is this normal?" David asked. "Talk to me!"

"Those beetles...it can't be...it can't be..." Sifran muttered.

"Sifran." David walked up to him. "I need you to pull yourself back together."

Sifran's eyes were wild. "This is only a dream. I need to wake up, is all. I need to wake up!"

"This is no dream! These are the things that killed our kafras, and now they're killing us. You need to sort yourself if you plan to live through this!"

Sifran was not listening. His eyes darted around the room, his cracked lips moving wordlessly.

David pinned his forehead against Sifran's and glared into his eyes. "Look at me, Sifran!"

Sifran obeyed, his little black eyes wide and filled with tears. He was trembling like a child.

"You have two options. Stay here and die, or snap the fuck out of it. What will it be? Do you want to live?"

"Yes, but-"

"Do you want to live?!" David slapped him and rammed his forehead against his again. "Look at me! Do you want to fucking live?!"

"Yes! Yes! Fuck, David!" Sifran's glazed eyes found their focus.

"Now what is wrong with Caige? Is this what happens with molki?"

Sifran glanced at Caige and licked his dry lips. "Might be, but if it was molki, he may never wake up, David."

"Gods damn my fucking eyes!" David growled bitterly.

"We need to escape," Ricker said. "We are not safe here."

"Those things are everywhere," David replied. "Fort Kai is swarming with them. There is no way out."

"There is," Ricker said. "I know a way."

David's fingers unconsciously dug into his pouches for a cuksar but came up empty. The soldiers had taken them. "You have a smoke, Ricker?"

Ricker shook his head.

"Fuck my ass! All right, how do we flee without being butchered?"

"There is a goat path near the Salka's claim," Ricker said. "I followed it once up into the mountain. In half a day's walk it spills out near the razorgrass fields to the northeast of the Peaks."

"You want to go towards the mines? Ricker, these vorxed things came from up there!"

"Well, we cannot stay here!"

"Yes we can!" Sifran interjected. "We bar ourselves in, blockade the door. We wait until they leave."

"They broke through the temple doors, Sifran!" Ricker said. "This fucking house will not hold-"

A bloodied black knife poked through the nearest window's wooden shutters and carefully lifted the hook holding it in place.

These things are intelligent. These fucking things are intelligent!

David's heart dropped when the creature squeezed its large frame through the small opening, its sharp claws clicking on the wall and floor beams. Mita and Sepi's heads were tied to its tear-shaped abdomen, held by wet fibers threaded through their empty eye sockets.

Those girls were inseparable in life. They shared their meals, their bed, their men, and now they shared their fate. Seeing their lifeless heads tied side by side, broke David's heart.

The creature vibrated its abdomen at them, making the bones and heads tied to it rattle. The sonic assault sapped the strength right out of him.

He wanted to kneel, lower his head, and resign himself to this fate. There was no escaping these things. They were all helpless prey, scratching hopelessly for time.

The wasp-beetle speared Ricker's meaty thigh, putting him on his stomach and dragging him towards its awaiting maw. Ricker screamed, digging his fingernails into the floorboards and leaving behind bloodied scratches and broken nail chips.

No! No! NO!

David roared, picked up a nearby chair, and broke it against the thing's plated head. A sweeping foreleg lunged for his chest. David reflexively blocked it with left arm, but he was not wearing a shield. The sharp tip of its foreleg cut through the meat and cracked the bones of his forearm.

Barking in pain, he stumbled back, holding his bleeding arm. The creature dug its mandibles into the small of Ricker's back, biting down so hard it drew a geyser of blood. Ricker howled in pain, his thick arms reaching out pleadingly towards Sifran, who stood fear-stricken and trembling, his back pinned to the far wall as if trying to

melt through it.

The creature whipped its head and threw Ricker's body at David, pinning him back against the western wall. David cried out, his legs and right arm pinned under Ricker's weight while his bleeding left arm hung useless and throbbing from the pain.

"Suck Kaxxil's cock!" he screamed into the thing's chitinous face as it crawled up to him, its foul black maw open wide.

With a furious cry, Sifran clubbed the creature in the abdomen with a lighted oil-lamp. Liquid flames spread along its plates and the heads tied to them. Mita and Sepi's heads caught fire, their skin blackening and their hair going up like torches. The webbing holding them in place burned off, releasing the flaming heads which hit the floor with wet thuds.

The monstrosity lost all interest in them. Flailing in desperate agony around the room, it turned and barreled out the same window it had crawled in from.

"Terra's stone," David huffed, hearing the thing's wails as it fled.

"David?" Sifran looked pale, his face drawn taunt and his lusterless eyes looking down at Ricker.

Ricker's eyes remained open and fear-stricken, but there was no light left inside them.

"He's gone, Sifran" David said, shaking his head. "Ricker's gone."

Looking around the room, he realized Caige was no longer among them. "Sifran? Where is Caige?"

Sifran looked around, startled. "I did not notice him leave."

"So does this mean he's awake?" David asked. "Is he going to be all right?"

"David,"Sifran said, "I cannot say what is happening, but I don't think what Caige swallowed was molki."

9

Of Broken Things

The Earthly Road lay littered with the corpses of familiar townsfolk. Dotpan Antep's half-eaten torso hung sprawled on his fence, his blood seeping into the wood and dust. His son's headless body lay beyond the fence near the flax field on red, broken stalks.

The mutilated remains of people he had spoken to, laughed with, or simply knew by name, lay everywhere. Sun-kissed, smiling faces replaced by masks of horror and pain, covered in blood and flies. His heart sank into a dark, hollow place where it put down brick and mortar to surround itself.

He shifted his arm in its makeshift sling, wincing in pain. He had dressed the terrible wound as best he could, but he would need to brace the bones soon. They waited until the sounds of battle and the terrible rattle-moan of the creatures finally died down. Then they waited a little longer.

"David?" Benny Salka came out of hiding, his amber eyes darting around the streets nervously.

"Benny! You hard-boiled bastard. Are you alone?"

"No. A few of us are still hiding in the Grit Mug. I left to take a look when the noise stopped. Are they gone?"

"Not certain."

"This is fucking awful," Benny said, looking around at the littered horror on the streets.

"Benny, is Caige with you?" Sifran asked.

"Caige? No."

David sighed. "All right, we need to check Fort Kai. You coming?"

"Yeah." Benny nodded.

As if the Vorx had opened its Maw and belched its horrors back into the world, the ravaged remains of Dorav's soldiers littered the old fort within — the earth and walls painted in thick red curdle. Captain Dorav lay on a patch of red earth before the motionless body of one of the monstrosities. David checked the Ashura's life-signs.

"Bastard's still breathing," he said.

Dorav had various minor nicks and scratches across his face and arms, a deep puncture wound on his inner thigh, behind his tassets, and a bloody gape on his left forearm, almost identical to his own.

"He got stung," Benny said.

"How do you know that?" David asked.

"They got me too." Benny showed him the wound on his upper back. "Nothing ever hurt quite like that. Felt like I was being burned alive. Would have preferred death, given the option at the time."

"So their venom's not fatal," David said, mostly to himself. "Donner?"

Benny shook his head. "Got stung in the dick. Pain killed him."

"Sifran, grab some of that rope and tie Dorav up."

"What?"

"We need to secure him before he wakes. Tie him, knees and elbows, and pull him out of his armor while you're at it. Benny, with me. Grab a weapon."

They left Sifran to his task, picked up two discarded xiphoi, and made for the Magalian's vault. One of the creatures lay sprawled near the building entrance. Not wanting to chance it, David stabbed into the back of its head, satisfied when it did not twitch.

The tangy pungency of decay was overpowering in the dry, enclosed space. The remaining marines and Magalian Guild counters were a dismantled splatter of gore on the vault floor and walls. Benny ran back outside and heaved. Another three dead creatures lay sprawled in the center of the chamber, bloodied swords and spears protruding from their limp corpses.

Despite the barriers he had placed to guard himself, the sight of Leina's eyeless head, weaved to a creature's abdomen, tied next to the heads of Eira Piril and Minkar Slen, gave him a cold sweat. He turned his head and vomited on someone's severed leg. The flies swarmed to feed on his mess.

Movement and a painful moan made David's heart leap. He turned, sword leading, and found the old man, his long white hair and mustache caked in dried blood, sitting up against the far wall, watching him. He held someone, a young boy laying across his lap, still and lifeless. The old man held him with the familiarity and kindness of family.

David sighed.

"Your kin?" he asked.

The old man shook his head. "No. His name is Lieutenant Commander Kathor of the-" a fit of coughing overtook him and David could sense a rattle in the man's lungs. "Archonwolf Fleet's Royal Seaguard, and he was my friend."

"And you are?"

"Lieutenant Kartecus."

"Well, your men are all dead, Lieutenant, but your Captain still lives."

A hint of surprise and hope entered Kartecus' craggy features.

"He's my prisoner," David said sternly. "You both are, understand?" Kartecus nodded.

"The sword." David pointed at the bloodied xiphos in the man's hand. Kartecus stared at it as if noticing it for the first time and tossed it at his feet. It clanged loudly on the floorboards.

Benny entered holding his sword in both hands. "What was that?!"

"Another survivor. Calm down, and go grab some rope from Sifran."

Benny gave no argument, looking between them a moment before leaving.

"Are you injured?" David asked.

Kartecus nodded.

"Can you lift him?" He motioned towards Kathor with the tip of his sword.

Kartecus looked at the boy's bloodied, bandaged face, and shook his head.

"Then put him down, so I can restrain you. Do not make me kill you, old man. There has been enough death here today."

Kartecus' face was gaunt and drained of color. "Yes. Yes there has."

"David! David, come out here!" Benny cried.

"What is it?" he called back, moving towards the door.

129

Tall pillars of black smoke rose from the northeast edge of town. The Coppertooth Road was on fire.

"Bloodrider's thorny cock," David said under his breath.

By the time they reached Coppertooth Road, the flames had consumed half the storefronts on the road and was spreading rapidly west. In a matter of hours the town would be a pile of charcoal.

"How many people remain?" David asked Benny.

"What?" Benny raised a brow at him.

"At the Grit Mug. How many people survived?"

Benny stared at the ground, making mental inventory. "A dozen or so."

"That's all?"

Benny nodded.

"Get them all to Fort Kai. We must leave."

"But David, the town," Benny said, pointing.

"The town is dead, Benny. We cannot save it. Besides, everything we owned of value is already packed on wagons, remember? We need to gather everyone and leave, or we all burn."

"But, where will we go?" Benny seemed hesitant, confused.

Benny was born and raised in Kaira. This arid, shit-hole, mining town was all he ever knew. David felt guilty for speaking so callously. It occurred to him that Benny was watching his entire world burn down around him.

"Listen," he softened his tone. "If anything could be done for Kaira, we would come together and save her, but not enough of us survived to stop this fire. Even if we managed to drown it or cut off its fuel, what then? Rebuild? Those creatures are still up there somewhere. They will return for the rest of us eventually."

"Up there?" Benny's face scrunched. "Up where?"

Up in the valley adjacent to Ricker's fucking claim, is where!

"The mountain. Where else would they be?"

"I suppose."

Ashen poked his head out of Nikos' bakery, surprising them. Black soot masked his face and his eyes were bloodshot and haunted.

"Ashen!" Sifran embraced him. Ashen received the hug stiffly, with no sign of emotion. His gaze seemed vacant.

130

"Ashen." David licked his lips. "Are you alone? Did anyone else...?"

Ashen lowered his head and shook it. "Dead," he said tonelessly. "Everyone is dead. Burned or eaten. No one left but me."

"And Nianah?" He knew he should not ask, but he needed to hear the answer. The thought would gnaw at him until he gave voice to it otherwise.

Ashen locked eyes with him, and David witnessed the raw emotion nestling inside the boy, molded by horror and rage. Ashen did not answer — he did not need to. David should never have asked.

"We need to leave town," David said. "Kaira is lost."

"Yes," Ashen said flatly. "Go on. There's one more thing I need to do."

"All right." Although curious, David had already crossed a line. He was not about to cross another. Not now. "Don't tally."

"I won't." Ashen walked back into the bakery.

As he and Sifran walked back towards Fort Kai, Benny headed for the Grit Mug to gather the survivors.

"Where could Caige have gone?" Sifran asked, his eyes searching the abandoned streets.

"I don't know."

"Should we try and find him?"

"Sifran, if even one of those things is still here somewhere, or one of Dorav's men, and he catches us off-guard, we are fucked. We need to sever our moorings and sail."

"Ah." Sifran ran a hand through his sandy hair. "Perhaps he'll show while we prepare the wagons?"

"Perhaps."

They walked the rest of the way back to Fort Kai through an uncomfortable silence.

Murciel was being dragged by something. He opened his eyes and immediately shut them as the day's light pierced them like acid-dipped thorns. The thought of that creature carrying him towards its lair made his heart catch. He carefully opened one eye, just enough to see what pulled him along.

"Buio?"

"Be quiet, Murciel. You took a wound."

"The others?"

"Safe."

Murciel tried to stand but his body would not obey. "I cannot move."

"You were stung. Be still."

Murciel remembered the agony of it like one would a vivid nightmare. His body was flooded with liquid suffering rising so sharply he blacked out. The wound on his lower abdomen still throbbed.

"Am I going to die?"

"No, if the poison was lethal it would have killed you by now. Remain calm, and be quiet."

Murciel sighed and tried to relax, wishing he could open his eyes. The relentless heat of this land made sweat run down his skin, soaking the inside of his leathers. His nose and cheeks stung and mouth tasted like sand.

A soft layer of darkness pressed up against his eyelids, letting him open his eyes. They stood beneath the shadow of a tree with thick, leafy branches. The world beyond was a golden inferno of light and indistinguishable blurry shapes.

Buio leaned him up against the trunk and stripped him of his leathers. Murciel forced himself to not cry out when the leather was peeled from the puncture wound in his gut.

"Hang on," Buio said, and placed him over his shoulder.

Buio climbed the trunk using his sharpened claws, carrying him as if he weighed no more than a cub. Nihengale and Escara both lay naked on the higher branches, protected by the tree's shade.

Murciel struggled not to stare at the curvature of Escara's pale legs, the firmness of her stomach, or the smooth shape of her bare breasts. "How did you find this place?" he asked to distract himself.

"Do not speak." Buio glared silently at him with those cold blue eyes. Taking drassil sap out of his pouches, he applied it directly to the wound on Murciel's stomach before covering it in majesty leaf wrappings.

"My thanks," he said.

Buio nodded and removed his own skerki leathers. His thick, taut muscles were crisscrossed with old pale battle scars, healed burns, and long pale lash marks. He applied a thin layer of sap to a few shallow cuts and grazes on his torso and legs.

"Indeed, thank you for this, Buio," Nihengale muttered weakly. "We would have perished today if not for you."

"Attempt to rest," Buio stated dryly.

"Do you think Rairi made it to safety?" Murciel asked, closing his eyes.

"She will be fine," said Nihengale.

"How can you be certain?"

Nihengale sat pensive a moment. "A year ago, Buio, Rairi, and I were sent to clear out a nest of socolinc crawlers. The Elders sent her with us because socolincs normally nest near generous sources of drassil moss. Before we ever found their nest, we were ambushed by a pack of kajaks. Have you ever seen a kajak, Murciel?"

"No."

"They resemble black jaguars, but are larger, meaner, and far more cunning. They have thick pelts, claws as long as your fingers, teeth like boar tusks, and thick bone plating around their skulls, spines and vital organs.

"Rairi vanished right as the ambush occurred, leaving Buio and I against five of them. We were as good as dead. A few seconds later, the beasts stopped their stalking and ran off, losing interest in us."

"How?"

"Rairi called it 'pheromone imitation'. She made the kajaks believe their cubs were in danger by using their own natural scents and sounds. The girl knows how to survive in ways I cannot wrap my head around. She may appear reserved, Murciel, she has a sharp, flaming sword in that mind of hers. Have faith. She will be fine."

"I will try," Murciel relented.

Rairi paced the dark cavern anxiously, awaiting Marca's return, with eyes heavy and mind tingling with exhaustion. When she heard someone approaching down the mineshaft, she closed her eyes and used ketter.

Every corner and sharp angle of the mine came back in crisp clarity. Marca made her way clumsily down the drift, oil-lamp in hand.

"Well?!" Rairi asked impatiently.

Marca was crying.

"What happened?" Rairi softened her tone.

"They are dead," Marca said softly. "Everyone is dead."

"Everyone?" The news hit her like a dousing of cold water. Those things killed everyone? What was she supposed to do now? For a rare, brief moment, her mind went silent.

"Well, not everyone." Marca wiped at her face. "A few townspeople are still down there."

"Elinel's tits!" Rairi threw up her hands. "Why did you use the word 'everyone' if you did not mean everyone?!"

"I am sorry, but you don't know what I just saw! There are bodies everywhere, and the fire is spreading so quickly!"

"Fire?"

In her own anxiety, Rairi had dismissed the hint of smoke wafting through the claim. Now she could not help but smell it.

"How big is this fire?"

"It has eaten nearly half the town. You can feel the heat from the road."

"Marca, did you see the others?"

"The others?"

"My kin, the other mepsiens."

Marca chewed on her lip and shook her head.

"They were not among the surviving anthrops?"

"Humans."

"Yes, fine! You are certain you did not see them?"

"I am, Rairi. I am sorry."

They were alive. She needed to believe they were alive. She would be lost, trapped in a foreign land without them. Her mind desired nothing more than to go rabid with fear and doubt. She forcefully muzzled the beast and focused on what she could control.

"What are the survivors doing?" she asked.

"Preparing the wagons by the fort. I believe they intend to leave."

"How many remain? How many of Dorav's men survived?"

"I saw ten or fifteen people, none of them wearing Vinergale's colors. I don't think any seaguards survived the attack, Rairi. What do we do?"

"We wait." Rairi ran a hand through her hair. "I cannot leave this mine while Siege is in the sky, and if those monsters remain nearby-"

"What if they come in here?!"

Rairi scanned the tunnel and saw no weapons lying about. She could fend off an anthrop attacker with her moonblade, but not one of those things.

"Bring me those stones. The bigger ones," Rairi said, donning her leather gloves.

As Marca brought her the heavy stones, she meticulously wrote a warding glyph on each with her sxill.

"What is that?" Marca inquired, bringing her another heavy stone.

"You jest. This is my sxill. Hardened chalk infused with shinn? You anthrops don't use sxills?"

Marca shook her head.

"Sari's mercy." Rairi shook her own head. "We use them to draw glyphs and seals. They are more reliable than infused dyes."

Rairi placed the stones side by side, with the markings facing out towards the entrance. Marca stood back and watched her in silent fascination.

The stones trembled as the refined shinn began to interact with their chemical bonds. Blue flashes lit the gloom and an acrid stink wafted around them as the shinn melted the markings into the stone surfaces. An almost imperceptible hum and a hint of ozone filled the air.

"What do those do?"

"They are sensory blinds," she said. "They seal in light, sound, and odor, forcing a blank space in physical perception. Go ahead, step over them and look back towards me."

Marca gingerly stepped over the humming stones and turned, lifting her oil lamp. The confounded look on her face made Rairi smile.

"A wall!" Marca said. "I see a stone wall, like if the cave ended here."

Marca put a hand out and it halted in mid-air. She ran her hand across nothing, a hint of concern entering the corners of her eyes and lips.

"This is an actual wall...but I...Rairi? Are you still there?"

Still smiling, Rairi stepped over the stones.

"Oh! I can see them now, and the tunnel behind them. How did you do that?"

"Like I said, the wardstones inhibit sensory information, so your mind is forced to fill in the details."

"But I touched it!"

"Everything you believe to be real is but a construct of the mind. What the mind believes, you believe. Bending the perceptions of the mind is the foundation of this type of alchemy. With the right amount of flare and the subtlest of changes to perception, you can make a crowd of bumpkins believe you are a storybook magician."

"So the wall was not real, but because I believed it was..."

"It became real for you. Once the illusion is broken however, like by seeing me step through a wall you thought was solid, it ceases to function. The mind fixes the gap, so to speak, realizing it was tricked. Go ahead, step over them again."

Marca did as she was told, and by her doing so, the wall vanished, revealing the stones she had placed and the empty space behind them. Although she was certain the wall was false, she was still a slave to her mind's perceptions, like anyone else. Forcing herself to walk through what her mind considered solid stone would have resulted in a fierce headache afterward.

"This will keep us safe if anyone or anything wanders in here." She stepped back behind the stones. "Make certain you don't disturb the line."

"I won't, but you must teach me how to do this! And about the sss... chssill?"

"Sxill. You wish to learn ward glyphs? There are so many..."

"Then teach me this one."

Rairi was not keen on sharing mepsien wards with an anthrop, but at least it would keep their minds from wandering into the possible horrors that awaited them after leaving this cavern.

"All right."

10

My Cairn

Caige walked barefoot towards the mouth of the ancient ziggurat temple. On the altar, where the wretched, shit-stained old man had turned and prostrated himself, stood a little girl with wild hair — her naked body covered in dried blood and smeared paints. When she spoke, her words sounded strange and garbled, but he could still grasp their meaning.

"Have you come to kill me?" she asked.

"N...no," Caige said.

"Then why have you come?"

"Cairn, my Cairn," came a whisper from behind him, hidden somewhere in the petrified wood. He turned back towards the forest.

"Tyn?" he called out.

"Yes. This way, Cairn. You are not safe there."

Caige glanced back but the girl on the altar was gone.

"Tyn?"

"I am here, come closer."

He walked into the deep shadows of the petrified forest, the light fading around him until he could barely see. When Tynisia's hands wrapped around his own with their familiar softness, his eyes filled with tears.

"Tyn, is it really you?"

"Of course," she said, wrapping her arms around him, her head pressing against his chest.

"Tyn! Oh gods, I've missed you!" His heart nearly burst out of his chest. "I have been so lost without you!"

"I know, but I am here now."

"Tyn, I thought-"

"Shh, Cairn." She put her fingers to his lips.

He kissed her, feeling her arms wrap around his back and the sweetness of her tongue dancing with his.

"There is something I need you to do for me." She kissed him on the chin.

"Of course. Anything."

"Take me to Aztan."

"Aztan? Why there?"

"I will explain everything on the way," she said with a smile. "Will you do this for me?"

"Of course I will," he said. "If that is what you want."

"It is."

Caige wept, his arms filled with the warmth of the woman he loved. He did not hear the hollow moan coming from within the temple behind him, or notice how it became progressively louder.

"We must leave," Tyn said. "We are in danger here. Do you trust me, my Cairn?"

"With my life."

"Then come. We must be away from here."

Tynisia took his hand and tried to lead him away, but he sensed someone standing behind him and he froze.

"Don't! Don't look back, Cairn," she said. "Just keep walking."

Tynisia tugged at his arm, but his every fiber screamed for him to turn — he did. The lion stood on the altar of the temple, eyes burning like emerald candles.

"Tyn, run!" Caige turned to face the beast and spread his arms in a show of defiance. He would not let the beast have her this time. "He comes for you! Go!"

"No, Cairn!" Tynisia screamed pulling at his arm. "He comes for you! We must go! Now!"

They sprinted together into the petrified forest. The green-eyed lion gave chase.

ACT II

11

Palidor's Throne

Chancellor Edger Cotaline had never been a man to tolerate discomfort. He was born into a powerful trade family whose financial might could be traced back to the Bergal Empire and the founding of Palidor itself. His short youth was spent surrounded by servants, books, money, and privilege.

During his formative years he participated in political reform, debated at the Gilder's Club, and read many of the great works including *Iorn's Magnum Logos*, *The Hekoret Trials*, and *Palladius*. He could recite twenty of the epic *Rhapsodes of Hechester* by memory before he turned fifteen, and fancied himself a disciple of the ancient philosopher Selenes.

His unabashed ingenuity made him a favorite among the Gilder's Fraternity, where he earned the title Jack of Coins on his twenty-ninth yearday — a title reserved for senior members. The Gilder's Club had heavily supported his rise to Chancellor of Palidor thirty years ago, and reaped the benefits of their trust in him to this day.

Long years of politics as the city's chancellor had not been kind to him. The corners of his piercing blue eyes were afflicted with thin film of rheum, and dark circles were etched beneath them. His once proud mane of golden hair was a speckled wasteland at the crown, with a cascade of snowy fibers dangling around his ears. Although his mind remained a lithe and formidable instrument, folded and sharpened in the forge of experience, his body had grown fat and soft from a life of indulgence. His generous folds pressed him down into his sturdy wicker chair, forcing him to shift his weight every few minutes.

Seeing as the day would be warm and pleasant, he ordered a pot of Gaeled black tea be brewed and left to cool. The kitchen had strict instructions to pour the tea over ice, only once his guests arrived and were seated. The ice was shipped down from southern Telkan at an outrageous expense to the people's coffers, but he wished to impress his visitors.

Lord Renot, Host of the Ashuran Knights, Lord Admiral Selliaro, Master of the King's Navy, and Headmistress Dyrcei of the Palidorian Academy of Alchemy, all arrived together, took their seats, and were promptly served their tea. Cotaline waited for them to take the customary first sip before speaking.

"Thank you all so much for coming," he said, putting his hands on his generous stomach. "I admit to having heard some disturbing news about our campaign in Tepley. I asked you all here today to clarify any misunderstandings."

"Very generous of you, Chancellor," Lord Renot said, holding the silver goblet to his face, enjoying its cold touch. "Please tell us of what you have heard, so we can unburden you of doubt."

Edger stroked his white, braided mustache which hung well below his chin. Metzial had taken the lead. The Ashuran Lord came wrapped in his cloak of office; long, white, and made of felt, invariably speckled with mud on its lower hem. His blue eyes stared with their usual calculating demeanor, betraying nothing.

"What I've heard, Lord Renot, is that our mission deployed with only one ship, carrying two Ashuran knights, a paltry unit of seaguards, and one alchemist...excuse me, one apprentice alchemist. Considering the difficulty of the assignment at hand, these rumors must be entirely false. Yes?"

"No, Chancellor, this is an accurate estimate." Metzial sipped at his tea and leaned back, as if his answer was more than adequate.

Edger's ire rose quickly, but he kept it hidden. Parda and Selliaro remained equally impassive to the Host's remark. "Would you mind explaining how you believe this mission will succeed with such a meager force, Lord Renot?" he asked.

"I retain complete faith in Commander Minos to execute the mission. He is more than capable."

Edger's skin prickled. The Host playing coy with him meant there was something here he was not seeing. He turned to Selliaro.

The Lord Admiral wore his red doublet of office, black breeches, and leather boots. His ensemble accentuated his flowing salt-and-pepper hair and well-groomed beard. As usual, the admiral seemed bored and retracted, sitting with his legs crossed, his gaze wandering the grounds.

"Lord Admiral," Edger said, "would you care to tell me why only one ship left port on this most arduous of assignments?"

Selliaro secretly loathed his appointed office. A man of the sea, born and bred — his current administrative duties might as well be a prison sentence.

"The *Merrigold* only required one escort, sir," Selliaro said. "Too many ships entering Tepley's seaways would create suspicion and undo delays. Better this way."

Edger's instincts stood on high alert now. "Escorting the Merrigold would only require one ship, yes, but what of the remainder of the mission? The true reason for the deployment?"

"I apologize, Chancellor Cotaline," Selliaro said, "but I have no idea what you're talking about."

Edger looked over to Metzial expectantly. The Host sipped his tea and stared back without expression.

He turned to Parda Dyrcei, breathing deeply though his nose to steady himself. The headmistress, dressed in her lavender and cerulean surcoat, with matching alchemist's overcoat, waited for him to speak. He imagined she must be enjoying the coolness of his expensive ice more than any of them in that ridiculous leather coat.

"Headmistress," he said calmly. "Might I ask what you were informed about this most delicate deployment?"

Parda took a long sip of her tea, laid it on the table, crossed her legs, and placed her hands on her right thigh. "Only that the trade ship *Merrigold* would travel to Relm escorted past Teplian waters by the *Kajak*. Lord Selliaro requested one of my more promising alchemists to serve as a surgeon's mate."

Edger was not prone to violence, but this insult scraped his every nerve. Beating Metzial to death with his patio table became a tangible possibility.

He drank his tea, allowing the cool liquid chill his boiling blood. He took the ice shards left in the goblet and rolled them around in his mouth, letting them slowly melt. To think he wasted so much on these insolent wretches.

"Lord Admiral, Headmistress, if I might have a moment with the Host of Knights?" He spoke with as much steadiness as he could muster.

"Of course." Parda stood, taking her goblet with her. Selliaro silently followed.

Once they had walked far enough into his estate's grounds, he turned on Metzial.

"I left this critical mission in your hands, Lord Renot, Did I fail to express the importance of its success? Did I not clarify this assignment was handed down by word of the King? Do I need to explain to you why what you have done is an act of complete incompetence?"

Metzial did not appear the least bit perturbed. He finished his tea and extracted the ice, breaking it between his teeth.

"Chancellor Cotaline, you did place this mission in my hands, and I gave it the exact attention it deserved, considering the circumstances."

"Those being?"

"You are the Chancellor of Palidor, Lord Cotaline. You hold direct authority over the Archonwolves, the Academy of Alchemy, and his Majesty's navy. You could deploy a force as vast as you deem necessary, without speaking to me, but you did. You asked me to take the lead, on your behalf."

"On the King's behalf."

"On a heathen's behalf, as I understand it."

"Lady Dal'dira is a Warmaster, Metzial! The King's Eastern Rook! She speaks with the King's voice in such matters."

"She is a mepsien heretic, Edger. The Aegis of Man does not answer to any xial, no matter how decorated."

"Are you saying you would exchange an accusation of incompetence for one of treason?" Edger's blood rushed to his face.

"I answer directly to Bishop Ducast, or his Holiness, the Archbishop. None other."

"Archbishop Dales serves at the pleasure of the King, Metzial!"

"The King, yes, but not his heathen witch." A hint of anger scuttled into Metzial's voice. "The order you handed me contained her seal and signature. However, it did not contain the King's, or the Archbishop's mark. It was not thrice given."

"You endanger this critical maneuver on a technicality, Metzial? Are you mad? This order came from the Rook's office alone because the Magalians are involved. Neither the King nor the Archbishop can be held partisan. Did I not make that clear to you?"

"Do you really think me so blind, Edger?! You handed me this mission because you understood damn well, whoever moves against the Magalians, answers to them. You thought to buy my allegiance with one hand and use me as a shield with the other. Did you honestly believe I would not grasp your little scheme? Well, you failed, Edger. This will all come right back to your doorstep. I have seen to it."

"What the hell have you done, Metzial?"

"The Eastern Rook gave you the mission to attack Sharn." Metzial pointed a thick finger at him. "The Queen of Tepley and the Magalians will know the Warmaster gave the order and that you were to execute it."

"There is no goddamn mission to Sharn, you imbecile! You saw to that!"

Metzial leaned back, ran his callused finger inside his goblet and sucked the water off his digit.

"You bastard," Edger said, in sudden realization. "You ordered the *Kajak* to attack Sharn? Alone?"

Metzial stared back at him, saying nothing, but his eyes were blue malice.

"But Captain Minos is one of your Knights."

"Commander Minos received orders to escort the *Merrigold* to Relm's seaway, nothing more. He does not have leave or writ of passage to attack Tepley or Magalian lands." Metzial's smile was a knife. "If someone gave him other orders, in secret, none of us were privy to it."

Edger looked over to where Selliaro and Parda stood, speaking by the edge of his pond, teas in hand. Both the royal navy and academy of alchemy were expected to play important roles in the attack on Sharn, which is why had he summoned them here.

144

"If you meant to send Dorav to his death, why involve the two of them?" Edger asked.

"Because they also had pests in their homes they needed to be rid of. One hand washes the other, you see."

"You are a goddamn fool, Metzial. You could have claimed the lands and wealth of the Norvan Peaks, as promised. You would have taken Ship-Breaker-Sharn, landing an important military foothold for the Archonwolves and your King. I would have paraded you through this city like a damn hero, and you throw everything away for fear of the Magalian's fucking displeasure? You coward! You spineless jellyfish!"

"You are wrong."

"Get out of my home," Edger shouted, losing his poise, "and take your co-conspirators with you! This is not over, Metzial, you snake! You worm belly! You have my word!"

Lord Renot put down his goblet, turned his back on him, and walked into the estate grounds to retrieve Parda and Selliaro.

Father Meyirdor Ducast had not always been a saintly man, or been born with the name Ducast. The son of a cobbler and his unremarkable wife, he was born impoverished in the Murkstone slums of Palidor. He had been arrested three times for theft by the age of eight and stood trial for murder by age twelve.

Father Peitren Ducast took pity on him during his murder trial and requested to be granted custody. The presiding Arbiter agreed, and the nameless, desperate slum boy became the priest's ward, and baptized with the saintly name of Meyirdor.

The homely life of an altar boy did little to curb Meyi's mischievous nature. The amount of coin that flowed through the Zoniran Church only fueled his untrained desires. Father Ducast struggled for years to instruct him on the advantages of Divine Amounting and convince him to stop stealing from the church's coffers.

Once properly instructed, Meyirdor demonstrated an uncanny ability to inspire the congregation. His words were like honey and silk, dancing in the wind. Within a matter of months, his ministering doubled the church's sales of penance disks and holy fetishes. His personal earnings allowed him to purchase his own atonement from his past transgressions within a year.

Rising like the sun itself, Meyirdor became one of the youngest priests to grace the pulpit — an inspiration to those who believed redemption beyond their grasp, just as Father Ducast knew he would be.

The story of his life convinced even the most destitute of sinners to relinquish the trappings of the world, and allot their meager earnings to reaching deserved salvation. The church's coffers filled to bursting, and though the people's stomachs were empty, their hearts and souls were lambent with God's light.

Meyirdor's assignment as a missionary to Telkan during the Purification War only enhanced the people's love for him. He carried the Ashuran writs of passage and the righteous intent of the Holy Church. The people of Telkan fell to their knees before him, grateful beyond words for their salvation.

Gigan Minos, the Holy Redeemer himself, spoke admirably of him after the war concluded. At thirty-nine, he became the youngest man to ever hold the titles of Bishop of Palidor and Keeper of the Golden Arch, second only to Archbishop Kreagan Dales and the King himself.

Even though he was the Chancellor's junior by three decades, Edger held a great deal of respect for the man. They were allies in the shaping and managing of the great city of Palidor. The bishop would set things to right.

"Hello, my friend," Meyirdor smiled, waving him into his spacious home.

Few were privy to the bishop's private abode. Beautiful tapestries from Clannidan hung from the foyer's walls, surrounding furniture of the finest ash, cedar, and felt. Every candlestick, sconce, and chandelier was pure Bullywall gold — shaped into items of religious reverence by Palidor's most celebrated goldsmiths. Edger found the bishop's taste a bit boorish, but such a thing was expected from a man of humble origins.

"Thank you for seeing me on short notice, Keeper." Edger said.

"I am ever at your service, Chancellor. Come, sit and unburden yourself." They sat by Meyirdor's fireplace. The mantelpiece was red granite, painstakingly chiseled to resemble The Maw.

Edger had read *The Pilgrimage of the Unclean* by the renown poet Burgein, which described the Vorx's Gate as a mass of fiery, writhing vines. Sinners were caught in its bladed thorns and torn apart, their naked souls bleeding into eternal damnation.

Curving around the fireplace, so that the center of the Maw was the lighted hearthfire, the macabre mantelpiece did Burgein's poem a fine justice.

"Would you like something to drink?" Meyirdor asked. "I just received the most succulent snowberry wine from Telkan."

"Thank you Keeper, but no."

"Water then?"

"That would be fine."

Meyirdor made a small gesture to a servant who stood waiting by the doorway. The young girl hurried off to fetch his water.

"Now, tell me what has you so vexed," Keeper Ducast said.

"Lord Renot, Keeper. He disobeyed a direct order from the Eastern Rook," Edger began, interrupted by the servant girl who returned with a pitcher of water. She kept her eyes lowered as she poured. A slum girl, Edger was certain, from Murkstone.

"A very comely girl," he said, momentarily changing the subject.

"You are welcome to her if you like, my friend." Meyirdor granted him a genuine smile.

"Oh, I'm far too old for such a ripe blossom," he replied uncomfortably.

"She has served men your age before," Meyirdor assured.

Edger sipped his water. "I appreciate the offer, but no."

The bishop smiled thinly. "As to your situation with the Host, I must ask, why did you not come to me before?"

"Before?"

"With the details of this assignment by the Warmaster. Did you not foresee the Host would come to me for guidance? The Aegis of Man is under the sole authority of the Holy Church, Edger. Their every action must be authorized by either myself or the Archbishop."

Cotaline's jaw clenched. He sipped at his water to give himself time. Meyirdor already knew everything. Metzial had covered his angles well.

"I placed the mission in the Host's hands for the good of the faith, Keeper. The wealth of the Norvan Region, the claim to land, and the glory of conquest would have all been his. The Aegis of Man stood only to benefit."

"You must understand, Lord Cotaline, the Aegis of Man cannot involve itself in maneuvers against the Magalian family. They are currently tied in a relationship of mutual interest."

"Dear God!" He slammed his goblet on the table. "Is there no one alive who is not in the Magalian's damned pocket?!"

"Watch your disrespectful tongue, Edger!" Meyirdor gave him a dangerous glare.

He sighed. "Forgive me, Keeper. I truly believed that if anyone in Palidor remained free of their influence, it would be the Host of Knights. Another reason why I chose him."

"We are all on Zenthien's Golden Stair, Edger, and few can boast such divine favor as the Magalians hold."

"So do you share Metzial's belief that the Eastern Rook's orders are negligible?"

"No order from a King's Warmaster is negligible, Lord Cotaline, which is why Metzial committed one of his finest warships to escorting the *Merrigold* south."

"Keeper, escorting the *Merrigold* to Relm's seaway was only the excuse to mobilize a force past Sawstone's patrol lines. Alone, the action is worthless. Worse, this removes the one-"

"Let us not play this game, Edger! You made a grave mistake attempting to hide behind the Aegis. You did not like that the Rook gave you this assignment, so you tried to wash your hands and dry them on holy cloth.

"You owe your station to the Gilder's Fraternity, and they owe their continued existence to the Magalians. You are just as caught in this web as anyone."

"Except Metzial said he intends to place the blame of this debacle on my doorstep."

"Lord Renot is angry with you." The bishop waved dismissively. "He was practically gnawing at the bit to attack Sharn before he came to speak with me. I made him realize the error in his intentions. You remain the ever clever politician, and Metzial is not a man who takes being used lightly."

So you did this? You are the one who fucked me?

"Do not despair, my friend. The fault of this does not lie with you, and I will make certain such is known. The King's Rook placed us all in this predicament. The blame lies with her. This Lady Dal'dira," Meyirdor spat the name out like a piece of pig fat, "holds a complicated agenda of her own. The King is wise, but he is allowing his ambitions to be used against him."

"Why do you believe so?" Edger asked, hating the flood of relief washing over him. If Bishop Ducast spoke on his behalf, perhaps he would escape this predicament after all.

"Since that heathen's appointment as a Warmaster," Meyirdor said "Vinergale has suffered three long wars and lost the King's heir under suspicious circumstances. A fortune in sovereigns is being poured into this fruitless war with Qanalar, and it seems the King now seeks some fairytale weapon of Neterian legend. Neterian, Edger. Neterian!"

Edger stared into the crackling fires at the heart of The Maw. Helicartia's political envoy being granted the seat of Warmaster was a controversial move by King Velen. The Holy Church, the Ceredyre Table, and the Chancellor's Circle all attempted to convince him of the dangers of such an appointment, but he ignored their protests. Shortly after being granted her title, Lady Dal'dira declared war on the Pirate Kingdom of Calimport.

"The Church benefits from her assignment, Keeper," Edger said cautiously.

"Indeed. Churches were erected on every island of Calimport and their populations were spared the gnashing teeth of the Maw. They are now among our most ardent followers."

"And I believe the same can be said for Telkan?"

"Despite our influence there, you must remember, we are forbidden the burning of Telkan's temples and libraries."

"Yes, but should such cultures not be allowed their history and identity?"

"Of course not. The purging of false influence by fire is not something that should ever be restricted, Edger. If the sickness is not burned out completely, it grows back, stronger than before."

"Even when it means burning innocents, Keeper? Women, children, and the elderly alike?"

"You think in too short a scale, Edger, and forget your scripture. All who die not on the Golden Stair will fall into the Maw and become

Vorxspawn. Every soul we do not save is a soul the Ashkandar must one day defeat in battle. Only by fire are corrupted souls cleansed. That is holy law. Our destiny is not to save most of humanity from the Maw. We are charged with saving everyone. To fail in this most holy affair is to fail God."

He needed to be careful. Father Meyirdor was a friend, but he would only condone so much doubt and criticism, even from him. He thought it best to sidestep.

"You mentioned the war against Qanalar. Have the Ashuras been allowed on the field in force?"

The bishop eyed him evenly, and or a moment, he feared he might have misstepped.

"They are not." Meyirdor sighed. "What a miserable campaign. Those savages are proving more stubborn than the Telkans."

"And prolific," Edger said. "My Archonwolves assist Mormi's fleets, but are being beaten back by sheer numbers."

"The paltry forces Lord Merubaris summoned for this war are not enough," Meyirdor said bitterly. "We would shatter their lines if the Aegis were summoned into battle. The Western Rook deprives us of our due glory."

"Perhaps he only holds his strongest forces in reserve, Keeper. Reports from the field tell that he leashes the Winterwolves and Direwolf Knights as well. The Qanalar Horde is a monstrous thing — its numbers overwhelming. He may seek to starve and weaken the beast before committing to biting its throat."

"The heathen witch wet her beak in that war as well."

"What do you mean, Keeper?"

"Lady Dal'dira has sent the Iron Crab as an envoy to the Isles of Kirre, with the premise of granting assistance to the Western Rook."

"I am ashamed to admit being in the dark in this matter."

"She means to summon a horde of over-sexed, hut-dwelling heretics to help fight the King's war. They'll share in the spoils while our forces remain beached and wanting for blood and honor. It is madness, Edger. Unforgivable madness."

"The parstans proved themselves useful in coastal battles before, Keeper. They are savage, as you say, but fearless in battle and most importantly, expendable."

150

"The Sisters of Kirre do not send their children out to die without first making hefty demands, Lord Cotaline. You would do well not forget."

"Yes, Keeper."

"I do enjoy your visits, Edger, though I would prefer to see you at mass more than I do at my home."

"I will try, Keeper," he said, knowing this was the bishop's subtle way of dismissing him. "Forgive my absence. I will make repentance this upcoming mass, you have my word."

"And you mine, that when the time arrives, all will be set to right. Do not worry about Lord Renot, but I will ask you not antagonize him either."

"Of course. I see now that I should have come to you first, Keeper. Can you forgive my foolish misstep in judgment?"

Bishop Ducast gave him a winning smile. "Forgiveness and atonement is my calling, Lord Cotaline. Let this incident burden you no further."

Meyirdor put his right hand in the air, index and middle finger up, and moved them from left to right in a straight line. The simple gesture was the symbol of divine forgiveness, and also happened to symbolize a repaid debt. "Place it far behind you. You are absolved."

"I intend to, Keeper, and thank you." He stood, willing himself to appear as calm and at ease as he claimed.

Bishop Ducast had, politically, just grabbed him firmly by the balls. His good friend had turned the situation with Sharn to his favor.

Both he and Metzial now owed this dangerous man a debt, and both Selliaro and Dyrcei were indebted to Lord Renot. Without leaving the comforts of home, Ducast had sat himself on Palidor's throne. Edger had no choice but to let him sit there, and kiss the royal feet, for now.

"Remember friend, you are always welcome in my home.

"I will, Keeper. Farewell."

"Farewell."

12

The Road North

"You have the devil in you, Dorav." Iridia panted, nuzzling his neck.

Dorav propped himself on his elbows to take some weight off her. He stared at her lovely face, cherishing every detail. They were adults now, Initiates of the Order, and in their last year before taking their trials of Knighthood.

Iridia began cutting her golden curls off when she turned fifteen. A third of the Ashuran initiates were girls, but most kept their hair long, either tied into war-braids, or wrapped tightly within their helms during battle. Iridia liked hers cropped short.

She enjoyed how uncomfortable she made some of the boys, and that they knew never to mock her. Bloody noses and cut lips were distributed to the first who tested those waters. Dorav loved her short hair, which brought out the honey color of her eyes.

"I was inspired." He ran a hand across her cheek and smiled at her.

"What do you think about, when you are inside me?" She teased, nibbling at his earlobe.

Dorav stared deeply into her beautiful amber eyes.

"Headmistress Akarni," he said.

"You swine!" Iridia laughed, punching him in the ribs.

"That beautifully pale, wrinkled skin." Dorav struggled with her, laughing. "That perpetually disapproving scowl! I grow hard again just thinking about it."

Dorav finally got hold of Iridia's arms and pinned her down, kissing the softness of her neck.

"You are a damned fool," she said.

"I am your fool." He kissed her along the collarbone.

"Dorav, you must keep your promise," Iridia purred.

"Which one?"

She bit his ear.

"Ah! Yes! I will keep my promise!"

When she let him go, he lowered his head between her breasts.

"But truly, which one?"

Iridia playfully smacked the side of his head. He nibbled lightly on her nipple, the soft pink bud hardening in his mouth.

"We must be assigned to the same Eshim," she said. "I care not if we serve under Holy Knight Jolis or even that cur Tassider, as long as we remain together."

"We will be." He smiled and pulled himself up to kiss her warmly. "We stay together...unless Headmistress Akar-ow!" Her savage pinch cut him off and they tumbled again.

The wagon hit a bump and rocked Dorav awake. The dull pain in his leg and left arm setting in immediately.

"Kartecus?" he said groggily.

Kartecus sat in a sweat-stained shirt and mended breeches, watching him from across the wagon. The wooden contraption creaked and bumped along noisily, rolling over the uneven road.

"Glad to see you back, sir," Kartecus said. "I began to worry."

They sat on the bed of one of their own wagons, bound hand and foot. One of the young men from Kaira sat behind the driver's bench with a loaded crossbow on his lap. Dorav's other wagons rumbled behind them, flanked by weary, harrowed looking townsfolk. They eyed him with a mixture of suspicion and open loathing. The sky above was bright orange with hints of nectar and blood painting the crests of the western hills.

"How long have I slept?"

"A day."

"David!" The dark-haired boy with the crossbow shouted. "He wakes."

"All right, come and take the reins."

David traded places with the young man and took the crossbow from him.

"Captain Dorav?" David sat down and pointed the gnarled bolt at his chest. "How are you feeling?"

153

Dorav stared hard at the red-bearded man and said nothing.

"Not so talkative now? Fine, I will cut straight. Where is your writ of passage, Ashura? I could not find it on you or among your things."

The clump of the horses' hooves and hollow rumble of the wagon filled the silence between them.

"Your men are all dead, Captain," David told him with a hint of solemnity, "except for Kartecus here."

Kartecus gave him a thin nod in affirmation.

"I will need your writ when I hand you over to the korgurate."

"What is a 'writ of passage' David?" A sandy-haired man sitting next to the driver glanced back.

"Something all Ashuras must carry, Sifran," David said. "A different kind of shield they wear."

"What do you mean?"

David scratched his thick red beard and grinned at him. Dorav held the look quietly.

"Thing is," David said, "Ashuras are considered above the law of man. Only the Zoniran Church can legally hold trial and punish them. So whenever they are sent on missions like this, their superiors give them a writ of passage as proof that their actions are divinely sanctioned.

"These bastards are granted authority above local military and the gentry. The writ is important to their Code because it keeps them from going rogue, and returns them to their own if they are captured by the enemy.

"The Queen ran the zonirans out of Tepley and burned their churches, so we need to turn him over to the korgurate. They will decide his fate."

"Will we see any coin for him when we do?" Sifran asked.

"Not a wager I would place," David chuckled.

"So what if he has no writ of passage?"

David shifted the crossbow on his knee. "Then he is not sanctioned to be here. He is a rogue knight.

"So, where is your writ, Captain?"

Dorav stared.

"Stubborn bastard," David muttered.

"The road darkens, David," Sifran called out.

"All right. Find a place to make camp. Tell the others."

"Right." Sifran leaped easily out of the moving wagon. "We make camp!" he cried down the line of wagons. "Everyone off the road!"

Dorav glanced down at the bloodstained bandage around his forearm and flexed his hand. The wound only hurt gravely when he made a tight fist, which was a blessing.

The man called David had a similar, splinted bandage around his forearm and a nasty gash on his head. There was knotted muscle in his arms, he spoke with easy authority, and held a crossbow with practiced ease. Dorav needed to be careful not to underestimate this man.

The caravan stopped under a shady copse of sandwillows a quarter mile from the road. David herded the wagons into a defensive circle and instructed everyone to build campfires to ward off nearby predators. The air of the camp was thick with tearful despondency. Kaira's survivors were broken remnants of a whole — the last living fragments of families, friends, and dig teams. Sifran sat at their campsite, tending the fire.

"Ashen?" David asked.

"Went for a walk."

David scanned the somber wagon circle and the shadows beneath the surrounding sandwillows. "The road can be dangerous, Sifran."

"You suddenly care what happens to him?" Sifran raised a thin brow.

David sighed.

Dorav and Kartecus sat near the edge of the fire's light, their hands bound to the smooth spokes of their wagon's rear left wheel.

"Did you check their bonds?"

"Yes. They are tight, despite their attempts to wiggle loose."

"Would you not do the same?"

Sifran nodded.

"We need to set up watches," David said tiredly. "We cannot all sleep at once."

"I'll take the first one," Sifran said. "I'm not tired."

"I will take second." He sat down.

"How is our store of food?"

"Fine. Telepi insisted on cooking for everyone and her children will run the pots out when she is finished. I believe she feels guilty."

"About what?"

"Being the only mother in Kaira who did not lose her young ones."

"Fuck." Sifran spat into the fire. "That is bleak. Perhaps we should all have run for the Grit Mug's cellars."

"Perhaps." David rubbed the back of his neck. "Perhaps Ricker might still be alive.

Sifran glanced up at him, then continued to poke the flames. "Did Benny and the others return?"

"No, and we need those toe-suckers here with the rest."

Sifran gave him a wry smirk. "You're just ornery because they wouldn't listen to you."

David searched his pouches, found a leaf-rolled perrin cigarette, and lit it in the fire. "I'm not. The food these cock-herders made us load is more than enough to get us to Nevine without rationing. Benny and those boys do not need to hunt. If we are stopped by raiders, we are four young, strong men short."

"Come on, David. No one here is going to put up a fight against raiders. We would be fucked regardless. Benny and them just need to be away to deal with what happened in their own way."

David took a long drag and passed the perrin to Sifran. He blew the smoke in his lungs out in a long gray billow over his head. "I know."

"You are good at this. Organizing people and making certain everyone has a task. You would have made a better sindaco than that piece of shit, Rint."

"Not my sack of grain, Sifran."

"Could have fooled me." Sifran took a deep drag of smoke.

David gave him a sidelong glance and put his hand out. Sifran passed him back the perrin.

"Thank you, for saving my hide back in Kaira," David said. "I know that was difficult. You seemed ready to shit your britches, but you pushed through. What is your problem with beetles anyway?"

Sifran's small black eyes stared back at him, his features creasing behind his shaggy blond hair. David felt suddenly guilty for broaching the topic. A log inside the fire snapped, sending a swarm of embers into the night air.

"As a child, in Bramen," Sifran stared back at the fire. "I had a friend named Renso. One of our favorite activities was walking by the pier where the old cobbles sat loose from the river's wash.

"We would take sticks and turn stones over to poke and squash the scrambling critters living underneath. We would run home up to our knees in river muck and the occasional bug bite. Mother used to scold me ceaselessly."

One day, we pulled over this big rock and found a deep burrow, like a serpent's nest. Being idiots, we poked inside to see what would emerge."

Sifran stopped to poke at the fire, his little black eyes haunted. "Something in there made a sound, like stones or sticks clicking together. I got frightened and backed up, but Renso laughed and kept poking. I...I wanted him to stop, but the words never left me.

"This black, slick beetle — yes a beetle, no bigger than your finger, jumped out and stung Renso on the foot.

"He cried out as if burned by a hot poker and fell, screaming in pain while his foot became fat and purple. I was paralyzed. I stood there, useless as a stake in a field, watching him scream until a dockworker arrived, asking what happened.

"I told him, 'he got stung. A beetle stung him,' and the man rapped his knuckles against my head, right here," Sifran tapped his forehead. "He yelled at me, saying 'beetles don't got stingers, you half-wit little shit! Where's this boy's da'?!'

"I walked them back to Renso's home and the dockworker walked me back to mine. My father gave me a beating that night I will never forget, David, I swear to you.

"The next morning we heard Renso died in the night, screaming until his voice gave out. No one ever believed me about the beetle. The adults all claimed a dozen different critters were to blame, but I know what I saw. Ever since, they have terrified me.

"What happened today...you must understand...those were the same fucking bugs that killed Renso, only larger — so much larger. I knew I was dreaming, I had to be. Even when you struck me, I could not accept what was happening.

"Then that thing killed Ricker, and I just stood there, like I did with Renso...I fucking stood there, David! Useless!"

David put his hand on Sifran's shoulder. "You cannot blame yourself for Ricker, Sifran. You saved me today. I would not be here if not for you."

"But I just stood there, David! Piss running down my damn leg!" Tears stained Sifran's cheeks. "He reached out to me. I could have helped him!"

"Sifran," Ashen said, walking into the firelight. "None of this was your fault." He pointed over to where Dorav and Kartecus sat. "It's theirs. They are to blame."

Sifran and Ashen shared a meaningful look. The deep scar of losing Nianah was painted clearly on Ashen's face. Sifran took a breath and wiped his eyes.

"You did one thing today that you must remember, Sifran." David said. "You saved my life. We are alive, and now we must keep each other alive."

David looked up and saw Ashen did not share the sentiment. The boy's eyes were cold and hard, staring through the firelight into someplace dark and void of life. He walked over and knelt by the fire.

"We should kill them, David," Ashen's voice was a throaty whisper.

Shit

"You said we needed to bring them along because Dorav was an Ashura — that we would be in trouble if we killed him, because he is protected."

"Right." David kept his voice down.

"But he is not protected, because he holds no writ, right?"

David looked over at Dorav. The Ashura stared back impassively.

"Ashen, the writ of passage is a tiny thing, kept in a safe, hidden place. If you had a sliver of paper that guaranteed your release from capture, would you surrender it to your captors?"

"No."

"Exactly."

Ashen's face crinkled in confusion. "Then why did you ask him for it?"

"Because he looks young and I meant to trick him. Turns out the ornery bastard has stones and brains."

"How can he be certain we won't kill him?"

"He understands that without proof of whether he carries a writ or not, we need to play a safe hand and turn him over."

"No we don't! No one would know we killed him!" Ashen hissed, pointing at the man. "No one would care! We can string them both up beneath this tree and everyone here would cheer us!"

"They would." David kept his voice level, "but we are not in Kaira anymore. If we do hang them, once we arrive in Nevine, Holy Parliament will want answers about what happened out here. Their barristers are not like the militia back home. They will take account of everything, and believe me, they are thorough. When they discover we murdered an Ashura in cold blood, we will hang right beside him."

"Tarrak's cock!" Ashen growled in frustration. "We should have killed them back in Kaira!"

"We are not murderers, Ashen! Believe that these men will know justice and be satisfied."

David understood Ashen's desire to see these men hang for Nianah's death. He did as well, for Leina and the other girls, for Ricker and for Caige. However, he also knew this feeling was born of sightless rage.

Although Dorav meant to burn them all alive, he did not kill Leina, Ricker, or Nianah. The creatures from the vale had. The terrible fate of Kaira sat on their shoulders, not Dorav's.

He wanted as much as Ashen to place that blame in the mouths of these two men and murder it along with them, but such a thing would not set them free of their guilt. This much he knew.

He motioned them closer and lowered his tone. "Speaking of Parliament, we must discuss our story."

"Our story?" Sifran asked.

"The barristers will demand we tell them what happened in Kaira, from the beginning. We three must say the same thing, or they will suspect we hide something."

Both of them gave him blank, confused stares.

"They will find out about the shinn statue."

That made them both raise their brows.

"We keep things simple. When you are asked, by anyone, about what occurred in Kaira, you begin your tale with us drinking at the Pick Rock.

"You do not mention anything before. You don't talk about the valley, the temple, or the creatures we knew were down there. You don't speak about that to anyone, ever.

"If you are asked about the hours before Dorav appeared, it was just another fucking day. We walked down the drift, struck the rocks until sundown, then went for a drink. That is our story."

Ashen and Sifran stared at each other, then back at him. Sifran nodded.

"I need to hear you both say you understand."

"Yes," Ashen said. "We cannot let them know about our shinn."

"Right," Sifran said, "I understand."

"You fucking better, the both of you."

13

Schism

Nihengale hung upside down from a thick branch within a lush, shaded forest. Rairi hung beside him, her black leathery wings wrapped around her small body protectively. Directly above her perched Murciel, his black, citrine-tipped feather wings tucked at his sides. On the forest floor, Buio and Escara padded through the underbrush, stopping before an elaborately decorated doorway of intertwining ivory and horn.

A pink blood mist filled the air beyond the aperture, obscuring his vision. At the foot of the doorway sat a muscular young man with dusty black hair and oak-colored skin — his attention absorbed by a snarling white wolf standing beyond the doorway's threshold. Escara's graceful, lupine dreamshade shared little in common with the thing beyond the doorway.

Deep gashes framed the white wolf's face, as if some deranged predator had gouged its eyes out, and replaced them with swirling, fuchsia orbs. The edges of its paws and mouth were afflicted with sores and its fur was matted and blood-flecked.

Murciel and Rairi opened their wings in concert, remaining still as totems before pushing off the branch in unison and taking flight. They disappeared above the canopy.

The white wolf's occluded orbs stared up at Nihengale — its predatory gaze and manic smile chilling his blood. The spiraling mists beyond the door formed shapes so twisted and cruel, Nihengale could not bare to witness them.

The young anthrop's head turned away from the portal, his eyes blazing like emerald stars. Recognition overcame Nihengale, as if

161

meeting an unfathomably powerful ancestor through the spirit veil.

Nihengale recognized the ornate white horn, hanging from a leather cord around the man's neck, but could not recall from where.

The intensity of their two feral gazes made him feel infinitely small — an awestruck, winged rodent before the fury of twin suns spiraling towards him. Their radiance scorched his tiny body's fur, melted his flesh and leather wings, leaving behind only bone and bubbling gristle. The woods became consumed in flames and ash, while his tiny bones clung to the smoldering branch.

Buio sprinted for the door, his sleek black muscles pumping as he leaped, sharpened claws extending from the tips of his paws. The white wolf released a sharp bark and the flames consumed Buio's dreamshade mid-flight, leaving behind a smoldering feline husk that collapsed to the earth.

From the remains of the burning trees around him, erupted the black monstrosities that had attacked Kaira. They crawled down the scorched trees towards the anthrop, rattling their abdomens and repeating a single word.

Negkrat! Negkrat! Negkrat!

Something unseen behind the doorway shrieked with concussive fury, causing the blackened forest to shatter into kindling and forming hairline fractures across the surface of Nihengale's mind.

When he woke from the nightmare, he nearly fell off the branch he lay on. He braced himself and looked around, terrified. His breaths came in short gasps and his heart sprinted like a mare.

The sun had escaped to the east, leaving the arid land to cool in its wake. A moment later, he recovered his bearings enough to remember where he was.

The others woke, groaning — their breath agitated. Escara let out a yelp of fear and frantically gripped the branch she lay on.

"Escara?" he asked.

"I nearly fell! Buio, could you please carry me down from this trolking tree?"

Buio moved lithely, being careful to not injure her further.

"Nirin watches us tonight," Nihengale said. "We need to be in open moonlight."

Buio nodded and climbed down the sandwillow, Escara's bare

limbs tied around him.

Nihengale leaned back and caught his breath. Unlike most dreams, this one did not appear intent on fading. The details, colors and impressions — the wolf, anthrop, and black monstrosities remained vivid in his mind.

"Negkrat," he muttered, the word tasting bitter in his mouth. "Negkrat."

Buio crouched on a high branch while the others lay naked in the open grass beneath the sandwillow. High above them, Nirin's half-light shown down on their skin.

The Noctural Elders called Nirin the Twin Moon. The Arisi called her Still Moon. Half her face was light and half dark. Nirin took no sides and accepted no prayers. She was the balance. A reminder that the xial must at times fend for themselves and not seek the heavens for assistance.

The others grunted and moaned as their cuts and gashes sewed themselves closed with a hiss as if burned. Buio had given them all a bit of dried calcama fruit to numb the pain, but the moon's ministrations could be cruel if the wounds were deep. Escara bit back a yelp and dug her fingers into the earth as her ribs crawled back into place and seared themselves together.

Buio kept watch as his pack healed. That creature had nearly killed them all. He had never faced such a thing before, and held no yearning to do so again. He kept a lookout for them along the foothills, but also hoped to spot Rairi.

When he brought Escara down from the tree, he noticed the thick pillar of black smoke rising over the town of Kaira. Although he wanted to investigate, Nihengale remained adamant about keeping the pack together.

Buio studied them, squirming in the moon's healing pulse. They would be helpless without him if attacked. He loathed not being able to search for his friend, but he was needed here. Rairi had survived her share of dangerous situations before, but this was different from anything they had ever faced.

Buio took a deep breath, put his ceramic whistle to his lips and cupped his hands around it, imitating the mating call of the male, crested mivyari.

All mepsiens were required to learn these calls, to communicate over the vast forests of Helicartia. This particular call was used to summon others to a meeting point. Hours of this with no response from Rairi made him increasingly anxious.

A female mivyari answered his call, promising to meet. Buio stood on his branch and surveyed the foothills, unable to locate its source. He changed his call, asking if there was danger near her tree.

Her calls returned. "Safe. Coming. Safe?"

He responded with, "Safe".

"Do you see her, Buio?!" Nihengale inquired from below.

"Not yet."

"Keep up the call. Mask it in case someone's listening."

Buio raised the whistle to his lips and repeated the mating call, doing his best to vary the sound while still sounding like a sexually frustrated mivyari. Every couple of minutes Rairi replied from somewhere closer, also masking her call. Finally, he spotted Rairi's silhouette in the moonlight cresting a nearby hill, followed closely by someone.

He put the whistle to his lips. "Danger?"

"Safe," came the twittering call.

Buio climbed down from the tree. "I will meet them half-way. She is with someone."

"Good." Nihengale's face was tense and covered in sweat. "Likely the anthrop girl, but keep whoever it is away until we know our situation."

Buio nodded and handed Nihengale the bird whistle. He sprinted, closing as much space as he safely could, then he crouched behind the trunk of a fallen sandwillow and waited.

Nihengale kept up the call, with Rairi replying every few minutes. When they crested the nearby hill, he saw the anthrop girl with Rairi. He patiently observed their movements as they shuffled downhill. The girl held no weapons, both their postures appeared relaxed, if tired, and their scattered conversation held an amicable tone, but he knew not to make assumptions.

He waited until they passed his fallen trunk and stalked them. Within moments, he crouched behind the girl, neither of them the wiser. He drew his moonblade, pinned the anthrop's right arm behind her back and put the blade to her throat, against her jugular.

"Giagh!" Marca cried out, startled.

Rairi whirled, moonblade in hand, her eyes wide and her posture low and tense.

"Elinel's tits, Buio!" Rairi screamed in xiasi, holding her chest. "You scared the spirit out of me."

After a moment of catching her breath, she said, "Let her go. She is with me by my wish and means us no harm."

Buio released her. Marca turned and looked up at him, her eyes darting fearfully.

He sheathed his moonblade.

"The others? Are they all right?"

He nodded. "She stays," he said in xiasi.

"Right...all right. Marca," she switched to calisthian, "you must remain here."

"What? No..."

"Only for a bit," Rairi assured her. "I will come back and fetch you, all right?"

Marca nodded meekly. "Please do not be long."

"I will try."

Buio motioned with his head and started back towards the others.

"Stay hidden and quiet." Rairi motioned to the fallen tree where Buio had crouched. "I will be right back for you."

Marca stayed at the bottom of the hill, glancing around like a sheep who lost her flock.

Nihengale, Murciel, and Escara were drenched in sweat, their skins clammy and feverish. The moon-healing was taking its toll on them. Thin wisps of steam rose from their sizzling wounds and a scent of ozone permeated the air.

Buio had applied a poultice and leaf wrappings to assist in their recovery but Rairi could tell some of the injuries were grave — mainly one on Murciel's stomach and another on Escara's side. Their irezu skrit was working at capacity.

"What happened to you, Nihengale?" she asked.

"One of those things hunted us down. We managed to slay it, if barely. Rairi, I am sorry. The decision to leave was mine. Our situation there-"

"Do not be," Rairi said calmly. "You protected the pack. I am grateful you trusted me to take care of myself, and that I was not eaten by one of those things."

"Tell us what happened."

"Let me see to your wounds first." She inspected each of them in turn, scanning every abrasion for signs of infection.

"You did well dressing these wounds, Buio. Apologies that I was not here to do my duty. Murciel, what caused this?" She touched the corners of his wound. There are signs of scorching."

"I was stung."

"By one of those things?"

He nodded.

The puncture wound was troubling. She could only surmise the venom itself had cauterized the wound somewhat.

"Does it hurt?" She pressed lightly against the skin nearby.

Murciel's eye twitched. "A bit, but I believe the moon-healing is the bigger culprit."

"You must speak out if you notice any change in its color or if the edges become overly delicate to the touch, understood."

He nodded.

Escara seemed distracted, her head turned away and her nose sniffing the wind. Rairi checked the wound on her side and was relieved to see the puncture wound was shallow, her ribs taking the brunt of the impact.

She gave Escara a vial and a length of silk. "Wrap the wound in this and apply a measure of this elixir to where they make contact. Wash the silk regularly."

Escara took the items with a nod and gingerly wrapped the silk around her torso. She placed a single measure of elixir on the silk where it touched the wound and looked up with her brows raised.

"Perfect. Are you well? You seem far away."

"It is nothing."

"All right."

Rairi dipped her fingers in a squat cedar jar of balm and retrieved a translucent glob. Escara raked it away with her own digit, sniffed at it, and applied it to the skrit lining her body.

Rairi gave each of them an equal portion until she stood back before Nihengale.

"Now, tell us," he said.

She nodded. "I accompanied Marca to the mines, like in every town. I thought it would be another short, fruitless expedition, but her springfinder pointed into one of the claims.

"She broke the lock to the entrance, and I suppose the noise woke those things...or attracted them to us. The sounds they made were so terrible, unlike anything of this world."

"We know," Escara growled.

"I thought if we ran into town, we would surely be caught along the way, so we hid inside another open mine. A dangerous gamble now that I take inventory. Those things could have come from every cave in that mountain."

"You chose correctly, Rairi," Nihengale said. "What happened then?"

"We remained hidden. The sun approached and I knew you were near Fort Kai. I had no way of reaching you."

"Or we you," Murciel interjected.

"Marca proved surprisingly valiant. She stepped out of the claim, hid under a mining cart, and spied what I could not."

"What did she see?" Nihengale asked.

"The creatures razed the town. Dorav's men, the town militia, everyone either ran or fought for their lives. Kaira lays decimated."

"The smoke coming over the hills?" Murciel asked.

"The town burned down. We took this long to escape waiting for the flames to ease."

"What started it?" Nihengale asked.

"I do not know."

"Were there survivors?"

"Marca could not identify them, but yes. Also, the wagons and horses we arrived in are now gone."

Nihengale turned his head but she could see the frustration in him painted clearly.

"How late was it, when Marca returned to you?"

"Cal-Siege sat on his throne."

"Midday?! Rairi, why did you not send the girl back out to

investigate?"

"Nihengale...she was terrified, and those creatures were still about. The fact that she went out there at all...she is not a mepsien."

Nihengale took a moment to regain his composure. "I beg Sari's forgiveness, Rairi. You did the best you could. Did you see Dorav's body before leaving town?"

She shook her head.

"So he may still be alive." Nihengale leaned back and stared up at Nirin, his face troubled. "Do you know which way the wagons went?"

"I noted fresh tracks heading north."

"Cursed luck. That means if Dorav is alive he is a captive, otherwise the caravan would head back to Sharn. We must give chase."

"He may well lie dead somewhere in that smoldering town, Nihengale," Murciel said. "Must we do this?"

"If even a possibility exists of his being captured, yes we must."

Buio remained silently resigned. Escara however still seemed far away, staring off with her nose in the air.

"I will need to go fetch Marca," Rairi said.

"No," Nihengale stated. "She is not our concern. She would only be in the way."

"Am I to leave her alone out here?"

"Yes. Go if you must. Tell her she must make her own way now, and say your goodbyes."

Rairi stood rigid, her fists clenched at her sides. "I cannot do that."

Nihengale groaned and stood to his full height, steam still rising from his skin. Their leader was evenhanded and at times, unassuming, but he was a dangerous man to cross. The others turned their gazes to them, wary and silent.

"Are you choosing to disobey me, Rairi?" His voice was flint and ice.

"No, Nihengale, but your order contradicts one given to me by Lady Dal'dira."

"Your mission, was to load a particular crate on to the *Kajak*. You reported that mission successful."

"I did." She kept her eyes locked on his. "Lady Dal'dira gave me one other mission, soon before we left."

"Rairi, do you speak truthfully, before the faces?"

"I do, Nihengale — before Nirin, my pack, and my Alpha."

Nihengale sighed and slumped back down on the grass.

"To keep this girl safe, I wager?"

"Yes."

Nihengale closed his eyes and steadied himself. "Buio, do you know these lands?"

"Not this far south, no," Buio replied.

"Can you guess where these anthrops might be headed?"

"There are a few villages out here they might head towards. No way to be certain."

"Rairi," Nihengale said, "you understand the path we walk next will be very dangerous. We cannot afford to nursemaid this girl. She cannot come with us."

"I understand."

"Nihengale, what are you saying?" Murciel asked.

"We cannot take Marca with us and Rairi cannot leave her behind. They must both return to Sharn."

"You place her before Alciren!"

"We live in Alciren's shadow, Murciel."

"Then allow me to travel with her."

Nihengale glanced at each in turn, appearing to consider their options. "Fine. Retrieve your things."

Murciel closed his eyes and the wisps of steam stopped rising from his wounds. He rose to his feet and stretched gingerly, flinching when he reached full extension.

"Still a little sore but I should be fine." He went to retrieve his kit.

While Murciel dressed, Rairi knelt and handed Nihengale a vial of Moonlight Pearl. "You will need this after the healing is done, and here are some supplies in case you are injured again."

"Are you certain?"

"I have what I need to make more."

"My thanks, Rairi." Nihengale swirled the pale white liquid in its vial.

"Remember, one sip each. No more." She placed her forehead against his. "Moon's blessing, Alpha."

"Moon's blessing," he repeated. "Please be careful."

Buio reached behind his armored gauntlet, and retrieved a long string of small black beads with a red feather attached to each end.

He offered it to her.

"Buio, no. I made that for you."

"You did, and I want it back." Buio hunched down so their foreheads could meet.

"Moon's blessing," they said in unison. He placed the beads in her hand and closed her fingers around them.

"You will get this back," she said.

He nodded.

Next she knelt beside Escara and they embraced.

"Keep your knife sharp," Escara told her, "and your eyes sharper still. You like this girl, but remember, anthrops cannot be fully trusted."

"I understand."

They placed their foreheads together.

"Moon's Blessing," they said.

Murciel returned, tightening the straps on his armor, his pack and bow slung over his shoulder.

"Murciel," Nihengale called. "When you reach Sharn, find Ser Isa, inform her what happened here, and seek passage back to Vinergale.

"Both of you, remain useful but do not allow the anthrops to place you in unnecessary danger. See them return you to the same place where we boarded. If they refuse, steal one of their skiffs and escape the *Kajak*. Do not let them take you back to Palidor and do not let them separate you."

"Understood," Murciel said.

"You must also make certain Rairi completes her mission, so keep Marca safe as well. As your Alpha I burden you with these tasks before the faces and before your pack. Do you take heed?"

Murciel stared at Nihengale as the weight of his words took seat. "I do."

"Do you accept?"

"I do."

Nihengale retrieved a fang from his pouch and gave it to Murciel. "Elinel's light keep you both," he said. "Return home safely, and tell our story if we cannot."

Escara watched Murciel and Rairi depart from the corner of eye.

Facing northeast, her nose in the air, she sniffed the wonderful scent that had persisted through the night. She sensed it past the scents of burning dactwood, fur, and flesh coming from Kaira.

She knew this to be a meaningful event — that she should consult her alpha, but she could not find words to explain it. How could she possibly make him understand this?

He smells like home.

"Escara," Nihengale said. "What is it? You are unusually distracted."

She took a long inhalation through her nose, the scent of the mysterious musk intensifying. It was intoxicating.

"We D'sabres can track by scent for about two miles."

"Yes, this I know," Nihengale said.

"I had the strangest dream. You were both in it — Rairi and Murciel as well. None of us appeared as we are now. We were animals." A smile crossed her lips.

"Nightglass, just like the Elders speak of. In my dream, this young anthrop, someone from that town, I am certain, sat-"

"Before a portal of ivory and bone," Nihengale said. "Staring at a white wolf with glowing pink eyes."

"Nihengale?" she turned to look at him.

He stared back, his jade eyes reflecting Nirin's light. The hairs on the back of her neck stood on end.

"A wolf with a scarred face and sores around its mouth and paws," Buio said.

"We shared the dreamsilk?" she asked. "But how? Was there a fire in your dreams?"

They both nodded.

"I pounced the wolf..." Buio said.

"But it killed you before you could reach it," Nihengale said.

Buio nodded stiffly.

"Those two flew away before it happened," Nihengale said, motioning towards where Rairi and Murciel had gone.

"You saw that too? How is this possible? Do you think they had the same dream?"

Nihengale seemed to consider his words carefully, looking between them. "Did either of you see a horn tied around the anthrop's neck?"

"Yes!" Escara said. "White and intricately carved. I remember it well."

Buio nodded.

"I have seen that horn before," Nihengale said, "painted on a scroll."

"The Horn of Dawn," Buio stated.

Nihengale looked at the taller D'kirn, surprise etched on his features. "Yes."

"Ariel's Horn?" Escara asked. "No. Are you saying Neteri's namida are real?"

Buio and Nihengale stared at each other, as if caught off-guard by the knowledge the other held.

"They are," Buio said flatly.

Nihengale's face darkened. "How do you know?"

"I have seen one before."

She could tell they were about to argue. Nihengale did not like Buio's answer.

"How did we all silkweave without an Elder's guidance?" she asked. "Does it have something to do with the namida?"

"What were you saying before, Escara?" Nihengale turned to her. "You meant to tell us why you appeared so distracted."

She took a second to gather her thoughts. "In my...our dream, I could smell the anthrop. He did not smell like any of his kind. There was an earthiness to him, like a field after rain, or like jasmine bloom and den musk — like menstrual blood, oak shavings, and bowel sickness, all mixed together."

The look on their faces made her laugh.

"It sounds strange but it is not unpleasant. Quite the opposite."

They gave each other worrying glances, the moment of tension between them forgotten.

"The point is!" she said sharply. "I can still smell him."

"He is near?" Excitement entered Nihengale's voice.

"No, and that is the most confounding part. If I had to guess, he is at least a day's walk northeast. There is no explanation I can give as to how I have his scent, but I do, though it grows thinner by the hour."

"Ariel," Nihengale spoke more to Buio than to her. "The lion that guards the World Tree. He is why we shared the dreamsilk. His horn must be calling to us."

Buio gave a pensive nod.

172

The implication that Neteri's Tears were real was terrifying. As a cub, Escara had been raised on stories surrounding the namida. Her father told her the tales of World Forger, the Seastar Gem, and Ramiel's Storm Drum.

Her favorite story as a cub was *The Fall of House Greyflame* — but now? The thought of the Decanter of Shadows actually existing made her nauseated. She wondered if the other tales her father told were real as well.

"Nihengale," Buio crouched next to him. "We must go after the horn."

Nihengale sighed and again stared up to Nirin's impassive duality.

She sensed his conflict. His mind burned oil looking for a solution to some internal dilemma. Fear did not normally creep up on Nihengale, but she caught a whiff of it now. Whatever arrested his mind was scaring him. Escara followed his gaze up to the Twin Moon, both light and dark — both friend and foe. He would find no answer there.

"Yes," he said at last. "You are right, Buio. Best if you both leave as soon as you are able."

"What do you mean by that?" Escara asked.

"I will not be traveling with you."

"Nihengale, what are you doing?"

"This is the only way, Escara. Just as Lady Dal'dira entrusted Rairi with Marca, she requested I see personally to Dorav. He might still be alive and I need to be certain if he is or not. I cannot walk away from this, but if that anthrop you smell carries the Horn of Dawn, then we must recover it. The two of you need to give chase."

Escara sighed. The Elders heeded against splitting a pack during a mission. This was no easy decision for Nihengale to make, but what choice was there?

"Parting under a Twin Moon is ill-fated, Nihengale," she said, "and now we schism twice."

"Escara," Buio said.

She looked up at Buio's hard, piercing blue eyes and wondered how much he had seen, and gone through, to give him such a menacing gaze. He was different from everyone else, even other D'kirns. She found him both frightening and oddly exciting.

"Get dressed," Buio said. "We need to move."
"All right."

14

The Elder Birch

Caige woke with a start — his breaths sharp, labored gasps.

"Shh, you are safe." Tynisia lay on his lap, reaching up to stroke his stubble. "You were only dreaming."

Caige lifted her small frame and buried his head in her black curls, sobbing miserably. He held her, anchoring himself with her presence as if she were a jutting rock in a raging river — keeping him from being swept away to drown.

Although his entire body trembled, he could not remember the vicious nightmare he just awoke from. He vaguely recalled there being terrible pain, a hot flash of blinding pink light, and a naked dread that rode him into his waking state.

"Shh, it is all right," Tynisia wrapped her arms around him and stroked the knotted muscles of his back. "You are safe. It was only a dream. Push it from your mind, my Cairn. Push it far away, and forget."

"Gods, Tyn," Caige said, slowly calming. "I've felt so lifeless these last years without you, and now I cannot keep myself from weeping. I must seem like such a woman."

Tynisia ran her fingers through his hair. "Do not fret so, Cairn. You can be soft in my arms."

"I missed you calling me that," he said.

"And I missed your hands on my skin," she said.

Caige smiled and kissed her, tasting her warm tongue. He held her close, cupping her breast and savoring the soft moan she released into his mouth.

Tynisia reached under his breeches and took him firmly in her hand, stroking him to hardness with her warm, soft fingers. He lifted her by the waist and placed her above himself, a moan escaping him as she guided him into her softness.

The impact of being inside her after so long sent a spark of pleasure up his spine. Her slow, grinding motions making his breath and thundering heart catch in his throat.

He grabbed her roughly by the ass, feeling the biting grief and desperation of knowing he would not last long, losing himself to the pleasure of her soft lips and grinding hips.

He growled, nibbling her nipple through her blouse. Tyn's hands gripped the back of his neck as her momentum increased. She panted and moaned in his ear, sending him unceremoniously past the point of no return.

"Tyn! Fuck! Tyyyn!!!" His body became its own instrument, thrusting violently into her as his hands gripped her, hard enough to bruise.

Her sex tightened around him, her legs wrapping around his waist and her nails digging into his back. She bit down on his shoulder, crying out in ecstasy.

They held one another, their bodies spasming, and then there was peace — like a thick blanket draping itself over them.

The cold tears of an overcast sky gave Caige a sudden chill, waking him. Tynisia slept with her head resting on his shoulder. He remained insider her, soft and spent.

For the first time, he took note of their surroundings. They sat under the branches of an elder birch which stood at the summit of a sloping hill — the tree's canopy shielding them from the light rain.

Around the elder birch leaned ancient, broken pillars, and the faded foundations of stone walls, which jutted from the undergrowth in a kind of grid.

Tynisia stirred and opened her eyes, stretching out contently like a cat awakening from a nap.

"Where are we, Tyn?" He kissed the base of her neck and stroked her dark hair.

"On our way." She gave him a sleepy smile.

"Something stood here before."

Tynisia turned to regard the stones. "There are many places like this in the wilds. Ancient stories forgotten by this world." She turned and sat with her back against his chest. "I wish it had rained like this in Kaira."

Caige tucked his manhood back into his breeches. He planted a small kiss on the crown of her head and wrapped his arms around her.

"Tyn, this all feels very strange."

"Why strange?" She stroked the hairs on his forearm.

Caige savored the peculiarity of the landscape. The rolling clouds in the overcast sky seemed to match his breathing — the dark nimbus thinning and thickening with his every breath. The leaves of the elder birch were lambent, and the raindrops on them glinted, luminescent and mesmerizing.

He believed if he stopped and let himself go, he could become lost to the beauty of this place, melting into the elder birch, and becoming one with its trunk. He could sit here and observe the world as it went by, forever.

"I feel as if I am somewhere between asleep and awake. Is that an odd thing to say?"

"No." She kissed the back of his hand.

"I cannot lose you again, Tyn."

She turned her head up to look at him. "I will not leave you, my Cairn."

He kissed her soft lips. She was just as he remembered her, beautiful and small, with dark wavy hair and soft, almond-colored skin.

Her yellow blouse and long orange skirt with its flower pattern hem was his favorite dress of hers. The only thing different were her eyes, which held the oddest shade of rosy pink.

Something struck him on the head, drawing blood. A chunk of ice lay by his knee. Hailstones began falling around them, splashing in the mud and clunking off the branches.

"What is this?" Caige shielded himself with his arms.

"Ah, ow!" Tynisia complained as a piece of hail struck her leg.

Caige placed Tyn against the tree and crouched over her, protecting her with his body.

"Cairn..."

"Do not worry." He smiled past the sting of a shard of ice hitting him in the back. "This is nothing. Pull your knees up."

"Caige!" The sudden shout startled him.

His father lay in a puddle of muck and blood just beyond the shelter of the elder birch branches. Corren reached out to him, the hail pelting down on his head and body.

"Corren? Father!"

"Caige, I am sorry! I am sorry! Please help me!" His father reached out, blood running down his face.

"Cairn, no!" Tynisia grabbed his arm. "That is not your father!"

"What?"

"Look! Look closer!" She pointed.

Corren's mouth was filled with sharp, yellowed fangs. His entire face appeared feral and his eyes were green lambent orbs.

"Do you see? He tries to trick you! We must go, Cairn. We must go now!"

Corren pulled himself towards them, struggling through the pelting hail and dragging his left leg as if injured.

"Caige!" his father roared in a voice not his own. "Help me!"

A violent shudder of fear ran through Caige's center, threatening to tear him in two.

Tynisia tugged hard on his arm, and they ran away through the hail.

"Caige!" The creature called out in a horrible, echoing mutation of his father's voice — more animal than man. "Caaaiige!"

15

On Disparate Roads

"Mmm, this tastes like Haran black brew, but spicier, earthier." Marca sipped at her sivin tea.

The sun was close to rising, so they decided to make camp in the sacked town of Portan. They chose a cozy little hovel with a hearthstone fire-pit.

The tables and chairs in the hovel were strewn about, chests emptied, and shelves stripped bare by Dorav's men. Even the beds were a shredded mess of straw and torn linen, but the door still hung from its hinges.

Outside, the night sky was deep azure with a few rogue clouds sweeping west from Enelysion. Murciel had gone out to sweep the perimeter.

"You could have asked for a taste before," Rairi told her.

"I could not! Buio and Escara intimidate me. I feared they would forbid it."

"And Murciel?"

Marca's face blushed. "He is not quite so imposing."

"Marca! Do you find Murciel attractive?"

"Perhaps a little." Marca hid behind her teacup.

Rairi shook her head. These anthrops maintained no boundaries when it came to race or species. Their libido was completely unchained. "I thought as much."

"You did?"

"I noticed you sneaking glances at him on our journey."

"His face is interesting, is all. Oh God Rairi, you must not tell him!"

"Of course not." Rairi gave her a mischievous smirk. "I prefer to extort you."

"You monster!"

"In truth, he likely knows, Marca. Little escapes his eyes."

Marca sighed and tugged absently at her hair. "You told me that before. That D'aerths have the keenest eyes of the clans."

"Yes, although even for a D'aerth, Murciel's eyesight is unmatched. I once witnessed him snipe a rider at full gallop from four-hundred yards."

"Impossible!"

"For an anthrop perhaps, but not Murciel." Rairi sipped her tea.

"We are called humans, Rairi."

Rairi scoffed. Anthrops denying their own origins was infuriating. Every high race knew them as the Children of Anthros, the anthropaki — born from the rage and madness of the Old World.

Anthrops insisted on their heritage placing them above all other peoples — claiming divine greatness and inherent sovereignty.

Misguided pests.

Marca sighed. "What special things can your clan do?"

"Simply because I agreed to discuss the clans does not make you my interrogator." Rairi narrowed her eyes at her. "I've told you more than I should already."

"Oh please, Rairi. They do not teach us about mepsiens in Palidor. We are told you are all dangerous, psychotic killers who worship daemons and practice vorxcraft. I wish to learn the truth."

Rairi sighed and sipped at her tea. "Every anthrop settlement owns enslaved xial. How do you-"

"Humans."

"If you wish me to speak do not interrupt me!" Rairi glared at her. "Sorry."

"How do you not know these things?"

"Because city sp...xial are so meek. They are nothing like you, Murciel, or the others.

"They run errands, do physical labor, and serve their masters however they are told. I never knew D'aerths can see for miles."

"Roughly a mile."

"Well, what about you?"

"Hmm, well as you now know, we D'tiri use ketter to navigate in darkness. Our claws also let us climb better than other mepsiens."

Rairi thumbed the thin claws on her right hand. "They are small compared to a D'kirn's, but we can dig them into almost anything. They grow from this first knuckle." She pointed to it. "And are reinforced by the bone structure of the second when locked in position, like so."

She pulled her fingers back as far as they would go to form a claw, showing her how the bones of her fingers aligned to facilitate climbing.

"Amazing!" Marca stared at her with childish wonderment.

"Our feet have claws too." Rairi took off her right sandal and showed her the bottom of her pale foot.

"I don't see them."

"They only extract when our toes at are at an angle while climbing. Observe." Rairi pulled her toes back as far as they would go and four black claws poked out of their slits, beneath where her toes met the sole.

"We call these our rakes."

"Oh my God!" Marca put a hand to her mouth.

"While we were slaves, the anthrops taught our clan to kill their enemies quietly and without leaving trace."

Rairi replaced her sandal. "We became assassins, bred and trained to kill in darkness. After our escape to Helicartia, we named the art Alci'tirnni, meaning 'Alciren's Shadow'.

"We continue its use for our own means now. Until recently, only we D'tiri could learn the shadow arts."

"What changed?"

"Elders Netapa and Ekido both passed. They were strict in keeping to the old ways, and opposed any measure of change within the clans.

"The Elders who replaced them believe our clans need to unite and learn from each other. They say division will forever keep us incapable of evolution. Because of them, I was able to enter the Sar'divri and become an alchemist."

"Which of your clans are usually alchemists then?"

Rairi wondered if she should answer truthfully or formulate a lie. She could be making a grave error, divulging so much to this girl.

They can never be fully trusted.

"All right, enough of this."

"No, but-"

"I said enough!"

Marca's face pinched in exasperation, but she held her tongue. They both sipped their tea.

"Will Nihengale and the others make it back safely?" Marca inquired.

"I do not know. They are on a very dangerous mission. I hope to see them again, but it may not be for some time."

Marca's gaze turned towards the small hearth-fire. "You and I should not have gone this far. We were meant to remain with the shinn."

"We were, but I am glad we came. Do not fret. How much shinn did you manage to gather?"

"The Magalian counters hid the true shinn counts from their ledgers in every town, effectively robbing their own people. I hold enough to perform my experiments and perfect my formulas, as I hoped."

Marca patted her travel sack, which was now considerably bulkier than when they began their journey.

"You are wrapping that shinn in kafra skin, yes?" Rairi asked.

"Of course. The academy teaches us to store shinn in quartz or copper. I never knew kafra leather was a viable substitute. I was skeptical at first but the hide is surprisingly effective."

"It is."

Marca swirled the remaining tea in her cup, steeling herself to ask a question. Rairi knew the look well.

"Speak your mind, Marca."

"I only wondered if I could one day have markings like you."

Rairi ran a finger across the thin tattoo on her cheek. "I fear that is impossible."

"Because I am human?"

"No, because you were not bathed in Arisia's spring."

Marca gave her a queer look.

"As you know, even purified shinn can be dangerous. If directly etched into the skin, the toxins can prove fatal.

"When we are but cubs we are placed through a ritual that binds us to Arisia's light. This allows us to be marked with irezu skrit, carry weapons infused with alchemical runes, and wear skerki leathers with protective glyphs sewed into their folds."

"I never heard of such practices with shinn."

"The xial retained knowledge your people destroyed during your Neterian Purge."

"Neteri was a blight, Rairi! An archdaemon of the Vorx!"

"She was a goddess and a teacher of secrets, you goat-hoof! Anthrops perverted her gifts and blamed her for their own transgressions. Now are we quite done, interrogator?"

"Yes, if you wish."

In a swift movement, Rairi unsheathed her moonblade and put its cold tip under Marca's chin.

"You will remember your promise to me, Marca, because I will remember mine. If you repeat these secrets to anyone, I will have your tongue."

"No, of course not." Marca tried to edge her chin back but Rairi kept the blade trained on her.

"I am honored you would trust me enough to speak frankly." Marca smiled timidly. "Your people have always been such a wonderful mystery."

Rairi flicked the blade up, nicking her.

"Ow," Marca sucked in breath but did not move away. A single drop of blood ran down the blade's black edge.

"So you remember your oath to me." Rairi pulled the blade away and returned it to its sheath.

"I will." Marca ran her thumb over the wound and sucked off the blood.

"You are such a peculiar...human." Rairi grinned.

Marca's smile filled her entire face.

Murciel entered the hut, shouldered his bow, and sat. "The night is quiet, but Siege rises soon," he said in xiasi. "We must rest."

Rairi translated for Marca, who made a valiant effort not to stare at Murciel.

"Do not worry," Marca said. "I will be awake for most of the day."

"Remember if you sense danger..."

"Call out, I know." Marca stood and made her way outside.

Shortly after leaving Kaira, the caravan entered the barren razorgrass hills of southern Tepley. At first, Dorav thought the hills of swaying yellow grass to be rather innocuous. Then two of the procession's horses had eaten the grass and become ill. They began shitting blood, foaming through their coats, and became so weakened, they could no longer pull their wagons. The young man called Benny and his friends cut the animals' throats, butchered them with axes, and salted their meat for the road.

As the men hacked at the horses, Dorav realized they were the same two stallions he and Kartecus had ridden into battle at Sharn. He observed the hot blood as it sprayed up the men's arms and across the tall grass, feeling like someone walked over his grave. Kartecus did not appear to recognize the dire omen. He watched the slaughter with resigned impassivity, his mustache twitching over his thin lip. A ludicrous fate, for two such young, able steeds to be undone by a few blades of grass — a stark reminder of how fickle life could be.

They had left the rolling hills of deadly grass behind after midday and now strode through a field of wild wheat.

"We must be near Borm," David said with a slur in his voice. He sat in his usual place with his back turned to the driver, his crossbow trained on Dorav's chest.

"David!" Ashen called back. "We have company!"

"Sifran, trade places with me," David said, not taking his eyes off them until Sifran sat in his spot, crossbow in hand. "Remember, if they try anything, aim for the gut."

"I know," Sifran replied and pointed the bolt at Dorav's stomach.

Dorav stared into the scrawny blonde's lusterless eyes and could still not read anything about the man. His expression was like a masquerade mask before being painted. Every night the men of the caravan would come together to drink bullhorn and palm wine — all except for Sifran. The man participated in the smoking and fireside banter, but Dorav witnessed him dumping his drinks out when no one else was looking. He hid things, even from those closest to him.

A group of armed men approached the wagon from the front. The caravan came to a full stop and David jumped down to meet them.

Dorav strained to get a better look.

184

"Sit still!" Sifran barked sharply.

Dorav obeyed, losing sight of the men. He could hear David arguing with someone, but could not decipher their words. Teplians had a vulgar way of speaking calisthian, using expressions and abbreviations that reduced the noble tongue to an awful, scratchy drawl.

"Come see for yourself!" David's booming voice reached him clearly. "You will inspect the wagons anyway, right?"

Two Teplian Sickle-Talon soldiers walked within view with David leading. Both men were armed with honed shortspears and battle-worn wooden scutums with a golden falcon's head painted over a red and blue base. At their belts they wore long, curved kopis blades in leather sheathes.

"Names and ranks," a man with a dark blue line painted across his eyes asked them bluntly.

Neither he nor Kartecus spoke.

"I said names and ranks!"

"They refuse to speak, sergeant," David said. "Before we caught them the young one identified himself as an Ashuran Knight and Captain in Vinergale's navy. I brought his armor, cloak, and shield along as proof."

"Show me."

David untied a leather sack in the wagon and showed the Talon sergeant their contents.

"Well, bugger my sheep." The soldier pulled out Dorav's shield.

Dorav could not believe his aegis rode in the same wagon with him this entire time. He eyed the sack, hoping to make out the shape of his wolfbert.

"So this is aegis steel." The sergeant ran his fingers over the sacred diagrams of protection engraved on its face and rapped his knuckles against the metal, nodding in approval.

Next he pulled out Dorav's breastplate with a grunt, turning it around in his hands, and appraising the engraved wolf's head on the cloak pin. "Not nearly as heavy as it looks."

A soldier with a black line across his eyes, barely darker than his skin, walked to the back of the wagon. He scowled when he saw Sifran holding the crossbow.

"They hold a crossbow, Qelwin," the man said.

"Are they pointing it at you, Deurn?"

"No, sir."

"Then shut up!"

Deurn's scowl deepened as he turned to scrutinize the caravan behind them. The survivors of Kaira appeared nervous, huddled together, and muttering among themselves. Dorav caught sight of other Talons, moving through the wheat, surrounding them.

"This is damn fine steel," the sergeant told David. "Wager I could trade this in for three bulls and plows, with enough left over for the brothel."

"Nobody buys Ashuran armor. You have to melt it down or fence it."

"I might know a blackguard or two. These belong to you boys?" Qelwin held the shield up.

Seeing his aegis in foreign hands made Dorav's skin crawl, but he kept quiet. Silence remained his greatest weapon for the time being.

"If this man was an Ashura, he would say so," Qelwin told David. "Loud enough for all to hear."

"He refuses to speak or show his writ. I believe he does not carry one, and is a rogue."

"And how do you know so fucking much about it?"

David sighed. "I was in the war. I faced my share of these bastards in Padive."

"Oh? What legion?"

"Storm-Talons, Third."

"Third legion? You mean the Darkstorm's lot? I heard they got properly fucked in Sentinel."

"Nice try, sergeant. We were under Legate Akata's command, and we got fucked in the Battle of Coiren. Those of us who survived it were disbanded after."

"So where is your kopis?" The sergeant tapped the hilt of his recurved blade. "Never met a war vet who didn't carry his wife on his belt."

"I sold her in Aztan for booze and pussy," David replied gruffly.

The sergeant's eyes narrowed a moment before he let out a hearty laugh. "Well, what about all this?" He pointed at the caravan of onlookers behind them.

"They're all that is left of Kaira."

"So who are you? The sindaco?"

"No! No, our sindaco was killed in the attack — as was our Korgur."

Qelwin came around the wagon and sized them both up. "So this one is the knight. What is this old turd's story?"

"That is his lieutenant, Kartecus."

Qelwin's painted eyes widened hearing the name. "Kartecus? As in Captain of the *Cidraster*? The Cortast Revenant? Hero of the Calimport Pirate War? That Kartecus?"

Kartecus stared hard at the man but remained silent.

"Deurn, get up there and grant me a gander at the old man's neck."

Deurn did as he was told. Kartecus shuffled in place but could do nothing to prevent the soldier from pinning his head back against the wagon.

"It is! Fuck my sister's pigs! Who is this then?" he asked David, pointing at him.

"He said his name was Dorav," David said. "Dorav Minos."

"And those two names mean nothing to you?"

David shook his head, his face darkening.

"All right, this flies over my shield," Qelwin said. "I need you to hand over your weapons. The Tribune is going to want to handle this himself."

David shook his head. "I rather you simply take the prisoners and-"

"Well I rather you suck my cock on the road north! You want to make a wager on who gets what they want?"

Hearing their commander's tone, the soldiers hiding in the wheat made a slow, dramatic appearance around the caravan. The people of Kaira shriveled at the sight of them.

David's face turned as red as his beard. "No."

"Good, hand over your steel and get in the wagon." Qelwin turned to someone out of Dorav's sight. "Bagra! Congratulations, you drew prisoner detail. Pick six men and secure this caravan. I want all their weapons and any contraband they might be carrying."

"Right," Bagra said.

"Golin!"

Another Talon with a black stripe across his eyes appeared at the wagon's side.

"You're in charge until I get back," Qelwin told him. "Finish patrolling the grass and get the men back to Fort Lornen. Tell Gallav I'm escorting a couple of high profile prisoners north to meet Alister. Dorav Minos and Kartecus Andalan. Think you can remember that?"

"Yes sir," Golin replied.

"Do not fuck my dog, Golin."

"Wouldn't dream of it, sir."

David and Ashen were ushered into the back of the wagon with him. Sifran was disarmed.

Qelwin and Deurn sat in the driver's bench while Bagra and his men inspected the wagons behind them. Deurn sat facing the back of the wagon, the crossbow laying on his lap.

"A fine fucking mess this is, eh sergeant?" Deurn asked. "We just rolled a serpent's gaze."

"You would not know the scent of lady luck if she sat on your face, Deurn. These two bastards are Vinergalian war heroes. We rolled a prince's hand out here — you wait and see."

Kartecus had the twitch in his right eye he got when he was nervous — his worst tell while playing cards. Dorav straightened his back and nodded to him reassuringly.

Being recognized was dangerous for both of them. They were sent here without a writ and on Black Wings. Had they been turned over to the korgurate and remained silent, they would be returned to zoniran hands eventually, writ or no. Now they were high profile political prisoners. Not for the first time in his life, Dorav cursed his family name.

David and his friends appeared even more nervous than Kartecus. They gave each other confounded glances but none of them dared speak. The Talon sergeant whipped the horses into motion and the caravan began its languid trek north through the wild wheat fields, caught in the Queen's Talons.

Buio awoke before sunset. After a long evening spent tracking their elusive prey, they found shelter in a shallow, unoccupied cave under a grassy hillock. There were signs the cave was used numerous times before by anthrops.

A circle of flat stones held the remains of accumulated cold campfires and the surfaces within the cavern had been scribbled on with colored stones — mostly misshapen penises and various women with over-sized breasts in a catalog of compromising positions. Buio stepped out and squinted as the sun's last rays disappeared into the western horizon.

As the last glorious shades of orange, rose, and lavender faded from twilight, his gaze found the moon. Nirin's duality was replaced by Elinel, the Harvest Moon.

"Grant us wisdom, sister," he whispered.

"Buio?" Escara rose, rubbing her tired eyes. "Why did you not wake me?"

"Siege only now takes his rest. Elinel rules the sky tonight."

"Which means we are missing the Meridian Festival — again."

Buio nodded. "Do you still have the anthrop's scent?"

Escara inhaled through her nostrils. "He still has some distance on us, but I do."

"Hungry?"

"Ravenous."

"We should eat sparingly."

"Piniri?"

"Yes."

Buio checked their small loaf of black bread for mold while Escara opened a plain wooden jar containing their piniri — a sweet mixture of peanut oil, mirni leaves, and ground ginger.

They ate in silence, each dipping their bread into the jar and savoring the flavor. Buio had never found anything in anthrop lands which tasted quite like piniri. The mirni leaves gave the paste its distinct flavor, which anthrops found unpalatable.

"Buio, I have meant to ask you something."

"Yes?"

"What is it like, being able to see in daylight?" Escara was genuinely curious, and he sensed her timidity in asking. The question however, made him uncomfortable. An inexplicable sense of alienation sneaked up on him.

"It is, simply different," he said dismissively. "The colors are different."

Her face darkened. "Ready to go then?" She placed the jar away before shouldering her bag. He nodded and stood, dusting himself off while observing her through the corner of his eye. She left camp without a word, and he followed.

The thought of chasing down the Horn of Dawn, whose blast would herald the return of Cala-Neteri, disturbed him. The fabled namida were more than divine relics. They were alive.

Buio recalled the time his pack had been unknowingly called upon to chase down one such relic. He was only a cub then, learning the ways of his people.

"It is called The Rakka," Nahkir told them as they left the boundaries of Helicartia. Baiera and Hiou flanked the alpha while Buio held the rear, gazing back at the shadows of his new home.

He had lived there for only a year, but already knew he would always be an outcast. The other cubs treated him like an oddity. Even his own clansmen kept him at arm's reach. Only these three, his pack, made him feel like he belonged.

"Keep up, cub," Hiou called back, "and pay attention."

Buio jogged after them.

"A tribe of anthrops worships the Rakka as an idol of their god," Nahkir explained.

"Anthrops worship all kinds of stupid things," Baiera scoffed, tightening the straps of her skerki. "Why would the Elders care about this particular one?"

"Because the wild tribes believe it to be proof of divinity. They unite around it, forming a single tribe and calling themselves the Rakshasa."

"Like the shape-shifting Ardian deamon," Hiou said.

"Exactly."

"So we are dealing with hundreds of anthrops here?" Baiera asked.

"Possibly thousands," Nahkir replied. "When we find their encampment, we enter at the darkest hour and retrieve the idol. We keep this as bloodless as possible, understand Baiera?"

"I do not initiate bloodshed, Nahkir!" Baiera growled. "I end it."

"We know, but if fighting does break out, kill only as many anthrops as needed. We must escape quickly, or we all die."

"Buio," Nahkir glanced down to him. "You will keep by my side. Close and quiet."

"I will, Alpha."

When they reached their target, the sheer size of the anthrop encampment under Arisia's night gave Buio pause. Twenty different tribes had come together around this idol, like a massive army awaiting battle. A force this size, so near Helicartia's southern border, was an undeniable threat.

The Rakshasa had set up their leather and fur tents deep within the Chenzat forest, surrounding a long, moonlit lake. A clutter of fish traps and catch nets lay along the lake's shores. Grim totems and flags with primitive markings established boundaries among the united tribes. Deer, rabbits, and wild boar hung from tree branches closer to the encampment's center, gutted, skinned, and smoked. Roasted venison, burning oak, and anthrop musk blended in the air around the camp. Baiera's face crinkled in disgust.

The deeper they ventured into the maze of primitive tents, the more anthrops they were forced to evade. Buio was grateful for Nahkir's unforgiving drills on silent movement. While anthrop senses were blunted compared to theirs, carelessness would prove fatal here.

Nahkir and Hiou moved with bows in hand, and Baiera gripped her spear and shield. Buio was told not to draw steel unless a fight began, so his vrin remained sheathed on his back. He tapped its hilt, seeking reassurance in its presence.

At the heart of the encampment stood the anthrop's sacred grove, bordered by eight differently carved wooden totems. Unlike others around the Rakshasa's camp, these did not represent animals, but sharp, symmetrical shapes, carved and sanded by meticulous hands.

Within the grove was a large square hut made of flat wooden beams and covered in layers of animal skins. Two anthrops sat flanking the entrance, speaking their guttural dialect in hushed tones.

They played some kind of game involving a handful of colored stones. Each would throw a stone on the ground, smiling or cursing when the stone rolled to a halt.

Nahkir and Hiou crouched and approached the distracted guards from behind.

Moonblades flashed and throats were slashed under the moonlight sky. Buio recalled the mepsien sing-song.

Nahkir and Hiou held the men's mouths shut until they ceased thrashing and pulled them into the hut. There was a faint scuffle within, then silence.

Hiou appeared at the hut's flap and waved them over. As they made their way, Buio noticed the eight totems were connected by lines of meticulously placed, flat river stones, forming a symbol with the hut at its center.

Remembering it now made his hairs stand on end, but back then it had been only a passing curiosity.

"Nahkir needs you," Hiou whispered. "We will stand watch out here."

Buio entered the hut where Nahkir stood over a chest-high stone obelisk. At the foot of the obelisk lay numerous offerings of beads, bones, flowers, and urns filled with odd oils.

Another two anthrops lay dead on the floor of the hut — likely holy men by the beads and feathers they wore. The flat stone lines connecting the totems outside all met at the obelisk.

"Come here, Buio," Nahkir waved him over. "These anthrops are more cunning than they seem. They locked their idol within this stone and placed the latch behind a hole only a child's hand might reach. Old Ren smiles on us for your presence."

Buio spotted the small hole near the top of the obelisk.

"What do we do here?" Nahkir asked.

"Check for traps."

Nahkir nodded as Buio examined the obelisk.

"Even when the situation seems dire, Buio. Even when your heart is beating furiously and fear rides you like a mare, you must always account for traps. Missing one can lead to calamity."

"There is nothing here," Buio confirmed.

Nahkir nodded approvingly. "You must reach in and upwards to find the lever."

Buio slipped his hand into the cramped orifice and turned his hand upward, finding the rough spoke. Growling with effort, he turned the stubborn contraption until there was a dry click and a thud within — the tip of the obelisk coming away in his hand.

Nahkir reached into the obelisk and retrieved the Rakshasa's sacred idol — a perfectly round metal sphere with engraved lines

192

and tiny, archaic markings covering its surface. When Nahkir raised the sphere, it took on life, segmenting itself into a dozen rings of varying circumference that spun fluidly within and around each other.

As the rings picked up speed, the symbols on their surfaces glowed an eerie silver light, and shapes began forming within their diameters. Perfectly symmetrical squares and triangles danced inside the sphere, forming a three-dimensional representation of the octagonal symbol on the sacred grove's ground. The rings multiplied this image inward, becoming a vortex of cubes within cubes, before transforming into a myriad of interconnected geometric patterns of uniform light.

The object's confounding geometry was so kaleidoscopic and unnatural, Buio became dumbstruck. He stood gawking childishly at the shifting metallic shapes, radiant patterns, and dancing silver lines. The sphere blossomed like a flower, forming an impossibly complex nexus around a single silvery star at its fiery core.

Buio was enraptured, pulled into that trembling, radiant spark which appeared to simultaneously create and destroy the very object containing it.

A strong crackling hum filled the wooden hut. Nahkir's hands, arms and face became a shimmering extension of the idol's geometry. His flesh fragmented into bits of vibrating light and were pulled into the relic's core, only to be replaced as motes of light that seamlessly synchronized with his remaining flesh.

Most captivating of all, was the look on Nahkir's enthralled face. His tearful eyes and bright smile expressed such profound joy and emotional release, it flooded Buio's heart to witness it.

He felt his own tears rush up as a geyser of pain and resentment buried within him found its way through his pores and tore free, becoming fragmented light spirals which danced into that sphere of oscillating brilliance.

A flash of half-remembered images, like forgotten dreams, passed before his mind's eye. He felt the orb speak to him, attempting to communicate in varying tones and vibrations, but he could not understand.

The surface of his young mind cracked like thin ice when he

realized that he too, was being pulled into the white-hot spark, his flesh replaced by motes of vibrating light. He too was being devoured by the object in Nahkir's hands.

As panic struck him, Buio screamed.

Nahkir stood staring at him in befuddlement. A metal sphere lay dormant in his grasp, gray, tarnished, and unremarkable.

"Buio, come see this!" Escara cried back to him from the crest of the next hill, snapping him out of his reverie.

When he reached her, he saw the broken, abandoned ruins of an ancient anthrop city, sprawling out beneath him, nestled between three hills. All that remained of the forgotten city were ruined columns, partial stone walls, and a patchwork of overgrown pathways.

The remains of a massive stone bridge once joining two hilltops high above the city had collapsed and lay shattered at the feet of its own foundations — its towering arches all but decimated. Massive blocks of masonry lay among smaller, habitat shaped squares of smooth, squat stones. Elinel's silvery light gave the place a quiet, haunting air.

"It is beautiful," Escara said. "Can you imagine what it might have once looked like? How old do you suppose it is?"

Buio shook his head.

"Anthrops terrify me sometimes, Buio. How can a single species be so savage and depraved and yet build places like this?"

"I do not know."

Escara's face became somber. "The Elders say these kinds of places are tainted by the rage and regrets of the anthrops who once lived here."

Buio nodded. "Did our quarry go through here?"

"No. He skirted around it."

"Then we should too."

"Are you certain? If we cut through these two hills we could gain half a night on him."

Buio studied the ruins. In the heart of the valley where the three hills met spread a black lake, defying the recent summer droughts. At its center stood a single, dark metal statue, jutting out at an odd angle from the black water.

The statue was of an anthrop, wrapped in flowing cloths and pointing a spear down at its own reflection.

Even from this distance, he could feel the subtle pull of the water, calling for him to approach and submerge himself into those cool, soothing, moonlit waters.

"No," he said. "We go around."

"All right. This way then."

As they made their way around the ancient ruins, Buio's memory returned to that fateful night among the Rakshasa. His terrified cry had given their intrusion away and brought the horde howling down upon them.

Baiera's face was savaged by a tribal woman's iron claws during their escape. The D'sabre's eyes and nose were spared, but the deep scars never faded. Half her face became a perpetual scowl, which earned her the moniker "Grimwright".

Hiou escaped the fray with a broken arm and a number of deep slash wounds, while Buio was left with bruises and a deep gash across his back — a scar he still carried.

His final memory of Nahkir was him laying face down on the grass with three arrows and a spear protruding from his back.

They returned to Helicartia with the idol, but the weight of Nahkir's death made it a bitter victory. Baiera laid the blame of Nahkir's loss on Buio and petitioned the Elders to banish him from Helicartia.

Hiou defended him however, claiming the relic would have never been retrieved at all without Buio, and placing himself before the mercy of the Elders on his behalf.

The idol the anthrops had dubbed Rakka, was actually the head of Rashnu's Scepter, also called Fulcrum — a fabled namida. For the acquisition of such a prize, the Elders allowed Buio to remain.

Buio wished to return to the lake and avenge Nahkir by killing every last Rakshasa, but the giant tribe did not survive the loss of their idol. As the Elders intended, a bloody conflict between them arose soon after and they splintered, the threat of their union decapitated.

Buio could not be certain if what he experienced in the anthrop's hut had been real — only that it was more palpable than anything he had experienced since.

He never forgave himself for Nahkir's death. It haunted him throughout his life, but he knew having been touched by a namida had changed something essential inside him.

Now that another of Neteri's Tears had appeared and made contact, he needed to find it and make some sense of its nature and purpose.

16

The Animura

When Nihengale and his pack had entered the private chambers of Vinergale's Warmaster in Tyoh Keep, she had greeted them with a table of towering finery. They shared azdarian bread, smoked piniri, plump, red, vidan grapes, and fine Camnoc wine. They ate, drank, and spoke of pleasant things over the course of the meal.

The Lady Dal'dira was dressed in flowing black nidvi silks and walked around her chambers barefoot, as was D'crin custom. Her straight ink-black hair was tied neatly behind her head, revealing her lustrous sunset eyes, sharp as knives.

She wore no baubles or gaudy powders. Her uncompromising confidence and genuine expressions granted her a haunting beauty no amount of colored dusts or greases could ever imitate.

While they ate, she asked about Helicartia and how the xial cities fared. She was saddened to hear Seer Netapa succumbed to his weakened flesh after many fine years of life, but was gladdened to hear he died with dignity and the love of his people.

Escara told her about this year's Blue Moon Kotilyen, and how she had almost tripped near the end of the dangerous knife dance — a move which would have cost her a hand if she did not recover quickly enough.

After the meal they walked into her study where she treated them to snowberry port and Bullywall sugar figs before bringing out an armful of maps and charts.

"I realize, what I ask of you seems ludicrous, but I have every confidence you will succeed," Dal'dira said as Nihengale and Buio studied the mass of maps and charts she laid out for them.

"Two outposts," Buio said, looking them over on the wide strategy table. "And a fortress carved into the mountainside. This anthrop Captain has only his one ship's crew to sack all this?"

"Yes," she said.

"This is a suicide mission," Nihengale said, looking up at her.

"Yes," Dal'dira said. "Without you, it is."

He turned his attention back to the tactical scrolls. "These two outposts should be no trouble. The fortress itself however will take a dozen infiltrators working as one."

"The five of you are as many as I can send without arousing the Host's suspicion. I am not supposed to know what Lord Metzial is plotting for Dorav and his crew."

"The five of us are not enough," Nihengale stated.

"Dorav has command of a full contingent of seaguards who can be equipped for a mission involving silent killing."

"Anthrops are inept at silent killing. I would rather have a handful of xial babes in the field than what they consider soldiers trained in stealth."

"I am sorry Nihengale, but Helicartia's young will need to remain where they are. Their mothers would skin my hide if I shipped them off for a night of bloodied murder."

Nihengale looked up, believing he had irritated her, but she gave him a playful smirk. He smiled back.

He had not seen Dal'dira since she became Helicartia's political envoy in Vinergale, which seemed like a lifetime ago. Since then, she had been named Marquise of Tyoh Keep, and most recently, Rook of the East.

She was the first xial to ever hold political title in Vinergale, not to mention becoming one of the four Royal Warmasters.

"Anthrop soldiers it is, then," Nihengale said.

Escara and Murciel sat near the fire, nibbling on their figs and whispering to each other. Neither of them held any interest in tactical affairs, and he had long given up on attempting to force them to provide input.

Rairi on the other hand stood to the side, quiet and attentive. He knew she would not speak unless addressed, but her sharp mind was working diligently behind those focused turquoise eyes.

"Is this route through the Devil's Spine safe?" Buio asked, critically detailing another chart.

"No route through that maze is completely safe, but this one proved successful during the Greenfire War. Sharn fought off the invasion and placed an outpost to the east in case Padive attempted another breech."

"I see," Nihengale muttered.

"You will board the Kajak just north of Palidor," Dal'dira said. "In a small fishing village called Deepsly. The bailiff's wife will be your contact there. Take anything you need from the table and share it with the good Captain if you like. Rairi, may I speak to you a moment?"

Rairi's eyes shot up from the charts. "Yes, of course Lady Dal'dira."

The Marquise shook her head and gave her a warm smile. "Dali is fine."

Nihengale knew how much Rairi admired the Lady Dal'dira. Before being chosen as envoy, Dali had become renown for her treatise; *Dragonbone. The Origins of Kelashin,* and for inventing some alchemical equation beyond Nihengale's comprehension.

They spoke in hushed tones by the chamber's floor-to-ceiling window, its thick curtains pulled back to let in Kiyo's glorious radiance. He observed them while Buio rolled up select charts and maps and stored them in a wide-mouthed scroll case. Rairi returned from the conversation with a solemn, determined look on her face.

After the briefing was concluded, Dal'dira escorted the others off and asked Nihengale to remain behind.

"There is something I can trust only you with, Nihengale," she said. Her tone softened and the tension in her stance loosened. She served him a goblet of Camnoc wine and a stick of hardened cinnamon sugar before pouring herself a glass.

"I handed the assignment of capturing the fortress of Sharn to Sarandi Cotaline, expecting him to send his Archonwolves, but the old fool got the Ashuras involved to protect his own political interests."

"How so?"

"The Magalians are a force of nature in Eastern Obsal, Nihengale. They are an ancient family of merchants commanding unbelievable wealth and political leverage. They are associated to the wealthiest noble lines, and many believe, the three Thrones."

"Old Padive as well?"

She nodded. "No family outside the royal bloodlines wields such power. These are very dangerous humans."

"You call them by their own honorific?" Nihengale asked.

"All but a handful are no more than anthrops to me, but I am a political creature. Etiquette demands I not insult them directly."

"So why are you attacking this family? If they are so dangerous?"

Dal'dira's lips graced him with a rueful smile. "This attack will incite many ramifications — but in truth — I attack them because of what Sharn holds in its fabled vault."

"You mean their shinn?"

"No. A box, wrapped in black chains, marked with ancient binding runes. The Palidorian Academy of Alchemy sent a junior alchemist called Marca Kaitner on this mission to count and catalog the vault's shinn. I asked Rairi to stay close to the girl and tasked her with making certain the chained box is placed inside the *Kajak's* hold.

"I need you to make certain she completes her mission. It is of the utmost importance, Nihengale. I cannot overstate it."

"You placed all this into motion over a single object? What is in this warded box?"

"I am afraid I cannot tell you, but it is vital for the box to reach the *Kajak*."

"Why not task us to guarding it then, if it is so important?"

"I cannot draw undue attention to it. Once the box is on the *Kajak*, you need not concern yourself. Another of my agents will see to its delivery."

"What other agent?"

"Better you not be burdened with it."

"Very well." Nihengale nibbled at the tip of the cinnamon, taking control of his growing exasperation. "Once we help Dorav complete his objective and acquire this warded box, our mission is over?"

"There is one more thing, about Captain Dorav himself."

"Yes?"

"If the mission fails, or Dorav is captured, I need you to kill him for me."

"I would need to understand why."

"Nihengale, as a Blade of Mepsia you understand secrecy in such matters is its own weapon."

"No, you are confusing the Alci'tirnni for an anthrop's assassin guild, Dali. While we were taught the killing art by anthrops and use them in similar fashion, we do not kill for coin, or without knowing the mark in complete detail."

Dal'dira leaned back a bit in her chair and sipped her wine. "You are asking me for his Animura, aren't you?"

"I am."

"For the sake of our history together, can I ask you to forgo this part?"

"I cannot, Dali. Not even for you."

"It is a long tale, Nihengale, and closely tied to his Lieutenant's. I would need to tell you both their stories for it to make any sense."

"Then perhaps you should, before the faces."

Dal'dira sighed and settled into her chair, staring at him in smoldering annoyance. Nihengale held her gaze.

"I swear before the faces, and my ancestors, this Animura is spoken truthfully and without deceit. Ayloros miru emerus. I speak with my heart."

"Because of the immense internal fighting occurring between the Zoniran Knighthood and the Queen's Admiralty during the Sundering War," Lady Dal'dira said, beginning her Animura, "a treaty was signed between them giving any ship's Captain full authority and mastery of his vessel, even with an Ashura aboard.

"Ashuras were consequently demoted to the rank of Seaguard Commanders, which is why few knights ever serve in naval warfare. During the Calimport Pirate War however, it became necessary for Ashuras to serve on warships, as so few battles were fought on land.

"Kartecus was the Seaguard Commander aboard the *Cidraster*, under Captain Afir Rion. A young knight then, Kartecus found he had a great affinity for the sea. While many Ashuras clashed constantly with naval officers, Kartecus became close friends with his Captain and the ship's crew.

"After years at sea, fighting the seemingly endless war with Calimport, Captain Afir promoted Kartecus to Naval Lieutenant. To replace him as Seaguard Commander, the Ashuran Order sent Holy Knight Metzial Renot.

"Metzial resented Kartecus for having authority over him. As a Holy Knight, he outranked Kartecus in their Order, but at sea, he was forced to take orders from someone he considered his subordinate.

"Their tempestuous relationship soured the *Cidraster's* morale and their open hostility created conflict and division aboard the ship. Metzial even sought to involve Holy Parliament, claiming Kartecus was breaking sea law by accepting the wartime field promotion to Lieutenant.

"Their conflict came to a head when a pirate slinger put a stone through Captain Afir's skull, killing him instantly. By law of the sea, Kartecus became Captain of the *Cidraster.*

"Metzial was so furious, he attempted a mutiny with his most loyal seaguards. The mutiny failed and Kartecus arrested Metzial along with his men. The *Cidraster* sailed back to the heart of the fleet and turned the prisoners over the justice of the Admiralty.

"All Metzial's co-conspirators were hung for mutiny. Metzial himself, being from the renown family Renot and a Holy Knight, was pardoned of all charges and transferred to the fleet's flagship, The *Levizo.*

"A young, newly knighted Dorav Minos replaced Metzial as Kartecus' Seaguard Commander, and the *Cidraster* went on to win many victories, earning great respect and infamy during the Pirate War.

"I first met Kartecus and Dorav during the taking of Felgrin, the Calimport capital.

"Kartecus was much more amicable in his middle age — a salted sailor through and through. His title of Ashuran Knight seemed like an honorary title he kept stored in his cabin. I realized right away that Dorav venerated him.

"Both men commanded the love and respect of their men, and their crew proved pivotal in the final battles of the war.

"It was during the Battle of Felgrin that I learned something very intimate about Dorav. Although he is an Ashuran Knight, he holds the title with utter contempt. He hates the very institution which raised him and holds no loyalty in his heart for their mission or their God.

"He blames them for murdering the woman he loved and never forgave them. He was eager when I offered him to become my agent within the Ashuran halls.

"Back then, the Ashuran Order believed Dorav would be the inheritor of his older brother's legacy. Gigan Minos, the Holy Redeemer, was already a living legend.

"The Order wished to groom Dorav to become a Holy Knight and follow in his brother's footsteps. They were so blinded by their ambitions, they did not suspect how passionately he worked against them.

"He fed me information about the Ashuran internal structures, their rituals and politics, and the missions his fellow knights were sent on. I learned many useful things in those first two years of our agreement.

"One report stated Metzial Renot had been promoted to Lord Vaulter. He sought to remove Kartecus from the *Cidraster*, but Admiral Vasamm refused the request, claiming Kartecus to be among his finest Captains. The *Cidraster* was instead sent north to fight in the Telkan Purification.

"Dorav continued to send me reports from Telkan. After three years of fighting there, Kartecus promoted him to Naval Lieutenant and brought on a native Telkan girl called Isa Blackclaw to be his Seaguard Commander.

"One of Dorav's later reports claimed he had discovered an underground slave market in the port city of Cortast. Telkan natives were being captured and sold as slaves in the ports of the Qanalarian Empire.

"Dorav made it his mission to unearth this network, and it was not long before someone sent a hired blade after him. Luckily, when the xial assassin struck, Kartecus was nearby and came to his aid. The xial nearly killed Kartecus, but they managed to capture her.

"After a lengthy interrogation, they discovered the man who sent the assassin and who was also behind the human market was the revered Bishop Oreb Santpor.

"There was no law which could punish the Bishop in Cortast. Dorav wrote to the Archbishop of Hara himself but soon realized no justice would be had. The Archbishop ordered the entire investigation ceased and the Bishop exonerated of all charges.

"One day shortly after, while the Bishop dined with his fellow priests, Kartecus walked into the dining hall, unsheathed his wolfbert, and drove it through Oreb Santpor and the wooden chair he sat on.

"The Arbiter who took the case found Kartecus guilty of murdering a Zoniran Bishop. The Admiralty stripped him of his title of Captain, but the Ashuran Order took things a step further.

"The Lord Vaulter Metzial Renot caught wind of the proceedings in Telkan and sent an order for Kartecus to be stripped of all titles and honors. All his wealth and holdings were to be confiscated, and he was to be excommunicated and burned as a heretic.

"The Court did everything Metzial requested, except burning Kartecus for heresy. Dorav intervened on his behalf and granted the man his family's protection by offering the Arbiter a hefty bribe. In any civilized city in Obsal such a thing would not be possible, but in a war-front outskirt like Cortast, it bought Kartecus a second chance."

"Kartecus Andalan died that day in all official record, but Kartecus Minos lived on. Being the new Captain, Dorav rechristened his ship as *The Kajak* and brought Kartecus on as an Ordinary Seaman. The *Kajak* continued to fight until the Telkan Purification was over, and then she sailed west to wage war on the Sea of Crowns against Qanalar. When word of Kartecus being alive reached the ports of Obsal, sailors took to calling him The Cortast Revenant.

"I believe Metzial is using this opportunity to kill off both Kartecus and Dorav for challenging his authority throughout his career. This is why he sent them and their crew on this impossible mission — and by doing so now threatens everything I strive to achieve."

Nihengale leaned back a bit in his chair when he realized she had finished speaking. He searched his mind, trying to find a gentle way to say what he was thinking.

"What is it?" she asked.

"You have never spoken an Animura before, have you?"

Dal'dira sighed, her eyes narrowing. "No. What did I do wrong? This is their story, as well and truthfully as I know it."

"I believe you, Dali. It is only...Animura means, 'A true understanding', meant to convey who the person is, in their essence.

You gave me a glimpse of who these men are, and I do understand much about them from their actions, and how they are bound together, but to kill Dorav as an Alci'tirnni, I must witness him as if through your eyes. I must perceive him as you do."

Dal'dira took a sip of her wine. "This is how I know him, Nihengale."

"I am sorry, but you do not know him, and so I cannot do this."

"Nihengale, I need you to understand this, Dorav has been vital to my work here. It is because of him that I am able to stay a step ahead of the Archbishop, who is dangerous beyond imagining.

"His desires for this nation are a horror, and I am the only thing in his way. If Dorav is captured and placed under torture — if he reveals that he is my spy — everything I fought for here will be for nothing.

"I will be at Tepley's mercy. And when the Church finds out, which they will, I will be tortured and executed."

"All Helicartia would avenge you," Nihengale said.

"Yes, I understand this. More death, more war, all because of me."

Nihengale finished the wine in his cup and took a steadying breath. "You asked me to forgo the Animura for the sake of our history, which I could not do, and I certainly cannot kill this man as an Alci'tirnni with what you gave me me. But for the sake of what we had, and because of what will happen to you if he is captured, if necessary, I will murder him for you."

Nihengale could see it took her a moment to understand what he was saying. She had been in anthrop lands for so long, she had forgotten the mepsien beliefs about the subtleties of death and the affect it had on the spirit.

To kill a person was to place a heavy burden upon the spirit if the heart was not certain that death was deserved. The Animura was created for this purpose. The true knowing fuses the hearts of the one who requests death and the one who deals it. The Alci'tirnni then becomes the knife of the contractor and the stain is shared.

"You would carry his death in your heart for me?"

"For you, yes."

"Nihengale..."

The look she gave him sent a hot spike of desire coursing though him. He absorbed the soft curve of her bare feet, the supple length of her legs, and smooth shape of her hips. His eyes caressed the softness of her breasts and smooth lines of her neck, but the predatory look in her sunset eyes made him boil for her.

She stood and walked to where he sat, leaned over, and kissed him, her warm tongue entering his mouth. He savored the kiss, running his thumb over the lobe of her left ear, one of her most sensitive spots. She moaned lightly in his mouth.

"This kind of thing is forbidden between xial of different clans in Helicartia, Lady Dal'dira." He stared into her piercing eyes.

"We are not in Helicartia, Nihengale."

"No," he said, grabbing her waist and leading her forward until she knelt on his chair, straddling him. "We are not."

Nihengale lay flat in the razor-grass, watching the anthrop soldiers tend to their camp — over a dozen men huddling around a handful of fires. Nihengale knew the stripes painted across their eyes were signs of command.

He kept close to their leader until he sat down at his fire. The deep chill of predawn carpeted the hills in a white rolling mist Nihengale used to hide himself from these men.

"Goddamn Bagra and fucking Deurn." One of the soldiers cursed. "They get to ride back to Nevine, eat fresh meat and drink cold ale while we are stuck out in the razorgrass chewing jerky and drinking... what the fuck is this anyway?!"

"Shut it, Nen," the leader rebuked.

"They'll probably hit the brothel while there and get their wicks good and wet," the third man at the fire coaxed. "I fucking would."

"Stop stirring the shit Roper, or you'll spit-shine chamber pots until your nose melts off."

"Golin, why did Qelwin get a sudden hard-on over those prisoners?" Nen asked. "Who were they? I never even heard of the Cortast Revenant."

"Neither have I," Golin said, "but remember, we hail from Borm. Qelwin hails from Aztan. The bards tell all kinds of tales in those taverns."

"Nevine minstrels know more hero songs than I can count," Roper said, "but I never heard of him either."

"Even so," Golin said, "if the pretty little blond really is an Ashura, and the dried old turd is a Vinergalian war hero, Qelwin's looking at a commendation for bringing them in."

"A commendation? Just for bringing in a couple of prisoners?"

"After the hell those Ashuran fucks put us through in the war?" Golin asked. "The Crown still pays high bounties for rogue Zoniran knights. The Tribune will make Qelwin a Centurion for this, and the Queen herself will stroke his shaft."

"While we sit out here eating jerky and drinking this horse piss," Roper said.

"Goddamn Bagra and fucking Deurn," Nen said.

"All right, both of you, go walk the perimeter. I feel like I'm out here with my wife with all your fucking whining."

Nihengale crawled back slowly away from the encampment. Once clear, he stood and headed north, skirting the road through the razorgrass.

The first pale rays of sunlight crested in the east making him squint. With a frustrated curse he moved west, walking away from the road while keeping the sun to his back. There was nowhere to hide from Siege's light out here, but the tall razorgrass was a safe enough place to sleep. Nothing lived in these hills except for this abrasive grass. He only needed to find a safe place to set up camp.

Nevine.

They were taking Dorav and Kartecus to the anthrop capital and now they had a soldier escort. These summer nights were so short, he could not make up enough ground to catch the caravan.

He caught a glimpse of it the other night, far off in the horizon, just as dawn crept over the eastern hills. They were breaking camp and preparing to return to the road. He almost chanced being Lightburned to make up some distance, but he could not risk it. Fear of permanent blindness made him take shelter instead.

He needed to catch up to them before they reached the anthrop city. He could not hope to find Dorav once inside, and his promise to Dali would be broken. He could not let that happen.

17

The Fabhcun

Tiliash Dainte strode through the airy corridors of the Fabhcun Castle with a carefree stride. Not even the sun's reluctance to escape from behind a blanket of iron clouds above Nevine could spoil this morning's mood.

Her long skirt danced around her ankles as she glided along the empty passageway. In a moment of exuberance she twirled, arms out, her short auburn hair dancing wildly about her head.

The heavy footsteps of the castle guard made her jerk to an awkward stop. She smoothed her skirt, patted her hair back in place, and walked with the refined eloquence expected of a lady. As the guards passed, she gave each a courteous nod, which they returned in kind.

No matter how many times she was summoned to the throne room, it always sparked a sense of awe in her.

The cylindrical chamber's domed roof, fifty-feet about her head, was supported by twelve marble pillars — each one a carved representation of an oracle of Methven — the twelve women who guided Queen Aviedeen Hervine in her war of independence against her husband, the Emperor of Bergal.

At the foot of each oracle stood a Royal-Talon guard, fully garbed in segmented breastplate armor, colorful red and blue scutums, and intricate falcon-head-shaped helms. Their bracers and greaves were folded steel, and their long red capes hung suspended by falcon crest pins.

Queen Alinia Meridomin stood away from her high-backed throne, dressed in fine regalia. Her flowing, red and blue silk stola was threaded with silver lace on the neckline, and had gilded falcons sewn into the long sleeves, diving towards her wrists, talons leading.

A delicate silver tiara, curved behind her ears and embellished with golden kestrel feathers, served as her crown. The royal jewel *Surya*, said to be worth a mountain in gold, shone from the crown's center.

The Queen's eyes were the color of burnt honey and her hair, once vibrant and black, was almost entirely white. Her stern face, though treated nightly with oils and herbs, showed the etched lines of a life filled with bitterness and concern.

To her majesty's right stood Magistrate Bacrus Aldemont. The imposingly tall magistrate wore his steel-gray robes of office, with the crest of Testament sewed proudly on the front. He wore his thick black hair combed neatly back, away from his furrowed eyebrows and generous mustache. His expression was as hard and dour as the queen's.

"Ah, Tiliash," Alinia's strong voice filled the room. "How very generous of you to join us this morning. I hope the walk to my chambers did not prove burdensome for your young feet."

"No, Majesty." Tiliash bowed with one hand holding up the rim of her skirt.

"Good, I would hate to think I am inconveniencing you."

"Of course not Majesty, it is my duty and pleasure to serve." She bowed once more.

Bacrus glared at her.

"I am certain it is." The Queen turned back to the group of men standing before her. "Tell me, do you recognize any of these men, Sarandi Tiliash?"

Tiliash glanced at each man in turn. "Legate Hokran of course, and Tribune Alister of the Sickle-Talon ninth legion."

The men beamed with pride at her recognition, their smiles brighter than the cast plates of their armors. The third was a Sickle-Talon sergeant wearing simple leather. She stared at him in silent embarrassment.

"That one is sergeant Qelwin of the ninth legion," the Queen stated dismissively. "He brought this matter to the attention of Tribune Alister, who in turn sought the council of Legate Hokran.

"Imagine the implication of the Legate seeking my direct

involvement in this matter. Quite the delicious mystery, would you not say, my dear?"

"Yes, Majesty."

"Either way, two out of three is reasonably mediocre. Try the others."

To her dismay, Tiliash could not account for any of them. There was a broad man with a thick red beard, his arm in a bloodied sling. A smaller one with dirty blond hair and sunken black eyes. And a young handsome one, with black hair and sad, brooding amber eyes. All of them appeared like common Teplian laborers.

The last two men in the group gave her pause. Their blue eyes, facial structure, and taller posture gave them away as Vinergalians. The older man wore his hair long while the younger wore his blond hair cropped short. Otherwise, she could not discern anything from them.

Reluctantly, she shook her head.

"You are a disappointing little thing," The Queen sighed. "This fine Vinergalian specimen before me is none other than the Ashuran Knight, Captain Dorav Minos of the renown warship, *The Kajak*."

"Minos," Tiliash eyed the man.

"Is there an echo in here?" The Queen frowned at her.

"No, Majesty."

"Save face kitten and tell me who this other poor bound soul is."

Tiliash's mind stalled. The old man stared directly at her but his tired scowl only worsened her state. Only one name came to mind in conjunction with Captain Dorav Minos.

"Lieutenant Kartecus Andalan?"

"Are you asking me, Tiliash?" Alinia's eyebrows raised. "I thought I was asking the questions here."

"No, Majesty."

"A close enough guess. This is indeed Kartecus, of House Minos. Kartecus Andalan perished in all but flesh two decades ago. Behold, the Cortast Revenant."

"Yes, Majesty."

"Yes what? First you ask a question and now you answer a question no one asked."

"Yes, Majesty." Tiliash cursed herself silently. "Apologies, Majesty."

"Sir Dorav, do you realize what I must put up with to run my Queendom?"

Dorav stared at the Queen with a blank expression.

"Where is your writ of passage, Sir Dorav? What are you doing in my lands and why do these men claim you attacked their homes?"

Dorav offered no reply.

"Lieutenant Kartecus, can you explain why your lord and savior here is ignoring me?"

Kartecus also remained silent.

"Now gentlemen, I must take your insolent silence as a deliberate act. You are being disrespectful."

"Begging your pardon, Majesty, but both men have refused to speak," Hokran interjected. "Even after we...insisted."

"That would explain the cuts and bruises. It is a fortunate thing you are better at leading men than you are at questioning them, Legate."

"Yes, Majesty."

"You." The Queen pointed to the red-bearded man. "What is your name, shinn-miner?"

The man fell to a knee and lowered his head. "David, Majesty."

"David Majesty? Now there is a fine name for a plebeian. How about you give me your real surname, David, and stop trying to rob me of my title."

David stared at the floor without giving an answer. Tiliash eyed him warily.

"Oh, never mind!" The Queen rolled her eyes. "By the time you wrap your head around your own name I will have died and been joyously buried. You say you captured these men in Kaira, yes? Do you hold proof there are more of them?"

"I do not, your Majesty," David said. "But the townsfolk will tell you the same."

"And what of these creatures you claim attacked your town? Some kind of nine-foot, wingless wasp? Black with yellow markings — human skulls tied to their backs?"

"They remain near Kaira, Majesty," David said. Tiliash could hear the pain in his voice.

The Queen turned to Bacrus with both brows raised. The Magistrate gave her a morose nod.

211

"I have never heard of such creatures in my Queendom, and yet I see you speak truthfully. I am thoroughly disgusted by the thought of such things."

The Queen turned to Kartecus. "David Majesty claims that before these giant insects attacked, you sacked Kaira. He also believes you marched from the west. Is this true? Are your men currently posted in Sharn awaiting your victorious return? Did you dare sack lands in my care?"

Kartecus held his tongue.

"I warn you against the dangers of boring me, gentlemen. Either answer my questions here before the Parliament's Royal Magistrate, or answer to my Inquisitor. Which will it be?"

Tiliash's heart skipped. The Queen would not invoke the Inquisition unless she suspected heresy.

Kartecus appeared physically ill. His eyes widened and his jaw tensed. The entire room tensed.

"The Inquisitor then," the Queen said.

"There is no heresy here!" Kartecus cried, incredulous.

"Kartecus!" Dorav glared at him.

"They speak!" The Queen announced mirthfully. "How wonderful! Now that we have established a dialog, we may chat."

Alinia turned to the Legate. "Hokran, choose a cohort of Talons and march them to Sharn. If they encounter any foreign forces, my orders are capture if they can, kill if they must."

"Yes, Majesty."

"Also, take a team of Range Seekers with you. I would know about these creatures if you encounter them. And send word to Aztan. I order the *Kajak,* and any other ship flying Vinergale's banner detained at Sawstone Island and searched, thoroughly. I wish timely, detailed reports of everything. Dismissed."

"Majesty." Legate Hokran placed an arm across his chest and bowed. He turned on his heel and left the throne room.

"Alister, what has become of the survivors from Kaira?"

"They await your command, my Queen."

"Place them in one of my properties here at the Fabhcun. Something spacious, and make certain they are well tended to while this situation with Kaira is resolved.

"Clean water and fresh bread, Alister — blankets, soap, and wine. If any part of this story is true, they will desire a drink. I am certain I would.

"Do not let me discover your men cut corners and pocketed coin or you will answer to me. Dismissed."

"Yes, Majesty." Alister bowed and followed behind the Legate.

Qelwin mimicked his movements and turned to leave as well.

"And where are you going, Sergeant?" The Queen's voice became hot venom. "I do not recall giving you leave."

Qelwin's face went as white as cotton. "I'm sorry Majesty, I only thought-"

"You are a soldier, Sergeant. You are not here to think, you are here to obey. Leave the thinking to your betters."

"Yes, Majesty."

Queen Alinia turned to her Royal Guard. "Please escort these men," she pointed to the three miners, "outside. You may cut their bonds. They are not my prisoners and should not be treated as such."

Two Royal Talons ushered the three Kairans out into the corridor.

Once the door closed behind them, the Queen turned to Sergeant Qelwin. "Report immediately to Quartermaster Cofreiz. Let him know you are my chosen brush for his sanitation detail."

"Yes, Majesty."

"And Qelwin."

"Yes, Majesty?"

"Do not let me catch you thinking again."

"Yes, Majesty. No, Majesty." The sergeant bowed and left the throne room.

Tiliash gave him a pitying look. The Quartermaster had requested a man to help him drain and scrub every latrine in the castle. The stench had become repugnant. Queen Alinia promised to send someone as soon as the opportunity arose. Poor Qelwin truly drew the shortest of straws.

"Tiliash."

"Yes, Majesty?" The tremor in her voice made her curse herself.

"Take those plebeians and have them bathed, clothed, and given a quarter in my guest wing. I will deal with them when I am ready."

"Yes, Majesty."

"Also, summon Inquisitor Sinitel and let him know I hold a pair of playthings for him to sharpen his tools on. Dismissed."

"Yes, Majesty," Tiliash grabbed the hem of her skirt, bowed, and turned to leave.

"I may call on you later, kitten. Make certain you are easy to find."

"Yes, Majesty." Tiliash bowed once more and gratefully left the Queen's throne room.

Once out in the corridor, David let out a sigh of relief. Mercifully, he remained unrecognized in Nevine. Legate Hokran was perhaps the only man who could have recognized him, but once the names Kartecus and Dorav Minos were spoken, his attention became absorbed.

When Qelwin left the throne-room, David wondered if the Queen had ordered him to throw himself off the parapets. He gave them a murderous sneer as he passed them in the hall.

Tiliash came out and greeted them with a charming smile. "Come with me."

"Excuse me...madam?" Sifran called to Tiliash when the Royal Talons were far behind them.

David glared a warning.

"Would it be permissible to smoke?" Sifran asked despite David's reproachful stare. "I am nervous and it helps calm me."

"My name is Tiliash." She smiled back at him. "Be wary of the ash. If you drop even a speck on the Queen's royal carpet, she will take your hands."

Sifran held his cravings in check until they cleared the rich red fabric. Once his fingers were safe from severing, he hastily lit a rumpled cuksar on a hanging torch. The ecstatic sigh that escaped him made Tiliash chuckle.

"I see he really like those," she said.

"More than the air we breathe, I fear," David replied. The last time he saw little Tiliash Dainte, she was knee-high to a knee. He cleared his throat and lowered his gaze. He could not risk too much attention.

"You men are very brave to bring in the fabled Cortast Revenant and Dorav Minos. Their exploits in Calimport and Telkan have inspired songs as far south as Sentinel. Dorav is almost as famous as his brother. How did you manage to trap him?"

Sifran and Ashen remained silent.

"We did not," David said. "The creatures injured them both. We only found them afterward."

"The nine-foot wasps? Sounds like something out of a campfire tale," Tiliash said softly.

"They were more like beetles with stingers," Sifran said.

"I hope to never see anything like that," she replied.

An awkward silence rolled in the wake of her words.

"Well, rest assured her Majesty will not tolerate an attack on her people. Not by another nation or by crawly things. Legate Hokran will sort everything out soon, I assure you."

"We are grateful, Sarandi." David said.

"Tiliash is fine."

David smiled behind his beard. Little Tiliash, so young and already the Sarandi of Nevine. Her uncle Barril Dainte, the Sarandi of Aztan, and one of the most powerful trade barons in Tepley, was likely responsible for her ascension. She had grown up a beauty, with careless joy in her eyes, so unlike her temperamental uncle.

Tiliash led them down to the Fabhcun's infamous baths. After the Sundering of the Bergal Empire, the first King of Vinergale built a marvelous bathhouse within the walls of Castle Harathal.

He filled it with some of the most stunning men and women in his city, whose sole purpose was to pamper and bathe the King and his honored guests.

In response to this, Queen Alinia of Tepley filled her own luxurious bathhouse with her most beautiful subjects to accommodate her own guests. Lasting bitterness and bad blood had caused countless such little differences between two countries which were once a single thriving empire.

"The Queen wishes them cleaned and groomed," Tiliash told the bathers. "I leave them to your expert care." She graced them with a smile and a bow before walking away.

As they stripped out of their grimy clothes, the bathers stared at them in horror. Except for Ashen, who kept himself clean for Nianah's sake, David could not remember the last time anyone in Ricker's crew took a proper bath.

Their odor was likely layered and exponential. It dawned on him, that as coarse as the Queen was with everyone, she never made mention of their appearance or stench. Neither did Tiliash.

The three miners entered the deep, steaming basin in the middle of the room and six male bathers began their arduous work.

"Quit fidgeting!" David barked at Sifran who kept struggling to get away from the men.

"They're scraping off my hide!" Sifran complained as the pretty men scrubbed layers of mine filth from him.

"You won't get it all," David told the two bathers who attended him. "After a while it just becomes another layer of skin."

"We will see about that," One of them growled as he angrily scrubbed David's hairy arm.

The Queen's baths were four spacious basins, each filled with water and kept hot by a stone furnace in an adjacent room. Dimly lit carvings on its marble pillars depicted men and women in sexual positions David never even thought to attempt.

Long red and blue banners with Tepley's golden falcon hung from every pillar. A number of candles surrounding the chamber burned with a pleasant lavender and spice scent, granting the chamber the aroma of a hidden meadow .

The miners soiled the water of two basins before the Queen's bathers left them alone to relax in the clean steamy water of the third. An hour after entering, their skins were red from both the water and the bather's stubborn sponges.

"Her Majesty is really something." Sifran sat up to his neck in hot water. "I am glad she spoke to you and not me, David. I think I might have pissed myself."

"Again?" Ashen asked.

"Eat my ass, Ashen!"

"That is why she is a fine Queen," David said. "She scares the shit out of people."

"Why all the falcons?" Ashen glanced around.

"How do you ask something like that?" David asked.

"Ashen has never been out of Kaira before, David." Sifran sniffed. "That town is the only place he ever knew until now."

"Right, shit." David softened his tone. "Sorry Ashen. I forget. That

216

falcon is Skyel."

"Who?"

"Queen Aviedeen's hunting falcon."

"Who is Aviedeen?" Ashen glanced between them.

Sifran could not suppress a chuckle.

"Fuck you both, spunk-chuggers!" Ashen splashed them. "Who is she?"

"Queen Alinia Aviedeen, you ignorant rock-fucker," David gave him a wry grin. "Was Tepley's first Queen. Skyel was her gyrknife hunting falcon — a gift from her sister, and Aviedeen's personal weapon during the Sundering War."

"The war that shattered the Bergal Empire," Sifran said, seeing the confusion in Ashen's face.

"Skyel would fly over battlefields," David continued, "screaming and flapping her wings. She would dive into the bloody melee and gouge Vinergalian faces with her sharpened talons."

"Terra's stone." A thin smile found Ashen's lips. "Mean bird."

"Some say Skyel was blessed by the Oracles of Methven," David said. "Which is why she could not be shot down, even with Vinergale's best archers hankering to pluck her from the sky.

"During the hardest campaigns, Skyel's cry would lift the men's spirits like no war drum ever could. Her cry could change the tide of battle."

"I never understood how they heard a bird call in the middle of a battle," Sifran said, "with all the clanging and shouting."

"You miss the point of the damn story, Sifran," David said.

"So what happened to her?" Ashen asked. "Did Vinergale shoot her down?"

David nodded somberly. "Death Arrow stole her from the sky."

"Death Arrow?" Sifran asked. "I never heard this part."

"He was King Hervine's personal assassin and the deadliest archer the world has ever known. The man never missed anything he shot at. Every arrow he knocked into his Scythebow became a grave Tepley had to dig."

"No one is that keen," Sifran scoffed. "Skyel was killed protecting Aviedeen from an Ashuran Holy Knight, so the story I heard goes."

"Either way, her death infuriated the legions. They named her a martyr, painted her on their shields, and sang her stories over their campfires. They fought ever harder in her name, and she became Tepley's rallying emblem."

"You tell the finest stories, you ugly old kafra dropping." Ashen grinned at him.

"Fuck yourself with a mace," David smirked back. He missed these banters with Ashen. Perhaps Ricker was right and he did hold a soft spot for this lazy little shit-stick.

"Do you plan to shave your beard, David?" Sifran asked.

"No, I will braid it properly, but I will not shave."

"Girls don't appreciate those things, you know?" Ashen stared up at the bath's ceiling. "Makes their faces itch."

"Shows how little you know," David grunted. "Girls may not, but women enjoy the feeling of kissing a man, not some pin-dick boy whose stones have yet to drop. Besides, a woman's face is not the only thing I like to tickle with my beard."

Sifran dried off his hands and lit a cuksar with a nearby candle. A passing bather offered him a small clay bowl for the ash.

"My thanks."

"May we have ale?" Ashen asked the bather.

"Of course."

"And, why is it only you men are in here with us?" Sifran inserted. "I thought there would be women in these baths. The most beautiful in the land, if the bards tell it right."

"That was not a privilege the Queen granted," the bather replied.

"Oh." Sifran gave a disgruntled sigh. "Ale then."

David glared at them as the bather left. "We are not here to get drunk."

"Relax David," Ashen said. "I just need a fucking drink."

David opened his mouth to retort but the look on Ashen's face stopped him.

Nianah.

In the end, David had not seen her corpse. He wanted to ask Ashen what he did with it. Had he placed coins on her eyes or simply left her where she lay?

There was not enough time to bury anyone in Kaira. No prayers were spoken for the dead — no final rites performed. Their town was not only murdered that day, but damned.

"I will take ale as well!" David called out to the bather.

Ashen and Sifran gave him a smile.

"Aranath's cock," David spat tiredly. "I hope this does not lead to another fucking war."

They stared at him, their soaked hair limp across their faces.

"You fought in the Greenfire War," Sifran stated timidly. "You must have gone through all kinds of shit, but you never talk about it."

"I do not talk about it because I do not wish to remember it, Sifran."

"Except when you're drunk," Ashen said.

"Come, David." Sifran insisted. "If what you say is true and war may break out soon, we need to be prepared. As a friend, you must tell us something about what war is like."

David glared at them, but neither seemed ready to back down. He took Sifran's cuksar, gave it a drag, and passed it back.

"I was an infantry spear man, like those men we met on the road."

Their eyes widened in delight.

"You told Sergeant Qelwin you served in the Storm-Talons," Ashen said.

"Correct."

"Third legion," Sifran said. "Under Akata Firestorm. You knew the Stormlords then? What were they like?"

"They were fair commanders. They made the best decisions they could and kept us alive when things became ugly."

"Oh come on, David!" Sifran splashed him. "I mean you spoke to them right? Or were they too high-blooded to drink with their own men?"

David sighed deeply. "No, they drank with the men. We would gather around the fires on nights colder than an old crone's cunnie and drink, curse, and laugh at each other's stupidity.

"We told stories of home, and the mundanity we all craved. We made jests of each other's wives, mothers, and sisters — even traded some of them.

"We sang songs and howled at the moon. The commanders always sat in the middle of it, the loudest of the lot."

"Which one was the hardest drinker?" Sifran asked.

"I thought you wanted me to speak about war."

"We do, but you served with the Stormlords! They are legendary!"

"Never heard of them," Ashen said, looking between the two.

"They were the greatest heroes in Tepley's army!" Sifran's narrow face beamed. "Akata Firestorm rode into battle with flaming sword in hand, on the back of a black Nightmare whose mane and hooves burned with pure vorxfire!

"Then there was Khine Darkstorm, the Blackwing Butcher!" Sifran stood, naked as his birthing day, swinging an invisible sword around his head with both hands. "He was an immortal who could hold off an entire army on his own and never tire — never fall. His armor was made from black dragon scales and his silver greatsword, Doombringer, could cut through anything!

"But the most frightening was Rien Bloodstorm — son of the Bloodrider himself! When Rien entered the field of battle, the blood of his enemies would drown the land in Aranath's name. His sword Skura held the captive soul of an ancient vampire, and she would suck her victim's blood out of the very air when swung!"

"Do not get caught up in the damn stories!" David slammed his fist down on the side of the bath. Sifran stopped mid-swing, staring at him in surprise.

"Only fools believe such tales! The war was not about heroic battles and glorious victories either! I lost friends out there! They died in my arms holding their fucking guts in! Grown men crying like children, scared out of their minds! Blood, flies, and shit everywhere! I saw women and children raped and quartered! Entire towns burned with people locked inside their homes, screaming and cursing our names! We did inhuman things out there! We...we..."

David took a deep, steadying breath. Sifran and Ashen's smiles dropped from their faces and Sifran sank back into the steaming water.

"War is not some great campaign of honor and valor, filled with the ranks and files of the hard and fearless. It is not a privilege, or a calling, or whatever other horseshit the bards sing about.

"War is long days, cold nights, and bad dreams. It is waiting, always the godsdamn waiting, and far too much thinking — wondering if today is your day to die.

"It's shitting your pants right before you run screaming like a crazed fool into a wall of swords and spears. It's pain, and fear, and fucking hating yourself for what you did that day to stay alive. It is the closest to the Vorx you will ever be without dying.

"You believe what happened in Kaira was bad? All those headless corpses and stinking gore? You better hope you never see the outcomes of war."

Tiliash stood before the Inquisitor's chamber door and hesitated. It was like standing in a black forest, staring into the gaping mouth of some ravenous beast, all teeth and bloodied spittle.

She rubbed some life back into her hands. She hated when the Queen sent her for Sinitel. He was the strangest and most unnerving person. Being in his presence made her terribly uneasy.

She rapped lightly on his door, secretly hoping he would not hear. There was a shuffle of movement and the clunk of the wooden beam barring his chamber. When the Inquisitor opened his door, Tiliash took an involuntary step back.

Sinitel was a thinly muscled xial with long raven-black hair, pale green eyes, and a hawkish, yet strangely handsome face. He stood at his threshold, his hair hanging over his face, bare from the waist up. His chest and hands were covered in splattered blood which partially obscured the complex array of winding tattoos on his face, arms, and torso.

To her understanding, some markings were from when he served the Blades of Mepsia. Others were seals and wards meant to keep out the taint of the Vorx. Every Inquisitor was required to be sealed against corruption, but she wondered if they were inscribed too late for Sinitel.

"Yes?" he asked curtly.

"The Queen- " Tiliash took a second to compose herself. "The Queen has summoned you, Inquisitor. She expects you in her throne room immediately."

"Immediately will need to be prolonged, Sarandi Tiliash. As you can see, I am in no state to stand before the Queen."

"Delay at your own risk, Inquisitor," she said sharply.

"Noted, my Lady."

Tiliash nodded and walked away. Sinitel had an almost inherit ability to disquiet her. She knew his aura of danger was a natural extension of his race and profession, but there was something unnatural about his pale green eyes.

Some members of court spoke of him as an apparition — a baleful creature who would swoop down from the sky, pry children from their beds, and take them up to his chamber of pain.

Despite his race, infamy, and the horror behind his work, others thought him to be quite pleasant company. He spoke with refinement, had impeccable taste, and was a witty conversationalist.

He greeted everyone he came in contact with by name, and was well known to inquire on people's personal affairs — like an upcoming wedding or the birth of a child. Tiliash found his acumen for court intrigue rather reproachful.

The farther she got from Sinitel's chambers, the better she felt. She made her way through the corridors of the breezy castle, intent on returning to the baths to check on the Kairan miners.

"Tiliash." A familiar voice came from an adjacent corridor to her right.

She tip-toed toward the sound. Finding a half-opened door she slipped within. Someone grabbed her roughly by the arm, spun her around, and thrust his tongue into her mouth. Tiliash returned the passionate kiss with equal fervor.

"What are you doing in here, Ondar?"

They stood in one of the castle carpenter's storage rooms. Beams of various woods from around the Queendom lay stacked high on groaning, ironwood shelves, while boxes filled with nails and carpentry tools rested on the floor.

Dim, gray sunlight peeked through the storeroom's shutters. Caulk, mortar, and fresh sandalwood overpowered the air.

"You left so suddenly this morning," he said.

Tiliash ran her hands over his smooth, dark skin. Centurion Ondar of the Royal-Talon's second legion was of Qanalarian descent, but a Teplian native, born right here in Nevine. He was a powerhouse of a man — with a tall, lean, muscular frame, dark-chocolate skin, and honey-colored eyes.

He was ferocious, in both battle and in bed — and her sweetest secret for the last two years. When they met during the Queen's annual gala, instant carnal desire blazed between them.

They kept their love secret for fear of her uncle, the Sarandi of Aztan. He was a stern and traditional man. He would never condone a relationship between his prized niece and a simple soldier like Ondar, despite his being a Centurion.

Both of her parents had died during the consumption outbreak seven years back. Her uncle Barril took her in, saw to her education, and most recently, advocated her promotion to Sarandi of Nevine.

She knew her uncle was slowly grooming her for the Crown. The Queen bore no children to inherit the throne and her age was a common, if unrecorded topic in court. In her uncle's mind, Tiliash was meant for greatness, but she could think of nothing greater than to be in this man's arms.

"I was summoned," she said. "You would know this if you could be bothered to wake."

"I was tired." He smiled at her. "And with good reason. Where are you going now?"

"To check on the miners."

"Who?"

"Kairan shinn-miners. It appears we have a bit of trouble brewing in the south."

"Oh? Anything involving my men?"

"Not if I have my say." She placed her forehead on his chest.

"You cannot keep me trapped in the nest." He pinched her sides, making her giggle.

"I can, and I will. You are staying here, warm and safe."

"Speaking of warm and safe." He ran his hand in between her legs, touching the wetness of her smallclothes with the tips of his broad fingers.

Tiliash smiled and kissed him gently on the ear. "Tonight."

Ondar pulled her against him, and the hardness in his breeches. She brushed at it with her fingers and smiled before leaving the chamber. Her smile remained all the way back to the baths.

Kartecus stood stoically before the Queen and her Magistrate when Sinitel made his entrance.

The Inquisitor wore a gray and gold silk doublet, black breeches, buskins, and his gray cloak of office. His black hair was combed and tied back and his fingernails well groomed.

Sinitel gave the Queen a sweeping bow, bending at the waist. "Her Majesty's beauty is as inspiring as ever. To gaze upon it is a privilege."

"A privilege and a curse in your case, Inquisitor." The Queen eyed him coldly. "Need I remind you, refusing to act promptly to my summons will result in swift retribution? I called for you nearly an hour ago. You kept my guests waiting. No one keeps my guests waiting."

The Queen's face was an iron mask as she observed the xial. "Name your punishment."

"I lament my tardiness, Majesty." Sinitel's tone was unconcerned. "I simply could not come into this grand chamber in anything less than my finest attire. Having been working when summoned, my grooming took a bit longer than anticipated.

"For my lack of expedience, her Majesty should see fit to cut my feet into clefts, like those of the ram, so I may be quicker when making my way to answer her call."

Queen Alinia laughed heartily at his reply, full-bellied and genuine, the hard lines of her face creating a paradox of expression. "Your morbid imagination never becomes tiresome, Sinitel. I would like you to meet our guests; the legendary Ashuran Knight, Captain Dorav Minos, and his second in command, Lieutenant Kartecus, the Cortast Revenant."

Sinitel turned to face them and gave an openly mocking bow. "A pleasure, gentlemen. I look forward to working with you to our mutual satisfaction."

Kartecus eyed the creature. This was not a city-raised spook. He had the mepsien markings on his skin, and his eyes were open and sharp during daytime. A Helicartian spy, no doubt.

"I certainly hope it will not come to that," Queen Alinia added. "I only summoned you so these men were made to understand, neither their station nor reputation will keep them from you if they choose to keep their mouths sealed about the matter of their presence in my Queendom."

"As much as I admire these men for their accomplishments, Majesty, the presence of Magistrate Aldemont more than ensures they will choose silence over dialog."

"Is this true gentlemen?" The Queen teased. "Are you so brave and foolish as to risk this fate?"

"You cannot do this," Kartecus hissed, glaring at Magistrate Aldemont. "You cannot condone this! There is no cause for an Inquisition!"

"Ah, but you are mistaken, Kartecus." The Queen's smile was a knife. "You see, I know the only reason you still draw breath is because of Dorav's family name. You killed a priest of your own faith, after all. You escaped your Inquisition once before."

"He was a heretic! A defiler!" Kartecus growled.

"You are the only one accused of heresy here, Kartecus," The Queen said. "You have dragged the name Minos into the grime with your stubborn existence. You brought shame to the Order of Ashura and inspired doubt in the hearts of the people. You were condemned, and after your release, you could not prove your innocence."

Kartecus' jaw clenched. She was right. For two years they tried to clear his name, but their attempts all failed.

"You are a festering boil, Kartecus, and now I find you in my lands, attacking my people, and you brought your old pupil along without the Church's permission.

"The name Minos may have kept you safe in Telkan and Vinergale, but this is Tepley. Here the name Minos is spoken mostly by drunken sailors and street-corner hustlers. People enjoy the war stories but care nothing for the politics of your family."

"If I am what you want, then take me, damn you." Kartecus' heart beat heavily in his chest. "I manipulated Dorav and persuaded him to come here with me. He has no fault in this."

"He is lying," the Magistrate said.

"Kartecus, you should know better than to lie before a Magistrate of Testament." The Queen spoke with mock disappointment. "You walk the surest route to the gallows."

"Queen Alinia," Dorav eyed her intently. "My family is more than a name. Lord Mathis will not stand for this."

"Your illustrious father may get sodomized by Qanalarian cock wrapped in broken glass for all I care. You are in my lands now. Lord Minos is free to seek retribution, if he dares."

Dorav's face dropped to a scowl.

Kartecus tried to think of a way to save Dorav from this, but nothing came.

"Sir Dorav," the Queen stated. "Have you brought an invading force into my lands?"

"Magalian lands," Dorav affirmed grimly.

"Magalian lands under my protection," she sneered. "You have come here without a writ of passage, killed my innocent subjects, and betrayed your Holy Order. You reek of taint, Sir Dorav."

"No!" Kartecus called. "He is not marked! He is not tainted! Dorav is loyal to the Ashura!"

"He is lying." The Magistrate's voice carried a hint of curiosity.

"Oh how intriguing!" The Queen appeared dangerously amused.

Kartecus could not understand why the Magistrate said that. As the High-priests of Testament, Magistrates were granted the perplexing ability to discern calumny.

No untruth could be spoken in their presence without them knowing it. No web of conspiracy or intrigue could hold them long. Adding to this, Magistrates notoriously ruled against anyone who lied in their presence.

But he had spoken honestly. Even if Dorav was somehow disloyal to the scriptures, Kartecus believed him to be...it dawned on him — the mepsiens. Their use in combat was not permitted by the Order. Their methods and magics were considered heretical.

Fuck!

Kartecus closed his mouth, wishing he never opened it.

"Nothing more to add, Kartecus? How many ships are docked in Sharn perhaps? A fleet or two? How did you get past my patrols? How did you sack a place fabled for breaking upstart vessels like yours? These answers will buy you lenience gentlemen. I am not a monster."

Neither of them spoke.

"As you wish. Lord Aldemont, you have listened to my accusation, and their defense, or lack thereof. How do you see us proceeding in this matter?"

Magistrate Bacrus Aldemont stared at Dorav a long moment before speaking. "Were you given a writ of passage to come to Tepley, Sir Dorav of House Minos?"

Dorav stared back but gave no reply.

"Are you here by order of your King, Church, or the Knighthood?"

Dorav said nothing.

"Are you here against your will in any way?"

Dorav shifted and looked away.

"Were you made to swear the Oath of the Black Wing?"

Dorav's face betrayed his turmoil.

The Magistrate's face remained hard, but his voice softened. "You must speak, Sir Dorav. You must reply for all to hear, or I can do nothing to help you. Were you made to swear the Oath of the Black Wing?"

Kartecus wanted to cry out, *Yes!* Dorav's mission here was by request of the Order, of that callous piece of shit, Metzial Renot. Dorav was not a heretic or a rogue, but sworn to secrecy.

As much as he wished to spare Dorav, he could not betray him. Dorav swore the oath, and Kartecus had done enough damage already.

Dorav kept his tongue still.

"The accusation holds merit," Bacrus stated. "As the accused refuse to defend themselves, I authorize the Inquisition to extract the hidden truths from them."

"No!" Kartecus felt his legs wobble. "No, you cannot do this!"

"My dear Kartecus," the Queen spoke as if to a child. "It is already done."

When Tiliash showed the miners the guest quarters, Sifran let out a soft whistle of admiration.

These rooms, normally reserved for the entourages of traveling diplomats and envoys, contained four feather beds dressed in red sheets, accompanying water basins, and a chest at the foot of each bed.

On the western side of the spacious room was a balcony overlooking the western districts of Nevine, flanked by thick red curtains.

"This is a great room to watch the sun set." Tiliash said.

She could tell they had been drinking. Their eyes were glossy and their steps unbalanced, but they were clean. Gods, they smelled clean.

She had never experienced a body odor that ripe before. It would have been crass and ill-mannered to make mention of it, but she had breathed through her mouth the entire way to the baths.

Now David's beard was combed, braided, and treated with scented oils. Sifran's hair was free of muck and was surprisingly fair, closer to snow than corn. Ashen could pass for a lower Noble's son with the grime washed off his face.

They were each given a set of journeyman robes at the baths. Red and blue linens covered them from neck to ankles, tied at their waists with brown sashes denoting their lowly status.

The rags they arrived in deserved to be stabbed with a ceremonial knife, drenched in holy oil, exorcised, and burned as heretical items, but she simply ordered them thrown away.

"You must come see the view."

They stepped out into the dry, sour-sweet air above Nevine. Below them spread Tepley's massive capital.

"Originally built to withstand an attack from King Hervine's legions," she told them, "the Fabhcun perches at the center of a dozen land islands, all separated by the same bottomless chasm.

"Every island is a district, united by those wood and iron drawbridges, designed to rise or collapse as needed."

"It looks so different from up here," Ashen said, his gaze wandering.

"Those bridges feel much wider when you walk on them." Sifran added.

"They are quite sound," Tiliash said. "The Gnomes have improved them over the years."

"Gnomes?" Ashen asked.

"The Guild of Builders and Engineers. They call themselves The Gnomes, after the *Song of Tollas*. Those bridges used to be extremely dangerous to cross with anything heavier than a single-horse-wagon, and even then, the traders pinched their butt-cheeks while crossing."

They shared a laugh at her comment, which made her blush. She covered her smiling mouth which only made the men laugh harder.

"I am sorry!" She fought back their infectious laughter. "I do not know why I said that."

"Do not be." David chuckled.

"During the Sundering War," Tiliash attempted to recover some

228

dignity, "the city was not built yet. Only the Fabhcun stood, with the surrounding islands used as a defensive measure.

"Queen Aviedeen kept the bridges leading to the castle up, and only lowered them to admit scheduled supplies.

"After the war, the city grew around her castle. She named it Nevine to honor her sister, and Queen Nevine named the capital of Padive, Aviedina, in return.

"Since their founding, Tepley and Padive were sister Queendoms — their fates bound together for centuries heretofore, until recently."

Sifran's head drooped. "My family lived in Bramen until Padive's Raptors sacked it."

"They are still rebuilding Bramen," Tiliash said gently. "I have heard the stories."

Sifran took a long drag of his cuksar. "I was too young to remember much."

"I am sorry," Tiliash offered meekly. "The war was horrible for everyone. Even here. See the northwestern districts?"

"Yes." Sifran squinted.

"The burned-out black part is the old Caravan district, that one there is the Valik merchant's district, and right beneath us is the Herek district.

"Padive's legions made it all the way to that last bridge — to the castle's doorstep. A city guardsman called Herek gave his life to drop the bridge, giving our forces enough time to regroup and push the enemy back.

"Now the road, the bridge, and the district hold his name in honor of his valor. By the time the fighting was over, a third of Nevine was ruined. Fifteen years later and the Caravan district is still being rebuilt."

"What about those houses and ropes on the sides of the cliffs?" Ashen pointed.

Every island was cluttered with tightly packed buildings which spilled over their lips and clung to the chasm walls like barnacles. The islands were further strung together by thousands of rope bridges swinging precariously over the drop, connecting the communities clinging to the underbelly of the city.

"That's The Fall," she said. "The city has grown over the years, and people will build where they can."

"Are those rope bridges not a concern?" David asked. "If there is another war?"

"Our main concerns are smuggling and contraband, but for every bridge we cut down, three more spring up the next day."

"This may be the most amazing thing I ever saw," Ashen said.

"It pleases me to hear it," she said. "Well, I must go. Please enjoy the room. If you require anything, someone will be outside your door at all times. Simply let them know."

"Thank you, Lady Tiliash." David said.

"You are all welcome."

"Um, Lady Tiliash?" Ashen turned. "What do you think she might want with us? The Queen, I mean?"

"Something pleasant, I am certain. You stopped an attack on Tepley and captured its commanders. You are practically heroes." She graced them with a lovely smile.

"You hear that?" Sifran grinned at David, triumphant. "Heroes."

David shook his head and leaned against the rail, his gaze returning to the city below.

Tiliash left them and made her way back towards her own chambers. She wanted two things for herself today; that Ondar retire early from duty, and that the Queen forget she existed.

18

Hands on our Moonblades

They had made considerable progress on their journey back to Sharn, arriving a few hours before daybreak at the coastal town of Vlislis. Like the other towns along the Counter's Road, it had been thoroughly sacked, leaving behind only a remorseful shell of its lusterless self.

They found an adequate hut on the town's outskirts and made camp for the day. Marca fell into a deep sleep shortly after arriving without eating or bothering to remove her boots. Rairi wrapped her in a musky woolen blanket and stepped out into the chill, cloudless night.

Murciel sat by the shoreline, watching the dance of Elinel's light over the Zaratan sea. Small fishing boats tied to the nearby pier rocked gently in the tide while the dreaded Devil's Spine loomed in the shadows, a hundred yards from shore.

"You grow fond of that anthrop," he said with a grin.

"She is nothing like what the Elders preach." Rairi sat by his side. "She is childish and naive, but there is no malice in her, and she is as smart as any mepsien alchemist. Smarter, in some ways."

"High praise coming from you." Murciel leaned back on his hands. "I witnessed a falling star just now."

"That is troubling."

While anthrops were awed by the sight of falling stars, the xial considered them malignant omens. When a xial died, their spirits rose into Cala-Arisia's heavens and became a part of her star-fire canopy.

When stars fell from her grace, they did so to warn their living kindred that something terrible was coming to pass. During their fall, they became sacred star-steel, to be forged into weapons and wielded by their people.

"You believe something may have happened to the others?" she asked.

"I hope not. I do not like that Nihengale divided our pack this way. They should have come back with us."

"Agreed." Rairi looked at him. "I never did thank you, for accompanying me back."

"And you do not have to." He gave her a warm smile. "We are pack. This is who we are."

She returned his smile. "If I speak truthfully, Murciel, I hate this mission. It was such an honor to be entrusted by the Lady Dal'dira, but as the nights pass, I wonder if she did not send us out here to die as certainly as Dorav's masters did for him."

"No," Murciel said, shaking his head and flinging a small stone into the black sea. "I believe in my heart that she knew we would succeed."

"But we barely did. By your own telling the battle for Sharn's gate was a coin toss. 'We tore victory out of Sharn's grasp but damn near broke our fingers doing it.' Your own words."

"It felt that way at the time, yes," he said, throwing another stone, "yet that all feels like it occurred an age ago. All that killing, at the wall and on the streets, made my heart race at the time. Looking back on it now however, I see why Lady Dal'dira sent us. Why she knew we would succeed in sacking Sharn. Does that sound odd?"

She leaned back on her hands and stared up at the canopy. "Perhaps some, but you were the one in the heat of battle. The anthrops at Sharn's dock surrendered bloodlessly. Marca and I stayed in our cabin distracting ourselves with an argument over sodius compounds."

"How do you suppose Isa and Myrkin will take the news of their leaders being captured?"

"Not well. We should be careful when we encounter them, and allow Marca to speak for us."

Murciel nodded pensively. "Agreed."

They sat in silence, Murciel flinging stones into the silvery black

232

water. He threw each stone a little further from the last but remained on the same line of trajectory. He was playing some kind of game with himself, testing his aim.

"I do not trust these anthrops, Rairi," he said, breaking the silence. "I will be happy when we are free of them."

"As will I," she said.

She considered herself an Arineri, guided by the Elders to build bridges among peoples, not remain in isolation and self-sufficiency, like the Nocturals. However, even Marca was someone she did not entirely trust.

The more optimistic of her faith believed they would one day live in equality and understanding with the anthrops. She did not.

Anthrops did not accept those they considered "other" as their equals, even among themselves. The xial would always be at odds with them. There would always be conflict.

She eyed Murciel. "Where do your beliefs stand?"

"About what?"

"The teachings of the Arineri as opposed to the Noctural."

Murciel gave her a questioning glance, then stared back up at the heavens.

"I believe the Arineri have the right of it."

"Are you saying so because an Arineri is asking? Would you say the same to Escara if she asked? You know she is a devout Noctural."

He smiled. "For a time I believed the Nocturals were correct to hate anthrops. Anthropy cursed us after all.

"They summoned their rape-daemons to taint our bloodlines and create the first half-breeds. After that they kept fucking us until our cubs became more and more like them and we lost our ancient grace."

"We grew arms in place of wings," Rairi said, quoting scripture. "And walked on two legs, not four."

Murciel nodded. "We learned to speak like them, follow their gods, wear their clothes, and serve their every little need. They took away everything we once were, and treated us like animals. Animals that could speak, learn their customs, and make them feel superior and in control."

"I did not know you were so knowledgeable about our history,"

233

Rairi teased.

"We never truly talked about it." He scratched his left foot under his caligae. "I even refused to wear caligae. For years I walked barefoot."

"Why?"

Murciel scowled deeply and he raised his hand as if speaking in forum. "Even after we freed ourselves," he mimicked Elder Netapa's long-drawn vowels and throaty r's. "We let them govern our minds by believing we need such foolish devices as caligae. They represent anthrop weakness, not ours! Toss them aside! Let Gaia feel the touch of your feet. Caress her so she may caress you in turn."

Rairi laughed at his foolishness. "And now?"

"I grew tired of my feet hurting. Easy for a D'kirn to speak of walking barefoot."

"Is that why you changed beliefs? Your feet hurt?"

He gave her a mock, withering glare. "Of course not! It was Elder Ermuis' speech during The Reaping that finally made me see the error in my view."

Rairi raised her hand solemnly. "Regardless of what our people's history may have been, or how the anthrops were involved, the wisest course is for the clans to move forward, not back. What is done is done, and cannot be undone.

"We must embrace the teachings of Cala-Neteri, who spoke of a world unified by the Sephira — who views all life as part of a single netrus.

"From these teachings, and those of Terra, we will find our place among the many races of the world. We must not isolate ourselves, lest we share the same fate as the Eldarin.

"Cala-Arisia will always be mother. The faces of the moon, our family, and the stars, our ancestors. We will never forget who we are, but new paths are required to lead us into the future. We are the xial, one people under Arisia's sky."

Murciel laughed. "Did you just quote him to the letter?"

"Word perfect." She smirked at him. "One of my many gifts."

Murciel threw another stone into the sea. "The stories the Elders tell of our ancestors' enslavement are horrific, but we must move away from this idea of who we once were.

"We are no longer Night Glass, and for better or worse, we will

234

never be again. We are the xial now, and we must find our place in this world."

"Are you among those who believe we will one day have lasting peace with the anthrops?" she asked.

"No," he said grimly. "I believe our clans have a place in the world as we are now, in Helicartia — but not alongside anthrops. Not while they hold our people as slaves in their cities. Do you believe in such a peace?"

"No," she said softly. "Simply because I favor Marca does not mean I champion anthropy. Even with the rare exception deserving the title "human", as a species, anthrops remain treacherous animals."

Murciel nodded. "We would do well to remain distrustful, Rairi. Best to watch them carefully while awake, and sleep with our hands on our moonblades."

Nihengale scanned the road to Nevine from high above the branches of an oak. Fifteen years after Tepley's war with Padive, broken engines of war still dotted the fields surrounding the city's walls. Disabled, overgrown trebuchets and catapults remained untouched as a testament to how close Tepley came to defeat.

Kaira's caravan had gained too much of a lead and managed to pass the city gates an entire day ahead of him. In the distance, the towering sprawl of stone, wood, and lamplight that was the city of Nevine was beautiful and terrifying to behold.

The Elders spoke of these massive stone cities with a sense of dread for good reason. He would never manage to find a single anthrop within such a place.

There was little he could do now except turn back and admit defeat. Failing Dali weighed heavily on his heart as he deftly climbed to the tree's lower branches.

A lone carriage approached on the road, pulled by two underfed mares and driven by a lone man in worn linens, whistling a diddy.

Nihengale knew Dorav had been taken to a man called Tribune Alister, which was a military title. Surely these anthrops had something akin to battle academies, like the Ren'koltor in Helicartia. Perhaps if he was patient and somehow found the academy this Alister belonged to, he might still find Dorav before he betrayed

Dal'dira's secrets.

As the trader's carriage passed beneath him, he leaped, landing silently among the goods tied to its wooden roof. The sealed carriage had no windows, so Nihengale slid down its rear and tested the door there. Sensing no resistance, he slid cautiously inside.

While his eyes adjusted to the new layer of darkness, he used his ketter. A bulbous anthrop frame and four small ones lay on the floor, wrapped in thick blankets and surrounded by an assortment of rugs, pelts, and bundles of wool.

Once his eyes adjusted, he realized the largest frame was an anthrop female, and the smaller ones were four anthrop cubs. Their uncoordinated breathing was peaceful and rhythmic, undisturbed by his presence.

Nihengale studied the carriage's ceiling for a hiding place but found it cluttered with hanging nets of personal affects, clanking against each other. He stepped lightly to the front of the carriage where the robust woman lay.

Carefully, he unrolled one of the coarse rugs. It was thick and roughspun, with little intricacy in its patterns or longevity in its weaving. He wrapped himself inside and stood perfectly still.

A simple glammer would help him pass undetected if the city guard opened the carriage for inspection. Once past the city's armed sentries he would escape this contraption and go about finding the Tribune.

The carriage lumbered over uneven earth until the din of anthrop voices rose from outside. Men and women called to each other in rough calisthian, making clicking noises and yelling commands to their horses.

"Whoa!" The man at the reins yelled as the carriage came to a sudden halt.

The jarring stop tipped the unsecured rugs over. Unable to hold himself upright, Nihengale fell with a curse.

He hit the floor, the thick rug unrolling and ejecting him right into the fat anthrop woman. Her eyes shot open. She blinked rapidly in the meager light, forcing her eyes to adjust.

Nihengale unsheathed his moonblade and put it to her throat. The woman stared sightless into the darkness before she spotted him, her eyes widening with shock and disbelief. Her mouth quivered as fear awoke inside her, stretching its tendrils throughout her generous frame. Nihengale shook his head and put a finger to his lips. She swallowed dry and nodded. The carriage began moving again.

"Ma?" One of her cubs sat up, rubbing his tired eyes. "Are we there?"

Nihengale removed the finger from his lips, glanced to where the child was sitting, and pressed the dagger against her neck, her blood pumping furiously beneath the blade.

"Almost," she managed with a tremble. Nihengale narrowed his eyes and pressed the blade harder against her skin. "Go back to sleep now. I'll wake you when you're needed," she said, finding her courage. "Go on, back to sleep."

"I'm thirsty," the boy complained and stood.

Nihengale's eyes never left the woman's. He nodded to her once, watching tears run down her face as she steeled herself. "Fetch some from the bladder by the door."

"Can you get it for me?" the cub yawned.

"Sorn!" the woman hissed, unable to restrain a hint of desperation in her reprimand. "I didn't raise no useless ninny, now grab your own water and go back to bed."

The wagon boards creaked as the boy stood. Nihengale used ketter to track his movement. The woman trembled in fear. She stared at him, mouthing silently. *"Please, no."*

She repeated them over and over, a sob escaping her.

"Ma?" Sorn asked from the darkness. "You crying?"

His voice rose a grumbled protest from another boy.

"No, now go on back to bed." The misery in the woman' s voice was frightening her cub. Nihengale let the knife prick her to focus her attention. She flinched and put her hands over her mouth.

"Ma? What's wrong?" Sorn's silhouette shuffled blindly towards his mother.

"Stop him," Nihengale mouthed menacingly in calisthian.

"Sorn! Go back to bed this instant!" The woman's overexcited shout roused the other cubs. They groaned and began to rise from their blankets. Nihengale eyed them.

Disregarding the knife at her throat, the woman lunged for him, her strength and ferocity catching him off-guard. She ignored the bleeding gash on her neck and pinned him to the floor.

"No!" she yelled and put her meaty hands around his throat. "You won't hurt my boys! I'll kill you first! I'll kill you!"

She pounded his head against the floorboards while choking the air out of him. Her grip was like a wrought iron vice.

"Ma? Ma?!" the boys rose, caught in the infection of their mother's terror.

The blows against the boards threatened to black him out and his heart thundered from lack of air. This anthrop woman was killing him. Nihengale put his left hand over her mouth and pushed her up. With a grunt he drove his moonblade between her ribs and into her meaty heart.

A muffled cry escaped her. She stared at him, eyes wide and terrified. Nihengale watched the light fade from her eyes, until only her burdensome flesh remained.

Blood poured down his hand, slicking his grip on the moonblade. Her jaw muscles relaxed and her tongue lolled out, resting on his palm. Nihengale groaned and pushed the woman's body aside, coughing as his lungs struggled for air.

"Ma?" Came the pitiful plea of one of her cubs.

Nihengale could not use ketter but the cubs' silhouettes were visible in the lowlight. They tensed, their blunt instincts sensing something dangerous in here with them.

He had their locations, his body already moving. Two thrown knives and two swift swings of his moonblade would end the threat of discovery.

Sorn sucked in breath, preparing a long, terrified scream which would alert everyone outside of his presence.

Nihengale cocked his arm back, his sharp throwing knives thirsty and ready.

"Maaaaaa!" Sorn shrieked with a piercing pitch only children can reach.

Both knives remained pinched between Nihengale's fingers. He could not bring himself to murder these cubs. The carriage came to a sudden stop.

With a soft curse, Nihengale sheathed his weapons and made for the door. Outside, he was met by the broad faces of two startled stallions. They screeched and attempted to rear up, but were held in place by their wagon's restraints and the quick reflexes of their driver.

Nihengale kicked off his sandals and crawled upside down under the carriage just as the driver came around to the open door. Suspended there, hidden from sight, Nihengale cursed himself for a fool. Why had he not thought of this earlier? That poor woman was only protecting her young. He might have avoided this if he had only thought to hide here first.

Buio would not have made such a string of amateur mistakes. Cursing himself again, he crept upside down towards the front of the carriage and crawled up into the driver's empty seat. Pulling his cowl over his head, he tried to get his bearings.

Two carriages and three wagons ahead formed a line over a broad drawbridge. Eight armed guards took up the left-most length of the bridge, asking the drivers questions and examining each wagon's wares.

Nihengale took the leather reins and whipped them repeatedly against the horses' flanks, yanking them to the left and into the narrow passage occupied by the guards. The mares reacted at once to his violence, running head-long, and ignoring the living obstacles before them.

The cubs still inside the carriage screamed as it plowed forward. The driver ran behind them, his arms waving uselessly in the air.

"Motherless dick-eater!" The driver of a heavily loaded wagon screamed as he rumbled by. "Wait your fucking turn!"

The guards leaped out of the carriage's path, while others waved their arms at the horses, trying to stop them.

"What're ya doing ya shit-kickin' lunatic?!" A woman pushing a barrel on a handcart cried as he sped by.

One guard threw a spear, opening a fierce gash in the left mare's flank. She shrieked and panicked, plowing forward at a full run, forcing her partner to keep pace.

Both mares ran in a lather, fear overpowering their senses. Losing control of the carriage, Nihengale climbed up to its roof and dug his rakes in for support.

One guard managed to wrap her fingers around the wounded

mare's bridle. She was dragged under Nevine's fortified wall and through twenty feet of thoroughfare before she finally let go.

Shouts rose and guards called out as he barreled down a broad, busy market street.

"Spook!" A woman cried out, pointing. "Wild spook!"

Someone was caught beneath the carriage's heavy wooden wheels. There was a wet crunch and a sharp yelp of pain.

Nihengale used the carriage's sudden lurch to propel himself up to the sloping roof of a pewter goods store. He scrambled up its packed thatch as the wild horses plowed further into the city, rugs and other bits of merchandise flying from the open door — the cubs within still screeching.

He scrambled over the city rooftops, keeping to the shadows. The commotion followed the wild carriage north while he skirted away.

Someone had spotted him. Only a matter of time now before a hunting party was formed to find him. He needed to be deep into this city by then.

Nihengale and Buio were once hunting a group of anthrop poachers deep in the northern woods of Helicartia — near the ruins of Helesta. Their tracks had been spotted by border scouts two nights prior and a flurry of bird calls were traded over the northern expanse attempting to locate them.

Anthrops from Qanalar had a stubborn habit of wandering too far into these woods and it could cause problems. This was Herandal territory, and the half-beasts did not care for the stipulations of peace written into the Law of Reigns. If they found the poachers before the mepsiens did, they would tear them to tatters and the hard-won truce with the anthrop empire would be strained.

"Do you know why anthrops become lost in our forests?" Buio asked, as they tracked the poachers into the Heleswood.

"No, I never understood it," Nihengale replied.

He was surprised that Buio chose to initiate conversation. He tended not to speak unless spoken to, and his answers were usually concise. These moments were rare and sometimes strangely enlightening.

"It is not their stupidity," Buio said. "They simply cannot hear the earthsong."

"I do not follow."

"They adapt rapidly to new places. They have a developed sense of structure, but their main trick when navigating is picking out landmarks." Buio tapped the side of his head. "They imagine crude maps in their minds which tell them where they are by using chosen landmarks."

"But why do they not simply sense their location?"

"They cannot, Nihengale, that is my meaning. If you place an anthrop in a city, even one they do not know, they will eventually find their way around by appointing landmarks in their mental maps. Place them in an unfamiliar forest however, and they become lost, as everything appears the same to them. They cannot blend with their surroundings because they do not know how."

"Why are they cut off from the earthsong?"

Buio went silent, his eyes scanning the path they walked. Nihengale figured Buio was ignoring the question, so he focused on the sounds of insects and the rustling of the underbrush, trying to detect anything which might give the intruding anthrops away.

"The Elders say their blood is so poisoned by vorxcraft, they are no longer part of Gaia's wheel," Buio said. "They are something different now, foreign. This is why Gaia's children seek to purge the great mother of their presence, and why the Nocturals fear the xial becoming too similar to them."

"Why are you telling me this, Buio?"

"Because you are Alci'tirnni, and the night will come when the Elders deploy you into one of their cities. If you do not know what to do, you will become lost."

"I do not see that happening."

"Because you have never been lost before. Anthrop cities are uniquely strange places. There is a strong vibration in them, but you must never touch it. If you attempt to commune with your surroundings, the city will assault you."

"So how do you find your way, if you cannot feel a place's pulse?"

"You do as they do, Nihengale. You hunt for landmarks, remember their locations, and build a map."

Nihengale observed his immediate surroundings and his heart

sank. The anthrop structures were all frustratingly similar, with no distinguishing pattern in their placement. The entire city seemed a random, ill-conceived mess.

Elinel hovered above, accompanied by a few pale stars, but her light seemed to end just short of Nevine's rooftops, held back by a hardened dome of lamplight. He was severed from both starlight and earthsong, which filled him with a steadily growing sense of dread.

Although Buio had warned against it, he needed to hear the city's song and achieve some sense of direction in this blotted maze. Sitting on the warm shingles above a smithy's forge, Nihengale closed his eyes and took a deep, steadying breath. His skrit tingled, sensing his intention. He slowly released the tensions of his body, cleared the agitated murmur of his worried mind, and let himself fall into the city's underpinning vibrations.

A discordant miasma of scraping nails and rancid teeth assaulted him from all angles. Anathema to the haunting synergy of Helicartia's vast forests, the city's dense vibrations slammed into each other with murderous aggression. Scourging each other with primal barbs, fear and desire blended into a thorny gruel.

He was being masticated by a howling beast who's only purpose was to devour and excrete. The sensation infected him so suddenly, he released the meditative state to keep from screaming.

Nihengale lay on his side and pressed his face against the smithy's warm shingles, struggling to regain his composure.

"Elinel's tits, these poor creatures," he whispered to himself.

There was no natural order present here. The city's vibration was a crater of bridled entropy, stitched together by terror and welded by the cold flame of isolation. The emotional mortar holding these anthrops together was a blend of ignorance and greed, infected with a grime of distrust and selfish interest.

As he lay attempting to recover, a metallic clang rippled through the air and echoed over the city streets. The sound originated from a stark cylindrical tower, topped with a sloped conical roof, peeking out from behind nearby rooftops. Curious as to its purpose, Nihengale made his way towards it.

Other such towers began to ring around the city, their deafening hollow chimes clamoring over each other in disharmony before

242

finally falling silent.

The anthrop temple was larger and more elaborate than any he had seen. The massive dome and temple walls were the color of old graphite, surrounded by bleach-white marble columns carved into the shapes of seven robed women, their hems stained with a crust of green and black mildew. The well-tended lawn surrounding the property was decorated with somber looking statues of anthrop saints and holy-men.

Behind the bell tower rose the first pale glow of dawn. His search for Dorav would have to wait until the following evening.

The temple grounds were lit by ghostwood lanterns housing small blue flames. Their glow highlighted the smooth features of the statues dotting the lawn.

Nihengale was surprised to see ghostwood in the middle of an anthrop city. The snow-white trees with sap that burned blue in moonlight were sacred to the xial. The anthrops had fashioned a dozen eight-foot lamps and placed them around the temple grounds.

The grounds-keeper leaned against the stem of one of the ghostlamps, his bullseye lantern shut at his feet while he enjoyed a smoke.

On the nearby streets, the city was languidly awakening. Merchants and their helpers dragged creaking, loaded wagons towards their assigned stalls, doors of homes and shops opened to the street, and window shutters were pushed open to let in the chill predawn air.

Nihengale climbed down to street level and measured the distance between himself and the temple. The sounds of the city rose like the morning tide and if he did not move quickly, the sun would catch him in the open.

He needed to use the Kiyo'dreiv if he expected to pass unnoticed, but entering the Sheir in a place with such a corrupted animus felt unwise. What might stalk the shadow realm in a place as befouled as this?

He steeled his resolve, reminding himself that he was Alci'tirnni, and no true Black Knife of Mepsia could show fear of darkness. He took a long steadying breath, pulled his intention away from the lamplights, and concentrated on the gentle darkness between them.

He surrendered himself to shadow, focusing his intention on

becoming as them, devoid of light and warmth. A shudder of raw fear ran through him as his body reacted to the imminent death-like sensations. He held firmly to his sense of present self, letting the fear run its course until it washed through him and faded altogether. His mind slipped into the Sheir as an echo, waning and hollow.

The world around him became a black, mirror image of itself. Every surface coated in darkness becoming clear and solid, while empty patches and craters appeared wherever the lamplight touched.

Entire portions of the city were devoured by the black cores of its lamps and candles, under a sky the color of blooming thistles.

As he feared, the comforting darkness of shadow, which was soothing and inviting in the deep woods of Helicartia, was oily, corrupted, and diseased in this place. The Sheir whispered to him in sultry, indiscernible hisses, promising dark and bloody pleasures which were his to know if only he was willing to pay their price.

His shade churned in the wake of the sensations like a woman caught in the tensions of imminent ecstasy. He wanted to commit terrible acts so he might taste these wicked pleasures, have them crawl over and into him, until he was one with their slick, thorny tentacles — until a syrup of liquid sin seeped from his pores and dribbled down his trembling chin.

Something nearby let out a gurgling growl, full of terrible menace. The frightful sound startled him out of his trance, and the reality of the danger he was in struck him like an open hand to the face. He sprinted across the bridge of granite which lay between two street lamps and went over the squat wall surrounding the temple grounds.

Once among the light of the ghostwood lanterns, the cold, grotesque sensations fell away and the light of the blue flames graced him with warmth. In the Sheir, the ghostlamps burned like tiny blue suns but their light did not distort the Sheir like the anthrops' oily flames.

Warding glyphs carved into their stems also revealed themselves. The tainted things of this poisoned city's Sheir could not enter this light. The temple was warded against them. Apparently, anthrops understood the secrets of Neteri's netrus far more than he was led to believe.

The grounds-keeper's blind shade stood under the same ghostlamp as its owner, with a half-burned black cigar in its spastic hand, blowing blood-red smoke through its blackened lips. While the grounds-keeper watched his sky turn from black to azure, Nihengale witnessed a black sphere of nothingness rise in the Sheir's twilight sky. The eastern tip of the temple's tower was reduced to fine dust and sucked into that approaching void.

Nihengale moved to the temple's western wall, away from the rising black hole that would soon consume the city of shades, and began to climb. Beneath him, desiccated anthrop shades followed their owner's motions, walking into voids of nothingness, being absorbed by the black-light lamps, only to re-materialize once their solid counterparts re-entered a shadow.

When Nihengale reached the temple's roof he glided over the shale shingles and made for the tower, climbing its rounded side as the sky above turned faded indigo.

He rolled over the empty stone window and sat within the belfry. The enormous brass bell, half-eaten now by the rising black star, was linked to a series of pulleys and ropes leading to the building below. A familiar squeaking brought his attention to the tower's inner ceiling and the sight made him smile.

The beams above the bell were covered in the shades of hanging fruit bats. They stretched and yawned, readying themselves to sleep throughout the day. A few of them glanced down at him curiously with their nacre-colored eyes. Bats, much like cats, wolves, and a number of other creatures, existed partially in the Sheir.

Nihengale closed his eyes and focused. Returning his mind to his material body was always a taxing endeavor. He sank his attention deep within himself, until he found the single white spark which served as the doorway back. He flowed easily into the warm white light, being led back into place as if by gentle, loving hands.

The erratic noise of his frightened mind returned first, followed closely by the warm tingling of the skrit on his skin, giving him an outline of the shape his mind was meant to fill. As he became aware of his muscles, pins and needles assaulted him from head to toe, his entire body going through a mild electric shock. His heart sprouted into his chest, and the first painful aortic thrusts coursed into his body, like a sleeping limb suddenly flushed with blood. The weight and solidity of his bones followed, grounding him back into his flesh.

The Sheir faded away around him, replaced by solid shapes and vibrant colors. The menacing black star became a far less menacing glow in the distant sky, now reaching its first hints of crimson. After taking a moment to compose himself, he breathed a shuddering sigh of relief.

"Never again," he said. "Never again."

The most important lesson he learned when first entering the Sheir was to be wary of becoming lost. Away from the tensions of the body and the constant jabbering of the mind, the Sheir could be a hauntingly beautiful place. Arisia's cloudless canopy was so mesmerizing in the Sheir, many Black Knives came to call it Nerubia, the Doorstep of Grace.

The Alci'tirnni learned to walk the Sheir to move undetected in the material realm. His teachers had explained that while the mind was in the Sheir, the body became extremely difficult to detect — not because it lost any solidity, but because the practice nulled the user's presence to such an extent, he became imperceptible while in shadow.

If discipline was not observed however, or if the journey was overlong, travelers ran the risk of having their minds trapped among the shades. Without the mind, the body became a husk unwilling to eat, drink, or move, until it dried and withered away.

None of that compared to what he had just experienced. The Sheir of this city had quite literally tried to devour him.

The enormous bell made him reconsider his decision to come here. The thought of the anthrops ringing that monstrosity while he lay within was a frightening one, but if the fruit bats could withstand the clamor, perhaps it would not so terrible.

Other than the bell, there was nothing that seemed important here. The system of ropes leading up from the temple meant the bell was rung from below. The anthrops would have little reason to come here. There was a trap door on the floor so covered in dust and guano, he knew it had not been opened in ages.

With the sun crawling up into the morning's sky and the city awakening below, he knew he was without options. He climbed up the tower's support beams and into the small ceiling space where the bats nested. They flapped their wings in annoyance but remained in place, sensing he was no threat.

He positioned his pack, bow, and quiver on the crossbeams and lay carefully on the thickest beam, using his water-bladder as a pillow. He crossed his arms and feet, and wiggled himself into a balanced position. His moonblades and throwing knives weighed him down uncomfortably, but he kept them on in case he needed to make a hasty escape.

The thick oaken beam felt familiar on his back — like sleeping on the broad branches of his home's vast canopy. Exhausted and hoping the following evening would bring better fortune, Nihengale fell fast asleep.

19

Inquiry

Kartecus opened his eyes and took inventory of his surroundings. The chamber was hot as a forge and mostly in shadow except for the light of a few squat candles. He was secured tightly by iron manacles that pinned his arms and legs to the stone wall behind him.

A giant sphere, eight feet in diameter made of sturdy oak beams and cast iron studs took up the center of the room. The hollow sphere had a wooden X in its center with built in manacles for its victim's arms and legs. The gnarled, wooden contraption wore a dried coat of splattered blood. Sharp, hateful looking instruments lay scattered on the tables surrounding it.

Kartecus tried to speak but had terrible cottonmouth. He coughed and moved his tongue around to get the saliva flowing.

"Dorav!" He finally managed.

He strained his ears but no response came, only the rhythmic clicking of chain-links touching.

"Dorav!" His voice sounded clearer the second time.

An unexpected caw echoed in reply. A one-eyed raven stood perched over the chamber door, inspecting him — its left eye occluded and unblinking.

"You should not bother Dorav just now," came a soft voice from the shadows.

Inquisitor Sinitel stood only a few feet away, choosing instruments from a shelf and placing them on a small table by Kartecus.

How had he not seen him there before? The Inquisitor stood wearing only a pair of black breeches, his skin covered in gray, black, and red scrollwork.

"What have you done with him?" Kartecus growled. While they were still in the Queen's throne room, Sinitel had stuck them with something. Kartecus had felt a dull pain in his arm, then an overall numbness, then nothing.

"Do not worry Lieutenant, your Captain is fine. I intend to let him rest for now."

Kartecus tested his restraints and found them painfully constrictive.

"No need to be impatient now," the Inquisitor said.

"Where is he?"

"Not far, I assure you. You really should be more concerned about yourself."

"We will tell you nothing, creature. You waste your time."

"Oh you will tell me everything, but not tonight. Tonight is for easy conversation. I never had the privilege of working on an Ashura before, even an excommunicated one. I stand blessed."

Kartecus eyed the man and scoffed.

"You have lived an extraordinary life, Kartecus. Your body tells your tale wonderfully. The calluses on your hands from pulling rope and swinging heavy steel, and the roughness of your soles, filled with long-buried splinters.

"I admire the variety of your scars. You had a jagged object rammed through your calf once, right here. A broken piece of mast perhaps? Or a broken bottle? I counted nine arrow wounds and a number of other poorly tended injuries."

Kartecus shuffled uncomfortably under the Inquisitor's gaze.

"Your most telling scars however are those left by whatever amateur medicus you frequent. A broken leg, two broken ribs, one which has been recently tested. Your nose has been reset at least four different times by clumsy, uncertain hands.

"I am quite surprised you survived this." Sinitel ran a finger over the thin pink scar across his neck.

Kartecus could not pull away from the vile touch.

"A deep, fine incision," Sinitel said. "Studied hands made this cut. Was it vescar steel? No, this was mitiri."

Kartecus glowered down at him in silence.

"This may hurt." The Inquisitor dipped a small curved blade into a flask, and ran it carefully across Kartecus' forearm, drawing blood.

"What was that? What did you do to me?"

"Try to relax, Kartecus," Sinitel said, pouring liquid on a cloth and wiping his wound with it. "I only seek to loosen you up."

Whatever the Inquisitor used stung for a moment, then became a warm sensation coursing through his flesh. His breathing softened and his muscles loosened their tension.

"Lieutenant Kartecus, you godless whoreson," he said.

"Godless? I am an Inquisitor of Testament. Your own faith bows to the judgment of Holy Parliament, Lieutenant. Try to remember this as we move forward." Sinitel put the blade aside and leaned back against the table.

"Where is Dorav?" Kartecus asked again.

"I told you not worry yourself. He is safe, I assure you. Now, I would like to begin by you telling me about the Order of Ashura you once served. They fascinate me."

"No."

"No?" Sinitel asked with an infuriating grin. "Then you pick a topic."

Kartecus could not understand this creature's methods, but the farther he could maneuver this farce of questioning away from himself, the better.

"I thought your heathen race groveled before the whore of the night sky," he said. "How are you allowed to be an Inquisitor?"

"You do my people an injustice binding us under so small a roof. We are as varied and colorful as any of this world's high races.

"Like you, most of us adhere to the gods we are assigned at birth, but not all are so bovine and pliable. I chose this calling."

"What you choose does not matter in the slightest. You are all lost, lesser forms of life!"Kartecus spat.

"Why do you believe so?" Sinitel eyed him curiously.

"Because you were born to serve *us*. We are God's chosen, and those of you who walk away from the Stair fall into damnation."

"The xial of Helicartia broke free of your chains long ago, Kartecus. If we were meant to serve, how do you interpret their victory?"

"Their rebellion will not last." Kartecus' mouth felt dry and his eyes itched. "We will put you all back in chains soon enough."

"Is this truly your belief?" Sinitel raised an eyebrow. "That humans are the pinnacle of life? Every other high race knows you as The Children of Anthros."

Kartecus knew the name. Anthrops, the mepsiens insisted on calling them. A demeaning slur he would have slapped out of their mouths if Dorav had allowed it.

"The name comes from the ancient *Sepher Ra'Malkuth*," Sinitel continued, "which depicts your creator as a beast with the body of a monkey and the head of a wild boar — a rabid thing, more from the Vorx than from Gaia. Anthros spread his poisoned seed throughout the Old World, perverting everything into his own grotesque image."

"Ridiculous," Kartecus sneered. "Primitive, superstitious drivel."

"You believe your scriptures hold higher truths? I imagine you read the *Liber Scidomini*?

"Of course I have!"

"Do not be so surprised by the question, Kartecus. More than a dozen baptized zonirans have passed through this room who did not know where the concept of Zenthien being the one true god came from. You do understand these so-called revelations are being spoken by a mortal man?"

"The Witness is a saint and a messenger of God," Kartecus said. "He bares a divine burden. An aberration like you would never understand."

"I must disagree. From what I have read of this would-be witness, the only burden he bares is ensuring the zonirans conquer the very institution of religion."

"Heresy! You fucking dare!"

Sinitel smiled back at him. "I decide what is heresy, Kartecus."

Kartecus sneered down at him. "You speak as if your title grants you authority. Your faith only retains power by leave of the Monarchy, Inquisitor. There is no divinity in your calling. You are a puppet of the Crown, but all men must answer to God."

"You are again mistaken." Sinitel smirked. "Your monarchs only hold what power the Holy Parliament grants. Our *Magnus Scripta* is the cornerstone of your society. From commoners to nobility, including the royal families and your precious Church - All must abide Testament's Law."

"No one governs the Church but God!" Kartecus coughed dryly. He was thirsty, but would die from it than ask anything of this cur.

"Oh Kartecus, how frustratingly little you know. Whatever you may believe, whatever poison you carry in your heart for my people, I am not your enemy. I do not follow Cala-Arisia as my kin do, nor do I care for the differences between Noctural and Arineri beliefs. Whatever pettiness you Zonirans hold against other faiths is meaningless.

"As an Inquisitor, I have studied the scrolls and doctrines of all your divinities. Zoniran, Calusian, Novarin, Kerron, Levite, Selian, Galvite, and Lortian, to name a few. I have immersed myself in your dogmas and lore, because aside from each other, you all suffer the same common enemy."

Kartecus eyed the Inquisitor. "The Ashura hold the wall against-"

"No!" Sinitel said sharply. "I will not hear you say the Aegis of Mankind assists to stem the rise of the Vorx. The Ashuras were overtaken by their faith's desire to own and rule. Your people worship coin and the power it buys, nothing more. Your beliefs are gilded but hollow.

"You dare refute God?"

Sinitel shook his head. "You are not listening. I do not refute any god, because I serve a calling far beyond their myopic scopes. While your Churches and Temples scramble desperately for dominance over each other, I dedicate my life to defeat the only true enemy of creation.

"My faith is not dictated by the ramblings of tainted priests who make claims of heresy on innocent peasants only to justify stripping them of their lands. I am not governed by the empty and immaterial, but by ink and blood and steel.

"We raze the fields of entropy and plant seeds of order. We hold the wall alone. The rest of you only become involved when it suits your selfish interests."

"You are an ignorant spook who knows nothing about man," he said, feeling a heavy exhaustion weigh on his aching shoulders.

"I hold no quarrel with you, Kartecus. I do not care that you are human, or what God's heel you were born under. To me no race is greater than the other, because all are bound by the eternal cycles of order and entropy. All gods are accountable, as are their bleating ovis."

"You pontificate to an old, naked man in chains, you fucking spook. You are nothing more than a butcher and a heretic."

"Perceive me as you will. I am here to find the taint in you, and extract it by any means."

"You might have cause to punish me, but Dorav is an Ashura of Zenthien. You hold no right to him."

"Your willful ignorance is vexing me, Lieutenant," Sinitel said, visibly exasperated. "You are deaf to anything but the sound of your own voice. Both of you broke the law, refused to cooperate with the Magistrate, and failed to present a writ of passage. You are mine until I deem otherwise. Our situation is simple."

"Enough of your ramblings, butcher. If you seek to torture me, get on with it!"

"Whatever do you mean?" Sinitel grinned. "Are you expecting me to hurt you, Kartecus?" He waved a hand over the wicked items on the table. "To use these primitive tools to cause you such agony you relent and say whatever I tell you to? Is that what they did to you in Telkan?"

Kartecus went silent. He did not know what game this creature played, but he would not be toyed with. He realized how plainly he had been speaking until now. He had nothing to say to this heathen, and yet he nearly talked himself hoarse.

"Your poisons."

"I told you these are not poisons I administer. They are simply meant to loosen your bonds."

Kartecus shifted in his manacles, making them clink against the stone.

"Not those bonds."

"You think you can break my spirit?" Kartecus said, sneering at him.

"No man can break another's spirit." Sinitel took something from the table and held it up for him to scrutinize. "Now your mind is a different matter."

The leather gauntlet in the Inquisitor's hand had small, razor-thin metal claws attached to it.

"No, is that?" Kartecus stared at the gauntlet, unable to mask his fear.

"Yes. It is the beginning of your Inquisition."

Over the years, rumors, stories, and songs had spread wide about the Royal Inquisitor of Tepley, some which reached as far as the northern shores of Vinergale. *The Komiran's Claw* was a particularly terrifying poem which depicted this gauntlet as made from tanned human skin and studded with the bones of stillborns. The Inquisitor was said to have sold the souls of five vestigial children to the daemon prince Komiran, in exchange for the cursed relic.

What Remains was a fireside tale in which the gauntlet was actually the hand of a maimed daemon. It bled a foul ichor which corrupted everything it touched and but to gaze upon it could cause madness.

The gauntlet in Sinitel's hand was a well-worn, doeskin glove with five sharpened, two-inch metal claws attached to the fingertips, which held none of the fabled embellishments of lore. The Inquisitor uncorked five different vials on his table and dipped a single metal claw into each one. He held the gauntlet up to the light and turned it until the viscous syrups fully coated the blades.

"Now, be still." Sinitel placed the blades against his face with the center one in the middle of his forehead. "Do not move. It is not my intention to damage your eyes."

Kartecus kept still as Sinitel ran the blades across his skin. Three cut into his forehead just above his brow, one across his left cheek, and another on the right side of his jaw bone. The pain caused by the shallow incisions was sudden and fierce, coursing over his face and down into his body. Kartecus tightened his jaw but could not suppress the small moan of agony and spittle that escaped through his teeth.

"Yes I know," Sinitel said watching him. "Do not worry. The pain will pass soon. I would prefer to mix the elements myself and save you from this, but they are stubborn concoctions. Inside a living body however, they mix efficiently."

The sickening pain passed, leaving his body trembling and soaked in sweat.

The Inquisitor's pale green eyes reflected candlelight more intensely than before. They seemed to burn with an infernal, white glow. When the creature smiled, his teeth seemed brighter, each ending in a sharp tip. His hair became sprinkled with black feathers.

"What did you do to me?"

"Only opened your mind to the truth, Kartecus. I am curious to know what that looks like for you."

"I see you creature. I see you for what you are."

"Wonderful. My first question, then. Do you believe Zenthien is the only true god, Kartecus?"

Of all the things this cur could ask him, this surprised him. "Of course I do! What kind of fool thing is that to ask? I was his Knight! I served him once and I serve him still!"

"Is this really what you believe?"

"Yes!" A part of Kartecus understood it was a hollow question, rhetorical at best, but he was compelled to answer all the same.

"And yet here you are, powerless. As powerless as he is to help you."

The Inquisitor's every word was a whetstone scraping across his skull. The sealed lid on the cauldron of his emotions rattled as his rage bubbled to the surface.

"You know nothing of faith!" Kartecus growled.

"On the contrary, lost sheep. I know more than you would care to believe, and unlike you, I hold proof of my faith's divinity."

"Your vorxcraft proves nothing."

"Call it what you will, Kartecus. What I can do is real. Lady Testament's power flows through me and has fierce tangibility. Her divinity is something you will soon experience, intimately. In fact, let us play a little game," Sinitel teased. "I will call upon my Lady Testament, and you call upon Zenthien. If your god is listening, surely he will save you from me."

"That is not how faith works."

The Inquisitor's face became feral and distorted. The gauntlet in his hand now bore the horrible details Kartecus had heard about in story.

The metal claws were daemonically inscribed, glowing in the gloom like shadowfire. Sinew and gut stitched patches of human skin together, and tiny human bones adorned the tops of its fingers and the back of its hand. How had he not seen them before? This was a daemon's tool he was touched with. The disease it carried poisoned him from within.

"Yes, it is," Sinitel said. "Only your god is deaf to your pleas, while my summons will be headed. Go on then, make the first prayer. Ask your mighty Zenthien to pull you free from these shackles, to give you the strength to kill me and escape this cell."

Kartecus began to feel vertigo watching Sinitel's inhuman eyes. "This is not how true faith works!"

"Your faith is weak if you believe it will not free you from your chains. Will you not at least try? What harm could there be?"

Kartecus wished he could boil Sinitel's eyes and pierce his skull with only his gaze.

"If you insist, I will go first." Sinitel put his warm, pale hand on his bare chest. "Lady Testament, hear your loyal servant. A Holy Inquisition begins. I humbly ask for the Black Satchel of Cleansing to be opened for this sacred work. As my first instrument of dissection, I choose The Tourniquet."

Kartecus always had a terrible fear of spiders, ever since he was a child. Their mere presence made his skin crawl and his guts pinch. He carried this shame around with him in secret, hiding it as to not appear weak.

A swarm of black arachnids dug themselves out of the Inquisitor's arm, lifting his skin into smooth white bumps before cutting their way through. Hundreds of them scrambled on to the white hairs on his chest, crawling down his stomach, and up towards his neck, biting him as they went.

Their venomous, hollow fangs pierced him mercilessly, leaving white-hot pain in their wake. Kartecus squirmed in his chains as the bites began to travel below his navel, over his shoulders, and around his ribs towards his back. Fear wrapped around his bowels and squeezed, making him convulse. They were eating him. They were eating him alive!

"See now? This is what true divinity is like, old man. I ask, and my Lady provides. Where is your god? Why not ask him to cease this torment? This is only the beginning, Kartecus — a small demonstration of the power of my faith. I believe it would be wise for you to begin asking for some proof to your own."

Bound by unyielding iron, covered in eight-legged carnivores intent on devouring him, Kartecus danced impotently in his irons. The hot fever of the spiders' venom rushed through his veins, making him violently sick. He vomited, spewing chunks of meat and broth on to the floor and his own torso. His body began to dissolve, inch by inch being liquefied by the potent venom in the spiders' every bite.

Terror pounced him, tearing at his heart and mind, rending his pride and resolve. He raised his head and begged his Lord for salvation, his mind drowning in bubbling despair. He screamed out for Zenthien to save him from this maddening torment, even if it meant his death. Death was a welcome escape from this.

"Yes old man!" The Inquisitor said, smiling venomously. "Pray to your god! Beg for his mercy! Let us see if he answers!"

20

A Human's Eye

When Caige opened his eyes, he lay under a rocky outcropping somewhere near the coast. Waves crashed nearby and evening sea-spray hung in the air like mist. The chill and subtle light of predawn had awoken him. Tyn lay with her bare back to him. He kissed her ears and neck, wrapping his right arm around her and cupping her breast.

"Mmm...awake are we?" She asked.

"Mmmhmm." He slid his manhood slowly inside her. She leaned back against him, pushing him in to the hilt. He grabbed her breast in his hand and pinched her hardening nipple.

Tyn let out a small moan as he swung his hips, his hands exploring the smoothness of her skin.

"You are my treasure, Tyn," he whispered into her ear, incrementally increasing his rhythm. "My greatest gift."

Tynisia pulled his hand off her breast and wrapped it around her own neck. "Squeeze," she moaned softly.

"What?"

"Choke me, Cairn," she said huskily. "Squeeze."

He kept his pace but was taken aback. He never heard her say those words before. Regardless of his confusion, he gently squeezed her neck between his fingers.

"Harder," she hissed. "Harder."

Tynisia moaned loudly and ground her hips against him. Incredibly aroused by her reaction, he began to increase pressure.

"Yes! Yes! Cover my mouth!" she cried, guiding his left hand towards her face.

A chill of loathing slithered through him. He stopped moving, his manhood losing firmness inside of her.

"Cairn? What's wrong?"

"Tyn...no."

A thunderous roar emerged from somewhere nearby, making his heart leap.

"He found us." Tynisia scrambled to her feet, bundling their discarded clothes in her arms. "We must go. Stand! We must go now!"

"How does he find us?" Caige rose awkwardly.

"No matter! We must get out of here." Tyn took his large hand in hers and pulled him along. He followed obediently, looking back the way they came.

"No, Cairn! Do not look back!"

The enormous lion stood under the outcropping where they lay moments ago. Corren was on the ground under the lion's muzzle, reaching out to him with a look of terror on his pain-stricken face. The lion stared directly at him as it fed on the flesh of his father's back.

"Corren!" Caige went to run back but Tyn held him in place. "Tyn let go! I have to help him!" He tried to pry his hand free but her grip was surprisingly firm.

"You cannot help him! We must go!"

The lion's heavy pads stalked towards him, his emerald eyes gleaming like candles and his muzzle wet with his father's blood.

"He cannot be allowed to catch you. Turn away and keep moving!"

"He's my father, Tyn!"

"Your father is dead!"

Caige glanced down at her small fingers wrapped around his bloodied hand, and at her soft skin and familiar face. Everything about her was as he remembered, except for her eyes. They were supposed to be the color of bark and honey, not this eerie, luminescent rose.

In a moment of lucidity, he realized he was dreaming. The weight of the revelation was heartbreaking.

"So are you, Tyn," he said.

The urgency of escape dropped from her features. She stared up at him.

"Why is this happening, Tyn?" he asked her timidly. "Why did you really come back?"

"Damn you, Cairn!" Tynisia pulled him with more force than he would have thought possible, throwing him roughly to the ground behind her. "Get out of here!" she said in an animal growl. "Run!"

The massive lion pounced, brandishing its fangs and unsheathing its claws. Caige's heart made a fist in his chest.

"NO! Tyyyyyyn!"

The lion's enormous maw clamped down around Tynisia, crumpling her small frame and sending geysers of blood in every direction. She fought back feebly as the lion whipped his head back and forth like a pendulum. He dropped her limp, misshapen body into the dirt.

"NO! NOOOOOO!"

The massive, imposing creature stared at him, its bloody maw panting fetid air.

"Run, Caige," spoke an unfamiliar man's disembodied voice. "Turn away! You are not ready to witness this!"

Caige's shoulders slumped and his crest fell seeing Tynisia's broken body at the lion's feet. He was alone again, and there was no more reason to run. Kneeling before Tynisia's remains, he stared up at the lion's feral, luminescent gaze.

"Go on then," he said. "I am done running from you."

The lion unleashed a deafening roar.

Caige's body shuddered as long fissures of fierce emerald light broke open beneath his skin, segmenting his flesh and burning his eyes out of their sockets. The world around him became distorted and brightly chromatic.

The grassy hills rippled like a metallic ocean, their waves originating from him and flowing outward until they collided with the distant horizon. Here they became red bolts of lightning, riding the sky's concavity and meeting at its heavenly center, where the back of a trembling hazel eye stared unblinkingly down at him.

My eye! I am inside my own eye!

Pain scourged his bowels, his body tensing well past its natural threshold. His knotted flesh exploded into oscillating silver light slivers, keening as they rode the pulsing waves away from him and upward towards that trembling eye.

A pulse of electricity ran a painful circuit through the length of his spine, gaining momentum, twisting him backwards at an awkward angle, until his every bone cracked open, releasing tiny auroras of pulsing luminosity that danced like bees around a honeycomb. The light-bees swarmed around his viscera, devouring it in a brilliant, golden display, leaving behind only a shattered, lambent skeleton kneeling on chromatic grass.

His skeletal arms fell to his sides and his chin tapped against his sternum. He was left spent, empty, and ragged. The ground beneath him gave way, and he tumbled into a fathomless void, spinning helplessly through complete darkness. A twisting landscape of rusted chains and iron thorns appeared in the distance beneath him.

Disfigured, pain-wracked faces and writhing naked bodies draped in blood and refuse were caught in metallic barbs, writhing and screaming. They reached out for him, their desperate hands like a madman's claws, long-nailed and filthy. A raw terror he had never known rattled through him. With a voiceless scream, Caige fell unwillingly into that living nightmare.

Escara's mind tingled with every breath she took. The long razorgrass had given way to shorter, green wild-stalks that crunched under her pads. The damp earth and the scent of all the creatures that dwell within rose through her nostrils. The breeze carried a bouquet of varying scents and the night-song surrounding her was the most beautiful of symphonies. The closer they came to Ariel, the more tantalized she became by his nearly tactile presence.

Buio stalked behind her, his cold eyes scanning the horizon. She wished he could share in what she was experiencing. The D'kirn were powerful and graceful, but some of their senses were dulled compared to a D'sabre's. She wanted to interpret the colors and subtle vibrations she was interacting with. She wanted to put them into words, or even song, but did not know how. She breathed in deeply through her nostrils and the darkness behind her eyelids filled with untamed light patterns.

"Oh goddess," she moaned.

"Are we getting any closer?" Buio asked impatiently.

"We are." Escara reluctantly opened her eyes. "He has not moved in quite some time."

"Might he be injured?"

"I do not know, but I do not sense any blood in the air."

"How far, Escara?"

She was not certain. Her senses were raw and overstimulated. The closer they came to their quarry, the less she was able to discern the distance. Her mind was swimming in the cascading scents coming from somewhere ahead.

"Not far now," she managed and closed her eyes again.

A small groan of pleasure escaped her as a cool eastern wind licked her skin, teasing her, playing with her hair, and tickling her ears. There was a hidden song playing in the wind, so intimate and sultry, it made her eyes brim with tears. She followed the melody until she was lost within it.

"There!" Buio called.

Escara snapped out of her reverie. She did not know how long they had been walking, but the terrain seemed somewhat different. The wild grass was taller and the stars in Arisia's heavens had shifted positions in the sky. She could hear the ocean roaring nearby and taste sea-salt in the air.

Buio drew his vrin and crouched low, closing in on their prey. Escara had no time to consider the perplexing lapse in time. She crouched and followed closely behind.

When they came within ten feet of the anthrop, all the ethereal wonder around her dissipated. With the abrupt finality of a bird striking a tree, the mesmerizing presence she had been swimming through ceased to exist, as if it had never been.

The gaping hole left in its wake was quickly flooded by a deep sadness and sense of abandonment. While Buio examined the man, Escara stood in a state of bewilderment.

"Ugh," she said, covering her nose and mouth. The stink coming from the man was vile. His unwashed flesh, the bouquet of urine and dried feces clinging to his trousers, and worse of all, the reek of sickness, all clung to him like mold. Dried blood covered his hands, and his breath was a broth of raw meat, vomit, and disease.

"This is what you wanted me to smell?" Buio looked at her

incredulously.

"No," she replied. "This is very different."

"Is it him? Is he whom we chase?"

Escara looked around helplessly. She had let her senses guide her here, which she trusted implicitly, but how could this be the same person she had been tracking? He stank worse than a corpse.

"It has to be," she said.

Buio used his foot to turn the man over. He was a young, strikingly powerful looking anthrop, wearing nothing but a pair of soiled trousers and frayed calcei. His skin was clammy and grayish, he had dark rings around his eyes, and his black hair and stubble were thick and covered in filth.

"He does not have the horn on him, Escara. Are you certain this is him?"

"It has to be," she repeated.

Buio took out his water-skin and poured a bit over the anthrop's face. The man did not respond. Buio put the tip of his vrin on the man's cheek, just above his thick stubble, and cut into his flesh. A small droplet of blood flowed down his face, but he did not wake.

Buio glared at her expectantly. She felt terribly confused. She knew there was an anthrop in the middle of the wonderful scents she had followed here, but their sudden absence, and this man's wretched stench and appearance made her doubt her own convictions. She opened her hands in a helpless gesture.

Buio stared down at the sleeping anthrop pensively. "We either take him back with us," he said, "or we kill him here and now."

"Predawn is nearing," she said. "We should find a safe place to rest and decide what to do."

Buio nodded. "I will bind his arms and legs just to be safe."

"He stinks," she said. "Sari's mercy, he reeks."

"I know. Come on, we will be safer closer to shore." Buio dragged the man across the grass by his leg. The anthrop's arms spread out behind him. He continued to snore.

Escara followed at a safe distance, avoiding the anthrop's overpowering fetor. She could not understand why she had not caught whiff of his filth before now. She could always trust her senses. Something was not right.

21

Gypsy Bells

Nihengale sat on the tiled roof of a three story tenement building, exhausted and utterly crestfallen. His search for Dorav had proved fruitless, and now he was deep in the bowels of Nevine, despondent and thoroughly lost.

His eyelids were heavy. The muscles of his arms and legs were sore, and his claws and rakes ached from climbing the sides of buildings and over rooftops all night. The early hours of the evening had been the most taxing. The anthrops were still out in droves after sunset and the rest kept candles and lanterns burning in nearly every window. Moving around undetected without using the Kiyo'dreiv took every bit of skill he possessed.

The sun would inevitably rise soon and his only achievement was to wander the city aimlessly, searching for some hint or clue as to where the anthrop soldiers had taken their Ashuran captive to no avail.

He tried to rub the tension out of his neck and cursed in xiasi. This was a foolish and dangerous venture. He should have never come here. He had failed his pack by splitting them in anthrop lands, and then failed Dali by not catching up to Dorav in time. The most he could hope for now was to escape this cursed city before being discovered.

He was being tracked. There were dogs everywhere in the city, but there was a noticeable difference between the yapping of street dogs and the throaty call of well-fed hounds. The anthrops also had their own whistles and horns they blew, trying to scare him out of hiding.

Noting the sun was nearing the horizon, he climbed down to street

level and stalked the alleyways for a place to sleep. Seeing the scores
of vagrants sleeping in the shadows of Nevine had given him the idea
to find rest somewhere other than a belfry.

The bell tower he slept in before had struck twice. At midday, the
onslaught had startled him awake and sent spikes of pain through his
eyes. The bats had flown away in a screeching cloud, leaving him to
suffer the punishment alone. Once it was over they swarmed back
and stretched lazily before going back to sleep.

He had found little rest afterward and his nerves were frayed. The
second time was at sunset. The bats swarmed out of the belfry and
into the twilight sky, leaving him behind in a huddled ball of misery
as the giant bell struck its thunderous notes.

As he searched the sour smelling alleyway, the jingle of tiny bells
warned him of someone approaching. He ducked behind a pile of
lidless, discarded barrels, and put his hands on his blades. A quick use
of ketter revealed two forms approaching from the adjacent street,
speaking in calisthian.

"Where is he then?" one asked.

"Close by, I can smell him," the other replied.

"We cannot go wandering out after every spook you smell, Lupio."

"His scent is not like a normal spook's, Dio, and he wears no bells."

Nihengale grabbed the first figure that came near, pinned him
against the wall, and put a blade to his throat. He was a white-eyed
D'sabre wearing tattered linens and hemp calcei, with no clan
markings or battle-dyes. He was a frail thing with no muscle. His eyes
went wide with shock.

"Don't hurt him!" The other scared, young D'tiri cried out. "We
mean you no harm."

Nihengale did not intend to hurt one of his own, but he knew better
than to trust xial who lived in anthrop cities. The rules were different
here. Everything was different here.

"Why were you looking for me?" He spoke in xiasi. "What do you
want?"

"I caught your scent a while ago," Lupio said. "You do not smell like
a city spook. I figured you were lost and could use help."

"We just wanted to make certain you were all right," Dio said.
"Could you please take your blade off him?"

Nihengale pulled his blade back and sheathed it. "How can you smell anything but piss and horse-shit in this anthrop stink-hole?" Nihengale asked, taking a step back.

"It takes practice," Lupio said meekly. "We cannot stay out here. If the guards spot you they will put you in irons. Come, follow us."

Nihengale followed the two xial briskly through a small maze of alleys, an unmarked open doorway, and down a flight of broken stairs leading to a poorly lit corridor. A number of spacious chambers lay below, each filled with ragged looking xial.

There were members of several clans here, sitting on stained cots and lying in tattered hammocks, all wearing rags and brittle calcei. A number of wrought iron pots cooked something which smelled like old, wet undergarments. The xial in the rooms turned to watch him as he passed, their eyes reflecting the dim light.

"Sari's mercy," he whispered. He had never seen his people in such a wretched state. "What is this place?"

"A refuge," Dio said. "We come here to be among our own. There are places like this all over the city."

Antagonizing glares followed him into the chamber. He walked behind his guides, eyes forward, not knowing how to react. The madness of this anthrop city was scratching dangerously at his nerves.

"Why are they looking at me like that?"

"You are a wild spook. Wild spooks do not come here."

"Wild spook?"

"What we call xial raised out in the forests. Here, this is our spot."

Nihengale watched them make themselves comfortable on two dirty cots near a cold fireplace. Their belongings hung in frayed nets above their heads.

"Sit down," Lupio invited. "What is your name?"

"Nihengale." He sat awkwardly between them. "Son of Nahkir."

"What are you doing this far into Nevine?" Dio inquired. "How did you even get here?"

"I followed the city's thoroughfares like rivers."

"How did you pass the guard posts at the bridges?" Lupio's eyes were like saucers.

"I used the unguarded rope bridges dangling beneath the city's

267

deeper shadows."

"The Fall is dangerous," Dio said.

"The fall?"

"The hovels built on the sides of the chasms and the rope bridges connecting them." Lupio said. "That's the Fall."

"I see."

"But why are you here?" Dio asked.

"I seek someone. A prisoner brought in by anthrop soldiers."

The two young xial gave each other a questioning glance.

"What's an anthrop?" Dio asked.

The question made Nihengale nervous. He had let his guard down while sitting here among his own kind, but he was not necessarily safe here. Others around the room still looked at him, whispering among themselves.

"Humans." The word tasted odd in Nihengale's mouth.

"Is this prisoner a wild spook like you?" Lupio asked.

"Please stop calling me that." Nihengale said.

"But that is what you are," Dio said with a bemused grin. "I mean, look at you!"

Nihengale glared at them both. "You demean the clans, mentioning them as if they were savages. Your people are a noble, proud-"

"Wild spooks are not our people!" Dio growled at him. "We do not stalk around the woods like animals and live in huts made from cow shit or what have you. We live in homes of stone and tile roofing, with chamber pots and furniture! We are a civilized people, unlike you."

"Dio," Lupio said, a bit shocked.

"No! This tree-climber thinks himself better than us?"

The color drained from Nihengale's face.

"I work in the estates of Dominus De'Caur," Dio said, his voice raising. "My room is in the master's wing, and is filled with holy statuettes, masquerade masks, and penance disks. I own my own coin scepter, nearly full! What have you Amounted that makes you so much better than us? Sticks and leaves? Those heathen brands on your skin?"

Nihengale sat aghast and speechless. This pitiful excuse for a D'tiri was challenging him while spouting gibberish and calling the attention of everyone present. Nihengale was uncertain of the customs here, but he doubted silent acquiescence was an acceptable reaction.

"Never would a 'wild spook' as you so put it, treat another of his people in such a way." Nihengale's voice was cold and stern. "You would be welcomed into the Sari'dei, fed, and given wine and shelter. Never would your worth be questioned. You are a xial — starfire born into flesh by Arisia's grace! What else is there to measure?"

Neither of them spoke. They sat, eyes unblinking and lips parted.

"I have not suffered the horrors of this place to be chastised and insulted by unproven cubs in anthrop rags. If you cannot help me then I will be on my way."

Pain and confusion crossed their young faces. He was an oddity to them. Some strange shadow crawled out of anthrop legend. Whatever they expected him to be, or in whichever way they expected him to act, he had caught them off guard.

"Forgive us," Lupio sighed.

"Lupio!" Dio hissed.

"No, we should not be acting this way, Dio! He is our guest. We sought him out." Lupio turned to him and lowered his gaze. "You shame us, Nihengale, son of Nahkir. Rightly so."

"You shame us all," came a voice from behind them.

An elder D'aerth dressed in their same ragged clothing and footwear approached them. She wore small wooden beads in her red hair but was otherwise unadorned.

"My name is Aguiria."

"I am honored." Nihengale rose to his feet.

"How courteous, to rise as an elderly female approaches." Her golden eyes watched him, smiling. "A tradition lost on our young, as you can see."

Shamed beyond words, the two boys stood, their heads lowered.

"Are you the Elder here?" Hope filled Nihengale's heart.

"There are no Elders allowed in human lands, only old xial like myself."

"I feel lost, Aguiria," Nihengale admitted. "I do not understand this place."

"Well, let us try to put you at ease then, Nihengale. Would you come sit by my fire with me?"

A sigh of relief escaped his lips. Finally, a respite from this madness. "I would like that."

"Please forgive my overhearing your conversation with those two cubs, Nihengale," Aguiria told him as she served him tea from a black kettle. "You are the first of your kind to come here in a very long time."

"It is fine, and thank you." Nihengale accepted the clay teacup, inhaling its odd aroma.

"That must be awful compared to what you are accustomed to." Aguiria sat next to him.

"It doesn't."

It did.

"There is no need to sweeten my ear. I have tasted wild sivin tea. I might as well be serving you cat-piss by comparison, but I hope it is well received."

"It is."

It was.

"The prisoners you seek are an Ashuran Knight and an older gentlemen, correct?"

"Yes." He stared into her watchful eyes.

"They were brought into the city two days ago and taken to the barracks."

"How do I find this place?"

"Allow me to finish, Nihengale. Legate Hokran was summoned to the barracks shortly after their arrival, and he took both men under guard, into the Fabhcun — the Royal castle at the heart of Nevine."

"The royal castle," he repeated. "The home of the anthrop Elders?"

"In a way. I do not wish to bore you with the particulars of how the two differ."

"And how do I reach this Fabhcun?"

"That is a complicated matter, Nihengale. You will need a lot of help to accomplish such a thing."

"And have I found such help?" Nihengale looked up from his tea. He was hesitant to allow himself hope, but it sprung on him regardless.

"Perhaps, but I do not intend to help you just because you are a xial. This is not Helicartia, Nihengale. Assistance always carries a price in human lands. You will realize with time that everything has a price, and to pay this price you must first Amount to its worth. Amounting is the most sacred of virtues. To Amount is not only a holy rite, but an obligation of all."

"I do not understand. I know close to nothing about anthropic faiths."

"Is their wisdom forbidden in your forests?"

"No, I simply never felt the need to learn."

"I see."

They both sipped silently at their tea.

"The steps to Celestia are paved in golden light," Aguiria said, with practiced tone and cadence. "What does that make you think of, Nihengale?"

"It reminds me of the Night of Gildasa," he said wistfully.

"What is that?"

An Elder D'aerth not knowing about Gildasa, saddened him. He had to remind himself that these xial lived in a different world from those raised in Helicartia.

"Once every three years," he said, "Kiyo's face shines golden instead of silver. We call this face, Gildasa. She is Kiyo's bride.

"Legend says that on this night, the Valasi Stag, covered in grass and vines, wanders the deep forests of Helicartia willing to grant a single wish to anyone who manages to grab his antlers. The Stag is known to be attracted to cassia flowers, so we wrap ourselves and our homes in the bright, yellow blooms in the hopes of attracting his attention."

"That sounds beautiful." Aguiria's eyes betrayed a hint of envy. "If you ask this question to a Solarin, he will tell you he thinks of the sun-god Siege and his life-giving light. A Calusian might speak of the Light of Ascension, which a worthy soul sees when nearing death, after a life committed to the Great Works.

"To a Zoniran however, the scripture speaks of actual gold. To reach the promised land, we must first pave our stairway in golden bricks, so says the Lord."

"As I said before — I know very little of anthrop faith, but I do know Zonirism is outlawed in Tepley."

"Not outlawed, Nihengale, only relegated. As the faithful of Zenthien failed to overpower the might of Tepley, it was decreed by the Crown and Holy Parliament that their faith would only be taught to those who serve."

Nihengale took a moment to scan the dim-lit room. Most of the xial had gone back to what they were doing, but some still gave him quick, distrustful glances. Dio and Lupio ignored his presence.

"You are all Zonirans?"

"All here are baptized in the gilded waters, yes."

"And why are you telling me this?"

"Because gold is what you will need to enter the Fabhcun, Nihengale. Do you have it?"

"What use would I have for gold?"

"You will require a hefty sum if you wish to enter the Fabhcun undetected. That is your intention, is it not?"

"And if it is?" he asked, sipping at his tea.

"I am certain that it is. The guards have been hunting for you since you entered Nevine. They have questioned many of the Doms we serve and now the Hounds are sniffing for you on the streets."

"No hound could keep a scent in this place."

"Not those kinds of hounds, Nihengale. Human Hounds. Blood Trackers and Bounty Hunters."

"What will I need then, to enter the Fabhcun and avoid these Hounds?"

"You will require certain things arranged for you. A gate must be momentarily unguarded, a bridge may need to stay up longer than usual, and the Nighthawks will need to be entertained while you cross it. All these things have a price which must be paid in gold. Amounting to such a task will take time."

If Buio were here, he would surely discover a more direct way of entering this fortress. The D'kirn was renown for killing dozens of guarded anthrop nobles within cities like this. No one in Helicartia knew how he managed such seemingly impossible feats.

"I do not have time, Aguiria. I must be inside the anthrop fortress by the following evening at the latest."

"Not possible. If you like, I will take you there myself and show you why, but do not lose hope, Nihengale. Amounting is a virtue because it is difficult and filled with tedium. The gold of the deserving must be earned through toil and sacrifice. Also, we call them humans here, as they call themselves. They do not accept the title anthrop."

"Yet I noticed you call yourselves spooks, as they have dubbed you."
Aguiria's eyes narrowed at his remark.

He knew he was walking a fine line here. He needed to be more cautious in his approach. "Tell me more about this virtue of Amounting."

Aguiria's smile slowly returned. "I will give you an example. Do you know why everyone in this refuge wear such wretched clothing?"

Nihengale shook his head.

"We do so to remember the frailty of life devoid of virtue. While in our master's homes, we wear fineries and wrap our feet in carbatinas, but without our masters and the coin they shed in our names, we would be reduced to this squalor. We come here on the day of rest to remind ourselves what life would be like without the protection of those we serve."

Nihengale sipped his bitter tea. "Dio mentioned he owned penance disks. What are those?"

Her smile brightened. "When we sin against God, we must seek penance. We use our earnings to purchase penance disks at our Churches. Each disk absolves us of a single sin. The more disks we amount, the brighter we shine before the eyes of God."

Nihengale ruminated on the idea. "If penance disks are seen as a virtue, would this not lead to more sin?"

"Sin is a part of our everyday lives. Atonement however is costly and must be achieved through struggle. Penance disks show our sincere desire for cleanliness of spirit. They are proofs to God that we are repentant for our misgivings."

He nodded pensively. "What about the coin scepter? What use is that?"

"The scepters represent acknowledgment of divine service. When we act in a way which pleases our masters and the Church, we are given special coins which we attach to sacred scepters. When the scepter is fully covered, we trade them for golden blessings — the highest form of Amounting."

"Golden blessings?"

"They vary. Dio is looking to trade his scepter for a golden sash soon, for example. I recently traded my own for a pair of gilded carbatinas."

273

"Gold paves the way into Celestia," Nihengale said.

"The more you shine, the closer you come to the divine." She smiled. "You begin to understand."

"What about the masquerade masks he mentioned? What function do they serve?"

"None. Dio enjoys owning them. They are a sinful little pleasure he sacrifices his Amounting for." Aguiria gave him a knowing smirk. "This must all be rather ludicrous to you, Nihengale. To hear of a faith so distant from your own."

"A bit strange, I will admit. How long would it take then, to accumulate enough gold for what I seek?"

"Ah, but you cannot accumulate, Nihengale, that is not the point. You must Amount."

"I fear you lost me."

"You must Amount to worthiness. Firstly you must Amount enough gold to buy proper clothes, embellish and accentuate yourself, so you may rise above your peers.

"Only then, may you Amount enough to accentuate your dwelling, so you may entertain your betters and let them acknowledge your worth to Amount to a higher station. As your station improves, so does your ability to Amount."

"I believe I understand," Nihengale stopped her politely. "How will I know when I acquire enough to enter the anthrop fortress?"

"Human fortress, Nihengale. That will be up to you to decide. Using your gold for things outside of Amounting can be a worthy sacrifice as well. The true value of your quest will come to be realized in time. If entering the castle is worth the gold you must sacrifice for it, then that is a choice you will make when the opportunity presents itself."

Nihengale took the last sip of his tea. "This all seems complicated, Aguiria. I fear I may not be a good student."

"It can be, but you are proving quite adept. Tomorrow evening we will both go to the market and purchase your first set of proper clothes, bells, and carbatinas. You will amount enough to fulfill all your desires in due time, my new friend."

"Bells? Like those the cubs wore outside this place?"

"They are called gypsy bells. When the gypsy caravans enter civilization, they are made to wear them, so they cannot steal from

274

merchant stalls or escape undetected.

"All city spooks must wear them while on the street, and at home, if the master wishes it. We would never be so foolish as to steal from humans of course, but they prefer to know where we are at all times."

Nihengale nodded. "I see. Thank you for teaching me all this, Aguiria. I am glad we met."

"As am I, Nihengale." She gave him a warm smile. "As am I."

The following evening, Nihengale shared a loaf of bread and putrid smelling cheese with Aguiria while the refuge's inhabitants changed out of the thread-bare rags and into their fineries, giving him a chance to observe the brutal scars many of them wore.

"The Lord's Lash is another path to redemption," Aguiria explained. "It is a difficult road, but a necessary one to clean the spirit."

"Yet the scars on the flesh remain."

"As a reminder of the trespass, yes."

As the xial left the refuge, they each dropped a few silver marks and iron chints in a wooden bowl Aguiria had placed out before serving breakfast. Nihengale took note of their fine clothes, baubles, and accessories as they passed. Neither Dio nor Lupio spoke or met his eye. They deposited their iron coins in the bowl and made their way out.

Once they were alone, Nihengale turned to Aguiria. "This is your refuge."

"It is."

"You bring them here to remind them of their place without their masters."

"And to enjoy each other's company while outside their compounds. Places like this exist because many xial choose to live in this squalor, refusing to accept the Golden Stair."

"I witnessed anthrops living in such a state here — sleeping in sour blankets among filth and refuse, but I saw no xial."

"They are not tolerated in the same way humans are. Homeless spooks are imprisoned and executed if not duly claimed."

Hot anger rose up inside of him, but he caged it in his chest, preventing it from showing on his face. He focused instead on chewing his bread.

"As a first step towards your new life, we must burn those clothes you wear," she said.

This time he could not contain his outrage. Shock sat painted clearly on his face. "You would have me burn my skerki?"

"For a number of reasons. Firstly, to demonstrate your conviction towards this new path. Secondly, because that is truly no way for a civilized xial to walk the streets of Nevine. But most importantly, because your garments are covered in blood, Nihengale."

The anthrop woman's blood still clung to his armor, dried and clumped near the stitchings.

"No," he said firmly, straightening his back. "That I cannot do."

"Blood Trackers are after you. They hunt you night and day. I imagine you kept yourself on high ground, as you would in your forests?"

"Yes."

"That has bought you time, but they will close in on the scent of that blood. The trail will lead them here soon enough.

"Afterward, they will question me and my Dominus. By then you must be shrouded in the cloak of his protection."

He considered her words. "If they will find me there anyway, what difference does it make if I keep my armor?"

Her eyes betrayed her frustration. "It is a matter of intricacies, Nihengale. A matter of tact and the strength of our argument when my Dominus grants you his protection and sends the trackers away."

"No."

"Very well," she sighed, softening her tone. "We will take this slowly. Here, you will still need to wear these." Aguiria gave him a bundle which contained a musky wool cloak and four sets of gypsy bells. "A long night awaits us, Nihengale, and if you are tracked down before we reach the estate, I will not be able to protect you."

"I will take that chance."

While Aguiria changed into her fineries, Nihengale donned the bells on his ankles and wrists, then wrapped himself in the cloak. He caught sight of the pale lash marks crossing Aguiria's back and rear-end before she pulled her dress over her head.

"They exalt you in this way, do they not?" He gestured to the bowl of chints and marks at her feet. "They sacrifice their Amounting to add to yours."

"You catch on quickly, Nihengale." She smiled back at him. "Yes, they honor me with their coin, and humble me in the same breath."

"I do not understand."

"When they shed their coin, they diminish their own Amounting to add to mine, but in so doing, demonstrate that they are of a high enough station to do so.

"While in this shelter, I hold a higher station than any of them so by shedding a bit of their coin into my bowl, they reclaim their status. A gold sovereign means they are above my station, marks demonstrates equality, while chints denote a lower rank."

"There are no gold coins in your bowl."

"Because I am a taskmaster, Nihengale. Only a handful of xial in this city hold a higher position. Now come, let us find you proper clothes." Aguiria placed the coins from the bowl into a leather pouch, and they made their way up and out into the streets of Nevine.

Being at street level and surrounded by anthrops was disquieting. Nihengale wore his hood up to detract attention from his tattooed face. Although their bells jingled noisily with every step, no one seemed interested in their presence.

Aguiria wore a red cotton dress embroiled in silver, her gilded carbatinas, and three thin golden necklaces. Her bells were just as plain and loud as his own, but she wore them with a grace and pride Nihengale could not understand. Over her red dress she wore a green vest with a distinctive blue emblem on the front and back.

"Lupio and Dio wore your same emblem when they left this morning. You serve the same master?"

"Yes. Dominus De'Caur is a wealthy and influential man. He retains many fortunate xial in his service."

"Which is why you run the refuge, and they praise you with their coin. You are his taskmaster."

"You learn fast, Nihengale." She glanced back at him with an approving grin.

"If I may ask, what does your master do in this city?"

"Dominus De'Caur holds many businesses in Nevine. He trades in lumber and erawas from Ticondria, honey from Palimon, oils from Aztan, and fine wines from the Shantal vineyards. But what you really

want to know, is what business he conducts at the Fabhcun, is it not?"
She smirked.

"It is."

"The greatest weapon smith in Nevine has his shop in the low city
of the Fabhcun. He makes beautiful swords and daggers with silver
emblazoned hilts. He is a gifted artist and Dominus De'Caur
purchases exclusively from him.

"If you ever wish to be sent on such an errand, you must prove
yourself more worthy than Lupio. He is the only one Dominus
De'Caur entrusts to pick out the finest weapons at the fairest price."

"But first I must Amount to that worth."

"Yes Nihengale." She beamed with pride. "With every passing
moment, I sense you will Amount to something extraordinary."

"Thank you." His own voice sounded flat and unconvincing. He
hoped she would mistake it for trepidation.

Aguiria walked him into to a shop with a sign above the door; "Xial
Tailor" in calisthian. It was a quiet and enclosed place, away from
anthrop scrutiny, and lit by dim candles encased in blue glass.

Inside the store, three D'sabre girls were browsing wares. They saw
him as he entered and turned hastily away, pretending to be absorbed
by garments on the opposite end of the shop.

Aguiria picked out a red vest and breeches for him, with black
leather carbatinas and soft leather wrist-guards to go under his bells.
He tried them on without complaint, noting how well they covered
his skerki leathers.

"You almost appear a proper citizen." Aguiria gave him an admiring
appraisal. "For now you must continue to hide your markings, but we
will remedy that in time."

The way she studied him was predatory. She lusted for him, but
was attempting to hide it.

"There is something missing however. Ah, here." She wrapped a
thick leather belt around his waist and secured it. His knives and
pouches pinched against him uncomfortably, but he made no
complaint.

"It is important to dress sharply, Nihengale, but you must never
dress above your station. This is a terrible sin."

"What do you mean?"

"This is as much Amounting as I can grant you. The rest must earned from Dominus De'Caur himself. He will decide how you dress from now on."

"I understand." Nihengale was entirely vexed.

"Oh and another thing, you need a new name."

"A new name?"

"Among my people, I am Aguiria, but humans call me Petra. They dislike our native names, so they give us names which sound more pleasant to them. What shall we call you, Nihengale?"

"I would not know, Petra."

She smiled. "Such a quick study. Let me see. Nikolas, that will be your name. Petra and Nikolas. It has a pleasant ring to it, does it not?"

"It does." Nihengale tugged at the fabrics a bit and adjusted the belt. The extra layers of clothing were a bit stuffy, and he felt himself sweat underneath them. "Is there anything else I should know, before I meet this Dominus De'Caur?"

"Oh I believe you will do fine; better than most I take to him, and you are not even city-born. He will be enchanted by you."

Aguiria paid the clerk and they walked back out into the crowded streets. Nihengale detailed the roofs, archways, and overpass bridges dotting the city, wondering how these anthrops could find their way around this maze.

She walked him over a broad wood-and-iron drawbridge spanning the chasm between two land islands. The guards gave him curious glances, but none challenged their passing.

Loaded carts, wagons, and riders on horseback shared the bridge with pedestrians, street dogs, and merchants. The amount of activity on the bridge made him anxious, but the bridge itself did not so much as creak under the terrible weight it held.

"Be calm," Aguiria told him as they re-entered the city's winding streets. "And keep your head still. You attract too much attention.

Nihengale did his best to walk straight-backed and keep his gaze level. He spotted the Fabhcun's towering spires as they walked. Aguiria gave him a playful smirk and led him to the shadow of the castle's imposing mass.

A twenty-foot stone wall surrounded the city's central island. The royal castle rose from its heart like a jagged stalagmite, reaching into

Arisia's night as if seeking to pierce her canopy. Amber lamplight shone from its every window.

"Impressive, is it not?" Aguiria asked.

He wanted to tell her that it was anything but. The oppressive mass and rough angles of the stone edifice held no appeal for him. Aguiria had obviously never stood beneath the emblematic girth of a Tiperidrassil and stared in wonder at its impossible size, the twisting beauty of its reaching branches and the stone-hard sprawl of its deep roots, spanning for miles in every direction. This castle might be the epitome of anthrop ingenuity, but it paled in comparison to one of Terra's Daughters.

"It is," he said.

"I want you to look up at the tops of those towers, Nikolas. What do you see?"

The easy way she used his false name irked him. The stone spires of the Fabhcun presided around the center mass — their conical roofs and circular shafts completely uninteresting. He could see nothing out of place.

"What you fail to see, are the Nighthawks. Our beloved Queen understands the abilities of your clans quite well, Nikolas. As we speak, both D'aerth and D'tiri guards are posted within and without those towers, keeping a careful eye on everything below."

The sweet tone of her voice wrapped itself around his throat. He had not considered the anthrops might employ their enslaved xial in such a way. If she spoke the truth, these Nighthawks would have their minds in the Sheir, making them impossible to detect unless he entered into shadow himself.

Petra was right. He had no hope of sneaking past such a defense undetected. The thought made him look towards the drawbridge which connected the Fabhcun to the rest of the city. He was not surprised to find it lighted and well guarded.

"By the cast of your face I take it you finally understand," she said. "Like I explained before, if you wish to enter this place, you will need time and coin. Arrangements will need to be made for you.

"Patience, Nikolas. This task may seem impossible, but all worthy causes do at first."

"You told me at the store to keep my markings hidden. What are the dangers of exposing them?"

"You are being hunted, Nihengale. While it is not unknown for tattooed xial to walk the streets of Nevine, the less attention you attract to yourself the better."

"Anthrops know how to etch irezu skrit?"

"What?"

"Scrollwork infused with shinn." He pointed at the delicate marking on his cheek.

"Good Lord, no! What a ludicrous idea, Nikolas. Shinn is poisonous. What I meant was, those who Amount to the privilege are allowed to mark their skin with ink as a form of tradition. Come with me a moment."

Aguiria led him into the mouth of a darkened alley and gave him a meaningful look. "This is not something I do lightly, Nikolas. This must remain between the both of us. Consider it a sign of my faith in you."

"Very well," he said cautiously.

She pulled the hem of her skirt aside and showed him the gentle vine of xial lettering etched just above her pubis.

"There is no Amounting in it, but like Dio's masquerade masks, it is a guilty pleasure for some of us."

When he met her eyes, the predatory look was there again, highlighted by a flush of excitement on her skin. He knew then that she shared in anthropic body-shame. Exposing her nudity to him was both taboo and an invitation.

"I see," was all he could think to say.

"There is one final thing, before we go."

"Yes, Petra?"

"I will need you to surrender your weapons. I cannot take you armed before Dominus De'Caur, and besides, you have no more need of them."

He tilted his head at her. "What do you intend to do with my weapons?"

"Lock them away until you are ready for them to be sold. I am certain you are still attached to them, but with time you will come to understand their true value. They will fetch a grand price and Amount a great deal for you."

"But I must deserve it first."

"Yes, exactly. Nikolas, you are so very bright. You please me more with every word you speak."

"Petra, I must thank you." He stared directly into her eyes. Her hunger stirred. "I would be flying blind here without your help. Because of you, I now understand the vibration of this anthrop city in more ways than I can easily explain."

"Humans Nikolas, and you are a surprisingly quick mind. You will do quite-"

Nihengale's hands came up with blinding speed. Two open-hand strikes beneath her ears jolted her head and her eyes rolled. He caught her before she hit the ground and lifted her into his arms. Petra groaned but did not awaken as he moved her further into the dark alleyway.

Placing her gently on the ground, he shouldered her heavy pouch of coin and yanked off her golden necklaces. After a quick glance to ensure no one watched, he took her vest, donning the emblem of house De'Caur. He left the alley and walked towards the Fabhcun's bridge, leaving Petra behind in the shadows.

"Whoa there, spooky," an anthrop guard with ebony skin and a thick floral accent stopped him at the bridge's entrance. "Why the hurry?"

Nihengale took a deep breath. "I am sorry. My Dominus sent me to pick up three silver daggers from the master smith. He bid I hurry before the shop closed for the night."

"Dom De'Caur? He never sends anyone other than Skip, and I never heard of a tattooed spook working for him."

"I was rescued recently, from the wilds. I am new in his service. Skip is on another errand and I wish to show Dominus De'Caur that I am worthy of this task."

"You treacherous little bastard," the guard laughed. "Going behind Skip's back to get a little rub behind the ear? I appreciate that, but no. I like Skip because he knows the deal. You will not get by me."

"Dominus De'Caur will punish me if I fail him here. Please, I do not have the coin for a penance disk if I displease him."

"Your problem, pale-skin, not mine."

Nihengale's mind raced. He pulled Petra's golden necklaces from

282

the bag. "These are meant for my taskmaster, Petra. God has blessed her with this Amounting. If perhaps, I was robbed on my way back, and this was all the thieves managed to take?"

The guard gave him a bright smile. "You learn fast, spook, but I think the thieves took a bit more. I think they took your coin as well."

Nihengale reigned in his eagerness. "I need enough to buy the blades. It will be unforgivable to return empty handed."

"You will need to haggle then, little spook. Drive a hard bargain. Think of what you will Amount to if you buy those blades for your master."

Nihengale let the silence sit for a moment, staring at the ground in mock indecision. "Very well."

He handed over the necklaces and gave the man a fistful of marks. The guard smiled and moved aside while pouching the gifts.

Halfway over the bridge, Nihengale saw a crowd of anthrops within the small inner-city of the Fabhcun's walls. He wanted nothing more than to strip the bells and belt and damnable vest off and lunge them into the void. The mighty Fabhcun towered above him behind the prestigious shops and homes of the city's wealthiest citizens.

The full weight of this task pressed down on his shoulders. He had no idea how he was going to find Dorav in such a place without causing suspicion, but he was far too committed now to turn back. He would either find Dorav in this place, or die in the attempt.

22

Dust in the Light

Murciel skirted the coast at the south edge of Portan, looking out at the graveyard of ships washed up against the jagged rocks of the Devil's Spine. He counted the remains of nearly twenty ships of various sizes, half-sunken and jammed between rocks in the shallow wash.

The people of Portan had built their town entirely out of salvage from those broken ships. Their homes were recovered bulkheads with roofs of taunt sail canvas. Their beds were sailor's hammocks, their tables salvaged barrels, and every oil lamp was invariably covered in barnacles. He was surprised by the anthrops' resourcefulness.

Back at their camp near the edge of town, Rairi and Marca were in the midst of a heated argument. Murciel marveled at Rairi's fluency in calisthian. He always felt awkward attempting to speak the anthrop's tongue, so he avoided it when possible. He could understand it when spoken, read and write it to an extent, but speaking it was his weakness.

"I am not saying your measurements are incorrect." Rairi perused Marca's notebook. "But you have not taken into account the impurities which will infect your shinn during aeration and that you will not reach critical temperature.

"Your formula would work within a Kessian crucible but you cannot simply modify the temperature scale to a slower burn in clay and expect the same results. Your instruments have a direct effect on your results, Marca. Clay cannot sustain the kind of temperatures needed to create altashinn."

Marca bit her lip nervously. "What if I sealed it so no impurities could enter?"

"The increment pressure increase would blow the crucible, destroy the sample, and kill anyone standing near it! Can you not be so impatient? Wait until your return to Palidor and attempt your formulas with proper instruments."

"I cannot! If the academy finds me purifying shinn samples in their crucibles they will place me in chains."

"You cannot achieve altashinn below perfect standard, Marca — it cannot be done. Your theorem is sound, but without a Kessian crucible you will not achieve results greater than senashinn."

"The Academy holds the secrets of creating Kessian crucibles in their vaults. I would need to steal one!"

"So steal one!"

"What are you two going on about?" Murciel asked a bit hesitantly in xiasi.

"Marca is attempting to depurate her samples to altashinn at below perfect eutectic standard."

"Mind repeating that in plain xiasi?"

"She's," Rairi switched back to calisthian, "she is trying to purify her shinn using a clay crucible she recovered from a blacksmith's shop, even though she knows damn well the level of purity she desires is not possible without a Kessian crucible."

Marca made a petulant face and looked away.

"We should go," Murciel said. "We have lingered here long enough."

The three gathered their belongings and made their way out of Portan, heading northeast towards Sharn. Rairi and Marca continued with their vexing conversation about measurements, standards and proportions.

Murciel let it fade into background noise, scanning the path ahead and looking for signs of an approaching patrol. The sheer face of the Norvan Peaks was to their left while the Devil's Spine and the Zaratan Sea remained to their right. The road began a steady incline, and within an hour the Zaratan Sea was far below the Counter's Road, foaming its ill disposition against the jagged coastline beneath them.

Marca yawned more frequently as the night wore on, her eyes struggling to remain open. She tried valiantly to hide her exhaustion but her hanging face betrayed her.

"She drags behind," Murciel told Rairi.

Rairi glanced back, a shadow of concern on her features.

"Tell her to climb on my back," he said. "I can carry her the remainder of the way."

"Are you certain?"

He nodded.

"Marca, Murciel says for you to ride on his back. We can see you are exhausted."

"I'm fine." Marca stifled a yawn. "Honestly."

"You stayed up all day for us, Marca — we understand. We are fairly close to Sharn's borders so it will only be for a little while."

"He truly wishes me to?" Marca looked at him timidly.

He gave her a reassuring grin and took a knee. She carefully wrapped her arms around his neck, and as he rose, her legs came around his waist. A small groan escaped him as he stood.

"Are you certain you can handle her weight?" Rairi asked in xiasi.

"I am no D'morra, but I am far from weak." He shuffled her until they were both comfortable.

"Try to sleep," Rairi said.

Marca let out a humming noise and nodded against Murciel's back.

"It appears you are a comfortable ride," Rairi teased.

"I have heard so before."

Rairi chuckled and turned to observe the tide crash against the shore, far below the cliff's edge. Here the Spine gave way to the open sea. An old broken galley lay lodged firmly into an unseen reef, serving as a warning to any seeking to cross that threshold.

"Rairi, why is this girl so important to Lady Dal'dira?"

"She is from an important anthrop family. Her aunt is some kind of Elder in Vinergale."

"Why would she be sent on this suicide mission with Dorav then?"

"I am not certain. What I managed to understand is that the headmistress of her academy considers her a wasp among bees. She is too willful, and does not fear the kind of knowledge her masters consider heretical. This may be a way for them to be rid of her while keeping their hands clean."

"So they snare-trapped her?"

"Yes, I suppose they did. Just like the others."

"Is this not an overly complicated way of killing people? There are simpler methods."

"There is nothing simple about anthrop politics, Murciel. When anthrop nobles wish to kill each other, they must go to unbelievable lengths to ensure no one can trace it back to them."

"Why is that?"

"Because of their Magistrates."

"You mean the legend of how Testament's Magistrates cannot be lied to?"

"It is no legend. Buio told me a story about how the Royal Magistrate of Vinergale discovered a ploy to abduct the Chancellor of Lilith during the trial of a horse-thief. They pull at threads until they reach into the very heart of what they wish to know. Can you imagine how difficult it must be to not be able-"

"Rairi, quiet," Murciel whispered, cutting her off. "An anthrop patrol is stalking the cliffs ahead."

Rairi stared ahead and clucked her throat. "They are too far for me. Can you tell who they are?"

"Dorav's men. Remain calm and keep walking. No sudden movements. They have crossbows drawn."

Rairi wrapped the long string of black stones Buio gave her around her left forearm.

"What is that, anyway?"

"A precaution."

When the anthrop scouts finally spotted them, they began making subtle animal calls to communicate with each other. Murciel mused he could pick them off one by one in the time it took them to organize.

"You do the talking," Murciel said.

"Are they nearby?" Rairi used ketter again. "I do not have them."

"They hide behind those rocks. Be careful."

"We come in the name of Captain Dorav Minos!" Rairi shouted, startling Marca awake.

Murciel put the girl down and stretched his sore back, feeling a few satisfying pops up his spine.

After no reply came, Rairi added, "We come with bad tidings! Who is in command here?!"

The eight anthrops in hiding let out a few more calls. The clanking of Isa's armor reached his ears long before she appeared on the road.

"Greetings, Ser Isa," Rairi said as the stern-faced woman approached.

"Where are Captain Dorav and Lieutenant Kartecus?" Isa asked curtly. "Where are my men?"

She wore her aegis strapped to her back and her left hand rested causally on the pommel of her sword, but her scowling face made for a grim welcome.

"I am sorry, Ser Isa. Your men died in battle, and we believe Dorav was taken captive."

"Taken? By who?! Explain yourself!"

Rairi described the events of Kaira to the best of her ability. She spoke of the creatures and the chaos they caused in Kaira. She told her of Nihengale's intention to rescue Captain Dorav, and of their own orders to report back here with the news.

"Sergeant Kathor? What of him?" Isa's voice strained.

"Killed by those things as well."

"I see." Ser Isa was unable to hide the turmoil the news caused her.

"Marca, is she speaking the truth?"

"She is, Ser Isa," Marca replied meekly. "I am so sorry."

Isa let out a deep exhalation. "I need to report this to the Order and Admiralty. You will follow us back to the fortress and report to Master Myrkin."

"Of course." Rairi nodded.

With a hand signal, Knight Isa waved the other anthrops out of hiding. They joined them in the moonlight, their loaded crossbows lowered.

"Marca, come to my side," Isa called to the girl.

"Yes ma'am!" Marca quickly sprinted past the dual columns of seaguards. As Marca reached the Ashuran Knight, the eight soldiers fluidly raised their crossbows and pointed them at him and Rairi.

"Loose!" Isa growled, and as one, her men fired a volley of bolts.

Two crossbow bolts struck Rairi in the stomach and another tore through the center of her throat. Murciel threw up his arms just as a bolt meant for his heart punched through his right hand and pinned it to his chest. A second bolt sank between two ribs under his left elbow and a third dug into his side above his pelvis.

"Nooooooo!!" Marca screamed in shock and anguish.

Rairi fell to her knees, gasping and clawing at the wooden bolt in her neck. Two soldiers dropped their crossbows and charged Murciel, swords drawn, while the rest reloaded.

Murciel glanced down at his pinned hand, turned, and ran headlong. The soldiers' boots slapped against the stones and their panting breaths drew closer.

Two bolts snapped by so close, he heard their hissing peel. Another bolt sank into Murciel's upper back, sapping the strength from him. He stumbled, barely able to stay on his feet — the space between the men's thirsty swords and his exposed back all but vanishing.

Knowing their blades were an instant away from carving into him, Murciel sprinted and leaped straight off the cliff's edge.

"What have you done?!" Marca shrieked at Knight Isa through bitter tears.

"Lieutenant Kartecus left specific orders,"Isa spoke offhandedly. "If the heathens came back without him or the Captain, they were to be executed as traitors. No exceptions, no excuses."

"But she told you what happened! We returned here to warn you!" Marca sobbed looking down at Rairi's lifeless body.

She had never seen someone die before. Rairi's eyes remained wide in an expression of shock and agony. Blood still spurted from the wound in her neck and her right foot twitched in a death spasm.

The fear and nausea turned Marca's bowels to jam. She vomited on the stones at her feet.

"He is dead, Ser." A soldier confirmed. "Hit the rocks below."

"Good, get everyone situated," Isa commanded, "and send a runner ahead to warn Master Myrkin. We are leaving Sharn."

"Ser!"

"You too, girl, unless you wish to be left behind to face the Queen's Talons." Isa's eyes were as hard as a graveyard gargoyle's.

Marca sobbed miserably as the seaguards fell in line behind the Ashura. Without another word they marched back towards Sharn.

Marca stared down at Rairi's motionless corpse in horror and disbelief. She knelt beside it, unable to believe her friend, who she had just spoken to moments before, was dead.

"Rairi...oh god, Rairi!" she wept, grief pouring through her in spasms. "I am sorry," she told the dead body. "Oh God, I am so sorry!"

The string of stones tied to Rairi's left arm began to release small slips of black smoke. They glowed red hot and released a foul, acrid smell.

Marca stared in horrified fascination as Rairi's skin began to sweat and take on a greasy consistency — her beautiful black hair curling into a wiry, misshapen, mess. A moment later, Rairi's skin began to bubble, portions of her skin rising like boiling curd.

"No!" Marca cried, watching the bubbles spread over Rairi's face and down her pale neck. She tried to rake the radiating stones off Rairi's arm with her left hand.

Marca yelped in pain and pulled her hand back, cradling it with the other. Hot agony flared in her left palm and up her fingers. She opened it and saw black, charred circles marking the top of her palm and every segment of her four digits. Her hand began to throb and turn a fiery shade of red around the burns.

Rairi's skin and muscles melted like candle-wax. Thick blood and a yellowish secretion oozed from behind her eyes as her skull collapsed — her mouth distending and her hair becoming a tangle of swirling smoke.

Marca's attention became split between the melted horror her friend's body was becoming, and the searing agony spreading across her hand — turning her appendage a bright crimson as if burned by the sun. With a horrible hiss and a wisp of steam, her fingernails peeled off her hand, making her cry out in pain and terror.

Rairi's body liquefied, her flesh oozing into a black bile which ran in rivulets over the stones. Her clothes and hair burned themselves into a short-lived cloud of wind-swept ash. The glowing stones cracked open by their own heat, blazed for an instant, and were reduced to black dust, floating in the moonlight.

The searing agony in Marca's hand settled when the stones dissipated, but her skin still throbbed painfully and the red stain now stretched to her elbow.

"My God." She stared at her scorched, throbbing arm. She touched it

290

gingerly, expecting it to sting on the surface like a sunburn, but found her flesh tender, as if she touched a bruise. Nothing but a dark, wet stain remained where Rairi had fallen.

Marca stood and walked to the edge of the cliff where Murciel had leaped to his death. The black tide below slammed violently to the side of the cliff, rising a third way up the wall in a spray of sea-foam before dragging itself back into the sea. There was no sign of Murciel's body, but considering how violent the evening tide was, she was not surprised.

Crestfallen, with tears of pain and anguish streaming down her face, she made her way up the path Ser Isa and the seaguards had taken. Back towards the fortress city of Sharn.

23

A Truthtelling

David had once spent two weeks in a Raptor's prison before his brother rescued him. His captors fed him greasy bowls of potato broth, and the old stone walls were so drenched in piss and slime he developed a rash on his back and a lice infestation.

He had spent the last few days locked in a luxurious room with Sifran and Ashen, eating like princes and drinking fine wine by the cask, but he knew a prison when he saw one. The guards outside changed in shifts every four hours, but there were always two outside, even in the dead of night. Servants brought them food, water, and emptied their chamber pots, but they were not allowed to leave.

Sifran and Ashen made no complaint. They relished the Camnoc wines, butter soaked breads, and succulent sweet meats. They were also given a small wooden case of thick blue cuksar cigars.

Blue!

David had once carried a blueleaf cuksar for two months, waiting until the legion's victory in Sentinel before kissing its end with flame. So far they had smoked six.

"This is the life we deserve." Ashen leaned back on his feather pillow, staring at the stone ceiling. "Hopefully the Queen forgets we are here."

"We can dream." Sifran puffed on his cuksar, sitting in a chair on the balcony and admiring the view of Nevine.

David sat on his bed, his mind far away. He enjoyed the gifts of comfort as much as they did, but a voice in his mind would not allow him to settle.

"I hope that pretty girl comes back to visit us," Ashen said, his cheeks flushed with wine. "What was her name again?"

David eyed him evenly, a knot tightening in his chest.

"Hey Red, I asked you a question," Ashen pressed. "What was that girl's name?"

"Nianah," he said dryly.

Ashen's playful smirk dropped like a stone. "You think that's fucking funny, David?"

"Why not forget her and tell us what happened in Kaira, Ashen. What happened to Nianah? Why did you allow her die?"

"Allow her? Allow?!" Ashen stood, fists tightening at his sides. "You fat piece of shit!"

David stood, looking down at the smaller man, his bottled rage rising like steam in his chest. "If I had been there, she would still be alive."

"Oh, you would have saved her, David? Like you saved Ricker and Caige?!"

The blow struck home. His right hand tightened into meaty stone at his side. His left arm was still splint and wrapped in tanned gauss. "You never deserved her. A cockless, one-eyed goose would make for a better husband. You cattle warble. Tarrak should have eaten you along with your fucking parents."

"Horsefucker!" Ashen swung for his jaw. David stepped aside and planted his fist into the boy's cheek, knocking him back.

"You pile of kafra shit!" Ashen screamed at him. "I always knew you wanted her. You rotting tooth! She knew as well! That's right. We laughed about you in bed once done fucking, you sack of spoiled wine! Did you think about her, while fucking that diseased whore of yours?"

David lost his leash. He punched Ashen so hard in the head the boy's eyes rolled back. As Ashen hit the ground, David continued his assault, his momentum building with every blow. He pummeled Ashen's head with a wanton blood-lust he had not felt in years.

"David! David! You'll kill him! Get off!"

Sifran was screaming in the distance but the joy of finally pounding on this whelp was overwhelming. He had dreamed of this moment.

Sifran's arms wrapped around his torso, trying to pull him away. David shrugged him off and kicked Ashen in the stomach. The boy

lurched from the strike. David slammed his foot into Ashen's torso
again and again, wanting to break his ribs open.

"David you fucking coward! Stop it! He is but a boy!"

"I had killed a dozen men by his age!" David pointed down at
Ashen's bleeding face. "He is a fucking waste of air! Ricker should
have fed him to the Guild!"

"You fucking pustule." Ashen spat a wad of blood. "You're a dead
man, David."

Sunlight caught Ashen's eyes, blazing a bright amber hue. He
appeared like a cornered beast, ready to pounce.

David lifted his leg to land another kick when a terrible pain
coursed through his back, and the right side of his body went limp.
Sifran had punched him in the lower back, right in the sweet-spot
next to his spine. He fell to a knee and looked up at Sifran's pockmarked face in surprise.

"Enough!" Sifran said. "Get a grip on yourself, David! He's had
enough!"

Tribune Alister burst into the room flanked by two guards with
their kopis drawn.

"What the merry fuck is going on in here?!" Alister demanded, his
voice like a thunderclap.

"Just a difference of opinion, sir," David said, standing with a grunt
as his right side regained sensation.

Having been stopped so suddenly was bewildering. He looked
down at Ashen, surprised by how much blood was on him. How long
had it been since he last saw red?

"You tend to kill everything that disagrees with you, David?" Alister
crossed his thick arms.

David took three long, deep breaths. "No, sir."

"Back off. Now." Alister's tone offered no compromise.

David looked down at his bloodied, trembling hand and sat on his
bed, his head bowed. He had nearly killed Ashen. As lucidity returned
to the raging corners of his mind, he felt a wave of self-loathing wash
over him.

"Get him out of here." Alister commanded.

David did not resist as the guards ushered him out of the room.
Shame weighed heavily on his shoulders as they marched him down

through the castle's corridors and stairwells.

Outside were the prisoner pits — a series of rectangular holes, dug ten feet into the earth and sealed with iron bars.

They would likely leave him locked inside for days, stewing in his own piss and shit until the Tribune decided he had learned his lesson. They bypassed the pits and herded him towards the Talon's barracks.

Sometimes, guards liked to entertain themselves with prisoners before throwing them in dark places. They planned to beat him nice and bloody before tossing him in a hole. When they opened the barracks door, David braced himself, ready to fight them off.

Magistrate Bacrus Aldemont stood patiently among the soldiers' cots.

"There you are, sir," one of the men said. "We'll be out here if you need us."

"No." The Magistrate shook his head. "I want you both away from here."

"But sir," one of the men went to protest. The Magistrate's glare convinced him otherwise. "Yes, sir." They left without another word.

"Magistrate." David stood before the most powerful man in the Queendom of Tepley, uncertain of what to say.

"Please, sit." Bacrus waved a hand towards the cots. "There is much to speak about."

David nodded and sat on the cot like a child about to be scolded.

"Let me begin by informing you that I am recommending your inscription into our Queen's armed forces."

David's eyebrows rose and his mouth dropped. "Why?" he asked, and as an afterthought — "sir."

"Because I never forget a face, even one as changed by time and circumstance as yours. I know who you are, Sir Rien Bloodstorm."

David swallowed dryly, his heart gaining momentum in his chest and his adrenaline spiking.

Fuck. Fuck! OH, FUCK!

"That is not me, sir," he said. "Not anymore."

"You would not remember me. I was not yet the Royal Magistrate when we first met — only a city Arbiter, earning my way through Testament's trials. I did however witness your honorary appointment to Tribune of the Queen's Storm-Talons third legion."

"I see. Did I wrong you in some way, Magistrate?" David asked wearily. "That was a lifetime ago. If I insulted you-"

"On the contrary, you were an inspiration to us all, Rien. You and your brother Akata, if that is his real name. I brought you here because of a pertinent question I wish to ask."

David dreaded what this man might ask him, but dreaded more not being able to lie his way around it. He never considered how disarming it could be, not being able to lie.

"What is it, then?"

"What happened during the Battle of Coiren? Why did you desert the Storm-Talons and abandon your brother and men?"

"I had good reason, sir, but I doubt you would believe me."

"You forget, I am a Magistrate, touched by the grace of Testament. I would know if you lied to me. If you speak truthfully, I will have no choice but to believe you.

"Consider this an opportunity to unburden yourself, Rien. I can see this secret has weighed on you for many years. It is chiseled into every corner of your countenance, so much so that you are barely recognizable."

"Being unrecognizable was the point, Magistrate."

"I would like you to speak the naked truth without fear of judgment, for your own words will carry the weight of your circumstance. Lie to me however, and you leave me no choice but to perceive you as a coward and deserter."

David feared it might come to this someday. For fifteen years, he ran from this moment, trying to forget that fateful night.

He had never grown his beard during his campaign with the Storm-Talons. He had never been as fat, or hairy, or old. He only wanted to do his duty and get the hell out of Nevine. Now the Royal Magistrate had him over a table with his pants down.

"Wait," David raised his head in realization. "If you intend to judge me, why meet me here? If I know anything about Parliament, you never act outside your jurisdictions of power. Nothing I say here is admissible in your courts. This questioning isn't legal."

Something akin to a smile crossed the Magistrate's features and he nodded. "You are correct. Nothing you say here is admissible in any way. Which is why I stated that you may speak and not be judged, and that I would perceive you as a coward and deserter, not condemn you as one. I wish to know the truth as a personal matter, not one of state."

"So what happens if I refuse to tell you?" David stared squarely at the man.

"We go our separate ways, Bloodstorm. I am left with an unanswered question, and you may take your secrets to your grave, if you so wish."

David wrung his hands, considering the Magistrate's words. He never spoke to anyone about Coiren. No one would have believed him, but Bacrus Aldemont was the Royal Magistrate — the pinnacle of judicial law in Tepley. Only the Queen herself was above his authority. Like the man said, he would believe him as long as he spoke only in truths.

The Magistrate was offering him a chance to finally tell his story, in exchange for satisfying his own curiosity. The statement he gave here could not be used against him in any way. He could speak without fearing consequence. In a cruel way, he was safer telling this story to the Magistrate now, like this, than to the korgurs of his own faith.

"All right," David said. "Please take a seat, Magistrate, and I will tell you."

Bacrus Aldemont sat in the cot in front of David, crossed his hands over his lap, and waited.

"My men were ambushed by a tribe of Meleco savages in the southern reaches of Grierloom," David reluctantly began his tale. "They snared six captives during their raid before escaping into the thicket. By the time we tracked them to their village, my men had been slaughtered and eaten by those animals. They hung their insides out to dry in the sun like a prime butcher's cut.

"We killed those bastards down to their newborns, and then burned their hovels. At the heart of their village was a sacrificial pyre to honor the winged, fucking serpent."

"Cala-Neteri." Kartecus nodded. "Faith is a difficult thing to extinguish, Sir Rien, especially through the use of force. In my experience, war only serves to galvanize faith, not deter it."

"Perhaps, but I am a Calusian, Magistrate. Neteri is evil incarnate. Her malice caused the schism between us and the Zonirans.

"She is a corruption, a blight deserving of being hunted and destroyed. I grew up hearing stories about her cults, but they never struck home until that day. Seeing my men hanging like slaughtered pigs has haunted me since. Of all the things I witnessed during the war, nothing left a darker stain in me."

"This is before the battle of Coiren, however," Bacrus said flatly.

"It is, but it is where my story starts all the same."

Bacrus eyed him. David did not look away.

"Then please continue," said the Magistrate.

"I will not drag this out. I do not like talking about it." David took a deep breath. "Do you know the Xthonian prophesy? The one claiming Neteri will one day return by way of her tears?"

"I do," Bacrus said offhandedly. "The fleeing Neterians wrote it on every wall they could after the Purge. An ill-scripted snippet of desperate hope. What about it?"

"It's a lie. I have seen the truth."

Bacrus pensively combed his mustache with his thumb. "Go on."

"Khine took something from the village before we burned it down. Akata found him with it a few days before the battle of Coiren and made him destroy it.

"A book of sorts, made of skins splint together with leather bindings. The savages had drawn a story on its pages, showing the serpent as a divine thing — a teacher. There were pictures of how she was brought down by Tekuryo's spear. As she died, she shed prismatic tears, which were carried away by the four winds."

"'And when her tears are reunited,'" Bacrus interjected, "'she will return, not as feathered serpent, but as blazing heron.' I am familiar with *The Reincarnation Codex*, Rien."

David nodded. "Khine did not understand what he held. The pictures amused him, was all. He had a childish quality to him at times. Akata and I were wary at first, but Khine did not seem affected. He laughed in our faces, in fact. Called us sheep dogs and Nan's boys for our concern.

"During the last battle of Coiren, among the screaming, clashing, and dying, I saw her," he said, his voice trembling.

"Her?" Bacrus asked stoically.

"Yes, Her! Her! The womb of all malice, the corrupter of saints, and

298

all the rest. I saw her being born into the world."

The Magistrate's eyes narrowed. "You are lying to me."

"Of course I'm not lying! Listen to me! I saw Neteri being born on the battlefield! She took human shape!"

"Calm yourself, Sir Rien. Take a moment and speak clearly. What is it you believe you witnessed?"

"It was Khine. The codex must have cursed him, or changed him somehow. I cannot say how, but she corrupted him through that damned book!"

"Try and be more precise. What exactly happened to him?"

David tried to rub a bit of feeling back into his hands. "Khine took his vanguard deep into the enemy's lines during the Battle of Coiren. He wanted to take the Raptor Legate's head himself."

"Legate Exandir of the Elian Raptors?" Bacrus asked. "Your brother was reported to have killed him in that battle."

"I was not there for it, but I did see Exandir run Khine through and leave him to die."

Bacrus nodded stiffly. "Go on."

David took a deep breath. "Khine was in Akata's arms when he took his last breath. The idiot even found the nerve to smile as death touched him, but then something happened.

"He burst into black and orange flames from the inside out. His flesh melted like a block of cheese, forming a pillar of smoke and blazing embers. Two smoldering wings spread from that black pillar and I saw her, as depicted in the codex — a giant, burning bird. She used my friend's body as a pyre for her resurrection!"

Grief overpowered him, his body shaking. He had buried these emotions for fifteen years, and now the pot was overflowing.

"Please continue." Bacrus leaned in. "What else happened?"

"It was strange. The bird spread her wings and disappeared a moment later. When the black/orange flames died down, there was a baby boy lying in the ash."

"A boy." Bacrus' brow furrowed.

"A boy," David confirmed. "She is the mother of deception, right? Of course she would choose a shape no one would suspect. I pleaded with Akata to kill it, then and there, but he refused to listen to reason, though he had seen the damned bird too.

"He thought it some kind of miracle — that Khine had been returned to us by the will of the gods. He refused to kill it, or let me go near it so I might.

"Sir, I tried! I even forced him to choose between the creature and myself, his own brother, and he still would not yield. So I left."

"Your brother claimed in an Arbiter's court that you died in battle, crushed to unrecognizable pulp by a catapult round."

"I might as well have died." David ran his palm under his wet eyes. "I do not know what I became after that night. I don't even know for certain if my brother still lives."

"He is alive and well. Shortly after the war he returned to Aztan with a wife and a newborn son."

"A son? Gods have mercy." David buried his head in his hands.

"This news surprises you?"

David's head was a molasses. The weight of his long-kept secret fell from him at last, but the idea of his brother raising the mother of carnage as his own son gave him pause. "I suppose it should not."

"When you spoke before the Queen and said your name was David, I detected no dishonesty in your claim, which means Rien was the lie all along. What is your true surname?"

David sighed. This was something else he never thought to say before a Royal Magistrate. "Both names are true. A tale I will not speak of today, but to answer your question, my father's name was Jacinto."

Bacrus studied him, as if making a mental calculation. "Not *the* Jacinto?"

"Jacinto Redknife." David nodded.

For the first time during his telling, the Magistrate showed a vague hint of surprise. "Jacinto Redknife was a very troublesome man in his time."

"I doubt you know the half of it." David smirked. "My brother and I grew up among his bandits. By our tenth yeardays we both saw more death than any boy that age has a right to. Then came the war, and we learned the true face of horror."

"Who came up with your names and those colorful titles? The Stormlords of Tepley?"

David scoffed. "Akata. He always had a flare for the dramatic. When we were boys he wanted to be a bard, not a soldier, but fate rarely cares about what we want.

"When we were on campaign he made certain there were minstrels in our follower camp, and kept them up to their necks in wine and cunnie. He wanted our stories told far and wide."

"Minstrels are not known to venture into fields of war," Bacrus said. "Your exploits are gross exaggerations and outright lies."

"They truly are, sir. Most of those singing dandies were either too cowardly or too hungover to go near the fighting. They remained back in camp — fat, drunk, and plowing any lass who lifted her skirts for them. Most of the crazier stories you hear today are Akata's own fresh-spun horseshit. He loved to spin a yarn, and the minstrels ate it up."

"You are a more interesting man than I would have given you credit for."

"Well," David said with a shrug, " I told you my story, Magistrate. What happens now?"

"That Sir Rien, or is it David Jacintoson? Is entirely up to you."

24

In The Maw

Caige hammered diligently at the stone of Ricker's claim, aiming his strikes carefully like the others had taught him. He was on point today, with his father Corren to his right flank and Sifran to his left, while David and Ricker shoveled rocks and dirt into the loaded wagon behind him. Everyone was sweating profusely in the shaft's stale heat, the dirt on their skin becoming a muddy paste.

His mind was clouded and his body tingled with small static shocks. The stones beneath his pick appeared to him as laughing faces. He hammered down at them bitterly, but the more he broke them apart, the more faces he created, and the louder their laughter became. Caige tore furiously into the wall of mocking laughter.

"Caige! Caige, stop!" Corren called out.

Caige turned and faced his father, his face flushed in anger. The entire cavern trembled and the Bird bounced off the bars of her cage, desperate to escape.

"Gaia's thorny ass! Tarrak!" Ricker cried. "Out! Everyone out!"

Both David and Ricker threw down their shovels and ran for the entrance. Rocks and broken earth tumbled down around them from the cavern's ceiling. Sifran threw his pick aside, quick to join the retreat.

"Move it, Caige!" His father grabbed him roughly by the arm. "He comes!"

Caige shrugged his father off. "No, I am staying." He gripped his pick in both hands and began striking the stone.

For a moment, Corren stood watching him, dumbfounded. The Bird lay at the bottom of her little home, silent and stiff.

His father grabbed him by the arms and turned him around. "The Bird's dead, boy! Tarrak's breath has gotten to you! We are leaving!"

Corren picked him up and threw him over his shoulder like a sack of grain. Halfway out, a rock hit Caige above his right eye, drawing blood. His pent-up rage and frustration boiled over in an instant. With a hateful cry, he swung his pick down and plunged it into the back of his father's left thigh.

Corren cried out in surprise, and they both crashed to the ground. Caige stood slowly, looking down at his father with one eye blinded by his own blood and the other overflowing with tears.

"What are you doing, boy?!" Corren shouted. "You kill us both!" His father stretched his hand out to him. "Help me up, Caige! Hurry!"

Ricker's claim trembled. Tarrak was near. Soon he would surround them and bite down, grinding them to blood and pulp.

"She told me," Caige said grimly.

"What?!" Corren stared up at him, confusion etched on his face.

A blast of hot wind and a roar of grinding stones came from the depths of the claim.

"Tyn told me what you did to her!" Caige could not contain his anguish and fury any longer. "You fucking bastard, Corren! You forced yourself on my woman! You shamed her! In my own fucking bed! You broke her! She is dead because of you! Because of YOU! How could you fucking do this to me?! Your own son!? I loved her! You drunken fuck! I loved her!"

Corren's face was overtaken by shock. Grief and regret flooded into his features as understanding struck him.

"Caige," he managed, his voice cracking.

"To the Vorx with you, Corren!" Caige stood to his full height defiantly, his face flushed and weeping. "You shit-stained rodent! I fucking loathe you!"

"Caige. Caige I am sorry." Corren lowered his forehead to the sand and wept. "I am sorry, son. Chen's cunt! I was drunk! I know not how it happened! I am sorry! Caige, forgive me!"

"Sorry will not do this time, old man."

Corren looked back up at him, his eyes shining like fiery emeralds. The violent shaking of the surrounding mine went still and the dislodged stones fell as if sinking through water.

"The lion who kills Tyn in my dreams," Caige said, "was you, all along. I finally find peace in this hell-hole — a woman I loved and wished to raise children with, and you took her from me. You squat on your haunches and took a shit on my fucking life!"

"Caige, no!" Corren growled. "You do not understand!"

Tarrak's massive obsidian teeth inched out through the length of the mine's walls, ceiling, and floor. Caige stood at the edge of a black-toothed meat-grinder running the length of the claim.

As time spooled back up to normal, Tarrak's maw closed in with blinding speed, shredding his father into chum. Caige closed his eyes and raised his chin, accepting the same fate. Strong burly arms wrapped around his torso and yanked him back an instant before the jagged obsidian maw snapped closed around him.

The anthrop was moving around. Buio's eyes shot open and were pierced by the sun's morning light. Being accustomed to daylight, the immediate pain surprised him. He heard the binds around the anthrop's arms and legs snap and tumble to the ground.

"Wait!" Buio stood warily. "We have come a long way to find you. We mean you no harm."

Silence filled Buio's ears. He could not hear the man moving, the wind blowing through the grass, or the nearby sea. Something strange was happening. His every instinct begged him to draw his vrin, but he did not want to show aggression.

"Please say something!"

"Buio?" Escara spoke drowsily in xiasi. "What's wrong?"

"The anthrop is awake but I cannot see him," he said. "Do not open your eyes Escara, the sun is still out. Can you smell him? Can you tell me where he is?"

"Buio, open your eyes."

"I cannot. The light-"

"Buio," Escara insisted. "Open your eyes!"

Buio tentatively opened one eye, then the other. "Kiyo's swinging cock."

As if waking into a dream, Buio stood in a dome of physical impossibilities. The earth at his feet was roseate quartz and the grass, bright silver and fuchsia slivers. The sun had dropped from the

304

heavens and hovered only a hundred yards away, fiery and glorious beyond description, its light staining every passing cloud in resplendent crimson, pink, and amber hues.

Emanating from the sun's warm glow were long ripples of silvery light, gliding over the sea of pink grass and electrifying his skin as they washed over him. A monotone hum in his ears crackled and split into beatific notes which escaped confinement, erratic at first, then coalescing into harmonic synergy. He melted into that magnanimous incandescence, guided by the secret music which lies between form and spirit.

"Buio!"

Escara's frightened voice pulled him back into his flesh, his survival instincts flaring. At the center of the semi-liquid landscape, stood the white daemon wolf. The imposing beast, with its deeply scarred face and flaring roseate eyes, bared its yellowed fangs at him menacingly.

Buio crouched and placed his hand on the hilt of his vrin. A vivid hysteria shone in the wolf's pupiless eyes — like a madman's laughter directed at the world. Behind the creature, the young anthrop walked through the pink grass and towards the fallen sun, enchanted by its radiance like a moth to the flame. He wore the Horn of Dawn tied around his neck.

The white wolf growled deep in his throat and the ripples of light emanating from the fallen star reversed direction and flowed inward. Buio's flesh became motes of silver light, swallowed by the hovering ball of fire and light, reminding him of his encounter with Fulcrum. The same urge to scream in terror prickled his flesh, but he was not a cub anymore.

Buio drew his vrin and charged the tainted creature, leaping to clear the distance. The mad wolf barked and snapped its jaws, flinging spittle on the pink blades of grass.

Buio's world fragmented before his eyes. Every particle of space between him and the wolf became a tiny window of chromatic light. Inside every window where a dozen smaller windows, and inside those smaller refractions, were hundreds and thousands of similar portals, spanning into infinite recursion.

Buio lost himself in that blossoming flower of vibratory luminescence. His mind could not maintain singular focus as it

305

traveled through a maze of intangible images and tactile sensations. His attention was pulled in every possible direction so rapidly, it tore at his sense of identity.

Buio clung to his sense of present self, unwilling to let the terror take hold of him again — not like before. His body aged impossibly fast, wrinkling and bending in on itself until he was nothing but a dry, withered husk. His desiccated corpse struck the ground unceremoniously, but Buio remained present and aware, hovering over his own body as a speck of dust in a living ocean of vibrating light. The gravity of the star pulled him towards the wolf's open jaws.

Buio struggled to regain control, fighting back against the inevitability of entering that terrible maw. He hung suspended in air, caught by a pulsing web of timeless jewels. The wolf stood before him with its yellowed fangs wide open, eternally patient. Refusing to relent and be devoured, Buio held fast and stared into the creature's lambent eyes.

The oozing insanity in those rosy orbs spilled out into the fragmenting landscape around him, but Buio did not look away. He locked eyes with the beast and willed himself to remain calm. The white wolf's face became a canvas of living horrors. Puss and blood exploded from behind its fur. Insects, spiders, and serpents broke out of its pelt, drenched in blood. A menacing hum and sharp cracks like peels of distant thunder roared from the animal, pulling Buio down a spiral of black primal fears.

Buio held the wolf's gaze.

The living madness of the white wolf's eyes popped like soap bubbles, and waves of furious, savage anthrops poured out of his hollow sockets, wailing and screeching, running down the length of its snout.

Between the wolf's eyes stood a lone figure, smiling knowingly at him.

"Nahkir? Nahkir!" Buio cried out.

Ripples of regret rode through him at seeing his old mentor. Nahkir, the cunning D'tiri who had taught him the ways of the Alci'tirnni, even after being forbidden to do so by the Elders. Nahkir, who had taken him into his pack after no other would have him. A great man he considered family, and had accidentally gotten killed.

The howling anthrops fell from the tip of the wolf's nose like a procession of lemmings, cursing as they plummeted. Nahkir stood alone between the daemon wolf's cavernous eyes.

"Stop wounding yourself, Buio," he said. "You did nothing wrong. What happened to me was out of your hands. In this place, beyond all time and reason, we are forever one. Soon, the day will come when all must see, but until then, live free."

Much like his experience with Fulcrum, a nameless but monumental weight fell away from him. Years of buried grief and self-accusation,like a pulsing tumor in his spirit, burst and bled away.

Buio wept with the openhearted sincerity of a child finding refuge in his mother's arms. He had not understood how much pain he was in until the moment he released himself from it.

Buio opened his eyes.

The sun dipped beyond the western horizon, leaving an azure trail of clouds the color of peaches and plums. Escara lay nearby with her knees up to her chest, sobbing softly.

The anthrop was gone. His binds broken and lying on the grass.

"Escara." Buio used his thumb and index finger to wipe the tears from his eyes.

"I am sorry, Buio. I had the most vivid dream."

"That was no dream. I have been through this before."

"What, when?" She turned to look at him.

The tearful, unguarded expression on her face was beautiful. He wondered if his own face seemed equally bare and unburdened.

"When I was but a cub," he said.

Buio told her the story of his pack's mission to steal Fulcrum, and what he experienced when Nahkir had taken the namida from its case. Escara did not seem confused by his retelling. She nodded to the necessary abstracts he used to describe the sensations of that night, and their similarities to this one. He told her about Nahkir's death.

"Buio," she said, at a loss for words.

"What did you see?" he asked her.

She considered his question a moment. "I am sorry, Buio. This is all so new to me. I need time to process and understand."

"I know," he said. "All too well."

Buio watched the last rays of the sunset, his mind still riding the waves of the vexing experience. His every barrier shattered, he felt in unison with the landscape, and with Escara.

They had been pack members for years, and yet they knew precious little about each other. The night Nahkir died, a part of him had died as well. It became impossible for him to become close to another xial. The fear of loss was too great.

Now, this missing fragment of himself had found its way back and settled itself seamlessly into place. He was uncertain of what to do with the tide of emotions currently foaming within him.

"What do we do now?" Escara asked.

"Do you still have his scent?"

"I do." She sniffed the air. "He smells wonderful again, somehow."

"How far?"

"More than a day's walk away. We are not going to catch him again, are we?"

Buio stood and stretched his muscles out. "We must try."

Escara rose hesitantly. "Buio, in my dream, I saw the Horn around his neck, but I also saw the white wolf again."

"As did I."

"And you wish to give chase after what just happened?"

He nodded. "Because of what just happened, Escara. Whatever that wolf daemon is, it has the anthrop enthralled. He is leading him towards Aztan, and we must find out why."

They stared into each other's eyes, and for the first time, Escara did not look away. Everyone except Nihengale refused to hold his gaze, which made him feel like even more of an outcast, as if they were afraid of being tainted by him.

Escara's lustrous gray hair hung disheveled and her eyelids were puffy with tears, but there was fire in her galena eyes.

The unfamiliar warmth of a smile came over his face. Escara returned it with a hint of bewilderment, never breaking eye-contact. She really was quite lovely.

"All right, Buio," she said firmly. "We see this through."

25

A Fiery Ring

David stared up at the nebulous night as the open wagon rolled steadily southward. He recognized the white star-cloud filled with bright blue lights in the northern sky.

"Ursula," he whispered. His father had taught him the name.

The soldiers heading for Kaira had placed him in the baggage train, at the rear of the column, with the livestock, grain, and equipment. He did not mind. He needed time to consider the choices he had made.

Magistrate Aldemont had offered to give him back his life as a soldier. What a thought; Rien Bloodstorm, back from the grave like the Cortast Revenant. What would they call him, he wondered? The bards would grow fat telling his tale in the taverns.

David patted his broad stomach. No, he held no wish to be Rien again. His life of soldiering was well behind him. That being said, he had no intention of living the rest of his days in grueling, abject poverty either. Before leaving the barracks, he made a different kind of deal with the Royal Magistrate.

"There is something I need to tell you, about Kaira."

"Go on," Bacrus said, his gray eyes hard as flint.

"There is something we chose not to mention when we told our story about what happened in our town."

The Magistrate simply nodded.

"Before the soldiers showed up in Kaira, we discovered a valley."

David told him about the strange carnage left in the vale, the Neterian temple, and the ancient broken statue made entirely of shinn.

"When we heard that noise, the sound those things make, we ran for our lives, locked the claim behind us, and made for the tavern. The rest you know."

The Magistrate sat pensively a moment. "How much shinn would you say lay there?"

"Two tonne, perhaps more."

"And why are you telling me this now?"

David wrung his hands nervously. "Not every day you receive a private audience with the Royal Magistrate outside his seat of power. If I cannot get a fair deal for from you, there is not one to be had in all Tepley."

The Magistrate's eyes never left David's face. "Two tonne of shinn is no small find. Do you know its purity?"

David shook his head. "We had no chance to burn any, but it appeared clean."

"The lands of Sharn and the surrounding claims all belong to the Magalian family," Bacrus said.

"This shinn was not in Ricker's claim. It lay in unmarked, unclaimed land, just west of Kaira as the crow flies. That is the Crown's land."

The Magistrate's face pinched. "If contested, there is room for a trial. The letter of law would decide."

"Yes, but in the meantime the Crown would hold the land in safe keeping, right? And everything within?"

"You are very knowledgeable in these matters, for a bandit's son."

David grinned through his beard. "My father was a simple man from a violent upbringing. Smart too — smarter than most gave him credit for. He knew his letters and loved to read about old wars, and how they were fought and won, but this was not his greatest weapon. What the bards don't know, is my mother was also a bandit, and far more dangerous than my father."

"How so?"

"Before she fell in love with Jacinto Redknife, my mother served a truly vicious master — an unholy power which over time has destroyed countless lives and brought entire nations to their knees.

"She belonged to a cabal of soulless wraiths and, was herself, the meanest kind of vile, cutthroat, backstabbing, creature there has ever lived in this cruel world."

"And what kind of creature would that be?" Bacrus asked, his interest peeking through his impassive mask.

"A banker," David said.

The indomitable Royal Magistrate of Tepley, Bacrus Aldemont, tilted his head back and laughed.

David grinned remembering that cruel laugh. He leaned back against a bag of grain and took a deep swig from a bottle of firedrake. The deal they brokered before he left was better than he could have hoped for. The Crown would take on the cost of retrieving the shinn, measure its purity, and provide him a finder's fee worth a quarter of the shinn's total worth.

Even after the three-way split, they would be rich men, and could cease breaking themselves against Norvan rock. A part of him did not believe Ashen deserved a fair cut, but after what he did to him...

David took another swig of firedrake and set the thought aside, preferring to watch the soldiers in their ordered ranks.

The Queen had sent the Sickle Talon's third cohort to Kaira. Six hundred men led by Primus Carn Pentalion.

David had briefed the Primus on the cruel, gut-wrenching noise the monsters made, their piercing arms, venomous stingers, and why he believed they might hold intelligence. He could tell the dour Primus scarcely believed him, but if those things reappeared, these soldiers would at least have a fighting chance. Unlike Dorav's men who were caught unprepared and slaughtered. He needed to believe they stood a chance.

The Queen's Range Seekers rode by his wagon in single file. They were three men and two women on thoroughbred stallions carrying ornate saddlebags packed full to bursting. They wore fine gambesons over expensively dyed silks, cured stormcloaks, and supple riding caligae. Even the hilts of their swords and daggers were ornamented. They rode with an air of self-importance, sparing him curios sideways glances as they cantered by.

"Bunch of fucking dandies," he muttered at them.

David held no love for the Range Seeker's Guild. They were nothing but overpriced mercenaries who built their fortunes during the horrors of the Greenfire War — selling themselves as caravan guards, envoys, bounty hunters, and military shock troops. They possessed too much coin and legal freedoms in his opinion. If left unchecked, they were going to become a problem.

Murciel groaned and opened his eyes. He lay inside a damp cave with a campfire burning. The crash of waves against rock boomed somewhere nearby. His torso, hand, and leg had been cleaned and bound in fresh majesty leaves. He gripped gingerly at his thigh. There was a deep gash under his bindings he could not account for. He stared at his bandaged right hand and attempted to make a fist but his fingers would barely respond.

"Careful. You will pull your stitches," came a voice from beyond the firelight. Only then did he notice the form sitting there, watching him, green eyes glinting in the firelight.

"Rairi?"

"Of course, Rairi," she said with amusement in her voice. "You worried me, Murciel."

"How?"

"How long were you out?"

"No, how are you alive?"

She waved a hand dismissively. "The soldiers killed my surrogate. I was never in any danger, but you were. They nearly killed you, Murciel."

Rairi had treated the wounds on his torso and wrapped them carefully, but they still stung when he tried to move.

"Rairi," he said. "You dropped with a bolt sticking out of your neck. A kill shot."

"You saw what I wanted them to see," she said. "Do not wrap your head around it, Murciel. Be glad you are awake."

He took a breath. "I am not as smart as you, Rairi, but I saw you die, and yet here you sit. I need you to explain this to me. Please."

She stared at him from behind the fire for a moment. "To even begin to explain it, I would need to teach you the principles of high alchemy, Murciel."

"Please tell me something!" Fear crept into his voice.

Rairi's eyes widened, and she turned to stare into the fire, her brow furrowed in thought.

"Very well. We believe our world to be a familiar place. Wonderful and strange, with mysteries and surprises, but to a measurable extent, tangible and predictable. There is a pattern, and solid rules, and there is no changing or challenging them.

"The sinister truth is we do not know the world at all. Our minds fill in the gaps of what it does not understand — and believe me the catalog of which, is extensive — with stories and plausible perceptions.

"The Silvin teaches us how wide and deep these gaps in our perception are. How very little we know and how much of those gaps our minds are forced to fill. With that knowledge, and a clever use of alchemy, I can produce effects the untrained mind would consider magical, even miraculous, but they are not. They are hard-earned knowledge and careful application."

"The stones you wrapped around your arm. They were a part of it, right?"

She gave him a patient look. "Yes."

He nodded and decided to drop the subject, and never bring it up again.

"Thank you," he said. "How did I injure my leg?"

"By jumping off a cliff, you idiot."

He nodded and sighed.

"I am sorry, Murciel."

"What do you mean?"

"I could not stop them. I am no warrior. All I could do was stay alive and hidden. The way they came after you, I-"

Rairi sat slumped, her tears glistening in the firelight. He stared at her in disbelief. This brilliant, intriguing woman who somehow came back from the dead, could feel as lost and helpless as him.

"Come here, Rairi," he said.

She walked around the fire and sat by his side. He put his arm around her and held her to his wounded chest, running his hand through her hair to comfort her.

"What are we going to do?" she asked, her tears streaming down her cheeks. "We are trapped in enemy lands without our pack. You are wounded and I cannot fight like you can."

"We will find a way, Rairi," he said, planting a soft kiss on her brow.

"Do you swear it, Murciel?" She stared up at him, pleadingly.

He gave her his most confident smile. "I swear by Kiyo's bow, we will get out of this together."

Rairi nodded and put her head back on his shoulder. He spent the rest of the evening staring at his bandaged right hand, carefully trying to bend his fingers.

Caige quietly stalked the forest of Ticondria, a hunting bow gripped in his small hand. The maple trees grew huddled together in this part of forest and the sweet aroma of last night's rain still lingered.

He knew Marin hid nearby, studying his movements. He took a few steps down a grassy hill and spotted a jackrabbit. Trying to be deathly silent he crouched low and aimed, pulling the string of his bow taut. Sensing danger, the jackrabbit stood up on its hindquarters and perked its long brown ears.

Caige let loose with a grunt. The jackrabbit jumped safely out of the arrow's path and darted into the underbrush. Caige stood and fumbled for another arrow, but his prey had fled.

"Terra's ass!" he cursed.

"You tense when you loose," Marin said, coming out from behind a tree. "And you punch out with your left hand."

"This is horseshit!" Caige complained and threw his bow to the ground. "I need a better bow!"

"What you need, is practice."

"I do practice, but this bow is bent."

Marin smiled and shook her head at him. Her auburn hair was tied a ponytail, and she wore light leathers exposing the caramel color of her arms and feet. He loved how her deep brown eyes smiled more than her lips.

At fourteen, only a year older than Caige, Marin was almost a grown woman, and developing in ways that made Caige's heart race.

"Do all lads from the city blame what they cannot do on objects that cannot argue back?" she teased. "Or is it only you?"

"I can hunt!" Caige said. "I tell you, this bow is crooked! Go on, you try!"

"Shouting and scaring every animal within a hundred yards is a poor way to begin a hunt." Marin laughed. "And nothing is wrong with Erin's bow."

"Erin? This is his?" Caige was assaulted by a pang of guilt. Erin was a renown pelt hunter and Merin's older brother. Caige idolized him.

"Yes, the bow he learned with. He always said he was a terrible shot, but that bow," she pointed, "made by our mother's hands, did the work for him."

Caige turned his gaze away, feeling unbearably small. If any of the boys back in Aztan had made him feel this way, he would have punched their faces bloody. With Marin, he knew he deserved it. He picked up the bow and cleaned off the leaves and dirt.

"Want to try again?"

"Yes."

"And you are not going to blame Erin's bow if you miss."

"No."

"Good," she said and smiled at him. "Now let us see if we-"

"Cairn!" came a faraway, disembodied woman's voice. "Cairn!"

"Tyn?" The sudden recognition confused him. Tynisia was not supposed to be in Ticondria. He met her years after this moment, in Kaira.

I'm dreaming.

Caige turned back to Marin, but in her place stood the black-maned lion.

"What are you!? What the fuck do you want with me!?"

The lion bared its menacing jaws.

"Cairn! Where are you!?" Tyn's voice seemed far away.

The lion turned towards the sound. With a growl he sprinted away.

"Oh no, no no! Tyn, run! He is coming! Run!"

Caige tried to run after the lion, but his feet were trapped ankle-deep in mud. He struggled to free himself, but quickly sank up to his waist in the murk. He clawed furiously at the earth which only melted in his grasp.

"Caige," came another voice from behind him, and something tugged at his clothes. His father's face emerged from the mud, his lambent green eyes blazing.

"Caige!"

When Corren spoke, melted gold oozed from his mouth and tears of boiling shinn poured from his eyes, making his skin hiss and smoke.

"Caige! Help me!" his father gurgled.

"No! No you're dead! You died! I killed you!"

"Cairn, I have you!" Tyn stood at the lip of the mud-hole, gripping him by the arm. "Cairn, you have to help me! You are too heavy!"

Caige tried desperately to wiggle himself out of the pit and away from his father.

"Caige," Corren groaned, grabbing him by the leg. "I am sorry. You must help me. Help me!"

"Help me pull you, Cairn!" Tynisia shouted, pulling frantically with all her might.

As he was tugged in two different directions, the sky became filled with giant glowing eyes of varying colors, all of them staring down at him.

The sucking earth became rich with boiling gold and silvery shinn. These rare metals he had spent his life seeking seared painfully into his skin, cutting through muscle and drawing blood. The pain was unbearable.

"Stop!" he yelled at his father. "Stop, Corren! You are killing me! You must let go!"

"Pull yourself up, Cairn!" Tynisia cried, digging her fingernails into his forearm.

"Forgive me!" his father croaked.

"You have to let go." A wild, naked girl with disheveled hair and faded grease paints stood at the lip of the pit, observing him without a hint of emotion on her young face. He remembered her from the temple's entrance.

"What!?" He tried to kick his father off.

"Surrender to this pain so it may cleanse you. This is the only way."

Caige tried to pry himself free of Corren, but was being dragged further into the broth of gold and shinn.

"See," the disheveled girl said, kneeling now. "You must allow yourself to see."

Tynisia was no longer the one pulling him up, but a snarling white wolf with shimmering pink orbs for eyes. With a start, Caige yanked away from the creature and was dragged backwards into darkness.

"You whore," Caige hissed, staring at the sandy floor of his home in Kaira.

"Cairn! How can you say this to me?!" Tynisia sat at the foot of his bed looking small and broken, her face red from hours of sobbing.

"You are no better than Leina and the rest," Caige growled, so drunk he slurred his words.

"He forced himself on me! What was I supposed to do?! He is so strong! I could not stop him!"

"My father would not do that, unless you provoked him."

"Provoked him!? He was drunk, like you are now!"

"Then why did you not leave? Why did you come in here?!"

"To look for you! He said you were home! When I caught on to his lie, he grabbed me!"

"He grabbed you? That is your excuse, that he grabbed you?"

"What is wrong with your mind!?" The fear and disbelief in her eyes cut into him, but the pain only fueled his anger.

"Be quiet," he said, holding his swimming head.

"How can you act this way? How could you ever think I wanted this!?" She stood up and struck him in the back with her fist.

"I said be quiet!" His rage boiled over, a red haze clouding his vision.

"You would take his side?! After what he did to me?!"

"Shut up!" He turned and yelled in her face. "Shut your whore's mouth!"

"You seeping boil! You are nothing but a drunken cur like your father, CAIGE!" She spat in his face. "You worm belly! Shit eater!"

He grabbed her by the back of the head and pinned her down into his bed.

Long black claws tore through the flesh of his fingers and his mouth began filled with long, yellowed fangs.

"Caige! No! NO! PLEASE!"

A savage grating roar escaped his blackened lips. In a blind fury, Caige bit down on Tynisia's small frame, hot blood filling his mouth and dripping down his chin. Her cries of anguish only served to fuel his violence. He bit down until he felt bones break and raked his claws into her back.

"Caige, no! NOOOOO!"

Like waking from a nightmare, Caige's eyes shot open. The boiling gold and shinn shrapnel were pouring into his open mouth, scorching his throat and chest. As he choked and gargled in agony, the white wolf sat on its haunches, staring at him.

Tynisia's limp body hung from a tree-branch above the daemon wolf's head. The sight of her returned the full weight of memory, unrestrained.

Tynisia came to him with her heart in her small hands, begging to be forgiven for something which was not her fault. His drunken father had taken her by force on his own bed. When she told him, he had cursed her, blamed her, and done for her the same as Corren.

He was a drunken piece of human shit, like his old man. That night, Tynisia had left his home, her hair disheveled and her dress torn, and hung herself from Maggie's branches.

What Corren did was unforgivable, but he was not the monster who mauled Tynisia's heart and soul. Tyn could have survived Corren's assault if Caige had stood by her, and loved her past his own selfishness. He was the monster. He was the lion, this entire time.

Caige sank willingly into the boiling, gold and silver laced mud, grateful for the agony of being decimated from within. He deserved every morsel of this torment. He was tired of hiding from himself.

Welcoming his punishment, welcoming being burned in the bowels of the Vorx, he was pulled deeper into the earth until there was nothing but darkness and excruciating pain.

A sphere of vibrant, multifarious runic symbols bloomed in the depths of the void, expanding brilliantly. The shaggy head of the hell-born, white wolf tore through the light-portal and wrapped his fangs around Caige's neck.

"No!" The wolf barked and dragged him through the opening.

The world exploded in a sharp peel of rose-white brilliance.

Caige woke with a start — his breaths sharp, labored gasps.

"Shh, you are safe." Tynisia lay on his lap, reaching up to stroke his stubble. "You were only dreaming."

Caige lifted her small frame and buried his head in her black curls, sobbing miserably. He held her, anchoring himself with her presence as if she were a jutting rock in a raging river — keeping him from being swept away to drown.

Although his entire body trembled, he could not remember the vicious nightmare he just awoke from. He vaguely recalled there being terrible pain, a hot flash of blinding pink light, and a naked dread that rode him into his waking state.

"Shh, it is all right," Tynisia wrapped her arms around him and stroked the knotted muscles of his back. "You are safe. It was only a dream. Push it from your mind, my Cairn. Push it far away, and forget."

ACT III

26

The Jewel of Tepley

Xandrane stared at the thick tome on the table and chewed pensively on his thumb. Everything appeared to be in its proper place, but a crucial aspect of this equation was eluding him. He rechecked his work, scribbling on loose pieces of papyrus scattered before him, then compared his equations to the ones in the worn, leather-bound sepher lying open on the table. The *Sepher Cognitas* was written in his father's clean, meticulous calligraphy, making his own scratchy shorthand appear sloppy by comparison.

Xandrane simply could not prove that the sterilizing effects of Blue-back spider venom and the pain numbing properties of the Vically leaf could be combined. He was certain he had every element needed for a clean fusion, but something was off. The equation would not come together, inelegantly or otherwise.

Frustrated, he ran his hands through his sandy blond hair and stared up at the ceiling. Numbers and symbols hovered before his tired eyes, refusing to coalesce. If only he could take a vial of Blue-back venom, a handful of vically leaves, powdered shinn, and cook them in a Kessian crucible, he could finally finish his work. But that was not how alchemy worked anymore. The whole process was damnably tedious.

Along with his own notes and the *Sepher Cognitas*, copies of both the *Sepher Asclepius* and *Sepher Drassilius* lay open on the work table, their thick vellum pages stained at the edges from a lifetime of use. The Order of Zenthis Medicus had pounded the *Sepher Asclepius* into his mind, but he still liked using it as a reference.

The *Sepher Drassilius* was a different matter. He was not supposed to know this book existed, much less have a copy open in front of him. His father Temar was not a man to allow the acquisition of knowledge to be constrained by Inquisition law. He owned a number of books — kept in a sealed vault under their house — any of which would get them both burned as heretics if seen by the wrong eyes. Temar would beat him bloody if he ever found out Xandrane had discovered and taken liberties with his secret library.

He stood up from his desk and made for the kitchen. He could always find an escape from his frustrations in cooking. Here he could take all ingredients firmly in hand, cut them to appropriate measures, employ the desired heat, and have an end product he could see and taste.

He tossed seasoned shredded rabbit, diced carrots, longpod peas, whiteheart beans, oricar spices, and caramelized blue onions into a pot and slow boiled them over his home's hearthfire. While he gently stirred the thickening broth, there was a loud thumping at his door. He went back to his desk and hurriedly hid the *Sepher Drassilius* in a compartment under the floorboards. Taking a deep breath, he steadied himself and opened the door.

"Hey, Xan!" His cousin stood at the doorway fresh off the ship, wearing a sweat-stained linen shirt, black breeches, and a thick leather sword-belt. His long black hair reached well past his shoulders, and he had fresh cuts and bruises on his face — some partially obscured by his growing stubble.

"Wyk!" Xan smiled, the gloom draining from him. "Damn, have three months already gone past? Come in. How was the run?"

"Murder, in the literal sense." Wykith tapped the dirt out of his buskins, tossed his leather satchel on an empty chair, and hung his sword-belt on a thick iron nail by the door.

"What happened?"

"A little problem with the crew of the *Swordfish* in Relm. Started out as drunken mischief but someone on their side pulled a knife and things became ugly."

"How ugly?"

"We lost one, they lost three. The constables rushed in and beat the living hell out of all of us. You realize you truly fucked the dog when you wake the constables in Relm."

"So what happened?"

"The Arbiter who ruled the case banned both our ships from trading in Relm for the remainder of the season. Captain Alferos is still frothing at the mouth about it."

"Wyk, did you start it?"

Wykith gave him an incredulous look, but the curve of his lip betrayed him.

"You did!"

"Not true," Wykith chuckled. "This drunken, lecherous old fuck placed his hands on my friend Dirnia at The Siren's Den, so I put my foot in his ass. He pulled a knife, Xan. He was old and salted enough to know better. You don't draw steel in a dock bar. Everyone knows this."

Xandrane chuckled and shook his head at him. "You're impossible, Wyk. So what now?"

"Alferos called in a marker and found us another run. We head to Calimport by week's end with a hold full of grain, wool, and erawa oil."

"That's disappointing. I hoped you were home for longer. You are hardly around of late."

"We have to keep working before the autumn storms pick up. Once they start hitting we will be docked for months."

"Does Shayra know you are here?"

"No, I came here first. I will surprise her tonight." Wykith's broad smile lit up his face. "I regret not being here for you yearday, Xan, but I got you something."

Wykith returned to his satchel and pulled its leather straps open. He came back holding an ornate, foot-long whitewood cylinder and handed it to him with a grin.

Xandrane looked at the artisan carvings on the object's surface and realized what the gift actually was. Taking it by both ends he tugged, revealing the intricate scroll-worked blade hidden within. Etched into the flat of the blade was a depiction of a tower, long and slender, reaching for the heavens in aesthetic brilliance, crowned by the sun.

"The Bergal Sunspire." He held the knife up the light. "This is a Solarin ceremonial knife. Wyk, where did you find this?"

"A weapon stall in Relm. The merchant said he bought it off a tinker from Kiwaller. He had no idea how valuable those are, so I haggled him into the earth."

"I thought you paid no attention during father's lectures. How did you remember this symbol?"

"Temar's classes are as exciting as watching slugs race, but a few things stuck."

"Thank you." Xandrane sheathed the blade and tucked it into his belt.

"My pleasure. I was afraid you might take issue, since it hails from Bergal."

"I'm not superstitious, Wyk. Did you expect me to ward myself from the Evil Eye?"

Wykith chuckled. "Perhaps. Well, at least we are finally the same age again. Both of us men grown now."

"True." Xan beamed. Although Wykith was his senior by half a year, they both preferred when their ages aligned. Felt right somehow. "Fifteen at last."

"So Xan, how are things here?" Wykith walked over to his work table and idly scanned his notes.

"Father's been at Sawstone for the last week, but he should be back later today. I have yet to prove my formula."

"Pity. I hoped you had by now."

"Why?"

"A salve which seals and cleans wounds without stinging like a sonofabitch? You'll be as rich as a Magalian when you crack that mystery."

"Wealth is not the point, Wyk."

"Whatever the point, I'm famished. Alferos had us on watered ale and hardtack all the way back from Relm. What are you cooking back there?"

"Damn!" Xandrane ran back towards the kitchen.

Wykith watched Xandrane scrape the pot and stir the thick broth with a frown.

"What?" he asked.

"I overcooked it."

Wykith sniffed the pot. While well-seasoned, he knew the scent of that succulent meat.

324

"Rabbit."

"Yes." Xandrane pulled the pot from the flame and set it down on a stone slab in the center of the table.

"Perfect." Wykith took a seat, his stomach growling at the prospect of hot food.

Xandrane served him a hearty portion, then walked to Temar's cask and tapped two frothy mugs of black ale. Wykith abandoned conversation and focused on filling his empty stomach.

"No desire to savor your food after a week of eating hardtack?"

"I fill up on carrots and onions to kill the sting in my stomach," Wykith said between hasty bites. "The rabbit I leave for last."

"Ah."

When he finished his vegetables, Wyk greedily slurped the broth out of the bowl, and only then did he deliberately chew each piece of savory rabbit meat. "By Aeros, this is pearl."

"I left the pot on too long," Xandrane complained.

"You did fine. Besides, after my last few meals, this tastes like goddess cunnie."

Xandrane chuckled and sipped his broth.

"I want to go out for a few flagons," Wyk said.

"My father has an entire cask of ale right here." Xan pointed.

"Yes, but does he have women here? Does he have drunken bards, gypsies, and fire-dancers?"

"Is Shayra here?" Xan gave him a mocking smile.

"Go fuck a goat." He smiled back.

Wykith knew he deserved the mockery. Sometimes he could not help but go on about Shayra Lamadsdotter, the most beautiful girl in Aztan. "We are not going to the Red Ale. I know you don't favor the place. We go to Two-Trees."

"Truly?"

"I'll pass by the Ale after and see Shayra. Right now I want to drink with my favorite cousin."

"I'm your only cousin, Wyk."

"Exactly."

"I suppose I could use a break from this house."

"Good. We are settled, but I need a bath first. I may be a little ripe."

"You smell like the insides of a dead fish getting fucked by an unwashed sailor."

Wykith almost choked on his rabbit. "Graphic."

"You know where the soap is."

"You are taking one too. You have not left this house in a while, have you? You smell like a old boot stuffed with moist shit that a drunken leper spewed into."

Xandrane laughed and sniffed himself a moment. "Fine, fine."

Temar's house was on the south face of Laurel Hill, where wealthy merchants and minor nobles clustered together to look down their noses at those less fortunate. His home was spacious and open, with numerous rooms chalked full of charts, scrolls, alchemical equipment, and books on every table and shelf.

Temar was a scholar, a man of letters and numbers, and the only man Wykith respected more than his own father. He had mentored him and Xan in history, politics, mathematics, philosophy, and medicine.

Wykith could not think of a question Temar did not have an answer to. It was frightening to consider how much the old man knew. An education like the one he had given Xan and himself were rare gifts.

Although Temar had remained in Aztan during the Greenfire War, he did so to train some of the best medicus hands in the field. Xandrane was going to be the greatest of them all, Wykith was certain.

Outside the house, the day was warm and overcast, with a scented breeze filled with smoke, pine, and erawa oil. Temar had built a privy and a bathing closet in the yard behind his home but neither of them cared enough to use the enclosures. They stripped their clothes off by the six enormous barrels of collected rainwater in plain view of Temar's neighbors. Wykith picked up an oily block of scented soap and inhaled its sweet aroma. Alchemists always had the best soaps. They filled and poured buckets of water over their heads, scrubbing themselves into a lather with the thick bars.

Some well-to-do ladies lingered by their windows, pretending not to notice them. Wykith imagined how they might have a guilty hand down their smallclothes, watching them wash. His own body was toned and hardened by his years at sea. Xandrane's skin was pale, but he still kept to his soldier's regiments.

Just as Temar had honed their minds, Akata had honed their bodies. His father was a relentless, thorough teacher of soldiery, putting them through uncountable hours of sword drills and physical training every day. Their lessons included battle tactics, archery, shield use, horseback riding, sailing, and hunting.

Wykith had fallen in love with sailing, and his cousin had been consumed by medicinal alchemy. They had spent their entire youths in the military fields of Sawstone Island, learning to be men.

"Have you heard anything from Sawstone?" Wykith scraped off layers sea-salt and sweat.

"Such as?"

"Seagull song is the crew of the *Merrigold* was escorted south by a Vinergalian warship, but only as far as Relm's seaway. I thought there may be trouble brewing."

"No, nothing." Xandrane worked the soap through his hair, eyes shut against the stinging brown bubbles. "Probably just seagull song."

"Probably."

After they finished scrubbing, they poured a few buckets of water over their heads and headed back inside. Wykith waved brazenly at a girl he caught staring. She flushed and hurried away from her window.

"I left my scorpion buskins here right?"

They made their way through the house to Xandrane's room.

"You left a damned trunk full of shit here."

"The trade routes have been good to me," Wykith shrugged. "You are not wearing that coat out again, are you?"

"The night will chill later."

"You only wear that stupid thing because it makes you seem important. How can you stand it during summer?"

"I am a medicus, Wyk. This is my coat of office." Xan winked.

"We are not going out so you can work, you cow's ass. We go out to drink."

"Being an alchemist has its privileges. There is no need to be envious."

"Envious? I'm a pirate-killer." Wykith put a thumb to his chest.

"You're a seaguard private."

"A pirate-killer private, you sawbones leech-eater."

Xandrane chuckled and shook his head. "Your trunk's in the corner. Get dressed, killer."

Wykith and Xandrane walked down Laurel Hill towards Two-Trees Square, ready for a night of merriment. The sun dipped behind the western hills, painting the lingering clouds with the pastel shades of oranges, honey, and red apples. While the cobblestones were still warm, the salty breeze coming from the gulf was beginning to cool.

During the damnable heat of summer, the people of Aztan enjoyed loose garments and comfortable footwear. Both men and women preferred fashionably loose fitting tunics, knee-length breeches, and skirts, but their caligae sandals defined each person's social status.

People of lesser means in Aztan wore caligae made of straw, hemp, or dried vines. They adorned them with flowers, sea-shells, and bleached bone chips. Wealthier citizens wore caligae fashioned from the supplest leathers, dyed in expensive hues, and adorned with silk threading and semi-precious stones. Women of note painted their ankles and calves to accentuate the art of their supple leather sandals.

In high society; belts, charms, necklaces, and bracelets accentuated the theme dictated by the caligae. Their beauty and care emblazoned a person's standing on the social ladder.

Wykith wore his finest blue tunic and black breeches, his favorite ornate leather wrist guards, and a red cotton belt. All of this only to complement his courageous, knee-high Ardian Scorpion-scout buskins, made of wide leather binds, and decorated with sandspider-thread and tiny bird skulls.

He had bought them on his third run to Relm from an Ardian exile who fell on hard times. They were rare, exotic, and durable, making him the talk of Two-Trees for weeks after buying them, and they could still turn an envious eye.

Not to be undone, Xandrane wore a white cotton tunic, tan breeches, and his oiled, reaper shark buskins. The Coral Reaper's skin reflected lowlight, making his expensive caligae glow faintly in the darkness. They were poorly matched with his leather alchemist's overcoat, which while decorated with the various brands and sigils of his vaulted profession, was also stained with splattered blood and alchemical resins.

They strutted down Laurel Hill and into Two-Trees Square like young lordlings. Market day was coming to a hurried close and already the taverns were full to bursting. Lamplighters stalked the streets putting their long, fire-sticks to every candle and oil-lamp. Outside the inns and taverns, servers glided from table to table, taking and delivering orders among a throng of flesh, leather, and steel. Glossy-eyed and jovial patrons waved their mugs and sang along with the minstrels' fervent tunes.

In the middle of the bustling square stood the two giant oak trees which gave the place its name. Young couples drank ale and wine under their cool shade, enjoying the music and each other's company. The shade of the two old oaks was said to grant fortune and fertility to any couple who shared a drink beneath them. A number of stringed fetishes and charms hung from their lower branches and were nailed to their trunks to ward away everything from sickness to malign spirits.

"Wyk! Xan! Over here!" The shout came from one of the tables outside the Grecker Tavern.

Sergeant Rild, another pirate-killer on Alferos' *Swift Pelican*, was sitting with three boys Wykith did not recognize. Rild was older than Wykith by four years and had seen his share of battle on the wild southern trade routes. Wykith tapped Xan with his elbow and pointed at the table.

"Evening, cutter," Wykith greeted him and smiled at the others as he took a seat. Xandrane nodded politely and sat beside him, putting the back of his hand to his forehead and making a fist.

"Evening cutter," Rild replied. Rild's heritage was Old Padivian. He had the same dark hair and tanned skin as most Teplians, but his calisthian was cut and heavily accented.

"Wyk, these nips are going to be our shipmates when we next sail. This is Krim, Dirn, and Adi."

"Adiverik," the boy corrected him.

"Listen nip," Rild said, "you're Adi now, so become accustomed. Anyway, I was just filling their ears with our little bout against the *Swordfish*."

Wykith smiled, putting a fist to his forehead. "A messy fight."

"For certain," Rild said. "Where was I? Right, so I took the old fool's knife out of his mitt and stuck him in the leg. He cried out like a little lass and tried to pull the blade out, swinging his empty mug in front of him. Then Wyk there drummed him in throat so hard he choked on himself and keeled."

"Was not my intent to kill the old bugger, Rild," Wyk said somberly.

"You killed a man with a punch?" Dirn asked in juvenile awe. He was about twelve and looked as green as summer razorgrass. He even had a little landlubber fat on him.

"I know you're a small apple but you can't be that stupid." Rild smacked the back of Dirn's head. This is Wykith Junitari sitting there. Legate Akata's son."

"Your father is Akata Firestorm?" Krim asked in equal awe.

"Yes," Wykith smirked halfheartedly.

"Who is that?" Adi asked sheepishly. Everyone at the table stared at him in silence.

"Adi here's from the Shadow Isles." Rild put his hand on the boy's shoulder reassuringly. "He doesn't know up from down about Tepley."

"Akata, young nip, is a living legend here. He's one of the three Stormlords. A son of Aranath, some say. Though others believe he may be a son of Infris — not born at all, but molded from fire, blood, and battlefield sand."

"Rild's got a real itch in his crotch about my father," Wykith whispered to Xan.

Xandrane chuckled, watching Rild who was too enchanted by his own telling to notice their mockery.

"He's feared and envied by men, and lusted after by their women. His sword Skaldri can melt through iron and turn flesh to gristle! He once cut through a Padivian heavy war horse and its rider with a single blow. In the winter, snow steams right off his enchanted armor, and if you make the mistake of looking him in the eyes for too long, his glare will scorch your eyeballs right out of your head!"

"The other two were Khine Darkstorm and Rien Bloodstorm," Krim threw in. He seemed like the oldest of the three. "Both killed during the Greenfire War."

"I'm telling the damn tale here, nip," Rild scolded him. Krim pouted and lowered his eyes.

"Why was it called the Greenfire War?" Adi inquired.

Wykith and Rild shared a glance and Rild's smile grew broader.

"Well you see," Rild said, "in the heartland of Padive, well, Old Padive now, stands a massive watchtower — so tall, it overlooks all the lands claimed by the great Queen Nevine.

"At the top of that tower lives a goddess called Spectra. She's a sacred flame, you understand? People make pilgrimage from every corner of Padive to ignite their candles on her flame and carry her blessing all the way back home."

"I still don't-" Adi went to speak but Rild knuckled him on the forehead.

"Don't interrupt when I'm spinning yarn! You see, young nip, Spectra's flame is green, and whatever her green flame touches, burns green.

"So when the Queen's Raptors began their march on Tepley, they brought Spectra with them. Their campfires burned green, their torches were green, and when they burned down towns, cities, and temples, everything burned green.

"Now if Padive had won the war, it would have been remembered as Spectra's Wrath, but since Tepley came out as victor, they named it The Greenfire War. Real imaginative, these Teplians."

Rild gave Wykith a good-humored wink.

A serving girl whisked by the table and placed flagons of ale in front of Wykith and Xandrane before hurrying off. They took their hands off their foreheads and raised their ales.

"To a memorable evening," Wykith said, and they all cheered, tipping back their mugs.

"Wait so what-" Dezzy went to ask something but Rild smacked the back of his head.

"Shush now," Rild said. "The big dogs are barking. So what are you going to do with the glint from the last run, Wyk?" Rild took a long pull of his ale.

"Keeping it under a rock for now. You?"

"I'm buying a horse."

"A horse?" Wykith's face rose. "You're a sailor, Rild. What the fuck are you going to do with a horse?"

"I'm going to ride it, Wyk."

"Yier goin' to roid it?" Wykith mocked is his thick accent. "When? You spend most of the year out at sea and live by the docks. When are you going to ride it? Where will it even live?"

"At Bittery's stable. She'll take care of it while I'm away. When I'm home, I'll ride everywhere, but not alone. I'll give every pretty girl in Aztan a ride on my horse," he finished with a wink.

Wykith laughed heartily. "Not while speaking like you have a mouthful of dicks. I've known you for years and can still make out only half of what you say."

"Bugger a trout! I know you save up your glint for that Shayra girl. You gonna convince Lamad to let his little girl marry a cask-head cutter like you?"

"Eat pig-shit on bread, Rild!" Wykith laughed.

"Are you going to buy some land," Rild went on, "build a little cottage, get a couple of ankle-biters under foot?"

"Alright, enough," Wykith said.

"He makes a point," Xandrane added. "What else would you be saving for?"

"A gang-up then?" Wykith scowled at them.

"I'm surprised you're not at the Red Ale right now, sucking her feet!" Rild chortled.

Everyone at the table had a laugh at Wykith's expense. He smiled, shaking his head at them.

"Ah, she's a good girl, Wyk." Rild relented. "You do well keeping that one in your vest pocket, heed my nose."

Xandrane tipped his flagon and drank his ale in one long swing.

"One of those nights then?" Wykith grinned at his cousin.

"Why not?"

Everyone at the table followed suit, drinking their ales in a single pull before slamming the empty mugs down with a chorus of hearty burps. They put the backs of their fists to their foreheads and waited to be served again.

27

The Catskull

Aztan.

Buio had not returned to Aztan in years. The southern trade district, crouched outside the city's high protective walls, had expanded noticeably. New homes, shops, and stables were erected where the gypsies once staked their tents for trade and spectacle.

The fires of the new gypsy camp danced from the border of the western wood. The clang of their instruments and the occasional belly laugh rode the night winds. Buio hoped the Catskull still stood as before.

Escara tensed beside him as they approached the borders of the anthrop city. The outskirts were mostly vacant at this hour but a single unwanted altercation could prove disastrous. Stumbling drunks, homeless vagrants, cut-purses, and the occasional guard patrol were all dangerous obstacles on their path.

"This way," he told her as they entered the shadowy back streets of the eastern quarter.

The young anthrop had gotten more than a day's lead on them, had entered the city, and could now be anywhere. They would need to move fast if they intended to find him.

"Ugh." Escara put a hand to her nose.

"Breathe through your mouth," he told her. "It gets worse."

"How is this vile stench possible? I cannot track anything through this horror."

"The filth here has nowhere to go. Anthrops hurl their rotting garbage on the street, where it lingers until the rains come. Excrement is not buried nor burned here either, but accumulates in-"

"Enough, please. I think I will be sick."

"Breathe through your mouth and do not worry about keeping the scent." Buio glanced back at her. Escara's eyes were white pools of light in the darkness. "You will not be able to anyway. Leave finding him to me."

"Buio?"

"Yes?"

"I think I may have stepped in something."

He forced himself not to smile. "Try not to think about it. We will clean ourselves later."

She nodded.

The outskirts of Aztan were composed of three broad roads which led east into the city and one road running perpendicular to all three. Everything else was narrow street and winding alleyway.

As they proceeded deeper into the district, they became surrounded by tightly packed doorways and hovering balconies, each one a threat to their discovery. The city's rambunctious nightlife only added to Buio's sense of danger.

A group of anthrops drinking and playing dice on a balcony forced them to detour north around a slaughterhouse. Another two men, drunk and chatting while being serviced by kneeling streetwalkers in a dark alley, required a longer detour through a chapel's cemetery. After traversing a maze of filth, garbage, and sleeping vagrants, they finally came to the back door of the Catskull.

The squat, two story building stood exactly as Buio remembered. A foot-long cat's skull still hung above the door, stained with bird lime.

Buio walked to the building's back wall and tapped a few bricks with the tip of his claw — one of them making a hollow sound when struck. He scraped away the thin layer of mortar and wiggled the false brick free. Inside lay a small wooden whistle.

"You may want to cover your ears," he told Escara.

"Why? What is that?"

"Shrill-whistle."

Her eyes narrowed and her countenance darkened at its mention. "You mean a dog whistle."

He nodded.

D'sabres had a long, spiteful history with dog whistles. Anthrops used these little things to summon them, communicate across their villas, issue orders during combat, and if blown loud enough, to punish.

Before there was peace, anthrop soldiers fighting against Helicartia carried these to improve their chances against D'sabre shield formations. It became such an effective tactic, D'sabres began stuffing their ears with bee wax before battle, which was a different kind of hindrance.

"Just blow the trolking thing," she said.

Buio put the whistle to his lips and blew small, sharp puffs. One, then two, then one. Immediately, three dogs within earshot began barking.

"Shut up!" a cry came from a nearby window.

"Shut those fucking dogs up!" Came another.

Buio put the whistle back in its hiding place and stepped into the shadows with Escara. Yips replaced barks as the nearby dogs were beaten into silence.

The Catskull's door bolt released and the back door creaked open. Aldin stood at the threshold, peering warily into the darkness.

The D'sabre pup had grown, nearing his nineteenth moonday now. He wore mended caligae, torn linen trousers, and a black leather apron. His snow white hair was cropped short, in anthrop fashion. He looked ridiculous.

"Buio!" Aldin smiled. "Who is that with you?"

Buio came out of the shadows and gave him a small nod of approval. "Aldin, this is Escara."

"Greetings, kindred," Escara said in xiasi.

"Moon's blessing," Aldin replied in kind.

"Casiopi wuxiil aquitis," Buio said.

"Buio, you spoke that wrong," Escara whispered, giving him a queer look.

"I know," he said. "It is code."

The customary xial plea had no exact translation in calisthian. It could be interpreted as "we seek food, water, and shelter", "we seek friendship and the warmth of your hearthfire", or "we seek refuge from those who would do us harm."

Escara refuted him because he had spoken the words with

improper inflections.

"Dankara." Aldin mispronounced the customary response, which meant they were safe to enter. "Come in, but please tread softly. The master of the house sleeps lightly."

Once inside, Aldin led them through a narrow hallway and down a narrower, creaky set of stairs. The broad cellar space below brimmed with wooden vats and stacked barrels. As they walked amongst them, Escara came to a sudden stop.

"That smell. What is in these barrels?"

"Erawa oil," Buio said.

"And what is that? I have smelled this since we entered the city. Aside from filth, this scent is potent, and everywhere."

Aldin smiled and took up the call. "Dominus Paralbo's erawa oil is the finest in Tepley. Used as lamp oil, for cooking, medicine, and in soaps. You can drink it, mix it with your food, and even clean yourself. I will bring you some later, with some erawa fruit for you to taste."

Escara nodded pensively. "I would appreciate it."

At the far end of the vat room stood a small door with another cat's skull nailed to its frame. Smaller than the skull outside, this one was black, with small white and purple stars painted on it.

"This way." Aldin ushered them underneath the skull.

The chamber beyond was half as spacious as the vat room, damp, and empty. A few hemp nets hung from the ceiling, and bedrolls were spread around the dirt floor. A single street level grate allowed a sliver of pale light into the musty air.

The room was recently used. Burned oil, charcoal, and unwashed flesh-stink still lingered. Escara's small lips parted and her eyes darted around the chamber.

"Aldin. I will need my things, and bring Whiskey."

"Of course." Aldin gave Escara a pitying glance and made his way back towards the house."

"Buio, what is this place?" Her voice was thick with fear and confusion.

He knew she could smell them — the xial who came here from their master's homes to wear rags and huddle amongst themselves like vagrants. She probably smelled the slop which passed for food here, the urine on the walls, and the refuse piled up in the nearby

336

privy.

"What is this scent?" Her eyes were pleading.

Buio looked around the dirty little room and sighed through his nose.

"Despair."

Escara sat on the bedroll Buio placed out for her and stared at her sore, blackened feet. Tracking the anthrop who carried Ariel's Horn clear across eastern Tepley was exhausting enough, but confronting the daemon wolf guiding him, had filled her mind with a hundred questions. Her thoughts had preoccupied her since the encounter, but now there was this place to consider.

When Buio explained how these places functioned, it broke her heart. The xial, the People of Arisia, brought down so horribly low. Not only serving anthrop masters, but believing they would be destitute without their owners' favor. She felt sickened and infuriated.

Aldin brought Buio a snugly wrapped bundle along with bread, clean water, and as promised, a bowl of green, purple, and black erawas.

Escara watched Aldin work in fuming silence, observing his graceless movements within his anthrop rags. Her mood spoiled to carrion. As he cleared out a spot to place the erawas, Escara pounced on him, grabbing him by the throat and pinning him back against the wall. The clay bowl of dark fruits shattered at their feet.

"Escara!" Buio rose to his feet.

"You bring our people here to fester in this filth!" Escara growled at the pup. "You feed them your master's lies and make them feel weak!"

"Escara, release him." Buio's voice rose hard and threatening but she was too angry to care.

"He is no better than the anthrops he serves!" Escara barked back. "Remember the teachings! He is a taskmaster! A slaver among slaves."

When she turned to face him, she found iron in Aldin's gaze, cold and deadly. Something sharp pocked at her leathers, above her liver. He pressed the tip against her to punctuate his intent.

"Escara," Buio said.

She released him and cautiously backed away. Her hand fell reflexively to her hilt, but she forced herself to release it. Aldin relaxed and hid the small blade behind his apron.

"I beg Sari's forgiveness, Aldin," Buio said. "I did not tell her everything as I should have."

Aldin glanced down at the scattered erawas and took a deep breath. "I will bring something to clean this with."

"He is not a taskmaster, Escara, although he plays the role well. He is part of a movement, built to help our kind escape from bondage."

"But we escaped our bonds, Buio! Helicartia is strong and prosperous. Why are there still xial who serve?"

"We did escape. Many of us did, but not all. There is no law which denies anthrops the right to xial slaves. The Law of Reigns forbids warfare between Helicartia and her surrounding nations, but says nothing of the slaves which remain. Since our revolt, entire generations of xial have been raised from birth to serve."

"How does running this filthy place help our people escape?"

"I will show you everything, but not tonight. We must rest."

"Very well." She wanted to press the issue, but had caused enough trouble already.

Aldin returned, swept the broken clay and erawas, and left them a fresh bowl. A white rat wearing some kind of pocketed harness sniffed along his shoulders. Escara gave Buio a questioning glance but received no reply. When Aldin finished, he handed the rat to Buio and departed.

"A rat?" she asked him.

The rodent appeared normal, except for its dark purple eyes.

"Yes, this is Whiskey." Buio took a small, square, bronze token from his pouches and handed it to Whiskey, who snatched and shoved the token into one of its little pockets.

"For the Dorje," he told the rat, then gave it a small coin with a hole in its center. "And for Qustil at The Blind Man's."

Whiskey pocketed the coin, then stared up at Buio expectantly, twitching it's whiskers. Buio took out his piniri, dipped his finger inside and held a generous glob under the rat's nose. Whiskey ravenously lapped the paste off his finger, then raised its nose back up at him.

"You will get more when the job is done," Buio said firmly.

The rat made a grumbled squeak and sprinted off towards the far wall, scampering through a crack and disappearing from sight.

"That is no normal rat," Escara said.

"Whiskey's a moon rat. They are smarter, cleaner, and more organized than their cousins."

"Was that a knife on its belt?"

Buio nodded.

"It knows how to use a knife?"

"Not only use, but fight with. Where she is going can be dangerous."

"It's a she?"

Buio nodded.

"I have never heard of such creatures."

"They rarely live outside anthrop cities. They were created by alchemists as smarter, more helpful pets."

"Anthrop alchemists can create life?"

"No, I do not believe so, only change it."

Escara stared at Buio for a moment and the realization struck her. His eyes. Those cold, blue, killer's eyes had not lost their sharpness, but she no longer felt their sting when their eyes met.

He also spoke to her more often and more openly than before. She knew it was because they had been naked together — not physically, but spiritually. Sharing the dreamsilk had disrobed them, twice now on this journey, and they were deeply bonded by it.

"What is the matter?" he asked.

She smiled at him. "Nothing. Can we please wash ourselves now?"

"Of course."

Buio unfastened and peeled off his skerki leathers. She admired his toned muscles and the lines of his body as he undressed. D'sabre men could be just as lithe and powerful as D'kirns, but there were distinct differences in their shapes. D'kirns were more pronounced in the upper body and thighs, and their hands and feet were almost disproportionately large.

Buio's waist was small, his stomach toned, and his hip bones prominent. He had a natural flexibility in his legs which took her years of stretching to achieve. His musk was also different from a D'sabre's.

Her attention turned to the erawas Aldin brought them. Swallowing a pang of guilt for her earlier behavior, she picked a green one from the bowl and nibbled at it. They tasted better than they smelled. She popped the erawa into her mouth and chewed.

"Mmm. Salty, juicy, soft, and somewhat tart. These are lovely." She ate one after another, savoring the sudden release and dance of flavors.

As Buio lathered himself with the erawa soap, the room filled with the aroma, overpowering all others. He glanced at her and smiled, not with his lips, but with his eyes. He had done so often in the last few nights. She would say something or do something, and he would give her that same look. He would smile without smiling.

"Would you like some?"

"A few, yes."

"Then you best hurry."

She ate a purple one, then a black one. The darker ones were juicy but dryer, like red wine. She tried two of each at a time, then all three at once. The salty fruit was not only delicious, but revitalizing. She ate them by the handful, her eyes closed in pleasure.

Buio walked by and grabbed a handful, leaving the bowl empty. She glared at him in reproach.

"Try the bread," he said. "Smother it in the oil first."

Escara obeyed, tipping the thin bottle of amber liquid over the bread before taking a bite. "Mmmm! Buio we must take some of this with us! It's delicious."

After a satisfying meal, she unstrapped her leathers, glad to be free of them. Her own musk filled her nostrils, mixed with the scents they had collected on their journey.

There was a separate scent they picked up walking through Aztan, which made her face pinch. The urine, horse-shit, and other godless refuse smells were vile, but there was also a taint here. Something old and sour which clung to everything like a film — like disease.

She took the thick bar of soap and busied herself, washing away the scents of the road and wet leather. She paid special attention to her feet, scrubbing between her pads until they were sore.

While she bathed, she sensed Buio's eyes on her skin. She moved deliberately, gracefully, but restrained. She wanted him to look at her, but would not allow him know it.

"Where do we sleep?" she asked once finished.

"You will sleep in this." He pulled out a thick, black bedroll made of stitched furs and cured leather from the bundle Aldin had brought him.

"Sleeping underground in an anthrop city can be difficult at first." He laid the bedroll out and untied its side stitches. "You would feel alone, in a small room away from all light and sound, with the walls closing in around you."

He opened the furs for her, revealing a warm looking pocket of darkness. "Inside."

"What is it?"

"A Zidai."

Escara had heard of Zidai weavings before, but had never seen one. Her skin tingled at the thought of entering.

"What about you?"

"I will be fine."

"Buio, you cannot expect me to leave you out here after that explanation."

"I said I will be fine. I've adapted."

Escara eyed him and sank into the Zidai, feet first. She held the flap open and stared back up at him.

"You will sleep here as well or neither of us will. Come," she said.

Despite his efforts, Buio's eyes grazed quickly over her naked body. She left the flap wide open, allowing him to see all there was. Her pulse quickened, but she forced her face to remain calm and her gaze steady.

Buio quietly slid in next to her.

Not designed for two people, Escara needed to place her arm and leg over him so they would fit in the Zidai. He tied the side of the bedroll shut, enveloping them in warm darkness.

"Now, close your eyes and concentrate," he whispered to her. "Think of nothing but Arisia and the light of the evening sky."

Escara closed her eyes, focusing her mind on her memories of a luminescent moon and blinking stars high over Helicartia.

She recalled a particular night, when she was but a cub, laying on her back outside her home, staring into the night's starry depths with awestruck eyes. Her markings tingled as they reacted to her focus and the stuffy warmth of the bedroll became suddenly cool.

When she opened her eyes, the formless darkness of the Zidai's inner lining had transformed into an ocean of stars. Countless nebulae surrounded them in every direction.

"Buio, this is beautiful."

"Yes," he said staring into the void.

Buio's body was warm against her skin, contrasting the cool touch of the Zidai. She could feel his slow, heavy heartbeat and smell his freshly washed skin. The forced intimacy was intoxicating. Her nethers warmed, and she was tempted to run her fingers over his chest but caught herself. This was wrong. These things were forbidden.

"Who made this for you?" she asked, trying to distract herself.

"Rairi."

"She made this?"

"She did."

Thinking about Rairi saddened her. She wondered if she would ever see her pack again. By splitting them up, Nihengale had placed them all in terrible danger.

"Why is this here? Why not take it with you?"

"Serves me better here."

"I see."

Buio shuffled in place, making himself comfortable. "I have been thinking, about your question from before."

"Which one?"

"About daylight. Describing such a thing feels odd. The day is as beautiful as the night, but the lighting is intensified. Colors are not in a slow, subtle dance like in the evening sky, but in a kind of furious celebration.

"The color prism of Arisia's deepest heavens and nebulae gather around Siege as he rises — huddling among the clouds and eastern sky.

"The eternal canopy becomes a dome of softest blue, and Aeros' clouds invert, becoming white with gray highlights.

"Silver-touched greenery is draped in golden light, and black waters become blue. It is like awakening to an entirely different world."

"It sounds wonderful," she said.

"We had best get some rest, Escara."

"All right."

After a time of silence between them, Escara found her eyelids becoming heavy. Buio's warmth and the cool comfort of the Zidai relaxed her tired muscles completely, pulling her into the deepest sleep she had enjoyed since embarking on this mad journey into Tepley.

28

Black Rock Trail

Murciel was dreaming about being a child running through a starlit clearing when the ice-cold water hit his legs, snuffing the dream out like a candle. Instinctively, he dragged himself away from the water and struck his head on a rock.

"Trolk!" he spat, grabbing at his aching skull.

"Over here!" Rairi cried out from somewhere in the pitch.

Murciel felt around for his things, a spark of panic igniting when his hands touched only wet stone. He crawled into the icy water on his hands and knees, searching frantically.

His pack was half submerged, the current attempting to tear it from him. He grabbed the thick leather strap and snatched the pack out, blindly searching its dimensions. Relief flooded him when the smooth contours of his bow filled his hand.

"Murciel, the tide is rising. Hurry!"

He deftly shouldered his kit, the bolt wounds on his hand and back flaring as the icy water rose to his knees. He sloshed towards the sound of Rairi's voice, his arms swinging blindly before him.

"Rairi?"

"Come! This way!" Rairi grabbed his forearm and pulled him, clucking her throat as she went. Murciel took a hold of her belt with his left hand, keeping his bandaged right hand in front of his face. The rush of water behind them gained momentum, consuming the space where their camp had been.

Rairi stopped. "Crawl, we need to crawl," she said.

"What?"

"Through the hole!"

"Rairi, I am blind in here! What hole?"

The cold water rushed up past their knees.

"There is a crevice in the middle of the wall before you. Feel around for it!"

Rairi shuffled around ahead of him. His hand slid down the length of her legs as she crawled away. He tried to follow but bumped his head again.

"Cock!"

"Hurry Murciel," she said, her voice echoing in the enclosure.

Murciel patted the stone and found the dimensions of the narrow gap as the water rose halfway up his thighs. He shoved himself in and crawled, one hand in front of the other, dragging himself forward using his elbows and knees.

"Come on!" Rairi called from further down.

Murciel's bow bumped against unseen edges in the tunnel. His pack and the corners of his skerki snagged every few feet, slowing him down.

The sea water rushed into the gap, cold as winter. He gasped for breath as his lungs crumpled from the sudden drop in temperature. Fear bit into him as he realized if this tunnel did not have an exit ahead, they were both going to drown.

The water rose quickly to Murciel's chin, forcing him to take a deep breath before his head became submerged. He half-crawled, half-swam through the tunnel, blind, in freezing cold water, and with no way of knowing how far this tunnel went. He tried to push the thoughts from his mind but fear anchored them in place.

His bow caught on something.

Murciel wiggled, trying to dislodge himself. He grabbed at his bow's edges, attempting to shake them free, but the water pressure held it fast against the rock. Air bubbles escaped him as he struggled in desperation to free his bow.

Nothing. He was stuck in place. Seeing no other recourse, Murciel unshouldered his entire pack.

As the rushing water launched him deeper into the darkness, he bit back his desire to scream. He struck something in the dark, his ribs saved from breaking by the hardened padding of his skerki. The force of the impact still managed to knock his remaining air out of him. He

345

grabbed his injured side and spun in the darkness, his lungs burning as they pleaded for air.

The rushing cold water flushed him out, sending him flying into a shallow basin of loose stones and wet gravel. He rolled to his side and coughed, taking long, grateful breaths. Rairi coughed and spat somewhere nearby.

"Are you all right?" he called out.

"I am alive," she wheezed.

They both took a moment to catch their breath.

"We were damn, damn lucky that tunnel had an exit," Murciel said, standing.

"Don't-" a fit of coughing hit Rairi as she stood. "Don't be stupid. I knew there was an exit. I saw it using ketter."

Murciel smiled at her, holding his throbbing side.

They were outside, in the rain. The wide bowl they were expelled into slowly filled with cold water, spewing from a narrow crevice in the mountain wall.

"We must climb out of here," Rairi said. "Think you can make it with your leg?"

Murciel tested putting a bit of weight on it. The bite of the long gash on his thigh was numbed somewhat by the cold.

"I believe so."

He turned to look back at the narrow gurgling mouth as it poured water into the basin.

"What's wrong?" Rairi asked.

Murciel stared at the gap in the stone patiently, unblinking.

"Murciel? What is it?"

"I lost my bow."

The night was warm and cloudless. Murciel walked into Boldon's shop in Helicartia, still covered in sweat from the night's rigorous training. He looked around the bowyer's shop, appreciating the many pieces of art hanging on those walls. Boldon watched him with a knowing smirk.

"You summoned me, Master Bowyer?"

"I see you admiring my work, young archer."

Murciel smiled and swung his head around to take in the shop.

Each bow, a precise and painstakingly crafted weapon. Boldon never made the same bow twice. Always experimenting, he used different woods and materials, mimicking different styles of bowcraft and then improving upon them. In his hands, the woods purred and bowed to his whim.

"They are beautiful. You are gifted by Kiyo, Master Boldon."

"I simply love what I do."

"The Elders say they have never known work like yours."

"So I hear." Boldon smirked.

"Being so recognized is a great honor." Murciel smiled brightly.

"I suppose it is," Boldon said, flat pan.

Boldon's change in tone surprised him.

The master bowyer shook his head with a smile and waved dismissively. "I wanted to congratulate you on being chosen for the Hunter's Cadre. Even being a D'aerth, that could not have been easy. Are you glad?"

"Thrilled, Master Boldon. It has been my dream since I joined the academy."

"Why?"

"Why, sir?"

"Why does it thrill you to be in the Cadre?"

"Because the Cadre are the eyes, high and low of-"

"Stop." Boldon raised his hand. "I do not need to hear the Cadre creeds. I know them well enough. Why are *you* thrilled to be chosen? What was the persistent thought, the child's dream, which made you seek such a difficult achievement?"

Murciel shuffled his feet. He was embarrassed, being asked such a personal question, but the warm cast of Boldon's face gave him courage.

"Because I love the bow, sir. I love archery, and no other academy specializes in it like the Cadre. They are our greatest archers."

Boldon's eyes studied him unblinkingly, glinting in the candlelight. The old master smiled.

"I figured as much. You see Murciel, I am good at making bows because I too love archery. I love the song a bow sings when strung and released. I love its weight in my hand and the power behind each arrow I let loose. I love the thrill of landing a perfect shot from a seemingly impossible distance."

Murciel's heart raced hearing the old master speak. He could not help from smiling, beaming — the smile of someone who has met a kindred spirit who shares in their most intimate passions.

"I see that same love in you, Murciel. I see how you behave during practice. You are careful, disciplined, and respectful. You string and unstring your weapon with honed attention. You never fail to check the wood for flaws, before and after practice.

"You never lean on your bow, or leave it laying about carelessly. Even when ordered to release it somewhere with nothing to lean it against, you place the bow down, you never drop it. These small details tell me more about you than you may know."

Murciel felt exposed and validated in the same breath. He stood speechless, rummaging his mind for something, anything to say.

"Thank you, Master Bowyer," he said finally.

"You are welcome, Murciel." Boldon gave him a smile. "Now, if you would do me a small favor, I would like your opinion on something."

"Of course, sir."

Boldon reached under the counter and produced the most beautiful thing Murciel had ever seen.

"The wood is mainly direwood, and the string, queen's silk, which means it can hold tension when collapsed," he proceeded to extend the ends, turning the composite hunting bow into a longbow. "And when extended."

"Boldon you are truly amazing," Murciel's eyes never left the bow.

"I will admit, I am quite proud of this one. I call her Manticore."

Boldon presented it out to him. Murciel's smile could not have been brighter.

"Are you certain I may hold it?"

The Master Bowyer nodded.

Murciel held the Manticore, testing her weight, gingerly pulling on the queen's silk cord, feeling the smooth slide as he pulled it back, not to full tension, but as close as he dared. She was wonderful.

"Do you like her?"

"Like her? She's," Murciel shook his head. "She's perfect, Master Boldon."

"Nothing is perfect, Murciel. The weapon is only as good as the

348

hand who wields it."

"She is a masterful bow, sir."

"She will be, in the hands of a master bowman, which I hold every confidence you will one day be."

The color drained from Murciel's face. His mouth went dry and his eyes were pulled away from the bow to meet Boldon's. He could not bring himself to ask. He did not dare.

"Yes, Murciel. I made her because you inspired me with your dedication to the art — something I have not seen on the raptor fields in many years. The Manticore is yours. A master bow for a master archer."

"Sir, I..." was as much as came out.

"Wield her well, Murciel, but remember what I am about to say. She is a fine bow, but never forget," Boldon pointed a finger at Murciel's chest. "You are the weapon. You. The bow will sing for you, she will serve you as long as you keep her in repair, but she will never kill for you. She will only grant you the means. Do you understand?"

"I believe so."

Smiling with a nod, Boldon handed him a sealed quiver, heavy with ammunition. "Then go, make her sing."

Murciel stood in the freezing water which had risen past his knees, staring at the cruel horizontal cut on the face of rock.

"Murciel," Rairi said softly. It may not have been the first time she spoke, but it was the fist time he heard her. His patient, sniper's eyes never left the gushing waterfall.

"Murciel!"

His eyes snapped to her, hard and bitter. Rairi stood up to her thighs in water, her arms wrapped around herself, shivering from the cold. Seeing her softened the tension in his shoulders. In his dead focus he had forgotten to feel cold.

"She has been mine since I joined the Hunter's Cadre. She was made for my hands."

"I am sorry Murciel. Did you lose it...her, very far in?"

Murciel stared at the mocking slash of rock and nodded. The cold of the water and rain bit into him. If they stayed here any longer, climbing the edge of the basin would prove difficult.

"Come on," he said with a mournful sigh. "We need to get out of here."

They crawled up the rocky, wet slope of the basin, being wary of their footing. His wounds and newly bruised ribs yelped with his every motion. He ground his teeth and bit back the pain until they went over the basin's lip.

"Look," Rairi said, "there is a path leading into the mountain. Perhaps we can find shelter."

The path was a natural deformation winding through jagged black rock, filled with black puddles and slick from the rain.

"All right," he said. "Not like we have other options."

They followed the narrow mountain path, sloshing through cold, ankle deep water for over an hour, lost and disoriented, until they found a pile of carefully laid stones on the side of the path.

"This path leads somewhere after all," he said.

"I was thinking the same," Rairi confirmed.

The winding path led on for another three miles, marked intermittently by knee-high cairns. At one point the deformation opened up and became a flat, dirt road broad enough for them to walk side-by-side. The black stone of the Norvan Crags climbed high above them on their left and a deep gorge followed them on the right.

They passed the shattered remains of a broad, wood and stone arch bridge, which once linked their path to a much wider road skirting the opposite mountain face. The remains of the bridge were worn away and decimated by insects, while its stone abutments were home to a colony of blue-winged-sparrows. The little birds chirped nervously from their nests as they passed by, shaking the rain off their colorful feathers.

They continued on for another four miles before the path finally ended at the box-cut entrance of a cavern. Abandoned tools, empty crates, barrels filled with brackish water, and half a dozen shredded hammocks lay scattered near the cavern's entrance.

"What is this place?" Muriel asked.

"An anthrop mine. It looks like the one Marca and I hid in during the attack on Kaira."

Remembering the vile insect thing that attacked them on the grass outside Fort Kai made Murciel's skin pimple.

"Is it safe?" he asked.

Rairi clucked her throat and stared into the depth of the cave.

"It goes down farther than my ketter reaches, but there is nothing dangerous down there."

Murciel looked up towards the heavens and saw gray clouds lined with silver sheet lightning, highlighting the curtain of rain pouring down around them. The first hint of azure touched the edges of the sky above the eastern mountains.

"It will be day soon," he said. "We should make camp. Well, not here of course, but we can take some of this wood and a hammock down to use for fuel. Do you have anything we can start a fire with?"

"I left my things back in the cave."

"What?"

"Murciel, the cave was flooding. I went to find an exit and the water took my kit."

Murciel sighed and patted the pouches on his belt. "I still have my flint."

They walked down the mine's drift until they were clear of the threat of morning's light. Rairi clucked her throat, claiming the deeper part of the cave as safe.

While Murciel busied himself with the fire, Rairi stripped out of her leathers. He stole a glance at her, admiring the curves of her body.

Her build was not a soldier's, like Escara, but she had a lovely shape. Despite her love for numbers and symbols, she was still a Blade of Mepsia. He found her thin waist, small, round butt, and long, slender legs especially attractive.

"What are you looking at?" she asked, bemused.

"N...nothing."

"Take off your leathers so they can dry."

Murciel unstrapped and stripped out of his wet, clinging skerki and spread it out near the fire. He stretched out his weary muscles and rubbed some warmth back into them.

Rairi poked the fire's logs and retrieved some of its smoldering charcoal. She ground the burnt wood chips into a fine powder, then poured a little water on it to make a paste.

"Apologies, Murciel," Rairi said as she applied the paste to his wounds. "I should not have abandoned my pack. My healing herbs were in there. I was careless."

"Don't blame yourself," he said. "I lost my things too."

After Rairi finished tending and redressing his wounds, she sat near the fire with her knees pulled up against her chin, her arms around her shins. "Come closer, will you?"

Murciel moved beside her and wrapped his arm around her shoulder. She felt small in his embrace. He placed his head on her damp hair and closed his eyes a moment, more exhausted than he had realized.

"Do you think the others are doing as well as we are?" She nudged in closer to him.

"We are lost, cold, and without most of our gear," he said, rubbing some warmth into her arms. "They must be."

"Not to mention we have no idea how far we are from home, or how to return."

Murciel sighed. "At least we have each other."

Rairi reached across his back and rubbed his arm, returning the favor of warmth. "Murciel, can I ask you something, as a pack member?"

"Of course."

"I have seen the way you look at Escara. You desire her, don't you?"

Murciel's hand stopped on her arm. The fire's crackling filled the silence.

"It is forbidden to lust outside of one's clan." He tried to sound matter-of-factly.

"That is not an answer."

"It is as much an answer as I have. And it should be enough."

The silence between them echoed with the snapping of burning timber. Murciel fed the fire a piece of broken crate.

"I have desired men outside my clan," Rairi said. "I actually find D'tiri males rather uninspiring."

Murciel was taken aback by the statement. No one spoke of such things in Helicartia. It was akin to admitting one lusted after goats, or a sibling.

"That is the Fel speaking," he said.

"Do you truly believe that, Murciel? That we hold some inherit taint in our blood?"

"The anthrops changed us, Rairi. There is no denying it."

352

"Perhaps, but I refuse to believe in this Fel nonsense, no matter what the Elders say."

Her speaking so brazenly gave him a strange sense of comfort. She was right. He did desire Escara. He had desired her for years but had no recourse but to feel wretched and disgusted with himself over it.

He tried to bury his feelings, but they only grew with time. He feared Escara might suspect his dark thoughts, or had seen a hint of them in his eyes. Now he feared his entire pack knew. What must they think of him?

"I find Buio intoxicating," she continued. "He has this dangerous way about him. I find it difficult to believe a female of any clan would not bend to his will, if he wanted her."

Her statement angered him. It had no reason to, but it did. He could not help but admire Buio, but he sometimes hated him for the same reasons he secretly praised him. As if sensing his aggravation, Rairi turned her head up to him.

"Does it bother you, my saying so?"

Murciel looked away, ashamed of his transparency. "It makes me uncomfortable. You should not be thinking such things. You are D'tiri, and he is D'kirn."

"Is that really why it bothers you?" Her green eyes observed him steadily in the firelight.

"Why is it important anyway? Why bring this up?"

She lowered her head back to his chest. "I have desired you as well."

He was caught by surprise. Quiet and aloof Rairi. He never expected her to say such a thing.

"You...have?" he wanted to slap himself for how foolish he sounded.

She nodded against him. "I think you are quite handsome. You never noticed me looking at you? Marca is quite taken by you too."

His heart quickened in his chest. He shuffled away, hoping Rairi would not notice.

"Rairi, if this is some kind of game, I want you to stop. This is childish. We are pack, and deep in enemy territory. This is no time to be-"

Her warm, soft lips on his silenced him. Her eyes were like a predator's, sharp and observing. Before he could react, she pulled away and put her head on his shoulder.

"I am not playing games." Her voice was strained with exhaustion. "But tell me, did that really feel so bad? Like a dark and wicked act?"

Murciel pursed his lips, tasting her there as he did so. It felt far, far from bad.

"No."

Her hand slid down between his legs and brushed his manhood. To his surprise, his flesh reacted immediately.

"Does this?" she whispered into his ear, her fingers gliding over his stiffening member.

"No..."

She kissed him gently on the neck, shoulder, and chest, her left hand stroking him rhythmically. He wanted to protest but his mouth would not find words. His lips moved but made no sound except to try to catch his breath as her lips made their way down his torso.

When her wet tongue and warm mouth wrapped around his hardness, her smooth hands stroking him, he abandoned all thought of protest. It evaporated into nothing, carried away by the smoke of their fire.

Rairi's eyes shone like jewels in firelight. She stared up at him intently as her tongue and mouth worked around him. The fire in her eyes was exhilarating. With slow and deliberate movements she rose and straddled him. Kissing him deeply, she took him in her hand and slid him inside herself. A groan of pleasure escape him.

His hands explored the milky softness of her skin, sliding over her small breasts, the curves of her hips and the roundness of her rear. Rairi's hips moved with increasing rhythm against him, making his heart race in his chest. He licked and nibbled at her small nipples.

"Rairi," he growled.

"Yes. More." Her motions increased in tempo. She grabbed the back of his head and rode him fiercely, firelight and shadow dancing on her skin.

Like a cat in the low light, her eyes shined with hints of green and gold. Her sex gripped his manhood tightly, her wild thrusting becoming involuntary as her body lost itself in the lightning-strike of ecstasy.

He gripped her rear firmly, a sudden shock wave of pleasure peeling through him. Rairi's small claws dug into his wounded back making him tense, but he was too far gone for it to stop him. The spark of pain made the fire of his pleasure all the more intense.

Rairi cried out, her hips thrusting and her legs shuddering. Murciel's final release was violent. He called out like a wild thing, holding Rairi in a death grip, thrusting himself in and out of her to the hilt.

Rairi's soft body melted into his. She lay with her head against his chest, panting — her heart beating in furious concert with his own. He leaned back against the rough stone, completely spent, his manhood still trembling inside her. Rairi swayed her hips, the small muscles insider her sex clamping and unclasping around him in a slow, sensual motion. In moments, he was hard again.

Rairi leaned back and stared at him, her hips beginning to sway. Her black hair was disheveled and her green eyes were alight, but it was her mischievous smile he found most enticing. Murciel forgot all about his wounds and his exhaustion. He began to move his hips in concert with hers.

29

This Is My Tree

As the sun began to rise behind Sawstone Island, Xandrane and Wykith stumbled up Laurel Hill, their arms around each other's shoulders, singing *Two Drunk Men by the River Bluff* to their lungs' full capacity.

"Liar! You Liar!
You filthy drunken sod!
Liar! You Liar!
You hooked her by the cod!
Soft sails! Hard pegs!
Your bird made nest between her-"

"Shut your holes!" Came a woman's voice from a nearby house.

Wykith and Xandrane laughed and continued their wobbling struggle up the hill. When they finally reached Xandrane's home, they noticed the candles in Temar's study burning.

"Liar, you liar, she kissed your willy's snout," Wykith sang, a bit more subdued.

"Father's home," Xandrane moaned. "Terra's sweet hole, I'm in trouble."

"Want me to come in with you?" Wykith offered.

"You won't make it anywhere like this. You have to stay."

"No, I'm meeting Rild at the Ale. Besides, I am far from-" He wobbled, nearly loosing his footing. "Right, guess I should stay."

The boys stifled their laughter and made for the front door, which was covered in the green blinks of fireflies. Xandrane smiled and opened the door carefully.

Once inside they made a valiant attempt at stealth, but were ambushed by the home's furniture. Every table and chair in the house tripped and poked at them.

"Xandrane?" Temar's stern voice came from his study.

"Yes, father." Xandrane tried to sound sober. "I am going to bed."

"Come in here, son."

"Fuck." Wykith leaned on a chair for balance.

The two entered Temar's study and found him sitting at his desk. In the dim light, Temar's wrinkled face, untrimmed beard, and glossy occluded left eye made him look like a storybook ghost. He glowered at them and shook his head in dismay when they stumbled into the light.

"Is this what you have been doing while I was away, Xandrane?"

"No, father."

"Wykith, when did you get back?"

"Today, uncle." Wykith managed to keep the slur out of his voice.

"Do either of you know this person?" Temar pointed at an unconscious man lying on the room's patient cot.

The man was covered head to toe in overlapping layers of filth. He wore no shirt or caligae, and appeared as if he had been beaten, stabbed, and dragged through horse shit. His short black beard covered most of his face and his clammy gray skin was wet with fever-sweat.

Wykith shook his head.

"No," Xandrane said.

"Either of you know how he entered my home and came to lie on my patient cot?"

They both shook their heads.

"I see. Both of you, take him outside and clean him up."

"What?" Xan swayed.

"Now, Xandrane."

They grunted as they picked the large man up by his arms and legs and carried him through the house. The unconscious man gave no protest as they bumped him into every article of furniture and wall along the way.

"Gods, he stinks! Is he dead?" Wyk asked.

"I don't know, perhaps." Xandrane's only desire was to lie down and find sleep.

"Why is Temar making us wash a dead man?" Wykith's voice slurred.

"Put him down over here," Xandrane said once outside. "I will get water."

"If we have to wash a corpse," Wykith's head bobbed from side to side, "why could it not be a pretty girl corpse?"

"Don't be ghoulish," Xandrane threw a bucket of cold water on the man's chest, splashing Wykith.

"Shit!" Wyk shot up. "Watch it!"

"Wyk, will you please help me?"

"Right, right." Wykith picked out a fresh bar of Temar's scented soap and began scrubbing the man's skin. "I think he shit himself, or maybe someone took a shit on him."

"Honestly, Wyk." Xan scowled.

As they struggled to clean the man, Temar stepped out with a wooden pipe in his hand, filled it with tobacco and calmly lit the bowl. He watched them work from the doorway while the new day's sun painted the sky in pink and aquamarine.

"Why are we washing a dead man, uncle?" Wykith complained.

"He is not dead, he just smells it. Xandrane, now that most of the filth is off this man, what can you tell me about him?"

"Father, I'm drunk, and half asleep."

"I have eyes, son. Answer the question."

Xandrane stared woozily at the man for a moment, trying to force his mind to focus.

"He's been hurt, but none of the wounds are deep. Looks like he got dragged through mud and shit for a bit. Someone's tended to his wounds, if poorly." He shrugged.

Temar leaned down, picked up a bucket of water and threw its contents into Xandrane's face. Before Xan could get the water out of eyes, Temar slapped him hard with the back of his hand.

"Do I have your attention yet, medicus?!" Temar glowered at him.

"Yes, sir!" The shock of the blow snapped Xandrane from his drunken stupor.

"Now, what can you tell me about him? Be specific!"

Xandrane looked down at the man again, his eyes struggling to focus. He scanned him meticulously, fearing another strike from his father.

As if conjured from nothing into existence, his long years of training spurred his mind into motion.

"He is a shinn miner, and has been on the road for days. He walked here, mostly if not the entire distance. He hails from the south. Sharn, most likely. He was beaten but his wounds are minor.

He is shi'da — very shi'da. He requires," Xandrane closed his eyes, forcing his mind to focus. "Grey leeches, and cannibal-trout oil. Venom for the wounds, vically for the pain."

Temar nodded, his demeanor softening. "Bring him back to my study and administer the treatment. I am going to bed."

Once Temar was out of earshot, Wykith looked at him in quiet shock.

"How in the Vorx did you do that?"

"I used a trick my father taught me."

"No, I mean tell me how! He hails from Sharn? How the fuck could you know such a thing?"

"Not now, Wyk." Xandrane rubbed his jaw. "Ask me again tomorrow. Help me put him inside, will you? I have to leech him and prepare the oil."

"What a falcon-dive!" Wykith laughed and lifted the man's arms. "You have a hundred ales in you."

"We can talk about it later!" Xandrane lifted the man's legs.

"Right, all right," Wyk relented.

The two carried the heavy man back inside and lay him on Temar's cot. Wykith sat at the foot of the cot, put his head against the wall, and closed his bloodshot eyes. "So, shi'da? A pox of a way to die."

"He will not die. Not as my patient."

"How did he walk here from Sharn with shinn poisoning? The Norvan Peaks are days away, even on horseback."

"I have no idea, but now I must make certain he recovers."

"That slap knocked the spirits right out of you."

"I deserved it. I am a medicus, Wyk. I must be able to work in any condition."

Wykith chuckled groggily. "Temar is making you do this because you wore your fucking coat out again. You wear the coat, you play the part."

"Cock in ass," Xandrane felt unbelievably foolish. "I fear you may be right."

"I tried to tell you."

"Please, shut up."

Wykith opened one sleepy eye. "Xan, this man will not survive. You must know that."

"I said he will live, and he will."

"Remember what my father used to say during sword drills?" Wykith made a poor impersonation of Akata's stone-hard tone. "'You fight! Wounded or dying, you fight! And if you cannot keep your petulant spirit in your fucking body, then you haunt the sonofabitch who killed you until he kills himself!'"

Xandrane ignored him. "Help me place him on his side so I can leech his back."

"Leeches are vile." Wykith shoved the man on to his side. "Wait, I thought you couldn't leech shinn poison? Do I remember the lesson wrong?"

Xandrane grabbed a jar of gray leeches from his father's cabinet. The creatures writhed around each other within.

"They are not normal leeches, Wyk. They are alchemical. They help treat shi'da by sucking out the poisoned blood so the cannibal-trout oil can clean his system."

"Cannibal-trout," Wykith yawned. "They're vile too."

"I have to warm the oil to match his blood's temperature or it will either boil through his veins or create clumps which will kill him as surely as the shi'da. Wyk could you — Fuck."

Wykith leaned back with his head against the cot, snoring contently.

Xandrane carefully applied the leeches to his patient's back. His mind and body ached for rest but his calling kept him focused. He could not allow this man to die. He toiled through the morning with Wykith snoring softly beside the cot.

When Wykith woke, it was early afternoon. His head was a marching drum and he had fetid cotton mouth. He smacked his lips in disgust, his back pinching and popping as he went to stand. He blinked the stickiness out of his eyes and tried to find his bearings.

He stood in Temar's study next to a blood covered cot. Rummaging his mind for why he had woken up here, he backtracked halfway through the night, his memories bouncing from scene to disembodied scene.

He had been drinking in Two-Trees with Xandrane and Rild. There was a girl with auburn curls, freckles, and a thin, pretty smile. He remembered her tongue exploring his mouth and the fullness of her breasts when he squeezed them.

They kept drinking.

Xandrane almost got into a fight with a tanner but no punches were thrown. Wykith placed money on a few throws of bone dice and lost every toss. They smoked spiced cloves and watched the fire-jugglers.

They kept drinking.

Rild left with the girl Wykith had kissed earlier, with a promise to meet at the Red Ale. He and Xan had walked up the hill singing-

The rest of the night came back to him all at once.

"Bloody snatch."

Wykith followed a trail of flecked blood leading from the cot, through the house, and down into Temar's basement. Xandrane was leaning up against the cellar door with his ear pressed against it.

"Xan?" he whispered down to his cousin.

Xandrane put a finger to his lips and waved him down. Wykith crept down the rest of the stairs and placed his own ear against the rough wooden door.

"Is beyond irresponsible!" came Temar's muffled shout. The old man was furious.

"He was not supposed to come here," came another man's voice, trying to soothe Temar's wrath. "This was not the plan."

"Plan! What godsdamn plan!? Do you not realize what you are meddling with here!? Have you lost your fucking mind, Cyrile!? Do you need help finding it!?"

"Dominus-"

"Do not fucking 'dominus' me! Do you not realize what will happen if, when, the Inquisition hears of this? Two guardsmen sent to the Teumathil after roughing this bastard up? The Hammers take note of such things! And you let him come here?! To my home?!"

"Dom Temar, please-"

"I believed him some lost drunk who had only hours to live, at most. I ordered my son and nephew to wash this sonofabitch, to teach them a lesson! What if he woke during the leeching?"

Xan looked over at him, his brows arched.

"I told you," Wykith mouthed at him.

Xan gave him smoldering look.

There was silence behind the door except for a slightly imperceptible clicking, scratching sound.

"There. It is done," Temar said. "I want him out of here, now. He was never here, you understand me?"

"Of course," came the other man's resigned voice.

The door swung suddenly open. Temar stood at the threshold, wearing his heavy leather medicus coat. He glared dangerously at them both, his occluded eye seeming more menacing than last night. Xandrane went deathly pale.

Temar took a deep breath through his nose. "Both of you, help us take this thing up the stairs."

In the center of Temar's basement, surrounded by long tables covered in vials, bowls, and boxes, sat an ornate, beautifully crafted oak coffin. Various strange markings were etched into the wood. Bones, feathers, and colored stones were tied and inlaid into its smoothed angles.

Wykith recognized the box as a vidarium. The legions traveled with them in their supply wagons in case a Legate or high ranking officer was mortally wounded in hopes of saving their lives. They were rare and expensive things to build.

Temar had scratched a few additional markings to the vidarium using the end of a charred witchwood stick. A charge hung in the air, like the kind the fills a field right before a storm.

Wykith glanced between Temar and the man called Cyrile. The stranger was older than him but not by much, with ink black hair pulled tightly behind his head and thin, bone rimmed spectacles sitting on his nose. He wore the same gray medicus coat as Temar but its cut and symbols were from the Teumathil, or the "Cracked House" as the soldiers and sailors knew it.

"Take it to the wagon outside," Temar said. "Damn you Cyrile, help them."

The three of them lugged the heavy coffin up the stairs. Wykith pulled while Xan and Cyrile pushed.

"Careful, careful!" Temar barked as they struggled.

They huffed and grunted and cursed the coffin with its decidedly heavy cargo. As carefully as their tired muscles allowed, they lifted the vidarium into the awaiting wagon's basket.

Temar threw a thick tarp of aged cloth over the basket to keep the vidarium safe from prying eyes. "Get it out of here, Cyrile. And remember-"

"Yes, dominus, he was never here." Cyrile seemed glad to be leaving as he jumped into the front of the wagon. The driver whipped the horses lightly and the contraption began to creak and wobble north.

"Inside, both of you." Temar stared at the wagon until it crested the hill, disappearing from sight.

Wykith looked to Xandrane but found nothing in his cousin's face but deep exhaustion etched with confusion.

Temar led them into his study. "Clean this mess up," he told Xandrane pointing at the bloodied cot. "Wykith, help your cousin."

"No," Xandrane said before Wyk could take a step towards the cot.

"Excuse me?" Temar whirled.

"You must tell me what this was all about."

Temar regarded Xan a moment. "This is not something to concern yourself with."

"No, father. You forget, you placed that man in my charge. You put his life in my hands. Which means you must tell me everything you know about his condition."

"This is not-"

"No!" Xan snapped.

Wykith felt suddenly very uncomfortable standing beside him. He looked between him and his uncle in tentative silence.

"You struck me last night, father, and you were right to. I am a medicus. My duty is to save lives and I serve my calling loyally.

"By your word he is my charge. Mine. You are going to tell me what is wrong with him, why you put him in a vidarium, and why he is on his way to the Teumathil. Everything. You had no right to discharge my patient without consulting me."

For a moment Temar looked shocked, taken completely off guard —

then his face darkened.

"Wykith I am certain your father is expecting you," Temar said. "Give him and Domina Melithi my regards, if you will."

"Of course, uncle."

"And thank you for assisting last night."

Wykith nodded and looked over at his cousin. Xandrane stood firm and resolute, his bloodshot gaze never leaving his father. "Later, Xan."

"Later, Wyk."

Wykith knew how much Xandrane loved and respected his father. Standing up to him could not have been easy. Even so, Wykith was glad Temar had politely hinted at him to leave.

The cycles of madness renewed themselves endlessly, retelling the same story without pause or mercy. Caige's love for Tynisia blazed as they traveled together through the razorgrass hills. His desire for her was as fierce every time they made love, and his fear of the lion stalking them perpetually pinched his bowels.

Then came the acrid memories of the atrocities he had committed — his assault on Tynisia and the murder of his father, like hot irons pressed against his heart.

Again and again, he faced the naked horror which had clawed at him from darkness his entire life. Crimes his mind had locked inside a black chest of denial at the bottom of a lake of cheap bullhorn tore free and screamed knives through him.

Like Vourseros, cursed by the gods to be devoured by wolves every evening, only to be remade by the morning's light so the wolves could feast once more, Caige was trapped in a perpetual loop. This was his eternity, with only one noticeable difference — the little girl.

The naked, bloodstained child with her long disheveled hair and smeared grease paints was the only thing that varied in his cycling torment.

Caige began to notice her in different places throughout the landscape of his nightmare. Once, she was hidden near the fir tree where he held Tynisia to him, sobbing like a child after awakening from his nightmare. Another time, he saw the glint of her eyes in the shadows of the underbrush, watching them make love. He caught a glimpse of her inside Ricker's claim once, right before Tarrak's black teeth tore Corren to bloody ribbons.

Caige's mind began to tie a flimsy strand around that one rogue pebble, desperate for some kind of purchase. He sought her out, focusing on her presence whenever she appeared. He could not know how many times he relived this terror, but each time he saw her, the nightmarish wheel he rode seemed to lose torque.

The sucking earth became rich with boiling gold and silvery shinn. These rare metals he had spent his life seeking seared painfully into his skin, cutting through muscle and drawing blood. The pain was unbearable.

"Stop!" he yelled at his father. "Stop, Corren! You are killing me! You must let go!"

"Pull yourself up, Cairn!" Tynisia cried, digging her fingernails into his forearm.

"Forgive me!" his father croaked.

"You have to let go." A wild, naked girl with disheveled hair and faded grease paints stood at the lip of the pit, observing him without a hint of emotion on her young face. He remembered her from the temple's entrance.

"What!?" He tried to kick his father off.

"Surrender to this pain so it may cleanse you. This is the only way."

Caige tried to pry himself free of Corren, but was being dragged further into the broth of gold and shinn.

"See," the disheveled girl said, kneeling now. "You must allow yourself to see."

The threads that had tied themselves around the girl in Caige's mind found anchorage, bringing the nightmare to a stall. This was his moment. Caige stopped struggling and let go of Tynisia's hands. He stared up at the girl, focusing entirely on her.

"Help me," he said.

"See." The disheveled girl knelt before him. "You must allow yourself to see."

"I want to," he heard himself say. "Show me!"

Their gazes held, and he was drawn into the cold depths of her emerald eyes. For a moment, he lost all sense of who or where he was — like falling into a dreamless sleep. Like a forgotten memory.

When he opened his eyes, Caige found himself sitting across from the wild girl, surrounded by a copse of petrified trees. The girl sat cross-legged on the roots of the plague tree, its hollow eyes and agonized mouth gaping above her head.

"Why am I here?" he asked.

"Because this is my tree," she said. "Under his shade is where my serpent was born. Among his roots is where I first took life, and in his mouth is where my bones were salted and burned."

"Who are you?"

"Regret."

A chill wind blew through the copse, disturbing the dead leaves carpeting the earth. As the leaves rose, they hissed as if angered.

Caige felt his mind attempt to return to the repetitive nightmare he had only just escaped. He focused back on the girl, on her features and hollow expression. Anything to keep from being dragged back into that churning spiral.

"What is happening to me?" he asked.

"You are being shown. As I was."

"Shown what?"

"That you are in a wheel. That you struggle."

"What am I struggling against?"

She did not reply.

"Did you bring me here?"

She shook her head. "You came here on your own."

Caige knew this to be true. The tension in his mind eased a fraction.

"You have been watching me," he said. "Who are you?"

"Regret."

"Regret what?"

"Do you wish to see?"

"I do."

"Then see."

The Vale of Azilial was in flames. The tribes were being decimated by famine and plague. The survivors of this nightmare killed each other over what remained.

They ate their healthy livestock, and then the sick ones. They ate their crops, stores, and seeds, until there was nothing left to sow. They ate their own clothes, and when they could find nothing else, they ate their young. They hunted each other like game, the strong feasting on the weak.

They built shrines to dark gods and summoned unnatural things into being, selling themselves to the whims of unspeakable horrors. Madness and horror reigned until there was nothing left to burn and no one left to kill. With nowhere else to go, the vorxfires burned themselves out, and the Vale fell silent.

At the heart of all this carnage, after the last fleck of ash floated to the ground, only one trembling, filthy, desiccated old man still stood, his eyes crazed with terror and his mind long since broken.

"The old man," Caige said. "The one by the temple."

"My brother. I kept him alive. I wished for him to witness, to live, and suffer, forever."

"You did all that?"

Tears streamed down the girl's cold, doll-like face. She nodded. "My brother took me into darkness when I was small — too small. He did so for many moons until he began to fear discovery, but by then I was already broken in two."

Caige's guts churned hearing her speak. He hated himself. Loathed himself beyond measure for the things he had done to the woman he loved.

"When I blew the Horn of Dawn with hatred festering within me," she continued, " my Other was set free. She seeped into everything like a corruption, and I took my people into Heleca with me."

"The Horn of Dawn?" Caige looked into the hollow eyes and mouth of the plague tree, ablaze with flames the color of jade. An old ivory horn stuck out of the tree's jagged maw, covered in ash, yet untouched by the flames.

"The emerald," he said, realization cutting through him.

"No. That was no emerald."

30

Two Temples

Wykith stood at Aztan's ferry pier and observed the contours of Sawstone with a sense of quiet dread. His head throbbed and he was in dire need of sleep, but he could not bring himself to board the ferry. The pier around him bustled with dock workers loading and unloading supplies.

"Wykith!" a call came from behind.

"Fair morning Bruss," Wykith greeted the familiar dock hand.

"Afternoon you mean." The man gave him a toothless smile.

"Right." Wykith smirked back.

"Going home? Ferry's about ready."

Wykith rubbed the back of his neck and made a sour face. "While I yearn for sword drills and to run around the island until dusk, I may wait another day."

"Suit yourself, sire." Bruss gave a nod and busied himself pulling a line from the water.

Wykith let out a sigh. His mother would have heard the *Swift Pelican* came into port by now. She had likely prepared dinner and organized his things. He wanted to see her, but once he set foot on that island, his ass belonged to the Storm-Talons, and his father.

Wykith turned his back on Sawstone and made way towards the Red Ale Inn. From outside, the Red Ale appeared as a large, three story building of flat gray stone spanning half a city block and cast the hard, grim facade of an armory. No signs or placards identified this as a place of business.

Wykith walked up to the main door and swung the heavy knocker three times against the knob. A viewing portal opened, and a man's rheumy brown eye looked him over before the door's heavy bar was removed. Wykith stepped into the poorly lit antechamber and faced the doorman.

Lote was a brute — a survivor of the gladiatorial pits. He bought his own freedom after countless battles, but not before the pits took their pound of flesh from him. He lost his left hand early on, which he replaced with a prosthetic fist of wood and iron. His right eye was an empty socket which he did not bother to patch, and only half his mouth held teeth.

The right side of his head was cupped in, hairless, and fiercely scarred. The mace-blow to the head had nearly killed him, but he won his freedom that day, holding what was left of his ruined face with his right hand while the wooden fist pumped the air in furious triumph.

"Fair afternoon, Lote," Wykith said.

"Welcome back, Wykith." Lote's voice sounded thick and runny, like hot gruel. "How fared the run?"

"Could have gone better."

"Are you here for blood, gold, or cunnie?"

"All three, Lote."

The big man gave him a half-toothed smile. "What have you brought for the altar?"

Wykith dug into his pack and produced a thick ear with small white hairs, crusted with blood. It had begun to blacken and smelled like ripe cheese.

"From a man who drew steel on me."

"Did you say the words?"

"Of course I did."

"Say them again." Lote pointed at the altar in the corner with his wooden fist.

At the altar, a half-full jar of eyeballs swam in vinegar and a sharp metal spike held over a dozen scalps. A shriveled human heart lay on a clay plate, and a wooden cuksar box sat open, full of blood-speckled teeth.

A few less vile offerings adorned the altar; Chints and marks, braids of hair, medallions, beads, bones, and semiprecious gems. A bowl of blood sat in the center, halfway full.

Lote would empty it into one of the six stone vases flanking the altar once the blood neared the brim. Blood remained the most common sacrifice.

Wykith placed the ear on a string with three others and took a knee. "Bloodrider, hear me. I bring you the flesh of my enemy as token, and give you thanks for my victory. Adeith Modein."

When Wykith stood, Lote held the inner door open for him. The shouts, jeers, and the clubbing of mugs on tables could be heard from within.

"You may enter the temple," Lote said solemnly. "Remember to enjoy yourself."

"I always do."

Two men dressed in black brigandine and armed with oval scutums, spears, and kopis swords flanked the entrance from within. Their black-beaked helms regarded him as he passed. Their armament appeared similar to those of the Queen's Royal Talons, but these were not men of the Crown.

The Bloodbeaks served only one power; Aranath, god of war. A dozen of them glided around the Red Ale, silently keeping order. If roused, these crows did not spare words. They acted quickly and decisively, and if you resisted their authority, you risked becoming a sacrifice to the Bloodrider.

The center of the Red Ale's main chamber was a wide fighting ring. Sweaty, drunken bodies crowded the Ring's circumference, howling, cheering, and cursing. Inside the circle, two men fought stripped down to their trousers.

Wykith knew many of the men who came here. This was a place for warriors who pledged their lives to Aranath. Those who came here saw war as more than an opportunity to earn coin, plunder, and pillage — they honored the very act of war. Aranath was their god and this was their temple.

Wykith walked to the quartermaster's counter and greeted the woman behind the iron bars. She sat on a high stool and made deft work of counting chints and marks, organizing them into neat little stacks and writing numbers on a thick ledger, all with only the use of her left hand. Her right arm had been cut off at the elbow when her home in Bramen was sacked by Padivian Raptors.

She was twice Wykith's age, but he found her lovely. Her long blond hair and dark eyes were a seductive match. He even told her as much once. She had not taken the compliment well. In fact, he was certain she hated him.

"Hello, Gana."

"Welcome back, Wykith." She did not bother looking up. "How much do you need?"

"Enough for food, drink, and a cuksar. I go into the ring later and wish to bet everything else on myself."

"You are being reckless." Her eyes were arrow-tips when they met his. "You do not know who you fight. You think Aranath favors such pridefulness?"

"I am not being prideful, Gana. I was trained to-"

"Everything then." She scratched her quill against her ledger and slid him a metal chip through the bars. "Rider's fortune to you." And under her breath she added, "you lame cur."

Wykith sighed and turned towards the Red Ring, pocketing the chip. The most recent duel had just finished.

A legionnaire peltast had soundly beaten a heavy cavalry spearman. The chamber trembled with the clamor of shouts and stomping boots. The wealthy, seasoned cavalryman was dragged off by his grim, cursing friends, while the lowly young peltast was drenched in ale and lifted on to hairy shoulders, his arms raised high in triumph.

"Wykith!" Rild called out and came to greet him. He sported a cut brow, bruised lip, and his left eye was half swollen. "What shit bucket did you fall into last night? I thought we were to meet here."

"I got pulled into something at Xan's. How fared your fight?"

"Gander at my face and wager."

"You got beaten, badly."

"Like a dog who bit the hand. I was far too drunk to fight and knew it. Serves me right."

"What about the serving girl?"

"She let me fondle her tits but when I went to finger her sweet nest she stopped me cold. Told me to come back and see her at the Grecker again if I wanted more."

"So you took your hard prick into the ring and fought like an idiot."

"Exactly right."

"How much did you lose?"

"Almost a third."

"Rider's cock, Rild."

"Indeed. One of his balls may still linger in my ass. Are you fighting today?"

Wykith nodded. "Need a drink and some food first. I suffer from Chen's morrow."

"Well, bet low, Wyk. Heed my nose." Rild tapped the tip of his broad nose.

Wykith arched a brow at him. "Why would I do that?"

"To begin, you look like a dry paddy run over by a wagon wheel, but the seagull song is the Master of the Ring does not like how your recent wins have tilted the odds. Your next fight is with Reur the Ram."

"Rider's cock!"

"Ah don't be such a cunnie, Wyk. A little beating will do your animus good. It needs pruning."

"I just bet everything on my next fight."

"Without knowing who with? Seems your animus does need trimming. Have you seen Shayra yet?"

Wykith shook his head.

"Don't tell her, Wyk. Heed my nose."

Wykith walked crestfallen through the musky room, giving the Red Ring a wide berth. The room's back doors led out to the courtyard, where the Red Ale's smiths and cooks plied their trade.

The courtyard was a hot, smoky area filled with the scents of soot, burning timber, and cooking pig flesh. The clang of iron hammers, the squeals of dying pigs, and the clucking of agitated chickens mixed with human chatter, cries, and laughter.

Lamad Turalson, the Red Ale's head cook, stood near the animal pens watching his daughter butcher a three-hundred pound hog. He was a veteran of the Greenfire War, with thick scars running over knotted muscles, black as night.

"Well fuck my pigs." Lamad gave a hearty chuckle. "Look whose back among us simple folk."

"Wykith!" Shayra's face lit up when she saw him.

Her chocolate skin was splattered with blood and pig-fat. She wore a thick butcher's apron stained in gore and her face was marked with sooty fingerprints, but the warmth in her honey-colored eyes was all Wykith noticed. She fell into his arms and they kissed deeply. She tasted of blood and salted pork.

"You turd!" Shayra punched him in the chest. "The *Pelican's* seaguard all came last night. Even Rild showed his face eventually. Where were you?"

"I meant to come," he chuckled, "but needed to help Xan with something."

"Help him drink an entire barrel of ale, you mean?" She raised a brow at him.

"At first, yes."

"How is he? I have not seen him since you left."

"Keeping himself busy."

"You are not usually here this early in the day." She glared at him knowingly.

"I wish to stay clear of my father, at least for one more night."

"Domina Melithi will not be pleased with you."

"Neither will Akata, but my shore leave cannot be all work and training. I intend to enjoy this time as much as I can."

"When do you sail off again?"

"In one week."

"Oh," Her warm smile descended.

"Xandrane gave me the same look. I will return before autumn."

"Wykith, do not fight today," she said. "When I am done here we can go to Two-Trees and have a drink together."

"I already placed my bet, Shayra."

Her lips pursed. He could tell she was attempting to be subtle, to not insult him.

"Did you bet reasonably? Considering who it is? And that you are obviously with Chen's morrow?"

Wykith shook his head. "I placed my wager before Rild told me I am to fight Reur."

"Before?" her eyes widened. "Wykith, you cannot be that foolish!"

"Yes, I truly can."

Lamad walked up, his thick arms crossing over his barrel chest. "How much did you wager on yourself, Wyk?" His brows were furrowed.

"All of it."

Behind them, pigs snorted and chickens clucked — the sound of hammers beating mercilessly on hot iron rang across the yard.

"You are a fucking helmet, Wykith Junitari," Lamad said flatly.

"Yes," he said. "I know."

Xandrane was in a poisoned mood as he rode through the streets of Aztan. He had never seen his father so angry with him.

He felt well in his rights to insist on knowing about his patient, but Temar would give him no quarter. His father was always clinical and logical about everything, but this was different. He had spoken with passion, clearly enraged by Xandrane's persistence. They had argued before, but never like this.

When Xandrane realized they would never reach an agreement, he saddled his mare, Pepperhoof, and rode off. He wanted to lead her through the eastern dock district. The wash of the sea and cry of seagulls had a way of calming him, but almost absently, he found himself leading her north instead.

Xandrane rode through the city in silence, listening to the hollow clunk of Pepperhoof's shoes on the cobbles, the rumble of scattered conversation on the street, and the cries and pleas of merchants. Despite his strange, busy morning, Xandrane was still very drunk and had not slept. Without meaning to, he fell fast asleep on the saddle.

"Hey, hey!" someone shook him, dragging him out of a deep dream which fizzled the moment he opened his eyes.

Xandrane looked around, startled and disoriented. He still sat on Pepperhoof, who had stopped at a water trough on the side of a tavern called The Hobknuckle.

Three city guards stood to his right. Two of them held a couple of street urchins pinned to the ground, while the third, a younger man with a patchy stubble, dark oak-colored skin, and a patch across his right eye, shook him.

"What?" Xan wiped the drool off his chin.

"Seems you fell asleep, dominus," the guard said. "We caught these two picking your purse."

Xan looked down at the boys. They could not be older than eight, both struggling against their captors. The guards had their knees to their backs and their faces to the dirt.

"Here." The eye-patched guard handed him back his coin purse.

Xandrane opened it and scanned the silver marks and handful of chints.

"Thank you," he told the guard, plucked out six marks from the purse, and handed them to him. "For your trouble."

"Mighty generous, dominus," the man gave a smile.

"Let us go!" one of the children screeched. "He got his coin back, now let us go!"

"Shut it!" the guard pinning him growled.

"Tell them to let us go!" the other one cried. "We ain't did you no harm! If you tell them, they'll let us be!"

"Is this true?" Xandrane inquired of the eye-patched guard.

The man gave the coin purse in his hands a meaningful glance, then looked back up at him and shrugged, a half-smirk playing on his lips.

Xandrane gave him another two marks, tied the purse back in place, and tugged at Pepperhoof's reins, turning her towards the street.

"A pleasant day to you, dominus," the guard said with a smile. The guards picked both boys up and kicked them in the opposite direction.

It took Xandrane a moment to gain his bearings. Pepperhoof had walked him southwest, to the south edge of the Markoli district. He decided to ride through it and put the event with the guards and street urchins well behind him. The Markoli was a pleasant distraction from his thoughts.

Gypsies, painters, musicians, and dancers came out in force after market day. Even under the hot summer sun, a small minstrel band crowded every corner, playing for their food. Merchants in street-stalls offered fresh sweetmeats, honey-glazed apples, smoked chicken entrails, baked yams, dactwine, and bowls of glistening erawas.

Two female jugglers stood on high stilts on opposite sides of the street dressed in motley and colorful feathers. Their gypsy bells chimed musically as they tossed small, colorful sandbags back and forth to each other. Even on horseback, the colored projectiles flew clear over his head.

Xandrane watched the women in fascination as he rode beneath their arc. One of them took a split-second to glance down and give him a mischievous wink before going back to juggling without missing a beat.

Past the Markoli, the wealthy Garnder district was noticeably more muted. Well decorated homes with flower bushels, clinging vines, and potted ferns sitting on open windowsills flanked him on either side.

Small iron and stone statues decorated the entrances to each home. An ivory heron, a statue of a small naked boy holding a bowl of erawas over his head, and an iron shepherd dog sitting in obedient stillness, were but a few. Xandrane entertained himself with the imaginative decor of the wealthy homes until finally reaching the slumping outer walls of the Teumathil.

The broad, three story building of black and red brick sat unevenly, sloped by some flaw in its design or the incessant weight of time. Once the home of a wealthy merchant, the old manse was falling into disrepair.

Its wooden roof shingles were stained black and weather-chipped. The unkempt clinging vine on its southern face smothered the wall, slipping insidiously into every crack it could find. The front yard of the property was lush, green overgrowth — its decorative statues and centerpiece fountain devoured by moss and black mold.

A shirtless old man in a wide-brimmed hat nodded curtly to him and took Pepperhoof's reins.

"Welcome young dominus, does your mare need brushin'?"

"No, only water, and some feed if I am long." Xandrane swung off his saddle.

"Aye, sire." The old man walked Pepperhoof towards the inner stables.

Xandrane walked the short stone pathway to the entrance of the Teumathil. Inside the hall was a cozy, well-lit receiving area with mahogany chairs around a varnished oak table. An oaken full desk sat on the far wall, flanked by the heavy, gray and white banners of the zenthis medicus. Thick bushels of lavender in clay pots sat on both the table and desk, giving the place a peaceful aroma.

"Greetings," the man behind the oak desk said with practiced sincerity. "How can I assist you?"

"My name is Xandrane Maeron, son of Prefect Medicus Temar

Maeron. I am here to see Cyrile Mcbane."

"Senior Medicus Cyrile Mcbane, young dominus," the man said. "A moment."

The attendant walked through the door behind his desk, returning a brief moment later.

"He will see you," the man stated as he stepped back into the room, gesturing for Xandrane to pass through the door.

Cool and well lighted, the chamber adjacent to the receiving room had generous daylight shining through the three tall west-facing windows. A blue crystal vase holding a bloom of white roses sat in the center windowsill.

Every other wall was lined with floor to ceiling bookshelves. Most were leather-bound, but a few were red felt. Comfortable reading chairs huddled around the chamber's hearth, and a solid cube of beautifully carved white marble served as a writing desk near the far north wall. Cyrile stood from behind the marble desk and greeted him with a bemused smile.

"Now this is unexpected," Cyrile said. "Please, sit." He motioned Xandrane into one of the broad backed chairs in front of his desk. "What brings you to the Teumathil, young dominus?"

Xandrane sat in the chair and took a moment to study the room. "Interesting collection you have."

"Thank you. Still, only a shadow of your father's horde." Cyrile gave him a cautious smile.

"I came here to see my patient."

Cyrile's smile dropped slowly.

"You misunderstand, young medicus. He is my patient now."

"My father placed him in my care. He had no right to-"

"Your father, is the Prefect Medicus of Sawstone Island. He has every right, and you know this." Cyrile eyed him critically a moment, then his features softened.

"Regardless, officially speaking the man was never in your home, and so never under your care. If you must know, Temar thought the man would die regardless of what you did. He only used him to teach you a valuable lesson."

"But he did not die," Xandrane said, "and you placed him in a vidarium, which means he is important. Then my father sealed him in with hermetic glyphs, which means he is dangerous."

Cyrile stared at him, his face betraying no emotion. He retrieved his spectacles from his coat pocket and put them on his nose. "How do you know about hermetic glyphs?"

Xandrane sat quietly in his chair, attempting not to fidget.

"You found your father's secret library," Cyrile said with a coy smile, "and helped yourself to some light reading. He will not be happy to learn of this."

Xandrane looked around the room again, carefully this time, then back at Cyrile.

"My father is not going to find out about that."

"And how do you figure?"

"Because you will not tell him."

"I will not?" Cyrile's thin brows rose past his glasses.

"No, and in return, I will not reveal to him that you told me everything you know about my patient."

Cyrile sat quiet for a moment, his small black eyes studying him. Xandrane matched his even gaze.

"Go home, young medicus," Cyrile said, "and do not return here. I will consider not telling your father you have been snooping in his personal affairs, if you behave."

"I have done more than snoop." Xandrane stood, stretched his arms above his head and walked towards the long windows, turning his back on Cyrile. The sunlight made him squint. He sorely needed to sleep.

"Any one of the books in my father's collection would bring the Inquisition down on both our heads, yet he chooses to keep them. The way I see it, if he is willing to place my life in mortal danger for this knowledge, then I have an equal right to it."

"A dangerous assumption."

"The markings he placed on the vidarium this morning are from the *Sepher Hermeticus*, which is considered an unholy text. When I saw father had written forbidden glyphs on a vidarium in front of you, it meant either he was certain you would not recognize them, or comfortable with the fact that you would."

Xandrane turned back to eye Cyrile, who had not moved from his chair.

"Turns out you not only know what those runes are, but also about my father's secret library."

Cyrile's expression darkened but he remained motionless.

"My father is not a careless man — I am certain you know this. He would not tell you about his library unless he trusted you with such knowledge, and knowing my father, he would not trust you unless he had something equally dangerous on you to balance the scale."

Cyrile smirked and shook his head in bemusement. "An entertaining story. Your assumptions are quite ingenious, but the truth is-"

"Rebis, Nigredo, Rubedo, Aether, Vitriol, Albedo," Xandrane said.

Cyrile's smirk sank, his gaze turning almost menacing.

"I honestly almost missed it," Xandrane grinned. "But this vase on your window, it reminded me of the old romance tale, *The Courts of Jannasa.*

"Princess Bidda would place a blue crystal vase with a white rose on her windowsill to let her lover know her father was away, and she would sing from her balcony-

Come play within my garden, love,

the Hound has gone astray.

We'll cast away the daylight glass

and drink among the fey .

Rada, Nada, Rada, Ada-'"

"I am not certain what you are getting at," Cyrile cut him off, "but I do not appreciate my time being wasted with nonsense. Leave, now."

Xandrane took a long deep breath and made to exit the room but stopped short of the door. With the index finger of his left hand he pointed at the spines of the books in the nearest shelf, making a zigzag gesture from top to bottom.

"Kal," he said, then repeated the gesture for the second bookcase. "Mur." He turned his body to the third bookcase. "Hast."

When he turned back to Cyrile, the man's eyes were wide as his spectacles.

Xandrane waved his hand in a single motion over the shelves behind Cyrile. "Tai, Marus, Thul."

Cyrile stood and slammed his hands against his desk, his posture menacing.

"Kal'mur'hast, Tai'marus'thul. 'Be welcome friend, to the phoenix nest.' Ingenious code, placing red-spine books in exact locations among the others."

Cyrile sat back in his chair. A moment later he leaned back and began laughing. He stood back up and lazily clapped, his smile bright and genuine.

"Inspirational!" Cyrile said. "Dominus! Temar said you were bright, but I doubt even he understands. You certainly did more than snoop!"

Xandrane nodded.

"Even so! Many of those books are encoded. How did you decipher them?"

"I have a way with patterns," Xandrane admitted.

"Master Xandrane, please, sit, sit back down," Cyrile urged.

Xandrane took his seat again.

Cyrile sank back and put his index fingers to his lips. "I understand why you came here, and why you are curious. But I feel I must warn you — this unfortunate man is part of something much larger. Something, which despite your blatant intellect, you might not be ready to accept."

"That is for me to decide, Dom Cyrile. What I learned from you today is that while you operate under the watchful eye of the Inquisition and the Zenthis Medicus, you are a Neterian — a heretic in the eyes of the Korgurate. A corrupter and consort of daemons."

Cyrile's cheerful mood dropped somewhat. He stared at him with a predator's eyes.

"Have you seen me balk or waver?" Xandrane asked. "Do I seem afraid to you? Whatever it is you have to say, I am ready to hear it."

"Perhaps." Cyrile appeared pensive, a broad smile filling his face. "Perhaps."

Wykith stood leaning against a support beam, watching the ensuing brawl within the Red Ring. A salty seaguard corporal stood toe to toe with a young Storm Talon scout. Of all the fights he had seen today, this was the most interesting.

Wykith could tell the scout was by far the more experienced fighter. Overzealous, the corporal put everything into his swings, trying to prove the tougher man. The scout was focused. He danced around the hard blows, using small, precise movements, letting the marine wear himself out.

Since he had been slated to fight Reur, Wykith's fight would be the last one of the evening. He took a drag of his cuksar, the acrid flavored smoke filling him with a rush of energy.

"My chest is fire, my breath smoke," he whispered before exhaling. "Bloodrider, accept my ember spirit."

He repeated the ritual two more times, taking his time with each inhalation, letting the smoke burn him as long as he dared before releasing it. After saying the words a third time he tossed the half-burnt cuksar into a brazier.

"Adeith Modein."

The fight turned out as Wykith thought. The scout remained patient, despite the disappointed jeers and curses of the men who bet against him. They tried to goad him, fluster him into committing, but the scout remained calm, jabbing only at obvious openings, further enraging his opponent. When the seaguard became winded by his blusterous attacks, the scout made short work of him with a series of combination strikes to the chin, temple, and solar plexus.

A roar rose among the Circle when the corporal went down, both from the men supporting the scout, and a few seaguards Wykith knew to be under the corporal's command. They hated the pompous bastard.

"The victory goes to the Talon scout, Vardin Chance!" the Caller roared.

"Chance!" the crowd echoed. His friends lifted him up and carried him out of the circle. "Chance! Chance! Chance!"

Vardin had no expression on his face. There had been no challenge in the fight for him. When they put him down outside the ring, Wykith caught a glimpse of a woman wearing soldier's leathers.

She had long blond hair and a face of such sensual beauty it almost made him forget where he stood. She noticed him staring and they locked gazes.

Wykith normally carried a casual confidence when it came to women, but her attention made him blush and turned his eyes away, utterly flustered. When he forced his eyes back up, she was gone. He scanned the crowd but could find no trace of her.

"Unstring those coin pouches, boys!" Hovis the Caller spat. "Our next fighter is none other than the Red Ale's crowned champion, Reur the Ram!"

The room roared. All around Wykith, men raised their mugs and joined in a united chant.

"Ram! Ram! Ram! Ram!"

Reur the Ram entered the circle like a priest before his congregation. His ram-skull headdress was marked in ceremonial paints, adorned with feathers and bronze rings. He wore an assortment of small bones, beads, and human teeth as a necklace.

Serpent rattles adorned his wrists, marking his hand's every motion, and black and red grease paints marked his copper skin. Wykith recognized the symbols "Strength", "Temperance", and "Iron".

Reur rose his hands in the air and the room trembled with the shouts of men.

"His worthy challenger, the son of Akata Firestorm himself, Seaguard Private Wykith Junitari!"

"Junitari!" He heard Rild scream from somewhere in the crowd.

"Junitari!" shouted Shayra and Lamad.

The men howled in approval, the ruckus only half of what they had given Reur.

"Junitari! Junitari! Junitari!"

Wykith entered the circle and removed his shirt.

The Ram studied him a moment, then lifted a single finger in the air. The crowd cried out in delight. Wykith bristled, his trepidation about fighting Reur curdling into seething anger.

Akata had started bringing him to the Red Ale since he was ten. For five years Wykith could only watch these fights, since only adults were allowed to participate. In those five years he had seen three different champions reign in the Red Ale.

The first was Heindal Nalpa, The Berserker Bear. A northerner from far-away Telkan, Heindal was a giant in Wykith's young eyes — an unstoppable force of nature. He watched Heindal pummel men into bloody pulp, having to be pulled off his victims with cattle lariats like some kind of wild animal. No one thought he could be beaten. Few dared go into the Ring with him at all.

To everyone's shock, it was a blind wanderer was who finally took his title.

The man was young, with straight black hair, and a lithe, muscular build. He wore a blindfold — though he moved like a man who could see. The blind man had beaten the fucking tar out of Heindal, taken his winnings, and walked out of the Red Ale — never to be seen again.

Some claimed Aranath himself had come to show his displeasure at Bear for disrespecting his opponents. Others said it might have been a grigori, or even a daemon in human guise. Whatever he was, Wykith never forgot the name the Crier had called him — Basardin Black.

Without a champion, the Master of the Ring declared there must be a melee to decide who would wear the crown. A dozen hand-chosen men entered the circle and beat each other bloody until only Reur the Ram remained. His title was heavily contested at first, considering how he achieved it, but in three years no one had been able to take his crown.

Reur's punches were so devastating, he began claiming in how many he could drop a man before a fight, and he was rarely wrong. He never needed more than five, and he had just claimed he could down Wykith in one. One.

Reur took off his ram skull, necklace, and snake charms. He knelt, muttering his prayers to the Bloodrider, hovering his arms around himself and making sacred mudras with his hands.

"May Aranath bless the victor!" the Caller said. "Begin!"

Reur stood to full height and faced Wykith. "Do you know why you are here?"

Wykith was surprised. Reur was not one to talk during a fight.

"The Master does not like my winning messing with his odds."

Reur shook his head. "That does not place you here before me."

Wykith eyed him warily but the Ram did not appear to be jesting. "What then?"

"I asked for you, son of Akata. I think you will prove worthy."

Wykith's eyebrows furrowed. "If you believe that, why claim you can drop me in one punch?"

"Prove me wrong." Reur settled into his battle stance.

Reur moved, his eyes cold and fixed. Wykith only barely got his arm up in time. The blow hit him in the side of the bicep so hard he felt it in his back.

He ducked under Reur's left hook but his right cross caught him on the side of the head and sent him flying.

"Rrrrraaaammmm! Rrrrraaaaaamm! Rrrrraaaammm!"

The sounds came from somewhere far away, as if his head had been dipped in a murky bog. Slowly, Wykith came back from the edge of unconsciousness.

"Rraam! Rram! Ram! Ram! Ram!"

Reur stood in the middle of the circle, hands in the air, taking in the pleasure of the crowd.

Wykith rose with a grunt and touched the side of his face, certain it was as dented as Lote's gruesome mug. It was fine, if a bit sore. He ran his tongue over his teeth and found them all still there.

Reur the Ram smiled at him. "You can take a punch."

"Fuck you, Reur."

"You are not my taste, boy."

"Junitari!" Someone called out. The crowd's cheers were mixed but enthusiastic as they cried out their names.

Wykith and Reur circled each other, their guards up. Wyk had seen Reur fight before. He had strange footwork and swung differently than a Talon. Not wanting to be caught on the defensive again, Wykith came in.

It took three missed punches for Wykith to realize how outmatched he was. Unarmed combat was a routine drill among all the Queen's Talons. No man who came into this circle did so without having been trained in striking, blocking, and grappling, but Reur was more than proficient. His every motion was deliberate and precise, as if he were dancing instead of fighting. He did not block with his arm, he blocked with his entire body — the arm served as an extension of the action.

Wykith spotted the position of Reur's body and leaped back, his guard high.

The Ram grinned and they began to circle again. "How did you know to do that? Leap back?"

"You were baiting me. I have seen you do it before."

Reur's leg snapped out low. Wykith leaped to avoid the sweep and cursed while in the air. He had seen this before too.

Reur's body turned and pivoted. His other leg flew out and struck Wykith in the chest, sending him tumbling backwards. He hit the floor hard and rolled up to his feet.

Reur was on him in an instant. Wyk's arms came up to protect his head. Reur's foot struck him in the solar plexus so hard it knocked the wind out of him and doubled him over. He gasped and kicked Reur's legs from under him, knocking the champion on his ass.

Wykith charged and slammed into Reur, pinning him to the ground. Before Wykith could land his first punch, Reur wrapped his legs around his back and pulled him in, delivering a massive elbow to Wykith's jaw. Wykith swung hard and connected against Reur's face. When Reur tried the elbow again, Wykith blocked and pummeled down on Reur's stomach.

Hitting Reur's stomach was like hitting bricks, and his legs squeezed him like an iron vice. The champion twisted his body and suddenly Wykith was lying on his back.

He mimicked Reur and put his arms over his head, leaving his stomach exposed to save his face. Reur's punches to his gut felt like a stone breaker's hammer. He coughed up a little vomit on his chin from the sheer force of them.

Without thinking, Wykith pulled his legs up, wrapped them under Reur's armpits, and kicked out, launching the Ram away.

He gasped for breath, blinking salty tears out of his eyes and wiping his chin. His muscles spasmed, and he felt like he might throw up again, but rose to his feet.

Reur was in the air, coming down with a massive right cross.

Instead of attempting to block, Wykith spun under the blow, closing the distance between them. In an instant he stood behind Reur, who was already fully committed to the punch. Wykith's right elbow struck Reur in the spine and his left fist caught the champion in the back of the neck.

Reur's body folded forward at the hip and his right leg shot backwards. The horse-kick caught Wykith in the stomach, throwing him back and folding him over. He hit the ground on his side.

The Ram turned to him with a grimace, rubbing the back of his neck.

"I guess you proved me wrong, Junitari," Reur said.

"Fuck you, Reur," Wykith groaned as he found his feet.

"Sifu."

"What?" Wykith arched a brow at him.

"From now on, you call me sifu."

"The fuck does that mean?"

"You will learn."

Reur rushed forward and leaped, spinning in the air so fast Wykith could not make out what he was doing. From that blurring ball of motion a foot snapped out and hit Wykith squarely in the chin. A cloud of bright white stars exploded in his vision and then there was silence.

31

Vashyn

Murciel and Rairi stood naked in the safety of the mine's entrance as the final remnants of gold, red, and aquamarine faded from the sky.

They had both fallen asleep after their night of lovemaking. By the time they woke up, the Siege was on his throne. Instead of moving deeper into the cavern, they decided to stay and wait for moonlight to help with Murciel's wounds

Rairi was insatiable. Murciel was exhausted down to his bones, and he might have pulled a muscle or two, but he could not remember a time when he felt more alive.

"Your wounds are healing," she said. "How is your hand?"

"My fingers can bend this far now." He almost made a fist.

"Good. Keep flexing, but take it slowly. The moon-healing will help."

"We must keep moving, Rairi. We are not safe here."

"No, Murciel, you need moonlight. Your hand is too important to let heal on its own. We stay here tonight so you can heal."

Murciel took a deep breath and smiled, looking at her with a sidelong glance. "So I can heal, Rairi."

She smiled back.

The storm clouds from the other night had made their way east, leaving him a clear night sky to heal by. Elinel was nearly full to bursting. Kiyo would rule the night again soon.

Murciel sat on the cool earthen path, bathing his wounds in light and grinding his teeth against the pain. His skrit used the moonlight to purge any infections and mend tissue that would normally take weeks to heal. His body began to sweat, his moisture turning into thin wisps of steam. The charcoal helped the process along, but he wished they had majesty leaf instead.

"Make certain you keep drinking water or you will shrivel and pass out," Rairi said, looking him over.

"I will."

"Your irezu skrit looks good. Are they tingling or hurting?"

"Tingling, though my wounds are another matter."

"They will hurt worse soon. Are you going to be all right?"

He nodded.

"I will check the fire and boil you some more water. Call out if you need me."

He nodded again.

Murciel knew he was meant to feel ashamed for what they did, but he simply could not summon the guilt. The lovemaking had been incredible. Rairi's lithe body melted into his again and again, their motions blending, their ecstasy fusing, as if they could read each other's minds through the unspoken language of sex.

He had never felt lustful towards her before. He considered her a friend and fellow pack member. His forbidden desires were reserved for Escara. Now, he could not stop thinking about her naked body in firelight. He recalled the taste of her skin, how her body writhed, and the small noises she made when excited.

Murciel smiled through the pain and focused on his wounds, willing them to heal faster.

Buio found the hidden lever and tugged it back. The mechanism within clicked loudly, allowing him to slide the false wall out of the way, revealing a small chamber with a square hole dug out of the floor's center. The rope and pulley system bolted in place around the opening was once used to retrieve water, but Dominus Paralbo had found other uses for it. A reinforced cage hung suspended from a thick hemp rope over the gaping orifice.

"What is this?" Escara inquired as he checked the ropes and pulley system for signs of wear. Everything seemed in working order.

"Our way under the wall."

"This how you infiltrate anthrop cities?"

"One of the ways, yes, but Aztan is unique for what lies underneath. You will see."

Aldin came into the room, watching Escara through the corner of his eye, and handed him a small, square parcel wrapped in oilcloth.

"This much?" Buio asked in surprise. He expected half the amount.

"It was a steal," Aldin grinned.

"Thank you, Aldin. Anything I should know before we head down?"

"Kalsto is still looking for you, Buio. He will know you are there."

Escara gave him a curious glance but kept her question unspoken.

"Yes he will. Anything else?"

"The new warehouse guard is called Dalro. Yaobi is living in Lushinder now. She found herself a lifemate."

Buio nodded and stepped into the metal cage, motioning for Escara to join him. She stared at the contraption with equal parts disdain and trepidation.

"It is safe. Come."

She climbed into the cage, tensing as it swung, the ropes creaking with her added weight. Buio closed the gate behind her.

"Take us down, Aldin. Until our paths cross again, moon's blessing upon you, and thank you."

"Sari's mercy on you, Buio, and you, Escara."

Escara's muscles were taut, her legs braced and her hands holding on the bars of the cage for dear life. She blinked up at Aldin as if unsure she heard him correctly.

"And you," she managed.

Aldin disengaged the system's lock bar and turned the iron crank, lowering the gently swaying cage into the darkness below.

"Try to calm yourself," Buio told her.

Escara narrowed her eyes at him but her fingers loosen their grip on the bars.

"Where are we going, Buio? I am without starlight."

He took a moment to gather his thoughts. "Where we are going is called Norzyn. A ruined city buried underneath Aztan."

"How large is this ruin?"

"In total? Larger than Aztan itself, but entire districts are inaccessible or have fallen into chasms over time."

"Anthrops live down here? In the dark earth, like worms?"

"Not only anthrops. The xial have found homes here too, as have the durodans and-"

389

"Buio, our people live in the earth? Cut off from Arisia's light? You jest!"

"Have you ever known me to jest?"

She was silent a moment, searching his face. "Who is this Kalsto Aldin spoke of? What does he want with you?"

Buio studied the hemp ropes above their heads.

"We are going to a place called the Silver Rat Market. The ruler there is known by all as the Dorje. The former Dorje had a female D'morra named Valtrea as his personal bodyguard. Kalsto was her lifemate-"

"That does not explain-"

"What he wants is to kill me, Escara, because I killed Valtrea."

Escara's face owned a catalog of ways to show her displeasure, and until now Buio thought he had seen them all. The naked disgust etched into her features gave him pause. She glared at him like one would a roach who crawled out of a half-eaten steak.

"You killed one of our own?! A xial?! Why?! Buio what possible reason could you have!?" Her face flushed and her teeth clenched. For a moment, he thought she might lunge at him.

"My objective was to kill the former Dorje. She was in the way."

The pale light of the antechamber they descended into stole Escara's attention.

The room was a cathedral, with a high ceiling held up by thick stone columns. The floor was choked with numerous crates, barrels, and shelves stocked with earthenware pots and ampules. On the far wall was a grand mural, obscured by distance and shadow. Beneath them, a single D'sabre stood in the dim light, holding a spear and shield, awaiting them.

When the cage came to a halt, Buio opened it and faced the guard. He was tall for a D'sabre, half a head taller than Buio and thickly muscled.

He carried himself with the easy tension of a seasoned warrior, his body covered in thin pink scars and his long black hair tied into braids behind his head. When their eyes met, there was no fear or hesitation there, only cold gray glass.

"You must be Dalro," Buio said.

"And you are Buio Vashyn."

390

Buio tensed even though the barb was expected. Ever since he killed Valtrea, the xial of Silver Rat knew him by the moniker Vashyn; Kinslayer. But there was something intentional about the cavalier way he threw the word out. Like a challenge. The silence between grew ripe with violence.

"Greetings, kindred," Escara said firmly.

Dalro broke their stare down to glance at Escara. His face softened at the sight of her.

"Moon's blessing." Dalro stepped back away from the cage, his posture easing. "Welcome to Dominus Paralbo's erawa warehouse."

"We may need to come this way again," Buio told Dalro, still watching him carefully. "Do you know the signals?"

"I know everything I need to, Vashyn."

Buio nodded and motioned for Escara to follow. Dalro stayed by the cage, striking the metal bars three times with the butt of his spear. The cage began its slow ascent.

Escara looked around the warehouse, sniffing the air as her gaze wandered. "Why would this anthrop put so many of his wares down here? Is it not difficult to take them back up?"

"These stores do not go back. They are sold here in the Silver Rat to avoid the Sarandi's collectors."

"I do not understand."

"Anthrops pay for the privilege of being ruled over. They call it 'taxes', though not all of them agree with the practice." Buio could tell Escara was confused. "It is not important."

Escara stopped when they reached the mural at the far wall of the cathedral. The floor-to-ceiling fresco was the masterful portrait of a giant, prismatic winged serpent. An ancient masterpiece, showing subtle hints of aging at its corners, but with surprisingly vibrant colors.

The hues and shapes of the mural seemed to dance and fold with the room's dim blue light. Buio watched the shimmering serpent take life and slither slowly towards him, eyes like golden bonfires, the glinting colors of its wings and scales mesmerizing him.

Fear and wonder swept through him in equal measure as she came within striking distance. He knew her intention was to devour him whole, and he wanted her to. He would willingly become her sacrifice, his flesh consumed and his spirit released into her eternal light.

Buio closed his eyes and took a steadying breath. When he opened his eyes again, the mural was still. The dim light danced off the colors of its contours.

"This is beautiful craftsmanship," Escara said breathlessly. "Beyond beautiful. It comes alive when observed. Did an anthrop make this?"

"Yes, but not just any anthrop. It takes a reiarista to create such art."

"And they are?"

"Gifted, tormented souls, touched by Cala-Neteri's grace. Their art flows from an immaculate source, though they are said to be all mad."

"I feel a sense of awe standing before this mural," she said. "Neteri, the great teacher. She freed us from our bonds and taught us to master alchemy, and our own selves. Without her we would still be slaves."

Buio could tell Escara was fascinated by the mural, but not enchanted, not like he had been. As D'sabres used their ears and noses far more than their eyes, he wondered what would happen to Escara if she ever heard the music of a reiarista.

Escara turned to look back at Dalro. "Are they all anthrop slaves down here as well?"

"He is no slave, Escara. The xial who live in Norzyn have been freed."

"But then why stay here, Buio? Why not flee to Helicartia? If they are truly free, why do they linger among their slavers? Why not come home?"

"Because freedom is not so simple a matter, and Helicartia is no home to these xial. You will see why."

As Buio led her outside Paralbo's warehouse and into an adjacent hallway, Escara perused the faded frescoes on the walls and domed ceiling which told an ancient, disjointed story. Images of fantastic creatures, weapons which shone as if possessed by their own inner light, and stoic beings radiating power in a variety of faded colors adorned the walls.

A short, narrow corridor led out into a makeshift stall where a short, stocky, black-skinned anthrop was crying out to all who passed her by.

"Erawas! Erawas! Erawa oil! Erawa wine! Spiced erawas, stuffed erawas! Erawa soaps and lamp-oil! The finest for the cheapest! Chints, chips, and scripts, all welcome!"

The woman glanced back when she heard them approach and quickly looked away. Escara could sense she was disquieted by their presence, but was making an effort not to notice them. They walked silently behind the anthrop, out of the stall, and into a wider hall where a number of similar stalls stood.

The hall was forty-feet wide and roughly eighty feet long, with a cathedral ceiling covered in chipped, faded frescoes. She counted seven other stalls where anthrops haggled, sampled, bought, and traded. The entire place reeked of moisture, stale sweat, and burning erawa oil.

"This is the Silver Rat Market?" she asked.

Buio shook his head. "There is more ahead."

Escara wanted to bury her bubbling emotions, to shrug them aside and carry on with the mission, but she absolutely could not contain the rage rising like sea-foam at the corners of her mind.

"Buio." Her bitterness echoed in how she said his name.

His head turned slowly towards her, and there they were — those cold killer's eyes. She had not felt their bite in so long they made her skin tingle. She held his gaze.

"You killed a xial, Buio. How are you allowed back into Helicartia? How are you in our pack? Do the Elders not know?"

She could not help her accusatory tone. The Elders were clear on this matter. The punishments for killing another xial were skrit-scourging and banishment. While Buio's body was covered in battle-scars, his skrit had not been scourged.

"They know," Buio said flatly.

"They know? I do not understand."

"Pray you never do." He went to turn away.

"No!" she snapped, her anger rising. "You are going to explain this to me, Buio!"

When their eyes met again, they did not meet as friends. Buio was deadly, she knew, but if he was a kinslayer who had forsaken the laws of Helicartia, she could not afford to see him as a pack member. He was tainted and a danger to her. Not a drop of fear emanated from him. She forced herself to remain calm.

"Valtrea was not the first xial I killed, nor the last." His tone dropped to a deeper register. "When the Elders speak in the circles about The People, they do not mean those still living in anthrop lands. In their own private language, they do not see these kindred as xial, but thropen."

Escara's resolve faltered somewhat.

"The Elders say The People are united," he went on. "That we are different from anthrops, but this is a lie, Escara. There are as many divisions among us as there are among them.

"We are not one united people under Arisia's grace, as they like to claim. We are either xial or thropen, noctural or arisi, of this clan or the other, of this or that academy. Each clan has secret factions struggling for control of Helicartia. The academies each have their own agendas. There is a silent, bloodless war occurring in the shadows of Helicartia's trees as we speak."

Escara took a moment to consider what he said. The D'tirnni were shadow workers, meant to keep the outskirts of Helicartia safe, to spy on potential dangers, and on rare occasions, eliminate threats to the xial as a whole.

She never imagined the xial fought among themselves. Were they so similar to the anthrops? Were they not meant to be better than them, in at least this way?

"Buio, have you ever killed a xial of Helicartia, or betrayed your pack?"

The dangerous glint in his eyes faded. "No, never."

She believed him. She nodded.

"We have to move," he said. "Keep your senses about you here, Escara. If you hear or smell anything you find odd, if something makes your instincts flare, you must tell me."

"I will Buio, but I will not attack my own kind. If this D'morra finds us-"

"I will deal with him. All I ask is you not get in my way."

Escara nodded, but she was uncertain, and she could sense that Buio knew. How would she react if confronted by another xial? She had fought others of her kind throughout her life but mostly in training and sparring.

She had fought her own kind in anger of course, even mepsiens were not beyond such, but she never fought a xial with an intent to kill. What if Buio attacked first? What was she supposed to do?

These questions plagued her while they made their way through the hall, surrounded by anthrops and unmarked xial. Thropen, Buio called them — "the befouled" — so different from the xial of Helicartia. They wore anthrop clothes, their skin untested and unmarked, and they reeked of ingrained fear. They spoke fluent calisthian and broken, heavily accented xiasi. It was pitiful and heartbreaking to witness.

Escara was also bewildered by what Buio had revealed. It challenged her core beliefs, to think such things occurred back home. She hated the idea of the clan Elders lording their powers and the academies scheming against each other, but Buio was a tool of their will. He was a shadow meant for shadow-work. Who would know the Elders' secrets better?

A sudden change in the general hum of her surroundings snapped her from her reverie. She had failed to be wary of her surroundings like Buio asked. They had left the market hall behind without her noticing.

The cavern they stood in now was not a part of the Neterian temple. This was a much wider space, with a massive ceiling, lit by greasy lamps and pig-fat candles.

Enormous stone columns punched through the ground and up into the dark rises, holding the cavern's grand dimensions. In the shadow of those columns was an agglomeration of ancient stonework and hodgepodge anthrop architecture.

The so-called Silver Rat Market was part buried ancient ruin, and part anthrop shantytown. Regal, two hundred-foot archways were chocked by wooden cabins stacked atop each other and connected by rickety stairwells and creaking bridges.

Strange, oily, scents lived down here, mixed together in a thick broth. She caught the lingering scent of uncooked meat, blood, urine, and scat, blended with herbs, spices, burnt oils, scented wax, potpourri, and anthrop musk. All these aromas, condensed and allowed no escape by the enclosure, became an assault on her nostrils.

She could hear the clicking, banging, and scraping of construction mixed with the cries of merchants and mongers, peddlers and fences, all plying their trade in an overlapping cacophony. The Silver Rat's claws scraped against her swollen senses.

She needed a moment to steady herself. There was no rhythm or pattern to this place. Nothing was in harmony.

"Are you all right?" Buio asked, sensing her discomfort.

"This place lies in Alciren's shadow. My mind swims."

"I know," Buio nodded. "Keep moving. This way."

The Blind Man's looked the same as always, and reeked of cigar smoke. Dried beer, spoiled wine, and crusted blood covered the tavern's woodwork. Escara put a hand to her mouth, her face pinching.

Blind old Qustil was behind his bar, smoking a cuksar and staring into the void with his dead white eyes. He turned his head as they came in, his left ear following their movements until they sat at his counter.

"Hello, Buio," he said with a half smirk. "Who's the other spook with you?"

"Her name is Escara," Buio spoke in fluent calisthian. "You received my marker?"

Qustil nodded grimly. "Whiskey brought it by. Listen, after the dung storm you summoned here last time, I don't think I can help you."

"My business is not down here this time. I need to find someone, topside."

"The great Buio lost a mark? That is a first. You know how big topside is, right?"

"Do not play games, Qustil, this is important. He came into Aztan alone and on foot, from the south. He is young, heavily muscled, and smells like he was birthed from a bison's ass."

"You just described the entire dock district."

"Your people would have taken note of him, if they are worth what you pay them. His clothes are in tatters and he is sick. Shinn poisoning."

The old man frowned. "Perhaps I heard something. What is it worth to you?"

Buio took the parcel Aldin gave him and thumped it on the bar counter. Qustil reached out and ran his fingertips over its dimensions.

"Seriously?"

"I said it was important."

"He was stopped by the gate guards when he tried to enter. He put up a fight, so they clubbed him and dragged him off towards the stocks. He got away from them on the street. That's all I know."

"I need him found, and I need eyes on him at all hours once he is."

"With what you're paying? I'll have him brought to your doorstep in a fucking bow by tomorrow night, Buio."

"No, I do not want him brought down here. I only want him found and followed."

"Is he some kind of spook weapon?"

Buio stared at Qustil but the man's frowning face gave him nothing.

"What makes you ask?"

"The guards from the scuffle with him. They ain't right anymore." Qustil tapped a finger against his temple. "Up here."

Escara gave him a concerned glance.

"Anything more?" Buio asked.

"This morning they found one of them hiding in the shitter by the barracks. Inside the shit, screaming to the heavens about doomriders and the end of time.

"The other one cracked a patron's skull open at a brothel and licked his gray stuff off the boards while giggling like a girl. They are both up in the cracked house now."

"Found and followed, Qustil."

The old man nodded. "Fine."

"Knife."

Qustil grinned and passed him a clean blade.

Buio cut the parcel in half and handed him one.

"You should give me the whole thing now." Qustil smiled.

"Why?"

"Because he is outside, waiting for you."

Kalsto stood out in the street with four armed men.

"That did not take long," Buio said dourly.

Escara turned to regard the D'morra and the anthrops flanking him.

"News travels fast down here, Vashyn. He means to kill you, you know?"

"I do." He stood and put the other half of the parcel back in his belt-pouch.

"Goodbye, Buio."

"Fuck you, Qustil."

"Keep that shit outside my place or our deal is off."

When he drew his vrin, Escara was quick to draw her blade and don her shield. They stepped out into the street together.

"Vashyn." Kalsto said, his voice as deep as a chasm.

"Kalsto."

Kalsto seemed even larger than the last time he saw him. When D'morra men are in mourning, they shave their beards and tie their long hair in a single braid around their necks. Kalsto had shaved his face and his head.

Shaving the head was a sign of deep shame and usually only performed during an exile. It was a powerful message, to inflict it upon yourself.

Kalsto wore no shirt, revealing the thick gnarled muscles and network of old scars that made up his arms and torso. Two javelins were sheathed in a harness on his back and the ax in his hands was a massive piece of iron, sharpened to a glinting edge.

The weapon's handle was a single piece of smoothed ironwood as thick as Buio's forearm. No anthrop could hope to lift an ax that massive, much less swing it. No xial for that matter, who did not happen to be a D'morra, and Kalsto was no small specimen. He stood with his legs shoulder-width apart, the pads of his feet planted deeply in the earth.

"You owe me a blood-debt, Vashyn," came his cavernous voice. "I am here to collect."

"And your lady-friends here?" Buio spoke in calisthian, motioning to the four men whose demeanor immediately darkened.

"I thought if you ever came back here, it would be with a full pack." Kalsto's honey colored eyes fell on Escara coolly. "One shieldmaiden. She is all you brought? I hope she's good."

"Kalsto, don't. This is between you and me."

"So she is important to you? Good. Kill her," he said to the anthrops.

"Actually, tear her tongue out, rape her in the ass, then kill her."

The four men drew their swords and moved towards Escara with wicked smiles on their faces. Before Buio could intercept them, he fell into Kalsto's massive shadow. The ax struck the ground with such force, it spat up a cloud of dust and flying pebbles.

Kalsto stood before him with the quiet certainty of an executioner. Escara fended off the anthrops with her blade and shield. Buio could not afford to take his eyes off Kalsto. He needed to trust that she could fend for herself.

"For Valtrea," Kalsto said coldly, squeezing the smooth handle of his ax. His eyes darkened as his pupils widened. His muscles shivered and his lips pulled back in a hideous snarl. "FOR VALTREA!"

"Shit," Buio muttered as Kalsto charged him.

"Gaia has not birthed a tree which can stand before an enraged D'morra's direct attack," he recalled Hiou telling him once. "If you ever find yourself before one, you have only one option. Run, Buio. Run, or you die."

Against his every instinct, Buio did exactly that. He turned tail and sprinted up the main street. Kalsto gave chase, his thunderous roar making Buio's balls jump into his stomach. He sheathed his vrin and leaped on to the nearest wall, climbing like a cat being chased by a rabid hound.

Kalsto's ax slammed into the corner of the building right below his feet, turning a thick support beam into kindling and leaving behind a baleful gash in the wall.

Buio climbed well out of Kalsto's reach, dug his claws in, and flicked two knives down at him. The knives sank neatly into the meat of the D'morra's back and drew blood. Kalsto did not seem to mind. He yanked a javelin out of its harness and launched it up at him.

Buio leaped out of the way. The missile struck the wall with such force, it broke through as if fired from a ballista. Buio climbed to the building's roof, away from Kalsto's line of sight.

"GET DOWN HERE, VASHYN!" Kalsto roared.

From this vantage point he scanned the street for Escara. One man lay on the ground in a pool of his own blood, his sword hand severed. The remaining three approached cautiously now, harrying her back in an attempt to surround her.

399

The fight was drawing a crowd. People came out from every corner of the Silver Rat to watch the action.

Buio drew his composite bow, knocked an arrow and let fly. The missile flew short, sinking into the earth behind one of Escara's attackers. He cursed, adjusted his aim and let fly again. This time his arrow found the flesh of his target's lower back.

The anthrop yelped, his body twisting towards the shaft reflexively as his right leg gave out. Escara's sword flashed in a violent arc, cutting through his undefended neck before he could hit the ground.

Buio raised his bow again but before he let loose, Kalsto's ax broke through the roof shingles behind him, cutting a support beam right through the marrow. The roof shook and buckled as Kalsto tore his way up like some daemonic baby chick emerging from its egg.

Buio turned and fired. His arrow hit Kalsto in the head but at an angle, deflected by the D'morra's thick skull. The shaft lodged itself into the side of Kalsto's head, held there by a piece of bleeding scalp.

Kalsto leaned on the roof with his ax hand, pulled his second javelin from its harness, and thew.

At point-blank range, Buio could only leap out of the way. The sharpened edge of the javelin tore into the back of his right thigh, mid-leap.

The pain was immediate and blinding. Buio struck the corner of the roof with his back and fell off the building, his stomach leaping as he plummeted through the air.

The butt of the javelin in his leg hit the ground first. Smooth wood sliced through his leg, scraping against his femur. Buio's agonized scream was cut short by his head hitting the ground.

The world went dark.

"Buio!"

Escara watched him plummet from the roof and the distraction nearly cost her an eye. She managed to lean her head back right as one of her assailants' blades sliced by. The two men grew tired of testing her defenses and began swinging in concert, looking to end the fight.

She took a defensive stance and blocked their advance with sword and shield. The men were well-trained, but their styles of attack differed. While it made predicting them difficult, they did not complement each other's momentum. Their unspoken tactic was to overwhelm her. She backtracked to keep them both in front of her, which placed her progressively farther from Buio's prone form.

The man on her left grew emboldened, gripping his sword with both hands, he came in with a massive side slash. She stepped into the swing with her shield, putting her shoulder behind it. The instant the sword made contact with her shield, she crouched and spun on her heels, bringing her sword around at knee level.

The Ayu's Hook was what her teacher would call a bird-shit move. It was flashy, risky, and would have gotten her in trouble in a sparring competition, but her muscle memory decided on it anyway.

Her sword cut into his knee, slicing tendons and breaking cartilage. He went down with a cry, releasing his blade and grabbing at his ruined leg.

Using the momentum from her spinning crouch, Escara leaped and brought her shield around in a devastating hook, connecting with the second man's jaw, breaking bone and sending teeth flying as he struck the dirt, limp as a rag doll.

Flashy and stupid, but it worked.

"VASHYN!" Kalsto's monstrous roar came from within the building before he stepped into the light, his massive ax in hand.

Escara sprinted towards Buio. The anthrops gathered around to witness the bloodshed moved quickly out of her way. She stood over Buio's prone, motionless body, and the worrying puddle of his blood seeping into the ground. A thick scent of ozone emanated from his markings, which were flaring to mitigate the damage.

As the massive D'morra came to stand before her, she caught whiff of his potent musk. His sour breathing was labored, he was drenched in sweat, and tiny drops of blood speckled his perspiration. The prolonged blood-fury had taken its toll on him.

"Kalsto, stop!" She held her arms out over Buio's body. "Please! This is not our way!"

With a snort of derision, Kalsto took the ax in both hands and heaved it over his shoulder. Escara leaped back right as the massive slab of iron swooshed by, picking up a cloud of dust and making her hair glide in its wake. If he had hit her, he would have cleaved her in half.

Merciful goddess.

"Kalsto, please! I cannot let you kill him! He is my pack. He is family."

"Then say your goodbyes." Kalsto's voice was like wet rocks tumbling down a pit. "It is more than he ever gave me."

Kalsto pulled his ax up and over his head, lining up for a vertical swing down on Buio's body.

"No!" Escara jumped into the path of the D'morra's ferocious strike. Instead of putting her shield in the direct path of the massive ax-head, she planted herself firmly and raised her shield at an angle. The ax clipped the surface of her shield and followed through. Dust, stones, and blood flew into the air as iron made contact with the blood-drenched earth, inches from Buio's waist.

Escara's body shuddered from the glancing impact. She growled, tightened her grip on the hilt of her xiphos and thrust up, cleaving through the meat of his right arm.

Kalsto roared and kicked out. She caught the big, padded foot with her shield but the force was enough to peel her off the ground and yank her hilt from her hand. She rolled backward and regained her footing.

Kalsto dropped his heavy ax and stared at the xiphos sticking out of his arm. He grabbed the hilt, winced in pain and released it. Escara deftly pulled a throwing knife from its sheathe and palmed it. Kalsto stared at her, seeing her for the first time as a credible threat.

"You want to die for him?" His pupils widened until they swallowed the honey of his irises.

"FINE!" He tore her sword from his flesh, holding it in his hand like a dagger, and charged.

Escara snapped the knife into his stomach, right below the solar plexus. Kalsto did not break stride.

"Trolk me!" Escara cried out and did as Buio had done. She ran.

Buio lay in a quiet glade under the shade of an oak tree, staring up into a star-lit sky. He did not know how long he lay here, but he had no intention of moving. He was exhausted and needed rest.

"And just what do you think you are doing down there, Buio?" Hiou hovered over him, his arms crossed over his broad chest.

"Resting, sifu," he said.

"There is no time for that, cub. Get up," Hiou offered him his hand.

"I'm tired, sifu."

"Rest will come soon enough. Now come on, get up!"

Buio groaned tiredly, reached up, and gripped his teacher's hand.

The first thing Buio felt when coming to, was the wound in his leg. Raw agony rode up to his crotch. He bit back his scream and opened his eyes, blinking away tears and stars. Noises came from somewhere nearby — far away echoes trying to make their way towards him, rumbling like an approaching storm. People were crying out, cheering on, yelling.

Buio's head cleared all at once, the misty dreamworld popping like a bubble. People stood around him, inching in as close as they dared. When he looked up, they pushed back and away.

Kalsto's javelin lay next to him, bloodied from tip to butt. His massive ax lay beside him as well.

The rumbling he heard came from inside the tavern he had fallen off of. Sounds of wood splintering and the sharp crack of broken glassware came from within. Kalsto roared from somewhere inside, followed by Escara's yelp of pain.

"No!" Buio tried to stand but the pain in his leg was like an iron chain tied to an anchor, pinning him down.

The wound was grave. The javelin had nicked his femoral artery, and he had lost a lot of blood, but his markings worked to sear and cauterize the wound.

"Goddess bless you, Rairi."

He reached into his pouch, grabbing the cut brick of molki Aldin had given him, pinched off a piece, rolled it into a ball, and pushed the soft, black sphere into the raw flesh of his wound with his thumb.

He groaned as his nerves flared. The molki took instant effect, numbing the pain in his leg.

Another violent crash. Kalsto's growls, like the sound of falling trees, echoed through the tavern's open doors. Wood splintered and there was a crash of metal against metal.

Buio tried to stand again. The pain was sharp, but the molki numbed it enough for him to stand. Another loud crash. Escara

403

screamed in fury.

The molki all but dulled the pain in his leg, the initial lulling effects massaging the corners of his mind. He fell away from himself, spiraling into a waking dream.

Buio pushed his foot against the earth until the pain sharpened his mind again. He drew his vrin and hobbled towards the building, leaving bloody footprints in his wake.

Before Buio could reach the tavern's doorway, Kalsto crashed through the window, flying backwards. Escara held her shield against his bloodied chest and was using her entire body to propel them both out of the building.

The huge D'morra fell on his back in a puff of dust. Escara was seething, bleeding from a number of wounds, and mad as a vorxstorm. When they landed, she punched Kalsto in the head with the rim of her broken shield, again and again, screaming with every blow.

She was in a blood-frenzy. Four of Escara's throwing daggers stuck out of Kalsto's body, puncturing vital pressure points.

Kalsto recovered his senses and punched Escara clean in the face. Her entire head whipped to the side, her loose hair snapping like a sail. Escara went suddenly limp and collapsed off Kalsto's broad torso.

Buio took the opening and leaped, plunging his vrin through the pocket of Kalsto's left shoulder, pinning him to the ground. The D'morra roared and hit Buio with a backhanded fist.

Buio's mind swung out over the bottomless precipice of unconsciousness, swinging back by sheer will alone. A tooth hit the inside of his mouth and fell on his tongue.

He spit the tooth in Kalsto's face and in a single motion, unsheathed his moonblade and cut under Kalsto's left armpit, slicing open meat, tendons and the artery. Kalsto's meaty right fist slammed into his ribs, snapping them, and putting him on the ground.

Kalsto pulled the vrin from his shoulder and stood, his left arm hanging uselessly at his side, drenched in blood. Buio's vrin was like a knife in the D'morra's massive hand.

Still laying on the ground, Escara yanked a throwing knife stuck in Kalsto's left calf and sliced it through his heel tendon. The D'morra fell to a knee, roaring in pain. Buio snapped a throwing dagger right into his mouth.

The deep baritone roar turned into a slurped, sucking of dry air. Kalsto's thick fingers dug into his own mouth in desperation. Buio extracted his sharpened claws and plunged them into the D'morra's thick neck, savaging his jugular.

Buio roared in his face.

Kalsto's eyes found his, and to his surprise, there was no more rage in them — only the frost of failure and regret. In his final moments, Kalsto knew he had failed to avenge his lifemate. His eyes rolled and his body collapsed sideways.

Buio watched in fascination as Kalsto's spirit rose from its mortal encasing. His spirit's thick, braided hair was waist length, and his coarse beard hung halfway down his chest. Kalsto's spirit stood in warrior's regalia; beads, and bones, feathers and ward wraps. His skin was slick with oil and covered in war-grease markings. He stood before Buio, regal and imposing.

Buio fell to his knees before the visage, suddenly overcome with remorse. He could not fight back the tears flooding his eyes.

"I am sorry, Kalsto," he said in xiasi. "I am so very sorry. I took your heart from you that night. I see now. I did not only take her life back then, but yours. Please...I..."

Kalsto's golden gaze gave him a pitying look. The D'morra shook his head and faded into nothingness.

"Buio, who are you talking to?" Escara was by his side, her face covered in blood. She wore the wolf headdress and fur cloak of an elite Shieldmaiden of Helicartia, her body covered in ceremonial beads and bones. She was beautiful, glorious. His heart swelled at the sight of her.

Escara began to age before his eyes. Deep wrinkles appeared on her face, and her luscious hair grew thin and frail, falling away from her scalp. Only her eyes remained unchanging, even as her skin began to peel away, revealing drying muscle and bits of skull. Then came the maggots, eating away at her flesh.

Haunting patterns of gold, silver, and flawless porcelain replaced what the maggots ate. A disk of radiance and sacred script materialized around Escara's head. Pearl white serpents with green glass eyes wrapped themselves protectively around her, watching him as they rose towards her crown.

Her wolf headdress became a living thing. A regal wolf's white face hovered above Escara's beatific visage, framed by the golden disk, silent and watchful, with eyes like sheet-ice.

A proud chime sounded, celebrating the fullness of Escara's transformation. It was like witnessing the birth of a goddess — a being of divinity rising from frail, mortal flesh.

The molki. The molki!

He had used too much. The convulsions hit him then, pitching him on his side. He tasted stale bile as white foam escaped his lips. His body felt like it was being crumpled into a ball by some cruel god's hands. He had initiated a spirit walk without respecting the rituals or having an Elder present to guide him. He was in terrible danger.

"Buio!" Escara's voice faded as he fell into a bottomless well. "Buio! Buio!!"

32

Revelations

Kartecus had no way of knowing how long Sinitel had worked on him. Time seemed to bleed back into its own mouth, forming unending loops which spun on for days, weeks, months. He would stare at the candles in the room after his frayed mind managed to coalesce, but could never assert the time.

The spiders were only a prelude to a damnable, unending chain of torments the Inquisitor had unleashed. For all he knew, he was born in this chamber and his past life was only a dream he devised to keep himself sane.

Sinitel tormented him endlessly, summoning serpents of flame and thorns to slither over his skin and sink their long fangs into his flesh. He summoned greasy shadows to whisper his darkest secrets and most painful mistakes into his ears. The terrible shadows spoke with the voices of his mother and father, belittling him for his every flaw and failing.

At one point the Inquisitor dug his fingers into his sides and ripped his skin right off his flesh, wearing it like a cloak, imitating his Vinergalian accent, and posing before him in mock chivalry. It was not until his screams became hoarse that the Inquisitor reluctantly gave him back his skin.

He did not understand how Sinitel managed to mend it seamlessly back in place, but he cried in relief when he could no longer see the bleeding muscles of his arms and chest.

In the quiet interludes, his mind swam with visions of blood and chaos. Long-buried memories flooded back with frightening clarity. The battles he fought in, the sins he committed, and shameful desires he indulged, merged like facets on a broken, stained-glass window, forming a macabre mosaic reflection of his soul.

"Kartecus."

Sinitel's voice startled him.

"What have you done to me?" His lips trembled. "How long have I been here?"

"Your Inquisition only just began, Kartecus. How much have you already seen?"

"Sorcery," he muttered. "This is no Inquisition. This is vorxcraft!"

"Your faith's dark threats have twisted your insides, old man. This is the corrosion you carry within you. Only by seeing can you be cleansed. You soiled yourself, Kartecus. Did you realize that?"

His body was covered in his own sick and filth. He remembered vomiting, but not the rest. His attention being brought to it made the pungency shameful and unbearable.

"This is inhuman!" He rattled in his chains. "You're a fucking animal! You cannot leave me here like this!"

"We are all animals, Kartecus. Not even your spiteful rape-daemons took that away from us. You must learn this lesson. You must know this to be true."

"Fuck you!"

"Much work yet remains I see," Sinitel sighed.

The Inquisitor dipped a small blade into one of his black vials and ran it across his skin, drawing blood.

Kartecus tried to rear away from it helplessly. "No. No more!" A thick haze began overpowering his senses.

"I do not intend to leave you in your own filth, Kartecus," Sinitel said. "Rest a moment. We will begin again soon."

Like being immersed in soothing hot water, his muscles relaxed, and he fell into a deep, black sleep.

When Kartecus woke, he was no longer manacled to the wall, but stood strapped inside the wood and iron sphere at the center of the chamber. He pulled at his restraints but found himself firmly in place.

"How long?" His mouth tasted dry and bitter. "How long have I been in here?"

"I gave some consideration to your plight as I cleaned your mess, Kartecus," Sinitel said. "I believe you are dealing with a strong adherence to a deeply rooted misconception. I wish to help you unburden yourself of it."

"Let me out of here, creature!" His head felt heavy, as if he drank too much wine the night before.

Sinitel dipped his claw in five small flasks and patiently coated the blades.

"No, no!" His muscles shuddered, as if remembering the horrors that glove had induced. "Take that thing away from me!"

"I need you to be still, Kartecus." Sinitel brought the razor-sharp claws up to his neck. "If you struggle I may nick your jugular and you will bleed out and die. Do you understand?"

Kartecus ground his teeth but allowed his head be guided upwards by the knife of Sinitel's palm. The Inquisitor raked his skin; one cut on either side of his neck, one under each side of his jaw line, and one under his chin. The pain, as fierce as the last time, made him rattle in his restraints.

"Do not go anywhere, Kartecus. I wish to show you something."

The Inquisitor left him to writhe alone inside the wooden sphere and returned shortly after with a statue of a Celestial Diva; an angelic female warrior of Zenthien, rolled in on a wooden cart.

The Diva was made of pure bleached marble. She wore a chain vest over her bosom, flowing silks over her arms and legs, and her feathered wings were pulled in closely behind her. In her hands, with its tip planted between her feet, stood an intricate greatsword with angelic scrollwork on the blade and six wings acting as cross-guards. Her exquisite appearance was marred only by tiny drops of dried blood-splatter on her sword and the hem of her skirts.

"Beautiful creatures these Divas," Sinitel said. "Stewards of the Ashuras, charged with passing judgment on the day of their deaths. What do you think, Kartecus? Will you be one of the chosen to stand among the heroes of old to fight against the Vorx?"

"Fuck you," Kartecus spat. He was no longer an Ashura and so no longer guaranteed to enter Celestia. It was not his place to be judged by a Diva, and the Inquisitor damn well knew it.

"I bring her out to witness the inquisition of every zoniran placed in my charge. She has never once lifted a finger to help anyone. What do you make of this?"

"She is a statue, you lunatic."

Sinitel's smile was a knife. "Is she? Are you certain?"

Despite himself, Kartecus gave the statue a more critical look. The Diva stood, a vision of beauty and danger. The feathers in her wings fluttered in the stale air of the chamber, her hair swept gently in front of her face, and her armored bosom rose and fell with her every breath.

Kartecus turned away, feeling a sudden pang of panic. This could not be happening. The very thought was lunacy. She was only, what? He knew she could not be there. The touch of that wicked claw had addled his mind.

"I cannot help but wonder," Sinitel continued. "Perhaps she will help someone like you; someone with the brass balls to kill a clergyman of his own Order in cold blood. Perhaps that is the kind of man my Diva will finally save. What do you think?"

Kartecus growled.

"What made you do it, Kartecus? Why did you really kill that priest?"

"Fuck yourself, heathen!" Even as the words left him, his eyes darted back to those of the Diva.

She glared back at him in silent disapproval. The cart Sinitel brought her in vanished — or had he imagined it? She stood with her bare feet on the chamber's stone floor, watching him with unwavering eyes of golden radiance.

Why was a Diva here with them? Did this Inquisitor really posses such power? No, something was not right here.

"God help me," he said. "I am losing my mind."

"Far from it, Kartecus."

"I cannot. I cannot go through this again."

"Before your inquisition ends you will need to confess all your sins. Not to me, but to her." Sinitel put a hand on the Diva's pale shoulder. She turned her head to regard the Inquisitor and gave him a nod.

"Take heed, Kartecus. She is here to listen for the sake of your soul. I will leave you two alone. Do not fail yourself at this most important of times."

As Sinitel turned and faded into the background, Kartecus gazed upon the Diva and his heart flooded. She spread her wings and floated into the air, more pristine and marvelous than any painting or mosaic he ever saw. Her pearl-white wings were dipped in gold, her shining hair was like a snowstorm, and her eyes were furious golden pools. Kartecus knew he stood in audience with the divine, the last fragments of doubt fading from his mind like an unremembered dream.

"Explain yourself, Kartecus." The Diva's voice was melodic and powerful. He basked in the sound of it. "I wish to know why you murdered a servant of God."

He stared in speechless awe at the beatific being of legend before him.

"My actions were not without merit, my, my Lady," he told her, tears welling up in his eyes. "Father Santpor was corrupt, possessed by something malefic. Dorav and I discovered his secrets."

"What secrets?"

"He consorted with criminals, took bribes from politicians, and stole from the Church's coffers to finance his inhuman trade. He sold Telkan prisoners to Qanalarian slavers and paid the constables to turn a blind eye."

"He stole not from the Holy Church."

"What?"

"Father Santpor's acted with the Archbishop's blessing. He Amounted a great deal for the faith."

Kartecus looked back up at her, incredulous. "But he was a heathen! A blasphemer! Those people were being defiled!"

"You forget, Kartecus, the path to Celestia is paved in golden light. Father Santpor worked for the good of the faithful."

Kartecus' insides hollowed out from shock. "No, no! How can this be!? He was tainted! He dealt in human slaves! In children! Babies!"

"Holy scripture does not denounce slavery, Kartecus. The weak are meant to serve the strong, each step on the stair serving the one directly above it. Wherever did you pluck the idea that this man of the cloth committed sin?"

His skin went cold, and he lowered his head in disbelief. "This cannot be."

He recalled the faces of the people in those cages, scared and covered in filth. He remembered the children, pulled screaming from their horrified parents to be sold off as playthings for the Qanalarian nobility. He remembered how they stared at him from behind the bars of their pens, pleading eyes brimming with terror.

"How can selling children to be used...how can such a thing serve God's will?" He raised his head to the Diva, his heart broken. "How!?"

"The flesh he sold was not of our faith or flock. They were irredeemable, unclean souls."

"How can you say such a thing? There was no attempt to save them! To teach them! They were thrown in cages like cattle and sold as such! That is the Vorx at work!"

The Diva's face seemed free of turmoil. She cast the calm certainty one would expect of such a being, which only demeaned his own wretched, conflicted soul.

"The Vorx is an insidious force, Kartecus. It corrupts whomever it touches, instilling them with the sole purpose of destroying all opposition. This is why everyone who works against the faith must be seen as a corruption — all which obstructs the Sacred Amounting of the Holy Church is sin. Do you see now, why you fell?"

"No." He shook his head. "No,this cannot be."

"You muddied the faith with your misguided sympathies. Had you Amounted enough in life, you might have bought the slaves yourself and decided their fates. Such an act would prove inviolable, even sacrosanct, but in your impotence and lack of Amounting, you resorted to the murder of a man who stood high above your place on the Golden Stair."

"This is God's will?"

"You are too absorbed by your immediate experience. You fail to understand that God spans the breath of all existence, in this life and the next. It is not your place to doubt or question. It is your place to serve. Your lack of faith led you here. You shamed your brotherhood, your Church and yourself. You are deemed unworthy of God's mercy."

Kartecus' heart beat furiously in his chest. Without God's forgiveness he was destined for the Vorx, damned for all time to a void of rape, murder, and madness. The creatures there would feast on him, tearing him limb from limb until the end of time, or until he succumbed and became one of them.

"I was so certain, that mine was a righteous kill — justified. I am damned? I am damned."

"Do not despair so, Kartecus." The Diva's voice softened. "You failed Lord Zenthien, but redemption is still possible."

"How?" Warmth returned to him, blazing in a sudden convulsion of hope. "I will do anything! Please!"

"You must be purified by fire. Your soul must be cleansed of the taint you placed upon it. You must be made to see the true light of God's design. Are you so willing?"

"Yes! Yes, of course!" His fear of the Vorx pricked his insides like steel thorns.

"You must place your faith unto me. Do not accept this trial lightly. It means surrendering a significant portion of yourself and entrusting it to the light."

"Whatever you want! I struck Santpor down because I believed I was doing God's will. I have always been faithful, and I will always be so. Please! Do whatever you must! Free me of this sin! I want to feel his love again! Please!"

"Very well, Kartecus. I hear your repentance and know it to be true. I will ask you one last time, and know that if you agree, there is no turning back. However, in the end, you will be saved."

"Anything, Diva. I want to be forgiven my sins. Whatever it takes!"

The Diva smiled at him, a look he found both beautiful and terrifying. She approached and reached out her hand. To his complete surprise, she grabbed him firmly by the balls.

"You made no significant use of these in your lifetime, Kartecus." She stared at him with her golden, unblinking eyes. "They only serve to get in your way. The first thing we must do, is pacify your rage."

"Wait," he heard himself say.

"I accept your sacrifice."

He was assaulted by the most unbearable, searing agony he had ever experienced. He would have chosen to be tortured for the rest of his days if he knew beforehand how this would feel.

He did more than scream — he rattled in his chains and garble-howled like a madman. A part of him knew he was not meant to survive such searing misery. Another part of him wondered why he did not black out from it. The third and final part simply prayed for death, coveted it, lusted after it as the pain broke something vital

413

inside him. He tried to bite off his own tongue but could not stop screaming long enough to find it.

Then as suddenly as it assaulted him, the torment transmuted. A thunderbolt of unhindered pleasure struck him so fiercely he lost bodily control. He shook in a violent, orgasmic seizure, his eyes rolling into the back of his head and he moaned. The sensation ended, leaving him hanging like a rung rag, incredulous about still being conscious.

When he opened his eyes, the Diva held a small orange globe in her ivory hand. "It is done."

He tried to move his lips, to ask what had just happened, but he was too weak, too spent, to do anything other than stare. He hung there, blinking like an idiot.

"Rest now, Kartecus," she said, her voice soothing his tired frame. "More work lies ahead of us. Rest."

As if her words were a command, he fell back into a deep, dreamless sleep.

33

Azilial

Once they were a mile from Kaira, Primus Pentalion had a chestnut stallion brought to David, with orders for him to ride up to the front of the column. David rode through the tall razorgrass to the left of the cohort, watching the men march in organized files. The sun had passed its zenith hours ago, draping the soldiers in the shade of the sandwillows lining the west side of the road.

It felt good to ride again. He had not ridden a horse in years, but it all came back to him naturally. He was tempted to kick the chestnut into a gallop but resisted. The soldiers eyed him as he rode by. A poor fat miner on a horse was all they saw, which was for the best.

"David, was it?" Carn spared him a sidelong glance when he reached the head of the column.

"Yes, sir."

"Kaira is your town, so I want you riding close. Tell me if you see anything out of place. Understand?"

David nodded. "Yes, sir."

Half a mile from town, the Range Seekers rode back from Kaira to make their report to the Primus. Their leader was a young man with long black hair, bronzed skin, and chocolate-colored eyes. He donned an expensive looking brigandine over a black gambeson for this little excursion, and wore two silver-hilted kopis strapped to his leather sword belt. A real piece of kafra dung, this one.

"The town is burned down and there are bodies on the streets," Vonner said. "No sign of the creatures this man mentioned." Vonner motioned to him with a flick of his head.

David glared at him silently.

"Any sign of the enemy?" Carn inquired.

"That much we did find," Vonner presented one of the banners which flew on the parapets of Fort Kai.

Carn stared grimly at snarling white wolf's face. "Archonwolves". Vonner nodded.

"Go on ahead, Vonner. Send a rider if there is trouble."

"On it, sir," Vonner turned his horse around, his four minions galloping behind him.

When the cohort reached Fort Kai, Vonner's gang entered first, followed closely by Primus Pentalion and his vanguard riders. David stuck close to Carn as instructed.

The fires had spared little in the old fortress. Charred skeletons in cooked leather and blackened steel were all that remained of Dorav's men.

David dismounted his stallion and walked to where Captain Dorav had killed one of the creatures outside the counter's vaults. The thing was reduced to a broken ball of misshapen, charcoal appendages with four human skulls scattered around it. Remembering its original, awful shape, David understood what happened to it.

"This is one," he told the Primus, who rode his horse closer.

"This?"

"It was dead before we left. The fire must have forced it to collapse into itself. Those skulls there were tied to its abdomen." David tried to grab a piece of the creature but it crumbled in his hands. "Fire. If they burn like this, fire must be their weakness."

Primus Pentalion did not appear convinced.

"Another pile like this will be inside the counters' vault. The old man killed one there."

Carn gave a small head gesture to one of his men who went to investigate the vault. The soldier returned and nodded, his face as pale as plaster.

"There are body parts in here too, sir. Everything is burned up."

Carn sighed and stared into the charred, ruined, husk of Kaira. "This place is cursed. We will set up camp outside the wall."

"Yes, sir!" One soldier ran off.

"Where is the shinn, David?" Carn asked.

"Up the mountain. Through the western-most claim on the Kafra

416

Road, and then down into a valley of petrified trees. I can lead you."

"No. Draw a map out for the Range Seekers. They will take care of it."

David wanted to argue but knew better. This Primus liked keeping to procedure, and he had to respect him for it, as much as he hated working with those fucking dandies.

"All right."

Vonner passed him some parchment and a quill. They walked over to a wide, pile of black bricks to give David a surface to draw on.

"Just do the best you can," Vonner told him.

David glared at him then looked down at the parchment, mapping the course in his mind. Nostalgic, he drew a tactical map, highlighting the trail starting at Fort Kai and putting in markers for things he knew they would run into.

He drew a marker for Ricker's gate, and another for the dead kafras at the end of the drift where Ricker's claim ended. He drew the cavern where the dead vine was and marked it, the path leading down into the valley, the dead trees, the pagan grove with its plague tree, and the path to the temple. He drew a mark for the temple itself, the ravine separating it from the rest of the valley, and the broken bridge. For the block of shinn he drew a thick black X.

When he turned it over to Vonner, the man gave him a curious stare.

"Done this before, have you?"

Idiot!

David cursed himself. "Seen my share. I used to soldier."

"Sickle Talons?"

David shook his head. "Storm Talons. Disbanded after Coiren."

"I'm from Coiren," Vonner's face sobered. "I was only a child, but I saw. You were lucky to get through that alive."

"I suppose so."

Vonner got back on his horse and his young gang of dandies lined up behind him, straight-backed and all business.

"Wait," David said. "You cannot go up there."

"And why is that?"

"Those things! They're up there somewhere, I'm certain! You need to wait and take the cohort!"

Vonner looked back at his riders, and they shared a chuckle. "The cohort is not here for you or your shinn, David. They marched because our Queen believes Captain Dorav to be the spearhead of a larger force. We are the ones with the mission to survey and retrieve the shinn."

"You children? Fuck my ass!"

"I will not, but Queray might take you up on it," Vonner said, looking back at one his riders.

"He's got too much blubber on him for my taste." Queray smirked and the others laughed.

"Take me with you. I mine shinn. That was my friend's claim and I have been in the valley before. I can be useful."

"No," Vonner said. "You wait here until we scout the area — Carn's orders."

"This is reckless. Those things-"

"If those things are up there like you say, we will report it back to the Primus. I understand we do not appear like much to an old soldier like you, but we are not inexperienced. We know better than to stick our necks too far out."

"Your horses will fit down the drift, but not through the hole to the adjoining cavern. Not unless you spend the whole night digging. You know how to safely widen passages in a mine? Can you tell the difference between hard and loose ceiling?"

Vonner frowned at him. "We will leave the horses outside the claim then. Anything else?"

"If you hear the noise, and trust me you will know it, clamp your ass firmly and run."

"We move!" Vonner shouted and kicked his horse forward.

The one called Queray blew David a kiss as he rode by. They rode straight into the Earthly Road, bold as brass.

"Fucking dandies," David muttered, shaking his head.

He watched them go and marked the sun's path. They would be entering the valley before dusk. He stared at the dust cloud picking up in their wake.

"Try not to fucking die!" he cried after them.

"This is my tree," Caige repeated the girl's words, tasting their strange power. "This is my tree."

Caught in the misshapen logic of dream, that one statement gave him a sliver of solace. A piece of himself kept trying to fall back into the circling horror he had managed to escape. He could sense the scar-eyed wolf somewhere nearby, hunting for him as if from behind a dense fog, growling in frustration.

"This is my tree," he said.

Caige focused on the wild girl sitting under the smoldering plague tree. Her eyes observed him dispassionately.

"This is my tree. This is my tree."

The daemon-wolf's sniffing and growling faded into the fog. Caige sensed movement from above and snapped his head back, fearing the wolf had somehow sneaked up on him.

He was sitting with his back to Maggie's thick trunk. Tynisia's bloated corpse swung from the branches, her bare toes pinched in rigor mortis. To her right swung his father, Corren — the pickax wound on his leg oozing puss and curdled blood.

"No! Why!? Why here?!" Caige eyed the wild girl.

"This is your tree."

Grief pounced on his heart, re-opening his wounds. He sobbed miserably, his self-loathing's hungry fingers digging into his flesh, hunting for his nerves — pulling, pinching, mining for pain. He banged the back of his head against Maggie's trunk, trying in futility to exchange one harm for the other. He punched down on Maggie's roots, seeking anchorage in the storm of his unfettered emotions.

There was no escaping it. He knew in his bones, he deserved every morsel of this torment. Self-hatred tightened its grip on his wounds, tugging at his nerve-endings, seeking to rip them out and expose new layers of agony beneath.

"Stop." The girl slapped him across the mouth. Startled, Caige opened his eyes and looked at her. Her features cast no expression.

"Stop struggling," she said.

"I killed her. I killed her! I killed them both!"

"Yes."

The flat tone of her statement surprised him. He searched her cold green eyes but found nothing except his own reflection.

"You must see," she said.

Caige looked up, taking in the full, horrible sight of Tynisia's limp, lifeless body — her purple, bloated face and tangled hair. He had raped her, his beloved Tyn. He had blamed his father for her suicide and killed him too.

They both hung naked, their flesh spoiled and covered in flies, all because of him. Neither of them were to blame, only himself.

"Yes," the girl said again.

Caige looked at her, angry now. Her face was like that of a painted doll. His fists curled up into thick balls of jutting knuckles.

"Yes," she said.

The anger drained from him as quickly as it rose. He opened his hands and stared down at them — his calloused miner's hands, covered in old blood.

"No." He took a deep breath. "No."

"You must cease struggling." She sat back down on the roots of her tree. The plague tree's eyes and gaping mouth, outlined by the green flames in its maw was like a guardian, wary and menacing.

"But I deserve to suffer for what I did! I deserve this!"

She did not respond.

The pain and grief drained from him, dripping over his skin like sour sweat, leaving behind a cold and hollow void. Hiding from this pain in the darkness of a shinn mine and the bottom of a bullhorn bottle had only widened the chasm within himself, making everything that made him feel human slowly seep out of him.

"What do I do?" he asked.

"Live. Or do not."

"I wish to live. I wish to live! But it hurts! It hurts so goddamn much!"

"Yes."

A warm, stale wind and the scents of ash and dry earth reached Murciel long before he saw the dead valley of petrified trees. The evening's trek through the cave system had been a long and winding one. He fought through the pain of his wounds to get over the steeper obstacles, and at times he was certain they were hopelessly lost, but Rairi kept them moving forward.

When they finally left the darkness of those tunnels and came upon the shadowy valley, Murciel was more intrigued than surprised.

The valley's surrounding peaks were pockmarked with caverns, some of them natural, but others the work of primitive tools and backbreaking work. The vast woodland below was dead, leafless and stiff as a corpse. A stout ziggurat hunched at the mouth of the valley, its flat zenith poking out of the gray, hardened canopy.

"What is this place?" Murciel asked.

"I do not know," Rairi replied.

"You do not?" The edge in his voice was keen.

Rairi looked at him quizzically.

Over the course of the last few hours Murciel could not shake the sensation that instead of discovering an unknown place with a fellow pack member, he was taking cues from someone who already knew where she was going.

"Something you want to ask me, Murciel?"

"Seems like you have known where we were headed this entire time. Like this is exactly where you wanted us to be."

Rairi smiled and shook her head. "I am using ketter, idiot. I know which tunnels lead to dead ends and which ones lead out. Things lived in those tunnels Murciel, and we avoided them. Are you honestly upset I got us through that maze?"

"Things? You mean the things from Kaira?"

"Sari's mercy, no! But one tunnel did lead to an orb weaver's nest. They made my skin crawl when I sensed them. They were big as cats."

Murciel opened his mouth but nothing came out. He sighed and forced a smile. "Apologies."

"No need, but the sun will be up in a few hours. Shall we set up camp here? It is safe enough."

"Do we have a choice?"

Rairi looked over the valley. "We could make for that ruin. It would at least put us halfway to the other side of this valley."

Murciel spotted the ruin, his brow furrowing. "Might not be safe. This entire place is unsettling."

"That is true."

He considered their options. There was still time before the sun rose and camping here would be a waste of time when they could make more progress tonight. On the other hand, something might be lurking in those woods.

"Can you tell if anything is down there?" he asked. "Anything we might need to worry about?"

"My ketter is unreliable in such an open space. You are the one with D'aerth eyes. You tell me."

The carpet of mist and thick knots of dead branches obscured the finer corners of the forest.

"I cannot see much from here," he said.

"Then we need to move closer."

"Fine. We head down and scout the area. At the first sign of trouble we retreat back here."

"A good plan."

They made their way down the winding mountain path until they stood at the shadowy edge of the petrified forest. A hollow, foreboding air permeated the area, like the entrance to an abandoned crypt. The mist slithered through the trees, like a living thing.

"I do not sense anything," Rairi said. "This place is deathly still."

"Anything could be hiding in that mist. This is an unsafe route."

"There were no other paths in those caverns. None that led outside."

Murciel sighed, feeling powerless without his bow. If something dangerous lay within, what could they do except run blindly through a misty wood? He drew his moonblade with his left hand and tapped the edge with his thumb. The blade still held a good edge.

"How is your hand?" Rairi asked.

"Better." He opened and closed his fingers with ease. "I still cannot hold a fist for long but at least I can make one."

"Continue to care for it. We still have some time before sunrise. Shall we head back and try again tomorrow night? Perhaps there will be less mist."

"No, we keep moving," he said. "Keep an eye out...or...you know."

She gave him a mocking smile and nodded.

"If anything happens, follow these marks back to this spot." Murciel used his knife to cut long gashes in the trunks of every other tree he passed. The petrified wood forced him to dig deep into their sides.

"Is that necessary?"

"Better to not risk getting lost in here."

Under the shadowy canopy of the petrified forest, the air had a thick, smoky quality. The earth under the mist was barren and dry, as if it had been salted. He could not make out any natural sounds coming from the deeper forest — not even insects.

"This makes no sense," Rairi said. "This valley has enough moisture to produce mist, but these trees appear to not have tasted water in years."

"I prefer to not think about it," Murciel commented, digging a mark into a tree.

A partial anthrop skeleton hung by its spine from a low branch nearby. Another six lined the tree branches beside it, then two, then four — most of them missing different appendages. The path ahead of them was a mist-carpeted bone yard.

Meticulously arranged skulls and long bones were tied to the trunks of every tree. The trees themselves had strange, deep markings carved into them, filling the spaces between the bones.

Murciel sheathed his knife and uncorked his water-bladder. He poured a little water on his left hand and ran his wet fingers over his forehead and the top of his head. "Great Terra, watch over me," he whispered. "I stand among the restless dead."

Rairi mimicked his motions and repeated the prayer.

"What is this place?" he asked.

Rairi examined the trees with a critical eye and scanned the hanging skeletons. "This is Old World black craft. These markings here are prayers, and these are wards."

"Prayers to who?"

"The Four Winds of Doom. They are supplications and rites of sacrifice."

Murciel regarded the hundreds of carefully placed skulls and bones, and a chill ran through him.

"Whatever happened here terrified these people," Rairi said. "Here, listen to this, 'The gods have turned their backs on us. Kaxxil's dirge echoes through our trees. Rakkis built his armory with our shattered bones. Locus dances on the shrapnel of our broken hearts. We are meat for the strong. Heleca is nigh. Damned is our Vale.'"

"Heleca?"

"An ancient name for the Vorx."

423

"They only named three of the dooms."

"Tharis is assumed. To write his name is to call his eye, so none dare."

"Is there anything you don't know, Rairi?"

She sighed and stood, wiping the dust off her leathers. "I do not know why these kinds of things happen."

"We should get away from here."

"Yes, please."

Deeper into the bone yard, the mists thickened and the ancient horror that occurred in this valley became evident. Bones littered the woods and ancient, broken weapons lay in disarray. Small piles of skulls sat under each tree, like offerings to terrible, nameless things.

One deeply marked tree-stump was surrounded by skulls. A crude stone ax was lodged in its center, the blood on its head still fresh.

"Rairi! Look!" he pointed at it.

"What?"

"That ax was recently used. Someone is in here."

They both unsheathed their moonblades and tread with caution. Murciel felt observed. He looked around for the source of his discomfort but found only the hollow sockets of skulls staring back at him. He was relieved when they finally cleared the bone yard.

"We should be almost to the ruin," he said. "We are not walking back through that."

"Agreed."

They made cautious progress through the petrified forest until they reached the shadow of the ancient stone ziggurat. The stars of Arisia's night were in retreat from the approaching sunrise. They needed to find shelter soon or they would be caught out in the open.

On the forest side of the ravine beneath the stone ziggurat, they discovered a fresh campsite with five bedrolls and a few simple cooking utensils surrounding an ashen fireplace. Whoever the camp belonged to had built a crude bridge across the chasm using logs, rope, and vines.

Across the ravine, before the main entrance of the ziggurat, lay the shattered remains of a moss-covered stone lion, wrapped in desiccated vines. Beyond it, surrounding the high, rectangular entrance, hung five dismantled anthrop corpses.

They had been torn apart, their skins stretched out and their segmented parts hanging by fibrous strands, forming five medallions of dead flesh — each circle of limbs holding a severed head at its center.

The four medallions on the corners of the doorway belonged to young Teplians. The crowning circle belonged to a very old man with leathery skin, a long stained beard, and a look of manic joy on his ancient, paralyzed features.

The kills were fresh. Wet, bloodstained, fibrous strands held them in place and fat black flies swarmed them in a ravenous buzz.

"Ren's swinging cock," Murciel said.

"Who would so something like this?"

"Not who. What." Murciel's voice was spiced with panic.

"What do you mean?"

"The fibers holding those bodies in place. They're the same kind the creatures from Kaira used to tie heads to their backs. We need to get out of here, now."

As if summoned, the petrified forest behind them came alive with the gut wrenching subsonic clip of the insects' rattling abdomens, sending a shudder of terror through Murciel's bowels.

"They are here!" Rairi's eyes went wide with fear. "Murciel, we are trapped!"

"Go! Go! Over the bridge!"

The sounds approached the edge of the forest as they ran over the creaking logs, over the ravine and towards the mouth of the ziggurat.

"Inside!" Murciel cried. "Go! Get inside!"

"No! Wait, what is happening to you?" Caige rose from his sitting position under Maggie.

Smoldering ash from the mouth of the plague tree had leaped out and caught the girl's wild, tangled curls. She made no move to extinguish herself. As the emerald flames consumed her hair, they expelled dry, dead leaves instead of smoke.

"My brother." A hint of wonderment entered the girl's voice. "He is dead."

"I do not understand."

"My brother's curse is lifted. She sacrificed him to let someone into

425

her lair. I am free." The girl's face lit up in a tragically beautiful smile.

"Wait! I don't know what to do! How do I get out of here?!"

"Will you live?" She stared up at him. The fire reached her face, eating away her right eye and the side of her skull. She did not appear to be in any pain.

"Yes! Yes! I do not wish to remain here! I wish to live!"

"Then your tree must die. You cannot linger beneath its shadow any longer."

"What? What does that mean? Regret!?"

"Miira," she said as the flame reached her smiling lips. "My name was Miira."

Relieved of its head, the rest of her small body crumpled on its side. As the fire consumed her remains, a whirlwind of dead leaves spiraled up into the starless night.

A haunting fear crept into Caige as she burned away. The green flames consumed everything except the girl's spinal cord and pelvic bone. The emerald fire burned itself out, leaving a single flame trapped inside her pelvic cavity.

Caige knelt and gripped the top of the abandoned spine. As his fingers wrapped around it, he was shown the tragedy of Miira's short life. He fused with her essence, becoming as one with her and participating in the weight of her memories.

He experienced their brother breaking them, dragging them into darkness under the shade of an ash. He shared in the horror of being defiled by someone they trusted and loved. In being irrevocably changed by the betrayal. A black serpent wrapped itself around their hearts, squeezing the light out of them as their brother grunted and thrust, his callused hand over their small mouth.

A bottomless chasm grew inside them every time they were left alone with their brother. The powerless loathing was like a disease, spreading its tendrils through healthy flesh.

One day, they experienced the sexual jolt of pleasure that came from murdering a mother duck and her ducklings. Killing was the only thing that made them feel anything, and so they killed. Every day they would hunt small game and smash them under rocks, wring their necks and stab them with the dagger their father had given them. They thought about their brother every time, wishing it was him — knowing that someday, it would be.

On the last day of their life, when they blew the Horn of Dawn in the shadow of Ariel's temple, that hateful serpent bared its fangs and slithered out, taking their murderous intent with it. In the timeless instant between the serpent leaving and the priest's flint knife slicing their throat, they both shared another life entirely.

They sprinted through a lush forest with the carelessness of youth. They squealed in pleasure as a mother duck chased them away from her young while hissing, her wings spread open in protective menace. They swam in the lake near their home under a warm autumn sun and ran circles over the roots of a sturdy ash tree, full of childish laughter. They sang, ate heartily, and helped their mother weave baskets.

When the Shapka proclaimed them as the chosen of Ariel, they cried tears of joy. Their family would be exalted. They would live forever, their name inscribed on the sacred tablets and their memory honored by her people for all time.

When they blew the Horn of Dawn on the last day of their life, they filled the Vale of Azilial with golden light and their people rejoiced, singing their name into the earth and the water. Fear was absent when the flint knife touched their throat, because they would be born again in service to the mighty Ariel.

Caige experienced the truth of both these lives; of light and shadow, hope and despair intertwined as a single, indivisible force, like opposite faces of a perpetually spinning coin.

By sharing in Miira's pain, he felt a calm sense of clarity about his own. The darkness of his life was not spiteful, purposeless cruelty. Something lined the edges of his fear and sadness, like an ineffable, benevolent presence which manifested as a web of light, interlacing existence itself. A web he was merely a strand of, but which without him, would be incomplete.

Caige opened his eyes and wiped the salty tears from his face, cradling the girl's spine to his chest.

"Thank you, Miira," he said.

He took Miira's spine to Maggie's base and placed the fiery pelvis against her roots. She lit up instantly, emerald flames coursing through every branch and igniting every leaf. The sudden blaze banished the shadows which lingered in the burrows and nooks of the gnarled old wood.

The shapeless things living in that darkness hissed and squealed in agony as they were burned away. The emerald flames rode down the ropes holding Tynisia and Corren, incinerating their mangled corpses.

Grief and misery poured out of Caige in waves, set free by the cleansing flames. As Maggie burned, the gore and grime in every corner of his being bubbled like boiling gristle. He accepted the fierce scourging with open arms.

As the pain passed, he fell to his knees and wept, his head bowed in silent gratitude. He felt like a slave whose chains had been melted while still wrapped around him, leaving him raw, exhausted, and grateful.

Nothing was left of Maggie but a charred husk, split in two as if struck by lightning. He stood and turned his back on her blackened remains.

"All right," he said to himself. "I am ready."

Miira's plague tree stood cold and dead, its inner fire extinguished. Inside its mouth, on a patch of black ash, lay the Horn of Dawn. Unlike the old broken horn he found before, this one was whole. He retrieved it from the tree, admiring the carvings and engravings along its ancient length, and the careful precision of its craftsmanship.

Caige wiped the marble mouthpiece clean, took a long deep breath, put the horn to his lips, and blew with all his might.

34

Greenfire

David stared into the eastern sky, watching the sun rise behind the Norvan Peaks. Although outside Fort Kai's walls and surrounded by armed soldiers, sleep had evaded him. The thought of those armored wasps made him jump at every noise in camp.

The surrounding cohort was having a busy morning. Primus Pentalion ordered out a unit of swift-riders to investigate the fate of Sharn while the remaining cohort busied itself finalizing the camp and running drills.

David walked towards the inner gate of Fort Kai and looked out at the black bones of his old town. Charred bodies still lay sprawled on the far edges of the Earthly Road. It hurt his heart to see his neighbors in such a state. He wished there had been time to bury them before being forced to flee by the roaring fire. The Primus assured him that by tonight they would gather Kaira's dead and give them proper funeral rites.

David picked up a seared Vinergalian xiphos and shield before striding quietly into town. The Range Seekers had come into Kaira looking for armed resistance, not venomous, man-eating monsters that might still be skulking in the shadows, waiting for a lone fool like him to wander near.

He remembered the pain in Donner's face when he was stung, and how Ladan had been ripped in half, his entrails dragging behind him as he crawled.

David's knees wobbled, and he straightened up, disgusted with himself. "Get yourself together, soldier!"

Gripping the sword and shield tighter, he walked up the Earthly

Road. When the creatures attacked, the townsfolk had spread out from the temple in every direction. Most headed south trying to flee Kaira, but a few made for their claims, homes, and shops. The streets lay littered with their carrion, burned and rotting in the sun.

The Pirils' dact palms had burned down. The Reens' kafras all lay dead on their sides, opened at the stomach with their entrails sun-dried and shriveled. Here and there, portions of the town still burned, even this long after the blaze.

David reached his old home, took a long look at the hollow, blackened husk, and let out a sigh. He held few fond memories of this place. The times Leina came by of her own accord to spend the night perhaps, or when the crew would stumble here from the Pick Rock to continue drinking. Other than that, this place was little more than a dank cave where a tired old animal fitfully slept.

David turned from his hut and walked through the wider alleys across Kaira. He headed for the Craftsman's Road, his head on a swivel — stopping at every crack of timber or shuffle of dust, his every nerve on high alert. Nothing stirred in Kaira except the wind.

The Pick Rock had fallen in on itself. The floor where old Noss and the girls lived collapsed and smashed the bar beneath it. David could see a few engraved picks still nailed to the surviving walls.

How many times had he dreamed of leaving his own pick on that wall? He always wondered whether he would mark his pick with the name David Jacintoson, or David Redknife, or just David. A whimsical part of him even wished to fuck with everyone and leave behind the bold burn-mark; Rien Bloodstorm.

"Fuck this piss-hole."

He walked south on the Craftsman Road. Citena's clay-works was burned to the ground. Her charred, mangled body lay just outside, missing its head and half her right leg. David recalled one morning they had stood outside her shop, just talking. She was content living in Kaira, but she yearned for a husband, for children.

He swallowed the lump in his throat and moved on, hating himself for taking this walk. He wanted to keep his eyes pinned to the road but could not restrain them. He glanced at the remains of Dendor's smithy. Built from brick to withstand the forge's heat, the building stood almost intact, except for the roof which had fallen in on itself.

On the east side of town, near the end of the Craftsman Road, was Elmir Salka's cock pit. To his unbelieving eyes, Deadluck, the big red and black fighting rooster, was still alive and in the ring. He clucked brashly, pecking at the dry earth. Three arrows stuck out of the earth nearby. Vonner's people must have entertained themselves here when they passed. Deadluck looked up and let out a mangled crow.

"You really are a hard cock," he said.

The rooster's head turned side to side, up and down in the strange erratic pattern unique to fowl. Deadluck's feathers were falling off in patches. He survived the fire and Vonner's crew, but looked likely to starve soon. David took some confiscated grain from his belt pouch and flung it at the ground before the once mighty rooster. Deadluck snapped at it greedily.

Deadluck's cage was broken open. The two other fighting roosters were not as fortunate and had cooked alive in their enclosures. David sighed, opened the fighting ring's wooden gate, and spread the remaining grain outside to lure Deadluck out. He decided then that he had seen enough.

On his way back to Fort Kai, despite his better judgment, he stopped to have a look at Nikos' bakery.

Nianah.

He wished he could have protected her. Wished he had not remained silent about his feelings for her, but what would have been the point? He was an old, fat, washed-up soldier with nothing to offer her but poverty, constant night-terrors, and a bad drinking habit. Ashen was young, handsome...lazy, good-for-nothing, kafra dingle-berry eating-

A blaze crackled somewhere deep inside the bakery and the fleeting flash of passing embers shown through the hollowed windows.

"Fuck."

If the Range Seekers missed this, they were not nearly as thorough as he hoped. He adjusted the grip on his shield and placed it before him, moving towards the bakery. The door stood ajar so he pushed it open with the tip of his sword, peering inside.

Nikos' store was a blackened ruin. The display stands, small wooden tables and chairs lay charred beyond repair. Like Dendor's forge, Nikos had built his bakery out of brick, so most of the building's infrastructure survived, but the roof was practically gone.

From the kitchen came another flash of embers and the crackle of burning wood. David stepped carefully around the display stands and through the door frame that led into the kitchen. He was so taken aback by what he witnessed that he failed to hear his sword hit the ground. He stood slack-jawed and wide-eyed, his mind scrambling to make sense of it.

Nikos' kitchen was on fire. Not a remnant smoldering, but a roaring conflagration. Bright orange flames licked at lacquered panels that had only now begun to char. The high beams were blanketed in bright flames that danced as they reached for the scorching ceiling.

In the center of the kitchen space, Nianah hung frozen in mid-air, her left arm stretched out towards him. Her garments had caught fire and were becoming floating ash. Her skin was boiled and blackened — half her face nothing more than bone and bubbling gristle. Her hairs danced like flame-tipped whips behind her ears. The part of her face that remained whole was caught in state of anguish and terror as she hung suspended in air.

One of the creatures stood behind her, its body in flames and already beginning to collapse into itself. One of its lancing arms was buried inside Nikos' mouth, gradually breaking through the back of his skull before David's terrified eyes.

The baker's scorched body hung suspended in air, falling backwards — his eyes wide with pain and fear. The creature's other arm was impaled through Nianah's blackened right calf. Noss and Citena's severed heads were tied to the creature's abdomen, their skin boiling before his eyes. Their mouths hung open, revealing black, lolling tongues.

David's heart pounded in his chest as the scene moved languidly forward in time. Nianah's remaining, pain-stricken eye turned and regarded him. He fell into that longing, pleading eye as it widened with recognition and hope. Her ruined mouth opened haltingly, as if to cry out to him.

David tore his gaze away and stumbled back into the store, hitting his head on the door frame. He realized he was screaming. He blinked the stars out of his eyes and looked back. The kitchen remained caught in that languid, perpetual moment. Golden embers danced before the doorway.

David's soldier instincts kicked in. He took quick, sharp breaths of air, regulating his adrenaline spike. Slowly, he deepened his breaths, calming his thundering heart and clearing the storm in his mind.

Vorxcraft. Vorxcraft!

This was same as watching Khine's body burn after he died. Time had lost its tempo then as well, and reality itself seemed to bend and tear at the edges. This was the mark of Neteri's taint. Someone from Kaira was a vorxer. The realization struck him like a closed fist to the stomach.

Ashen.

Ashen did this. David remembered the look in his eyes while he beat him in Nevine — the hot flash of light behind his irises. David mistook it for reflecting sunlight, but the day's sun had not yet reached their balcony.

Ashen was a vorxer — a bloodtaint.

David picked himself back up. A part of him wished to go back into the kitchen and try to help what was left of Nianah, but he could not bring himself to do it. He feared for his sanity if he tried.

He left the bakery and made his hurried way back towards the cohort's encampment. A force this numerous would have a korgur in their ranks. The bakery needed a holy benediction.

When nearing Fort Kai, the echoed screams of panicked horses reached him, coming from the direction of the mountain. Vonner stumbled down the Earthly Road, half-crazed and holding his bleeding side.

A moment later, the subsonic tremor those murderous creatures produced struck him. The sound came from far up the mountain, but even at a distance, was enough to make his mouth turn to ash and his balls shrivel like raisins.

"Alarm!" Vonner cried. "ALARM!"

David ran behind him towards the encampment.

"To arms!" Vonner's voice sounded manic. "Talons of the Crown! They are coming! Those infernal fucking things are coming!"

Rairi led them through the black corridor of the ziggurat, clucking her throat as she went. Like in the sea-cave near Sharn, Murciel held on to her belt and kept his left hand out, searching the empty darkness.

The creatures had not followed them inside the ziggurat, which only disquieted him further. What could be so dangerous as to keep those monstrous things out? After a long time of walking, a terrible sense of emptiness engulfed him, as if they had been swallowed by some gargantuan worm.

"Rairi." He stopped.

"Yes?"

"Where are we?"

"In the tunnel."

"Still?" He looked back. Not so much as a dot of light remained from the way came. "Are we in a drift?"

"A what?"

"The tunnel, is it sloped downward?"

"Why would you ask?"

"Because we should have reached the other end of this structure by now. We must be walking down, into the earth beneath it."

"I suppose it is possible," Rairi said.

"I cannot be in this blackness anymore," he said, patting his pouches in search of his flint. "I need to make light. Are we safe where we are?"

"I do not think that a good idea, Murciel. I do not sense them now, but if those things are in here you will surely call them down on our heads. We probably should stop speaking as well."

Murciel swallowed dryly and nodded. A second later he realized his foolishness.

"All right."

Rairi continued using ketter as they went deeper into the structure. He tried to trust in her guidance and remain calm, wishing his mind would keep from chattering, but the darkness held other plans. Clicking, shuffling, crackling sounds echoed all around him. He was on edge, his head swiveling back and forth with every noise.

After another long stretch of walking, Rairi stopped. "Hold on," she said, her voice raw. "I need water."

He could hear her gulping from her water-bladder.

434

"Where are we now?" he asked.

"Still in the tunnel."

"Still?!"

"Shh, Murciel."

"No, no this is wrong. Have we been going in a straight line this entire time? I cannot tell anymore."

"Yes."

"And this does not strike you as odd? What are the dimensions in here? Is it still as wide as when we entered?"

"No, it is much wider now."

"So we entered some kind of chamber?"

"No, Murciel. The tunnel simply became wider. The farther we go the higher the ceiling rises and the wider the walls are from each other."

Dread, which he had fought back up until now, wriggled its way into his spine.

"How far?" he asked.

Rairi remained quiet.

"How far away are the walls, Rairi?"

She clucked her throat sharply, thickly. Once, twice, three times.

"I do not know."

Murciel's skin went cold. "Why, why would you not mention this? Why not tell me?!"

Silence again.

He went to grab her, to hold her firmly, but his hands found nothing.

His fingers hunted empty space, fear blossoming in his heart.

"Rairi?"

Nothing. Not so much as an echo.

"Rairi?! This is not funny! Say something!"

Nothing.

He took long deep breaths, needing to calm himself and clear his mind. Why did Rairi not answer? Where was she? He realized he was turning in circles looking for her, and cursed himself for a fool.

There were no walls, no light, and now he had no idea which way he faced, or how to return to the doorway. He was lost and trapped in here. Panic set in, hot and unyielding.

"RAIRI!!"

"Shhhhh," came a woman's disembodied voice. "She is not here. She never was."

The voice was cold, sultry, and near. Murciel's instincts pinched down on his nerves, screaming for him to run. He was blind, defenseless, and in danger. *Run*, his body pleaded. *RUN!*

"Who are you?" He scraped his moonblade from its sheath. "Where is Rairi?"

"She died, Murciel, choking on a crossbow bolt lodged in her throat. You know this. I took you to shelter when you leaped from that cliff. I saved you, and I have been with you every moment since."

"No!" Even as he spoke, he knew her words to be true, as a thick fog in his mind waned and lifted.

He witnessed himself in the darkness of the cave near the sea, tending to the wound on his hand and the bolt wounds on his side and back, crying out as he yanked the shafts from his own flesh. He saw himself crawling sightless through the darkness as the tide approached, then crawling out of the muddy basin after the water spit him out.

He walked the black rock path alone, until finding shelter from the rain in the anthrop mine. He saw himself huddled near his fire, one hand rubbing his arm for warmth, the other stroking his manhood.

"No!" He could bare it no longer. He blinked, forcing himself out of those thoughts and back into the hollow darkness within the ziggurat. "What are you?"

Something cold pressed against the center of his forehead. He snapped his knife in an arc but hit nothing.

"What are you?!"

"Open your eyes Murciel, and see."

Surprised, Murciel realized his eyes were indeed closed. They were heavy and sticky, as if they had not been opened in days.

The woman who stood before him captured his attention completely. Her naked body was beautifully sculpted, her muscles toned and her breasts high and firm. Her waist-long hair, black and thick, danced wildly around her like a living thing. Her eyes, black as onyx, held a hint of emerald green, and the tips of her pointed ears peeked through her thick black curls. She held a single candle in her right hand.

"No," Murciel said. "I am dreaming. I must be."

"Life is a dream, Murciel."

"But you cannot be. The Eldarin, they are all-"

"Dead?"

"Yes."

The woman said nothing, as if her presence alone framed her refute to his claim.

"You're a moon-elf?" he asked.

When she gave him a small nod in response, his eyes watered. The Elders claimed the moon-elves were Arisia's first children. They built great cities of crystal and silver light in the deep forests of the Old World, when the xial were but beasts known as the Nocturalis, or "Night Glass".

"Who are you?"

A small smile touched the woman's lips. "You may call me Chrysalis."

The meaning behind the name was not lost on him. He shuffled his feet into a better position, sensing danger.

"Why did you bring me here, Chrysalis?"

"To cleanse you."

David was impressed by the organized fluidity of the Sickle Talon cohort. Centurions stood at the center of each phalanx, organizing their numbers into tight-knit files. Two ranks of archers stood directly behind the shield wall, a rank of peltasts and slingers hovered to the rear left of the phalanx and thirty mounted cavalry lancers huddled together at the rear's right.

Primus Carn ordered David and Vonner to join the skirmishers under Sergeant Stenner. A good call. David was fat and out of shape. The phalanx was a fiercely trained wall of shields and spears. He would only get in their way.

Vonner did not quite fit the phalanx either. His wounds had been seen to, and he now stood with the skirmishers, both silver-hilted kopis in hand — all his straight-backed bravado scared right out of him.

Primus Pentalion had taken heed to their warnings about the

terrible noise the creatures make. As the ranks formed, the Primus ordered his war-drummers to beat furiously on the stretched leather of their instruments.

His horn-men's faces flared red with effort as they blasted long, hard notes, and the war-chanters and banner carriers sang the loudest, brashest, battle-songs they knew.

Every soldier in the phalanx banged their spears against their shields, archers stomped their feet, and the skirmishers called out curses, cries, and taunts to the unseen enemy. The roar of the cohort was deafening.

When the first creatures came over the wall and scrambled through the open portal of Fort Kai's entryway, rattling their skull-covered abdomens in concert, David's fragile hopes dropped like a stone. A wave of terror passed over him, snatching the voice from his throat.

The surrounding skirmishers grew quiet and pale, their jaws slacking and their eyes like saucers. The boisterous chanting of the cohort began to fade, the drums slowing their beating and their song withering away, replaced by the desperate neighing of the cavalry horses, and the terrible rattle of the wasp-like monstrosities.

"Steady!" The Primus called. "Do not let the fear have you! Drummers! Horn-men! Do not let us down! Chanters! Give us a song to kill these fucking things to!"

One brave drummer bit down, found his balls, and began to drum.

"Come on you lilies!" he called out to the others. "Help me fight! They need us now, more than ever!"

Bolstered, the other drummers followed suit, finding the rhythm. The horn-men blew hard notes, discordant at first, then in loud, unified blasts. The brave drummer picked up the song from where it lay in the dirt, and others were quick to help him lift it.

"Smoke beneath her regent wings!" the drummer sang.
"Plume of golden light we see!" joined the chanters.
"She dives to pierce the bleakest night!"
The entire cohort sang as one.
"Skyel! Skyel! Skyel!"
"She who fights when darkness falls!
"She whose cry ignites our call!
"To her Talons all will fall!

438

"Skyel! Skyel! Skyel!"

The song fed the embers of the men's courage and the shield-wall stood its ground. A war-horn gave off a quick series of blasts that David remembered well. The archers lighted arrow.

"Good," David said under his breath. "Come on, please fucking work."

"Loose!" Came the call.

A cloud of flaming arrows sped for the walls. Many missiles snapped on Fort Kai's battlements, or sank between the old stones' mortar. Others rebounded off thick, black carapaces, but a handful struck home, sinking their fiery tips into flesh between the monsters' black plates.

The things let out hideous cries and fell from the ramparts, squirming in agony. Once having tasted their flesh, the fire spread voraciously, consuming the creatures like dry kindling.

"Loose!"

Another volley struck the creatures and another score of them fell. Their sinister rattling was punctuated by rasping screeches as the beasts fell to earth, squirming and burning, compressing into balls of smoldering charcoal. A triumphant cry came from the phalanx as the things fell.

A swarm of monstrosities suddenly overran the parapets of Fort Kai, their bone-rattling moan indelible. By the dozens, the creatures scrambled down the wall and trampled over the charred husks of their own kind, forming a mist of ash.

Their first impact against the phalanx was horrific. The creatures fearlessly crawled over the shields of the first line defenders, ignoring the poking of their spears.

They brought their vicious lancing arms down on the second and third ranks in the formations, while stabbing at those beneath them with their stingers. Blood erupted from deep puncture wounds and men screamed in pain and horror. The phalanx became overrun in moments, their tight formation ripped apart.

"Loose!"

The archers kept their volleys going, aiming over their companions' heads and into the growing horde or monsters crawling over the walls.

"Skirmishers, harry!" Stenner cried out to his men. "Assist the left!"

David and Vonner ran with the skirmishers towards the front. The left was trying desperately to regroup and form a solid line of defense.

"Light'em up!"

A company slinger placed a clay pot of oil on the ground and pulled off the lid. While the peltasts dipped the tips of their javelins in the oil, one man lit a torch and held it high for them.

"Make them count, boys!" Stenner said.

Flame tipped javelins flew into the horde. Most bounced harmlessly off their slick, chitinous plates, but the few that found purchase scorched the creatures and brought them down.

"Aim, you cross-eyed sheep fuckers!" Stenner's voice rang hoarse from shouting. "Aim! Get them behind the armor!"

"Don't just gawk, you flaccid tits, throw!" Stenner thrust three javelins into David and Vonner's arms.

They sheathed their swords and baptized their javelins in oil and fire. David lifted the javelin over his head and threw with all his strength. The flaming tip struck the corner of a creature's carapace, snapped left, and sank into the ground, hissing as it extinguished. Vonner and a few of the skirmishers saw better luck. They shouted in hate-filled joy when their missiles struck home and the things fell to writhing balls of agony.

"Move, move!"

A Corporal harried a group of boys who worked in pairs to bring heavy clay pots of oil to the back of each formation.

One pair tripped over themselves and dropped their pot, smashing it against the earth. Another pair reached the back of the right phalanx only to have the nearest infantryman accidentally kick the pot with the back of his foot and spill half its contents.

"You cock-hole!" One of boys cried.

David sank his second javelin in the oil, passed it through the torch, and aimed.

"Fucking die!" David screamed as he threw.

His javelin broke on the creature's torso plates. Vonner's missile flew true, striking a creature between its plates and sending it into a spasm of fiery agony.

"Come on, fat man!" Vonner cried, manic with battle lust. "Hit something! Whose fucking side are you on?!"

David went to stick his last javelin in the pot, but the oil was seeping through a break at the bottom. Someone had stabbed through it in their haste to wet their missile.

"Who? Which one of you? COCK!" Stenner groaned. "The earth is still wet! Stick it in the dirt you monkeys, before the ground drinks it all!"

Vonner and the peltasts stabbed at the earth and turned their javelins, hoping to slick their weapons enough to catch fire.

David shook his head and regarded the battlefront. "Eyes up!" He called to the men. "Company!"

Three of the creatures breached the brittle phalanx formation and came towards them. The phalanx had managed to wet their weapons in oil and now stabbed at the monsters with fire, but only the strikes that pushed past their plates took any effect.

David turned to face the three wingless wasps closing in, rattling their abdomens. He did not feel the dread in his guts like before. His blood ran hot, and the roaring clash of battle filled his ears. Battle fear clung to him, but he had learned long ago to overcome its press.

"Come on, you turd-flies!" He lunged his last javelin and drew his sword. The missile lodged itself in the shell of the creature's thorax.

The lead monster cleared the distance between them and reared up, slicing down on David with its dangerous forelegs. He put his shield up, bracing himself against the powerful blows. The creature's spear-point appendages tore holes through the shield with the power of heavy crossbow bolts.

David raised his sword in time to deflect the thing's stinger as it came up. He cut up and across, slicing between the creature's thorax and head plates. The blow was too shallow to kill, but forced the thing back. David crouched and put his shield up in front of him.

A javelin bounced off the creature's thorax and a stone struck its plated head.

"What the fuck are you two doing?" Stenner called out to them. "Run, you sewed up cunts, run!"

David suddenly remembered he fought alongside skirmishers. Standing their ground was simply not their way. They had already sprinted away from the incoming threat.

Vonner had remained beside him, equally oblivious to the protocol. The three monsters were on them. Stenner and six skirmishers rained stones and javelins on the things, trying to distract them.

"A pox on your children! MOVE!"

Vonner sprinted up towards them. As David turned, one creature's arm lashed out and sliced him across the lower back. He cried out as his legs gave out from beneath him.

He kissed the dirt, stars exploding in his vision. The three creatures reared up and brought their murderous forelegs down on him.

He curled into a tight ball under his wounded shield. When the blows landed, the pain was overwhelming. One thing stabbed him in his exposed left calf, punching straight through. Another lancing arm went through his shield and sank between his ribs. A third clipped the side of his skull, drawing blood that blinded his left eye.

He was a dead man.

His heart thundered in his chest so hard he felt it in his toes. His muscles trembled so badly his entire world seemed to shake. There was a thunderous crash.

Something heavy struck the side of his shield and forced him into a roll. Half a dozen horsemen had engaged the creatures. Their lance-tipped charge had impaled two of the beasts right through their thick carapaces and laid them out, squirming in spreading pools of blood.

The horsemen tried to fight the last creature off but had trouble with their mounts. The poor things trembled in terror. Though hearty and well-seasoned, the rattle of the beast's abdomens was making them panic.

Behind the struggling horsemen, fires blazed, and all sense of order in the ranks dissipated. Dozens of bodies littered the ground, covered in blood and ash. Men screamed in pain, either gruesomely wounded or being punished by the viscous venom coursing through their blood. Severed body parts lay scattered everywhere, squirting crimson. A dense blood-mist hung over the battlefield.

Watching the brutality with which these creatures tore the Queen's Talons apart, David wondered why in all creation had he chosen to come back here. He cursed himself for letting greed overpower his reason. How did he think this was going to end?

The creature fighting the horsemen reared up and stung one of their horses in the chest, then scythed its rider in the face, fish-hooking his mouth and flinging him to the ground. The man screamed horribly, his teeth and gums visible behind the ruin of his gored face.

The wasp-thing then plunged its arm through another rider's chest, the tip of its appendage protruding from the man's back, covered in blood and gore. One rider turned his horse and sprinted off, leaving his comrades to deal with the beast without him.

David tried to stand but the pain in his back kept him grounded.

The stung horse screamed and sprinted away, trying to outrun its pain. The three remaining horses were trying frantically to throw their riders. Two horsemen stayed valiantly saddled, but the third was thrown and landed on his back, hitting his head on a jutting rock. By the way his body twitched, David knew the man was dead, or would soon be.

The creature swung its deadly arms, slicing across one horse's lower flank as it reared up. Steaming viscera flopped out of the mare's stomach an instant before she hit the ground, landing on her rider's leg.

The man cried out and struggled to free himself from the heavy pin. The monster bit down on his neck and ripped his head off in a geyser of arterial spray. The last stallion fled, taking his furious rider with him.

A flaming javelin hit the creature on the head at an angle and broke its shaft. Two fire-tipped arrows struck armor and scraped innocuously aside. Stenner, Vonner, and the skirmishers had returned.

The creature hissed menacingly and scurried after them. They sprinted away again, trying to lure it. The wingless wasp-thing did not take the bait. It stopped halfway and turned back towards David.

"Tarrak's cock!" David crawled, his legs dragging behind him.

The thing reached him in an instant, lancing its arm into the back of his thigh beneath his right buttock. David screamed and reached for the broken javelin with its still burning head, his fingers inches from it. He stretched and cried out in pain as his fingertips brushed the smooth wood.

The thing pulled him back, away from the weapon.

"Aaaaaah!" David's empty hands grasped blindly.

David turned his upper body in time to see the gaping maw of the monster dropping to rip his head from his shoulders. He swung his arm out as the maw came down.

His blind, grasping hands had found an arrow on the ground. He drove the broken arrow's head between the plates of its neck as it lunged. The thing's jaws scraped across his head and face, drawing blood.

With a hideous screech it released him and scrambled back, squirming in agony as fierce green fire consumed it from the inside.

David stared in awe.

Spectra!

Murciel soared on the night's warm updrafts. Below him, the high, silver-needle spires of the Eldarin city rose high above the forest canopy. All around him, hundreds of aerthi eagles soared in a circle like a black halo, waiting for the call that all knew would come.

A long horn blast sounded from far below. Like an unwinding serpent, the cloud of black-glass wings dove. Past the tree line, the vanguard of the Eldarin army charged.

The moon-elves rode the massive sabre wolves and muscular jaguakirns, firing their bows at the incoming enemy with deadly accuracy. The massive morrabears roared as they ran, kicking up patches of grass and earth in their wakes.

The incoming anthrop horde was gargantuan, taking up the fields beyond the woods as far as his eyes could see. Anthrops screamed in unison as their army of horsemen charged the Eldarin — shields up, lances leading. Behind the cavalry charge were the anthrop archers, arrows knocked, waiting for the Eldarin to come within killing range. Once they saw the swarm of incoming aerthi, they raised their bows and fired.

Murciel knew his part. As the arrows took flight he tracked their paths, tucked his wings under himself, and dove. The screams of his kindred rose around him as arrows found flesh within the diving black cloud. Murciel locked on to his target, opened his wings and dug his talons into a horseman's chest, swooping him out of his saddle.

The flight of aerthi fanned out mid-flight, slamming into the anthrop horse-line, and breaking its forward momentum. Thousands of riders were lifted into the air or knocked off their sprinting mounts. When the Eldarin riders reached them, what was meant to be a head-on collision became a massacre. The sabre wolves and jaguakirns tore the fallen riders apart, sparing their terrified horses.

Murciel dropped the anthrop in his talons, the man screaming in terror as he plummeted to his death. Murciel rode the updrafts as he turned, tracking the flight of incoming arrows. He locked his eyes on the archers, tucked his black wings in, and spun, dodging three arrows that would have otherwise pierced his wings.

He collided with the archer's line, knocking them over, clawing and pecking down at their necks and faces. Blood filled his beak. Other aerthi joined in the attack, swarming the archers like locusts.

An Eldarin horn-blast told him it was time to disengage. The aerthi flapped their wings and began to climb away from the engagement.

An arrow tore through his flank. He cried out and plummeted, stunned by the hot spike of pain. He hit the ground in a thump, and as he tried to rise back into the air, two more arrows plunged into him, and he crumbled. The last thing he heard was the rumbling approach of the Eldarin charge.

The vision cleared from Murciel's mind, leaving him disoriented. His wounds throbbed, as if chafed by the vision's assault. Chrysalis stood patiently, watching him recover.

"Xialsadria," he said, "the last Eldarin city."

"Where the Nocturalis became the xial," she said, "and were enslaved to mankind."

"So it is as the Elders say," he said. "We once served the Eldarin."

"No, the Nocturalis served no-one, Murciel. The alliance was mutually beneficial, much like Helicartia's alliances are now."

"Why show me this?"

"Because it is Gaia's will that we take her world back from them, Murciel. They are not of her children's seed. They are a corruption that must be cleansed."

"The anthrops?"

"Yes."

Murciel shook his head. "No, there must be another way. What happened before — this is all ancient history. The xial are their own people now. We live free."

The Eldarin's eyes became hard and menacing. "Some of you are free, but most of your kind still lives in bondage. The Eldarin tried to live in peace with anthrops, Murciel. They even fought as allies against mutual threats, but in time, the anthropaki grew tired of sharing this world."

"They are not all sinister, Chrysalis. Condemning them all for the actions of a few would make us no better than them."

"Gaia's will is irresistible. Her wisdom immutable. The anthrop infestation must be exterminated. I have brought you here for this purpose. You will be my instrument."

"What?"

"You and I will venture from here together, and together, will give the peoples of Helicartia, of your home, the means to kill every anthrop nation that surrounds Gaia's Grove. We will swarm over them and reclaim the world they stole."

"I cannot," Murciel said. "I will not. This is not the way."

"This is the path that was chosen for you, Murciel. You cannot resist your fate."

He tightened the grip on his dagger. "I do not believe in fate, Chrysalis."

"Then you are a fool."

The candle in her hand did not grow any brighter, but its light began to spread, or perhaps it was the darkness receding like a curtain, until Murciel could see that he stood in the center of a broad stone bridge stretching over a bottomless chasm.

As the light spread farther, the impossible size of the spherical chamber revealed itself. Every inch of the cyclopean sphere crawled with the things that attacked Kaira. They crawled over each other like ants in a hive. They built bridges across the unbelievable distance with their own bodies, forming a loose web of death around him.

"This is how the anthropaki die, Murciel," she said.

"What are they?" Fear crawled beneath his skin.

"Look closer and you will see."

The creatures' skull-adorned abdomens cracked open, blossoming like macabre flowers. Each one contained an anthrop from the waist up. Some were adorned with feathers and bones, their bodies covered in dried paints and dead blood. Others he recognized as Dorav's seaguard and the people of Kaira. The rest he could not account for. None had eyes, teeth, or arms.

"Tell him what you are," she said to them.

"Negkrat!" the anthrops' voices were hideous, hollow and inhuman — the bony, plated abdomens of the creatures that held them rattled in concert.

"Negkrat! Negkrat! Negkrat!"

So many of them, all making those terrible noises at once, seized Murciel's nerves. He fell to his knees, primal fear twisting his insides like a wet rag. A piercing pain lanced his stomach where the creature they fought outside of Kaira had stung him.

The pain traveled through his veins like molten metal, scorching his innards. The agony spread like a fibrous vine inside him, searing his every nerve-ending, and throbbing in concert with the chitinous rattling.

"Can you taste their fear? Their pain? Can you see the depths to which it reaches?"

"Negkrat!"

The cacophonous cry rippled through him, body and mind.

"Negkrat! Negkrat! Negkrat!"

The sound vibrated through his spine, from stem to stern, turning his mind into a bloody syrup that oozed through pain's thorny fingers. The oscillations flayed him mercilessly. He cried out for Buio, Nihengale, and Escara, tears streaming down his face. He screamed Rairi's name in anguish, but no one came. His hand reached out to the woman, the pain searing his every fiber.

"PLEASE!"

"Every Queen needs a King," she said, watching him. "And you are mine. Rejoice, Murciel. It has been an age since the world witnessed what you will become."

The pain became too vicious. He preferred to die than allow this to continue.

"Negkrat! Negkrat! Negkrat!"

"This is what the anthrops planted within you," she said, "when they changed your kind into something nearer to themselves."

His dagger was still in his hand. He could make out the shape of its hilt past the agony coursing through him.

"Negkrat! Negkrat! Negkrat!"

"You will be cleansed of this fear, Murciel. Walk through madness and be renewed."

Murciel aimed the tip of the dagger towards himself. One quick motion, and it would be over. Better death that than this. Better anything than this.

"Negkrat!" Murciel cried in a voice not his own, the blade trembling in his hand. "Negkrat! Negkrat!"

The words were torn from him, as if he were an instrument being played by cruel hands. He focused his intention on his moonblade's edge.

The oscillations suddenly stopped, releasing him from their merciless talons. His muscles went limp and the dagger fell from his hand.

"No!" Chrysalis hissed.

Something was walking towards them. With an incredible effort, Murciel turned his burdensome head.

A towering, black-maned lion padded towards them with a human head clamped in his drooling jaws. The Eldarin's focus was entirely on the massive predator. Around the sphere, the negkrat's abdomens began to seal, hiding the anthrops within.

The lion dropped the severed head at the Eldarin's feet. It was the old man who had been dismembered and tied to the ziggurat's entrance. Chrysalis glanced down at it, then up into the lion's emerald eyes, their gazes level.

"This is no longer your temple, Ariel," she said. "They tore you from your perch and threw your horn into my tree. You are forsaken. You have no claim here."

The lion released a menacing growl that rode through Murciel's body, making his body shudder and his heart ache in his chest. The lion spoke, not with words, but intent. Murciel saw an image of a serpent, coiling around itself before biting its own tail.

"NO! I am Gaia's will!" Chrysalis became furious, her voice as hollow and inhuman as the anthrops trapped inside her creatures.

"My purpose is written on her roots!"

Ariel tilted his head back and opened his massive jaws. A roar like a thunderclap vibrated through Murciel's marrow.

Every monstrosity filling the impossible space became engulfed in bright emerald flames. The dying monsters hanging across the sphere screeched as they plummeted from their perches. The cyclopean chamber lit up in a roaring green inferno, like the heart of an emerald sun made of Padivian Greenfire.

Chrysalis' scream was an unholy thing, coming from a deep chasm of heresy and madness. Her veins turned blue, then green, before bursting into emerald flames. She fell to her knees, her body broiling until nothing remained but a smoldering pile of charcoal. Out of that mound of hot ash slithered a black-scaled serpent, coiling itself at the lion's feet.

Ariel's massive maw snatched the snake's body in a single bite, and as he did, the viper sank her fangs into the side of his face. The lion whipped his head about and gnawed on the serpent until she disappeared into his bloodied maw.

The enormous lion looked down at him and growled, sending another ripple through him. Murciel received an image of a tiny viper wrapped around his own terrified heart. They stared at each other for a moment, then Ariel collapsed on his side, breathing heavily through his open mouth, his breath a curdling blast of blood and carrion.

Ariel's breaths became long and rattling, before ceasing entirely. His massive body dissipated, becoming blackened leaves carried away by a spiral wind. In the wake of those leaves, a young, muscular anthrop lay naked on the old stone bridge.

Near the chamber's entrance, a large white wolf sat on his haunches — the same scar-eyed creature he had seen once before, in a nearly forgotten dream. The daemon wolf stood, turned towards the chamber's exit, and padded silently away.

Murciel opened his eyes.

He lay on a carpet of old dry bones in the middle of an ancient stone chamber. Two giant white trees clung to the inner stonework of the enclosure, reaching for the sunlight that poured down on him through the broken ceiling. He squinted reflexively but found the sunlight did not hurt his eyes as always.

He was in the main chamber of the ziggurat, surrounded by faded carvings. Behind him towered a statue of Cala-Neteri, her wings broken at her sides, and her elongated body swarming with lichen. A ceremonial flint knife had been plunged into her stone belly with incredible force, creating long, jagged cracks beneath her broad head. The sight of her visage filled Murciel with simmering dread. Feeling confused and exhausted beyond measure, he lay back and stared at the day's blue sky, wondering if this is what it felt like, to lose one's mind completely.

The monster that had nearly taken David's head compressed into itself, its body seizing and churning, until only a giant clump of black charcoal remained.

David breathed hard, staring at the thing's smoldering remains. He noticed he had pissed himself.

"Well, fuck," he muttered.

A roar of victory made David turn from the wet patch on his pants. Every creature on the field writhed, being eaten by emerald flames, trampling over each other as they were consumed.

David sensed someone walking towards him and turned. No one stood near, only the faintest hint of a familiar presence. He looked around, both surprised and strangely hopeful.

"Caige? Caige, are you out there?!"

No reply.

"They're dead!" Someone cried out. The shout grew in size and number like the roar of a gladiatorial amphitheater. "They are all fucking dead!"

The cohort cheered in unison, the sound echoing around him. David lay on the ground feeling drained and feverish. He had lost a lot of blood and felt disoriented. He could barely catch his breath.

"Hey! Hey!" Vonner called out. "Something is wrong with David!"

"Get that man to the medicus!" Stenner cried. "Fat fuck fought like a bull. I won't see him die like a stuck pig."

A group of men, quick to obey, lifted him up and placed him in a stretcher basket. He bit back a yelp of pain as his wounds flared.

As they wobbled him across the bloody field, his body began to shake with cold. He wanted to curl up but the pain in his back would not allow him. He desperately needed to sleep.

"Do not sleep!" Vonner yelled, startling him. The boy walked next to the men who carried him. "David, if you fall asleep you may not wake up. Stay with me."

"Shut up, fucking dandy," David growled.

"Not what your mother calls me," Vonner retorted.

Incredulous, David opened his eyes. Vonner smiled down at him.

"My mother would not have wasted her time on a pin-dick like you, boy," he said, rubbing his arms for warmth. "You even packing anything in those tight leathers of yours?"

"And you call me a dandy? Stay alive old man and I may let you have a peek."

"I'll take you up on it," David said. "My money's on you secretly being a lass passing for a man."

Vonner shrugged. "If imagining young men as women excites you, that's between you and the gods."

David would have let himself laugh, but he feared it might kill him. "You have a fucking mouth on you for such a young little shit."

Vonner's features grew stern."A dagger was my first toy as a child. Such a thing spoils the fruit of youth."

"It does," David frowned. "I know."

They placed him in a massive, blood-splattered tent with two dozen other wounded, screaming men. A procession of the injured was being hurriedly carried into the enclosure. The place already smelled like blood, shit, and alchemical resins.

"Water," he told Vonner. "I need water."

"Hold on." The boy walked deeper into the tent and returned with a brimming ladle. He put it to his lips. It was barely enough, but it helped.

"I will get you someone," Vonner said.

"Don't bother. Look around you. Some of these men are ready to bleed out. I am on the wrong end of the triage, boy."

Vonner's eyes widened before he ran back into the tent. When he returned, an older woman in a medicus overcoat walked by his side.

"He might be delirious," he told her. "I don't think he can feel his wounds."

A chill went through him remembering the slash he received on his lower back. He had witnessed wounds to the back take the use of men's legs before.

The medicus looked him over critically, then gripped him near the wound on his calf.

"Ow, fuck! What are you doing?"

"He can feel them," she assured Vonner. "He is just a tough old dog, but even tough old dogs bleed to death. Help me bring him into the next tent.

They picked up his basket and carried him among a throng of wailing men wrapped in bloodied gauze and stinking of burned flesh.

The zenthis medicus used flat-head pokers similar to cattle brands, glowing red-hot within coal braziers, to cauterize the soldiers' graver wounds. They passed one young man whose left arm had caught fire during the melee. It looked like a long piece of burned steak hanging from a white shoulder joint, with fleshy pieces of the bicep and forearm gone missing.

"I need my kit, vically paste, a vial of aqua vitae, and fresh gauze," the medicus woman cried as they placed him on a cot.

"And Maeron's clay," Vonner told her. "He needs clay, or he might lose his legs."

She looked at him, noticeably curious. "I can save his legs without it," she told him, though she did not sound convinced by her own words. "We only have a small allotment of clay. For the officers."

"You have enough for him," Vonner said, unbuckling his sword belt.

"What are you doing?" she asked.

"The hilts on these are Padivian silver," he said, offering up the sheathed blades. "More than enough to cover the cost."

The medicus gave him a stiff nod. "And bring the clay!" she called out.

"What the fuck are you doing, boy?" David was taken aback. "Those swords must cost a fortune."

Vonner shrugged. "Not like the blades are vescar steel. They're just fancy knicker-wetters for when I ride into town."

David smiled and shook his head at the brash little shit. "Goddamn dandy."

"You are welcome, you ungrateful old fuck," Vonner grinned.

"Your friends?"

Vonner's smile dropped like a stone, his eyes darkening. Pain and fear painted his features like blood-splatter. He shook his head grimly.

"Sorry, lad. I shouldn't have asked. Got a bad habit of it, seems."

"Get some rest," Vonner said and turned away.

35

Sunhoney

The black kajak lay on the bloodied earth of the proving grounds, groaning softly and exhaling pink mist through its crimson jaws. Iridia lay nearby, drenched in blood and motionless, except for the occasional twitch of an arm or leg. Her shield and spear both lay broken by her side. The two had fought each other to a standstill and were too exhausted and injured to continue.

"It is over!" Dorav cried at the foot of the Council's chairs. "The fight is over! You must pull her out of there!"

The Council of Knights turned to regard Lord Metzial, who sat digging the dirt out of his nails with the tip of his dagger.

"Master Dorav," Lord Metzial said coolly. "I decide when this is over."

"My Lord," he nearly spat, "the kajak is defeated. If she is not tended to quickly, she will die. Please!"

Lord Metzial sighed and stood, sheathing his dagger in a practiced, fluid motion.

"My Lords! My Ladies!" he called out, raising his hands above his head to arrest everyone's attention. "I must inform you that Initiate Iridia Atinara stands accused of tainting herself by lying with a man outside of holy wedlock."

Dorav's teeth clenched. There were gasps and a rank breeze of whispers coming from the witness stands.

"As a test of maidenhood for Knights cannot be considered valid," Lord Metzial continued. "It is this Council's decision that this Proving serve not only as a test of Iridia's worthiness, but as a trial to determine her innocence.

"If she survives, not only will she ascend to knighthood, but this accusation of sin will be burned away and forgotten. If she does not, then her unworthiness in the eyes of Zenthien, and her taint upon this sacred Order, will be known by all those present."

For a moment, Dorav could not formulate a response. He stood watching the Lords mutter and nod their approval as Metzial sat back down and unsheathed his dagger. Iridia's mother sat in the witness stands, watching her daughter slowly die.

"My lord!" Dorav said.

"Master Dorav," Metzial did not bother looking at him. "Those who prove false in the eyes of God must be allowed their fate. God's Will protects his loyal flock. Your own trial will commence soon enough. Patience."

"Dorav," Isa put her hand on his shoulder and looked him in the eye. "Come sit down."

"They cannot do this," Dorav growled, fighting back his tears. "They cannot!"

"They can, and they did." Isa's stern features softened for a moment. "Now come sit down, before her mother suspects what the Council already knows."

"No!" Dorav shouted, unsheathing his sword and raising it above his head. "I will kill you all first! Every last one!"

His sword blazed with golden radiance, its light arching across the chamber. Metzial screamed as the light from Dorav's sword scorched his skin and melted the flesh from his bones. The Council of Knights wailed as they shared his fate, writhing in holy fire.

"Goddamn you! Goddamn you all!" Dorav screamed as the Hall of Proving, and everyone within was consumed.

Dorav replayed the dream in his head over and over, refusing to let his mind forget any details of it. The only real part of the dream was Iridia lying next to the fatally wounded kajak.

He had not pleaded with the Lord Vaulter that day, and it had not been Metzial. His mind placed the old fucker in that seat during his dream. No, Dorav sat in the witness stands with the other initiates, as shocked and silent as the rest, pleading silently for Iridia to stand back up. She never did.

Dorav sat in his chamber's leather-back chair, staring out at the black skyline above Nevine. A bowl of olives, three different cheeses on a silver platter, and an amphora of Ardian wine sat untouched on the desk by his bed. He could not eat or sleep with the guilt and self-loathing grinding away at him.

The Queen had been bluffing after all. She never intended to turn him over to the Royal Inquisitor. He stood and watched as they drugged and dragged Kartecus away from the throne room, all because he would not admit he was sent on Black Wings. If he gave them what they wanted, he might have saved his old mentor from Sinitel.

The thought of what that animal might be doing to his friend made his eyes water. He let his tears flow freely for the pain Kartecus must be enduring.

The meaning behind his nightmare became clear then. He sat in the same spot as with Iridia, waiting helpless as someone he loved was brought to ruin.

He grabbed the silver platter of cheeses and threw it against his chamber door. The platter clanged loudly and the cheeses thumped around the threshold.

"Get your ass in here!" he called out. "I dropped my fucking cheese!"

The door opened slowly and his door guard looked at him, his eyes smoldering. "I will get you some more then, sir." The man's voice had admirable restraint.

"Fetch me some fucking olives while you're at it!" He threw the bowl at the door, which crashed against the thick oak, sending the green and black fruits flying. "Ewawas, or whatever poxed name you call them!"

"You wish for more wine as well?" The guard pointed at the ampule, some of his restraint falling away.

"Not yet," Dorav said. "Perhaps when you return. And I believe I want mutton. Juicy, black, and peppered."

"I will wake the cook." The guard closed the door.

"Petulance does not suit you, Captain," said a disembodied voice from behind him.

Dorav grabbed the Ardian ampule, turned, and threw it in the voice's direction.

Nihengale snatched by the handle in mid-flight, keeping it from tumbling out into the night. The mepsien stood in his balcony like a budding girl's secret lover, sneaking past her parents for a vigorous tryst, wine in hand.

"Nihengale? How, what...what in God's name are you doing here?"

"I am here for you, Captain." Nihengale placed the ampule on the balcony's stone balustrade.

Dorav shook his head in disbelief. "And the others?"

"Off on missions of their own."

"Nihengale, you came all this way? I cannot begin to imagine what you went through to get here."

"No, sir. I do not believe you can."

"Good god, man." Dorav walked up him. "You are bloody tenacious. If you were part of my crew I would promote you as far up as possible."

Nihengale remained silent. The mepsien's right eye was surrounded by intricate markings, similar to those on his body. The tattoo was freshly imprinted, the skin raised and red at the edges. A translucent ointment had been applied to it.

"That is new," he remarked.

Nihengale only nodded.

Dorav leaned up against the balustrade next to him and looked down at the fatal drop below. "How did you make it up here without being spotted? How did you know where to find me?"

"The Queen's Nighthawks are well-trained, but they are no Blades of Mepsia." Nihengale turned to face him.

"I meant to ask you before, what is that all about? The Blades of Mepsia. Who, where, or what is Mepsia?"

Nihengale gave him a strange, pensive look. "Perhaps a story for another time."

"As you wish." He grabbed the ampule. "Do mepsiens enjoy wine?"

"Very much so."

"Well you saved this one from an early demise. It is yours by right." He offered it up to him.

Nihengale stared at it quietly but did not take it.

"This is Ardian Sunhoney. White wine, Nihengale. The very rarest."

Surprise and desire filled Nihengale's eyes but he would still not take the ampule, so Dorav placed it back on the balustrade.

"Alright, Nihengale, speak your mind. What is wrong?"

"You are not a prisoner here, are you?"

"I am, and I am not," Dorav sniffed. "I am what we call a political prisoner. I cannot leave this room but in every other regard I am treated as an honored guest."

"I understand." Nihengale positioned his hands on the balustrade. "We disarm our prisoners and keep them away from our young, but unless they prove hostile we allow them to roam free."

"That is more trust than they will ever place in me. Armed or no."

"Were you questioned upon arrival?"

Dorav noted an odd inflection in the mepsien's tone. "Yes, but I have nothing to say to her Majesty the Queen, or her lackeys."

"And Kartecus?"

Dorav wrapped his fingers into tight fists. "The Royal Inquisitor has him."

"The Royal Inquisitor. Sinitel?" Nihengale's pose seemed more relaxed, leaning against the balustrade now, taking in the city view.

"You know him?" Dorav mimicked his easy posture.

"A lifetime ago I called him friend. Now he is dashunda — a traitor to his people."

"What did he do?"

"He stole something of irreplaceable value from Helicartia."

"And his punishment?"

"His skrit was to be scourged and his moonblade seized before being banished, but he escaped."

"You did not come all this way only to rescue us, did you, Nihengale? You came here for him."

Nihengale's face became disquieted. He pursed his lips and tapped one small claw against the stone. "Is rescue possible?"

"No, but it is not required, at least not for me. The Queen already sent a ransom letter to my father. When he replies they will escort me to Aztan and place me on the early tide back to Palidor."

"What will happen then?"

Dorav looked up at the moon's glorious light. "As much as it will vex that bastard Metzial, I will report my mission here completed. Although, because of my capture, he will likely make a dramatic gesture and cast me out of the Order. No matter. My true concern now is for Kartecus."

"You fear his fate in the dashunda's hands."

"Yes."

"Does he have something to reveal that you fear may be coaxed from him?"

"No." Dorav shook his head. "I know he can seem crass and difficult, especially to you, but he is a good man, and is like a second father to me. He does not deserve whatever that...dashunda, is doing to him."

"Perhaps not."

"Nihengale-"

"Before you speak," the mepsien cut him off, "there is a question I need you to answer."

"Yes?"

"Why did you decide to sack the towns on the Counter's Road, and commit the act yourself? Your place was in Sharn with your crew. You could have sent anyone on such a mission, even my pack.

"No one could predict the disaster Kaira became, but you should never have been there in the first place. So why? I need to know why all this happened."

Dorav took a deep breath through his nose. "Although I do not retain the privilege of company, this room still holds two wine goblets. Care to drink with me?"

Nihengale's green eyes stared at him evenly for a moment. He nodded.

Dorav retrieved the two steel goblets from the table and brought them out to the balcony. Nihengale broke the seal on the ampule and poured them each a generous serving.

"When I was a young man, I knew a woman called Iridia Atinara, who I loved more than words can explain. The kind of love you would sacrifice everything for. Have you ever known that kind of love, Nihengale?"

Nihengale gave him a sidelong glance and nodded.

"We were laying in bed one night, drinking a stolen carafe of ceremonial wine, flushed from hours of lovemaking, and she told me the story of how her family ended up in Palidor. Her grandfather was a Norvan shinn-miner called Feayn. No surname. Just another boy orphaned by the cruelties of this world.

"Long before the Magalians stripped the Norvan Peaks for its worth, Feayn was breaking his back against that rock with his brother and a team of six men.

"One day they came across a beautiful, fat vein of marrow. Coreshinn, as they call it down here. Once they realized what they were due to earn, Feayn's crew tried to kill him and his little brother. They both grabbed pickaxes and fought the bastards in the still, dark heat. By the end of it, only Feayn stood.

"Once the dust settled and coin had exchanged hands, Feayn walked into his favorite watering hole, a little shit-hole called Black Rock Tavern, and hammered his bloodied pickax right to the wall, with his and his brother's names carved into its hilt. Then he boarded a ship in Sharn and sailed up to the shores of Palidor, rich as a lord."

They each took a swallow of wine. It was like drinking sunlight reflecting off a cool meadow stream.

"Iridia swore that one day, once she became a knight, she would sail south and find her grandfather's pick, so she might hang it in her family home — somewhere everyone could see, and she would tell them the story of how a nameless orphan created the legacy of House Atinara.

"I went with the expedition because I needed to know if that pick still hung where her grandfather left it. I could not walk away from that, or give the task to someone else. It was too personal.

"Now, imagine my surprise when I saw that not only was the tavern still standing, but Feayn's pick was still nailed to its wall, right along with a number of others. Iridia's grandfather had birthed a tradition in Kaira."

They took another sip of sunhoney.

"You must think me a goddamn fool," Dorav said.

Nihengale unsheathed one of his daggers and placed in on the balustrade.

"Regardless of what academy we join, every Blade of Mepsia is granted a moonblade at the end of training. It is a personal and guarded thing in our traditions. If we ever discover one misplaced, say, in the hands of an anthrop, or in a merchant's stall, we will go to great lengths to recover it."

Nihengale sheathed the blade. "An item that is bonded with us in such a way cannot be easily disregarded."

"So you understand then, why I needed to go, personally?"

"I do."

"It feels good to say these things out loud," Dorav said, feeling lighter. "It has weighed on me, how wrong everything went, at the end."

"I am glad you feel that way. And I give thanks to you for sharing your Animura with me, Dorav Minos. It allows me to finally see you with knowing eyes."

Dorav took a long pull, finishing the wine in his goblet. "What do you mean by Anim-"

As if the world suddenly decided to drop away without consulting him, his feet left the stone balcony, and he tipped over the balustrade, the empty goblet flying out of his flaying hands.

His heart shot up into his throat, choking the scream that wished to erupt from his lungs as his legs cleared the balcony. His arms swung wildly as he flipped forward but his hands caught only the wind.

Finally, as the terror of what occurred struck him like a fist to the chest, Dorav screamed. He plummeted through the warm, summer night wind above Nevine, and witnessed Nihengale's impassive face at the edge of the balcony, watching him fall. In a matter of seconds the mepsien's face was too far away to see, and for one terrified instant, his eyes registered the brilliant silver glow of the moon high above the Fabhcun, also watching him die.

Then nothing.

Epilogue

Marca's lamplight began to dance and flutter off the stained bulkheads of her cabin. She listened curiously at the suckling pops which meant her lamp was almost out of oil. Leaning back in her cot, she rubbed her tired eyes. She did not like having to read in this dim light, but she could not risk reading above deck.

The first time she tried the weatherdeck, a wave had climbed over the bulwark and drenched her. If her books were not still in their leather satchel, she would have lost weeks worth of notations. She would be somewhat safer from the hard, frothy waves up on the quarterdeck, but she refused to be near Ser Isa. She surely was not going to climb the shrouds and sit on the beams like the fearless topsail men, so her dim-lit cabin would need to suffice.

The journey back to Palidor was proving difficult for the crew of the *Kajak*. They were well away from the trade route they used to escort the *Merrigold* south, sticking closer to the Enelysion coastline.

Captain Myrkin insisted they take this route until reaching friendly waters, but that meant braving the perpetual storm over the infamous Stormthrone Peaks. More often than not the ship was forced to furl the storm-sails and row against a hard current.

At first, Marca found the sight of the black mountain range of the eastern Enelysion coastline mesmerizing. A perpetual display of sheet lighting danced over its tips and dozens of silvery waterfalls made the mountains appear as if dipped in quicksilver. Sometimes the lightning cast blue, sometimes violet, and sometimes it cast hot white, changing the color of the entire sky.

Now, she began to loathe Enelysion.

The low, crackling booms after each faraway lightning strike was an unspoken threat. The innards of the *Kajak* would sporadically light up, white brilliance cutting through the vessel as if it were being visited by some luminous deity, followed instantly by a concussive blast so overwhelming, it made her ass clench and ears ring. Hedego told her if the ship got hit by lightning, even once, they would likely not survive it.

The crew of the Kajak took mass every morning under the rain and Ser Isa would stand boldly on the quarterdeck in full metal battle dress, assuring the crew they were in Zenthien's loving hands. That no harm would come to them in these heathen lands as long as they held tightly to their faith and showed their commitment through prayer and the shedding of coin.

The sailors placed handfuls of their meager earnings in a bowl and passed it around, muttering prayers as they relinquished their pay in hopes of salvation. Marca made sure to throw a few chints into the bowl to keep Isa's eyes from lingering on her. She could not look the dangerous woman in the eye after what she did on the cliffs outside of Sharn. She feared her hatred would show plainly on her face.

Some sailors made secret sacrifices to Aeros, the Great Sky Serpent. They threw small portions of their food and firedrake rations into the sea while whispering their pleads. The *Kajak* groaned in frustration as it cut painstakingly through the fat, frothy waves of Enelysion's coast.

Marca gingerly undid the bandages around her left forearm and found the skin still flushed and delicate to the touch. She had soaked her hand in aloe sap but she could still feel the burn of where Rairi's beads had scorched her. What kind of terrible alchemy was contained in those beads? What had she done by gripping them so?

With a sigh, Marca took the sputtering lamp into the companionway. Most of the ship's crew was above, fighting against the coastline winds. Without their boisterous presence, the ship's interior had a vacant, ominous air. Her bulkheads groaned like a perpetually settling house, or the belly of a hungry sea monster. Marca made her way briskly astern and below towards the quartermaster's chamber.

The troublesome weather of Enelysion was only the beginning of the *Kajak's* troubles. A rumor had spread that the ship was cursed; damned by Zenthien for leaving their beloved captain stranded in heathen lands. The ship was being haunted by ghost rats.

The *Kajak* was a military vessel, and nothing excited military officers more than watching people clean. The *Kajak* was scrubbed down tirelessly every day. Her rotting beams were replaced, her bulkheads scraped, and every feasible surface varnished. The caulker and his mate were always somewhere, patching holes, emptying the piss pots, and scrubbing the officers' privies. Marca had not heard so much as a squeak on their journey south. Now the scuffling and squeaking around the ship was so unnerving, it kept people up at night.

The ship had been searched stem to stern after Captain Myrkin's first sleepless night. The pantry and kitchen were emptied and searched, the cargo in the hold hauled up to the weatherdeck and inspected, and the hold itself thoroughly combed.

Denirce and her mate inspected the masts, bulkheads, and companionways for signs of hollowing, and even the filthy bilge was searched. Not a single rat or signs of scat were found anywhere. By the end, the crew was bitter and exhausted, but the rats continued to squeak and scratch, just beyond sight.

The endless days of fighting against Enelysion's coastal waters and the scratching of the phantom rats placed a terrible strain on the crew. Both Dessa and Garit looked more worn and tired with every passing morning. Kivan, who she met with every day in the ship's hold for counting and cataloging, had grown dark circles under his eyes. Even Isa, fucking Isa, looked more withdrawn and irritable than usual.

"Hello, Marca." Kivan looked gaunt.

Any chance of them ever being friends ended when Marca left him saddled with the counting and categorizing of shinn alone while she ran off on the Counter's Road with Rairi. He was not unkind to her, but she knew he did not like her much after that.

"Kivan. I am out of lamp oil."

"That is your fourth bottle so far."

"I do not like sleeping in the dark. The rats, you know?"

"You must ration your oil or your room will be in the dark for the remainder of the journey. Rats or no."

"Yes, fine." She rolled her eyes.

"I do not believe you are hearing me." He deposited a green-stained bottle of lamp-oil on his desk. "That is your last bottle. You will not receive another for the remainder of the voyage."

"What!? You cannot."

"Yes," he said. "I can. So again, learn to ration, or learn to live in the dark."

"You're being childish, Kivan!"

"No, you are being wasteful. The oil is for everyone, and you have reached your allotment. Now, did you require anything else?"

"I cannot make this last so long! Can you give me one more after it at least?"

"No."

"Kivan, do not force me to speak with the quartermaster."

"He is ill, Marca. I am in charge until he is well."

"Well you are being-"

A loud commotion rose from the companionway outside Kivan's office. As slapping feet ran amidships, they both turned towards the sound.

"What's happening?" Kivan asked her.

She left the question unanswered and moved to investigate. A throng of sailors huddled in the ship's mess, near Stapes' stove.

"Back up!" Hedego barked.

"Make room! Make room!" Dessa ordered from somewhere in the throng.

With Captain Dorav's abduction, the tier of command had shifted on the *Kajak*. Myrkin had been field-promoted to Captain, and his first mate Dessa was now acting Lieutenant.

The sailors backed away obediently. Private Ging lay unconscious on the deck, his sword still in its scabbard. Marca recognized him at once as one of the men who had fired on Rairi and Murciel outside of Sharn.

"What happened to him?" One sailor asked.

"What did he eat?" inquired another. "Did somethin' go spoilt?"

"The fuckin' curse got'im," a third spat.

"All right everyone out, now!" Dessa said. "I swear, any man standing here in three heartbeats gets double duties for a week!"

Marca leaped out of the sailors' way as they fled. Only Hedego, Stapes, Dessa, and herself remained in the mess.

"What happened to him?" Marca asked.

"I'm not certain," Hedego stood, wiping his hands on his medicus coat, "but his death was not swift."

"Oh, God," Marca put her hand to her mouth.

"Was it something he ate?" Dessa asked.

"No!" Stapes shook his head. "Cannot be that!"

"I am asking the medicus, Stapes," Dessa said flatly.

"I need a better look at him," Hedego said. "There are no wounds I can see, and there was no struggle. He did not choke or hit his head. His teeth and gums look relatively healthy and his eyes lack jaundice. I have no idea yet what killed him."

"Do whatever you need to," Dessa said. "Find out and report to me the moment you have something."

"Of course." Hedego glanced at her. "Marca, remain and assist me."

"Aye," she said. "Of course."

"I need to know what happened here," Dessa told the medicus. "Work fast, sir. Deliver me an answer."

"I will, Ser."

Dessa left the mess, heading for the weatherdeck.

"Help me move him, Stapes," Hedego said, "and be gentle please."

"Aye." Stapes picked Ging up by the shoulders.

Marca followed them out of the mess.

Kivan stood by the doorway. "What happened?"

She considered leaving him without answer, but it would not be wise to further antagonize someone who could deprive her of things as crucial as lamp oil.

"Private Ging is dead," she told him. "We do not know why yet."

"Damn."

"Can I return later for my oil? I must assist Hedego."

"Of course."

"Thank you, Kivan."

"Was it the curse?"

She turned back and looked him in the eye. "Kivan, you must not say that, to anyone. Not even in jest or in passing. You will ignite a panic."

"Aye, you're right."

Marca caught up with Hedego and Stapes, and stared at Ging's sunburned, peaceful features. She almost believed he slept. As they moved through the companionway, rats began to scratch and squeak from behind the bulkheads, following their progress.